... OLD, AND FULL OF DAYS

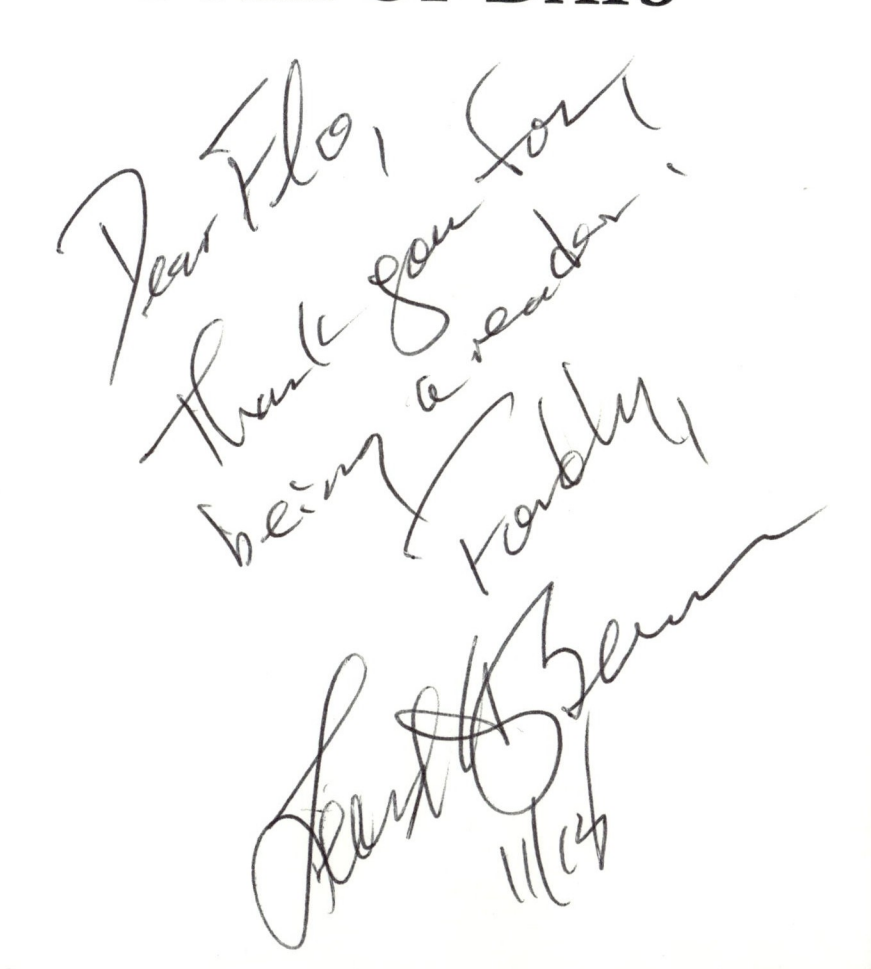

Also by Leonard H. Berman

Consider My Servant
A World of Secrets

... OLD, AND FULL OF DAYS

Leonard H. Berman

Copyright © 2015 by Leonard H. Berman.

Library of Congress Control Number: 2015919481
ISBN: Hardcover   978-1-5144-2823-8
           Softcover   978-1-5144-2822-1
           eBook   978-1-5144-2821-4

All rights reserved. No part of this book may be reproduced or transmitted in any form or by any means, electronic or mechanical, including photocopying, recording, or by any information storage and retrieval system, without permission in writing from the copyright owner.

This is a work of fiction. Names, characters, places and incidents either are the product of the author's imagination or are used fictitiously, and any resemblance to any actual persons, living or dead, events, or locales is entirely coincidental.

Any people depicted in stock imagery provided by Thinkstock are models, and such images are being used for illustrative purposes only.
Certain stock imagery © Thinkstock.

Print information available on the last page.

Rev. date: 01/2/2016

To order additional copies of this book, contact:
Xlibris
1-888-795-4274
www.Xlibris.com
Orders@Xlibris.com

DEDICATION

Jacob Wetchler
May 17, 1989 - October 15, 2009

Jacob Wetchler, a student who came into my classroom and into my heart, was lost to us at the age of nineteen to cancer. He was a young man who relished intellectual banter with friends, and one who reveled in toe to toe debate with teachers. Jake had the indomitable spirit of a Ulysses, and the courage of a David, and loved the challenge of learning and the joy that comes with discovery. Potential and enthusiasm exuded from him, and that powerful handshake, that sonorous voice, or hug when he said hello let you know how genuinely happy he was to see you. Jake loved his music and was always looking to expand his talents. He delighted in physical activity, and in the wonder of what the human body could accomplish. Jake was young man who loved deeply and championed the right of all people to think independently and speak out for a world free from superstition.

In his memory, his parents created *The Jake Wetchler Foundation for Innovative Pediatric Cancer Research*. Jake was the inspiration for the character, Aaron.

Stan Kaplan
September 4, 1925 - April 8, 2015

Stanley Kaplan, my cousin, grew up in Crown Heights, Brooklyn, and attended the High School of Music and Art. After high school, he fought in the Battle of the Bulge during WW II, and attended Cooper Union and NYU on the GI Bill. He was involved in the formation of the American Graphic Workshop in NYC which was a collective of left-leaning artists that worked to further social movements and progressive political causes. Stan was a freelance commercial/fine artist, working for individual and corporate clients, and a professor of art at Nassau Community College for 30 years. Stan's work graces the book covers of my three novels.

In Memoriam
Paul Berman
Sylvia Berman
Abraham Epstein
Clara Epstein
Gilbert Fonfa
Eddie Hoeger
Barbara and Gilbert Lenett

ACKNOWLEDGMENTS

To Toby, my beloved wife, whose encouragement, suggestions, opinions, editing skills, and taste were invaluable in assisting me in writing this novel.

To Steve Silverman and David Soowal, whose technical expertise with my computer was very much appreciated.

To Rob Kaplan, who pieced together a collage of his father's work so Stan Kaplan's art might once again appear as the cover on the final novel of this trilogy.

Resources

Bernstein, Arnie, *Swastika Nation*, St. Martin's Press, 2013.
Cohen, Rich, *Tough Jews*, Vintage Books, 1999.
Edsel, Robert M., *The Monuments Men*, Center Street, 2009.
Galbraith, John Kenneth, The Great Crash 1929, Houghton Mifflin Co. 1961.
Kaplan, Stan, *Images; Between the Lines*, Tortoise Press, 1997.
March, Joseph Moncure, *The Wild Party*, Panthon Books, 1994
Meir-Levi, David, *History Upside Down*, Encounter Books, 2007.
Miller, Rabbi Israel, *Our Israel At Forty*, World Zionist Organization, 1988.
Puner, Helen Walker, *Freud: His Life and His Mind*, Howell Soskin Publishers, 1947.

Response - Switzerland's Unwanted Guests, Wiesenthal Center, Vol. 19 No. 1, 1998. *Who Profited From Nazi Genocide?*, Vol. 17 No. 3, 1996/97.
Wikipedia
The National Jewish Museum, Philadelphia, PA.

CHAPTER 1

The Chernov kitchen in Brownsville, Brooklyn, N.Y. 1904

The samovar Jonah Chernov had carried across an ocean gurgled and steamed its announcement that the water for tea was ready. Rachelann, now nineteen, having taken her mother's place in the kitchen, carefully poured the steaming water into the small memorial glasses for her father to pass out to the men of the Krivoser Society who had assembled around his kitchen table in the back of the store. On the table were cubes of sugar that some of the men would put between their teeth as they sipped the amber brew, and for others, strawberry jam would sweeten the hot liquid for them.

"You will not believe what this so called 'man of God' said to me," Jonah began, trying to control the obvious emotion that was pushing its way out of his gut. "He was sitting in his kitchen pouring himself some schnaps into a teacup and he didn't even have the courtesy to ask me to sit down."

The men at the table leaned in to hear the story, neither surprised that a priest would be drinking, nor that he would not ask a Jew to sit at his table.

"You maybe expected something different, Chernov?" said Shepsa Silverman. "You think they're any different here then they were in Krivoser? Only here they're Catholic, not Russian

Orthodox. But it's all the same. So he wasn't courteous. Big deal. What did he say?"

Jonah did not expect the interruption and stared at Shepsa with a look of annoyance that masked his disappointment that indeed, in America, he thought a priest might be different.

"You know what he said after I told him about my Harry and Sammy being beaten by the Irish hooligans from his church? Do you know what he said? He said it was 'divinely sanctioned,' and as proof, he quoted this saint or somebody. I could not believe, that anyone who presents himself as a man of God could say such a thing."

"That's because you believe what you want to believe that religious people are better people, but underneath, nobody is better than anyone else. So get to the point, Chernov. What does 'divinely sanctioned' mean?" Shepsa responded, "My tea is getting cold."

"All right, all right," Jonah continued.

"He actually blamed my boys for getting beaten up! He actually said it had to be God's will that my sons were beaten because nothing happens without God wanting it to happen, and if Irish boys beat up Jews, they did it because God allowed them to do it." Jonah felt the heat in his cheeks. "Then he said that the church teaches their children that God controls all, and the boys of this parish could not have dared do what you say they did without it being what God wanted. Do you not believe in God's will?"

"But isn't everything God's will?" Pinkus Osterman ventured. "Don't we teach our own the same thing?"

Jonah was about to blurt out that Osterman was a fool, but decided not to embarrass the man in front of the others, making a mental note that this was a person to avoid.

"There was nothing to say after that and I left," he continued, ignoring the comment. "How do you counter such an insane belief? Such crazy ideas like that can give any insane person the justification for mayhem because they think what comes into their head must be God's will. And now you know why I don't believe that God has anything to do with anything."

"This is no time Chernov for a lecture on goyish theology or yours for that matter," Brenner interjected, sipping the tea that had spilled into his saucer, "and I feel I have to remind you that this is the board of a benevolent society, not the board of a vigilante committee. Keeping the streets safe is a job for the police. We are here to make personal loans, advance the social welfare, and to provide a place for people to be buried. That's what we do and that's all we should do. You expect us to change the charter because your boys get beaten up? Kids get beaten up all the time. Let him stay away from where the Irish are and let the police handle it."

"The cops ain't worth a fart, and the Micks wait after school for the Jewish kids to come out. And they like to come in especially on Friday night when the old Jews come out of shul. You know that as well as I do because you all know that the old men get their beards pulled or get knocked down. Only you're too damned scared to make some noise about it. So I guess you must think it's God's will that you do nothing."

Abraham Chernov, Jonah's eldest son, stood in the doorway with a sneer that was an indictment of what he heard. "You're like sheep, and if you don't feel responsible for keeping your kids safe on the streets, what about the old Jews you pray next to?" He laughed at them, seemingly to punctuate his indictment and his contempt.

There was an uncomfortable silence and a creaking of chairs as the men turned to the young man in the doorway and then to his father with the expectation that he would berate his son for being rude to his elders. Jonah bristled at his son's disrespect and clenched his teeth, but at the same time recognized that his son had voiced a criticism of the group that he himself did not wish to make. "This is for adults, and we'll take care of this, Abe. It's none of your business."

"Harry and Sam are my brothers," he retorted, not seeming to care about the look of anger that melted into embarrassment on his father's face as the elder Chernov stood before his friends and listened to his son's castigation of them. "So it is my business," he continued. Jonah also perceived the same contempt from other recent encounters with Abe since Leah's death. These confrontations were most acute when he expressed his profound disappointment in Abe and when he received reports of Abe's behavior in the streets or at school. His son overwhelmed him. The children overwhelmed him, and he felt he was losing control of them.

"You ain't gonna do nuth'in 'bout this and you know it," Abe said flatly.

The men around the table shifted uncomfortably again knowing full well that the brazen teenager who berated them from the doorway had more integrity at that moment than they had. "This is America," Jonah continued trying to pull the hostile looks back from his son, "and there are protections here that weren't there for us in Russia. I'm going to the police tomorrow and report the attack, and I think it might be a good idea if we form some sort of group to watch out for our children, at least when they come home from school. If the Irish kids knew that people in the neighborhood were watching, maybe they will stop coming after them."

"Are you saying, Chernov, that we should leave a customer and stand outside so we could watch out for your kids?"

"How long would it take? And it's not just my sons you'll be watching out for. You'll be watching out for everybody's children. They get out from school and they walk home past all the stores. What would be so terrible if we all took some time to look out so they know they're safe?"

"The Micks don't beat up the Jewish kids by the stores just like they don't attack the old men near the stores," Abraham interrupted again, this time his voice filled with exasperation. "You just don't understand. They jump the kids in the alleys or in the lot by the school. You have to take it to them where they do it." Abe's look challenged and condemned what was to him his father's naivete. "Besides, going to the cops is a waste of time. Did you ever meet a cop in this neighborhood who wasn't Irish? They're all Irish. They protect their own. They'll do nothing for you, Papa," and saying that, turned around and slammed the door behind him.

"That's the son you need to watch out for my friend," said Mr. Yavnah. "Harry and Sammy will heal, but your Abraham acts like he's been beaten up on the inside where you can't see the bruises."

"All right," Solomon Smolin interjected, slapping both hands on the table. "It's getting late. I can stand outside my store if there are no customers, but I can't walk over to the school or go looking in alleys. I have a business to run." The men around the table nodded their heads in agreement.

Jonah felt his momentum fading as the men sipped their tea and began changing the subject to what they thought were more pressing items confronting the community. To Jonah, the safety of children was paramount, but it seemed that his only option was to report the incident to the police and wait for something to be done. It was the only right thing to do, and all the while he thought of it, he knew the futility of the effort. He picked up a cube of sugar, put it between his teeth and sipped his tea.

Abraham Chernov, taller than his father by six inches and darkly handsome with his mother's coloring, her curly auburn hair and her dark topaz eyes, sat down on the cold stone stoop leading from the back of the store apartment to the street. As he ground his fist into his hand, imagining fantasy Irish faces there, he thought that the only way he might end the threat to his brothers was the way he had ended the threat to himself.

The street lamp flickered then sputtered and the shadow it cast on his delivery bicycle that leaned against the post cast a fantastic shadow across the square pavement blocks upon which he and his friends had played when they were younger. He couldn't be interested in kid games now even though he smiled briefly at the memory. This neighborhood didn't allow much time for staying a kid. Kids got pushed around, and though he never pushed, he was not afraid to push back. Now, on this same pavement where he once played box ball and Johnny on the pony, he tossed dice and dealt out cards. Money was to be made on these stones, and the less savvy were there to be hustled.

He sat there and thought about the men around the table and blanketed them with his disdain for their disinterest and seeming cowardice. But mostly, he was annoyed at his father for his inability to understand how things worked in the streets. They had been in America for eight years now, and even at sixteen, he saw clearly what his well meaning father chose not to see. The first time an Irish kid bothered him in the upper grades, he broke a bottle over the kid's head without thinking twice about it. The Irish kid thought a Jew wouldn't fight back. When that same kid brought others back, Abe had picked up a metal pipe and brandished it at them. Someone made a move towards him, and Abe smashed the pipe over the kids arm, opening up the skin and fracturing the bone. Abe's slender frame belied the muscular arms and torso he had developed from hauling cases of soda bottles and buckets of coal from the cellar up to the store and apartment for his mother. He menaced the others, and when another kid braved the circle, he too felt the pipe and screamed at the force of the blow. They cursed him and avoided him in school. After this incident, the word spread that he was a crazy and a dirty fighter who would just as soon as bash you over the head with anything he could get his hands on as well as look at you. There was also the rumor that he always carried a knife, so even nice kids who might have wanted to befriend him, stayed away. These rumors were picked up by the faculty, so he was watched more closely than any of the other toughs, and frequently told to empty his pockets. Besides, there were no nice kids in his assigned classes.

For as long as he could remember, he had difficulty reading. He knew all his letters by the time he was three, and his parents were so very proud, but when it came to putting them together and reading them, they didn't make any sense to him. So he memorized what was read to him, and what he memorized, he fed back to the teacher. He told them his sight was bad and that his family too poor to afford the operation that would get his eyes fixed. The ruse worked for most of elementary school and, out of compassion, his teachers read him his tests, and he always did very well. But in the upper grades, the teachers were less accommodating. His difficulty was revealed, and the principal, Miss Mary Delaney, seeing an opportunity to rid her school of one more tough kid, called for his parents and suggested that they take him out of school and teach him a trade where reading was not involved. Leah and Jonah would do nothing of the sort. In America, children were educated for free, and his children would have the education he was denied. Other than his reading problem, Abe had done nothing wrong to warrant being thrown out of school, and though he had been accused of being implicated in vandalism at the school, Miss Delaney could never prove that he was involved.

So Jonah went to the Irish district councilman who was always eager to make the Jewish vote happy, and got him to pressure the principal to let Abe stay. The fact that Abe was quite intelligent with a superior memory and a knack for numbers, seemed not to make a difference to Miss Delaney who clearly did not like Abraham Chernov. She relegated him to the class everyone knew was the dumb class, and true to form, the most disruptive in the school. There were two other Jewish kids in that class, twins Myer and Yitz Morganstern, but all the others were Irish, Italian, and Polish boys.

It was shortly after he was put into the same class as that Irish kid whose arm he had broken, that an incident happened which would change his life and make him a best friend. It came in the form of an Italian boy named Joey DiAngelo. It was on the way home from school when DiAngelo and his friends called out to Abe to stop. There were no epithets used about his people or his religion. This was pure bravado by this young Italian tough also trying to make a street reputation for himself. Abe looked around for something to use as a weapon, but saw nothing. He did not have a knife because he never carried one. He recalled putting down his books, turning slowly and seeing Joey's fist come at his face. He stepped aside and his own fist connected with Joey's shoulder as it passed him. DiAngelo winced, and his friends stepped towards Abe. Abe thought quickly.

"I'll fight you one on one," Abe said, "but if your gang jumps in, you'll never know if you could kick my ass, would you?"

Joey stopped and considered the truth in the statement and the proposal. "Nobody moves in on him," he said with authority, still massaging the shoulder and measuring the strength that belied Abe's slender appearance. Abe, sensing that this new adversary had some sense of street honor and that he could possibly talk himself out of a beating, motioned for the kid to step closer. Di Angelo moved cautiously.

"Now," Abe whispered so the others could not hear. "If you kick my ass, you'll keep the respect of your friends, but if I kick your ass, you'll lose it. So consider this. I punched you and I can tell it's still hurting, so you know I can really damage you if I connect. Believe me that I will connect. But if we step back and you punch me, we're kind of even and no one is the wiser for it or loses any face."

Joey half smiled at the suggestion Abe offered and considered the throbbing pain in his shoulder. This is a smart Heeb, he thought, and let Abe have one in the shoulder that he knew would leave a bruise. Abe accepted the punch that seemed to level the encounter, and both slightly nodded in respect. A friendship was born. "See y'a tomorrow, kid. You got moxie," Joey said, as he turned and walked away. "The kid's got moxie," he said to his friends. "Let's go."

Because of his reading problem, Abe listened intently as his younger brothers, especially Maurice, and sisters read aloud to one another from the library books Jonah insisted each take out weekly. From the stories he pieced together, he formulated something akin to a script with himself secretly starring as the gallant knight riding into battle, or a swashbuckler swooping down from the ship's yardarm brandishing a sword. He especially liked the stories of Robin Hood and of knights slaying dragons and rescuing beautiful girls. This was a secret that no one knew because such secrets belong to childhood and if he shared his fantasy with anyone, he would be laughed at. He could not tolerate being laughed at.

It was the Robin Hood in him who knew something had to be done about those Irish punks, so he assigned them the role of the Sheriff's men who were always riding into the village of Sherwood to terrorize the peasants and collect the taxes. If he ever needed to justify to his father any trouble making behavior that came along with his secret hero fantasy of saving the underdog, he would defend himself by spouting back, "You must not stand idly by upon the blood of your neighbor" which was one of the laws his father had taught his children at the Sabbath table. Though his father may have backed away from and frequently ridiculed the old traditions as not being helpful in America, he never seemed to doubt the truth of those laws and would often say that "without such laws, people would eat one another." At his parent's table he also learned to respect the elderly for their white hair. But the seemingly disinterested men around the table had no white hair on their heads and did not deserve his respect. He would have to do something about the Irish hooligans himself and do it soon.

Since the day his father found his mother at the bottom of the cellar steps, his father seemed to become less and less involved in the day to day running of the family, and though physically present, often seemed disconnected and unavailable. At times his father would disappear for hours without any explanation as to where he was going. Always, the children assumed that his moods and physical absence had something to do with his mourning and grief for their mother, so they said nothing. But Abe followed him one day into Manhattan, and saw him greeted at the door of a fancy townhouse by a woman. Abe chose not to tell this to anyone.

At those times when their father told them that he had business to attend to in the city, responsibility of overseeing the younger children and taking care of the store fell to Abe and to Rachelann. It was she who tried to maintain the traditions their mother loved, even as she watched her father move further and further away from synagogue involvement. Still, it puzzled her that her father insisted that everyone attend Shabbos dinner and all holidays that were celebrated in the house. The man made no attempt at daily prayers or attendance at the synagogue, but strangely enough, insisted that the prayers and rituals remain the same. No longer did he talk about the Torah stories at the table as when her mother was alive, but on occasion he did when there was something happening in the world that seemed to relate to a Torah tale. Current events often took the place of the Torah stories at the Shabbos table and was always prefaced with, "There is nothing new under the sun." Conversations not only about what was happening in the world, but also about books read, art seen, new inventions, new music heard, and where appropriate, the laws on proper Jewish behavior if these related to what was going on in the world as related by the newspaper, were topics. Cultural and history making events came to the table through *The Daily Forward*, the daily Yiddish newspaper. Their father would read the Yiddish and translate the story into English. It was through this that he intended to improve his children's English vocabulary. He would pass the paper around to those who could translate from Yiddish to English. If there was a word they did not know, it would be looked up in the dictionary and he would write it down even though he knew that writing was forbidden on Shabbos. He would also translate the sad letters, *The Bintle Brief*, sent from other Jews to the editor so his children could also learn compassion for others and gratitude for what they had. It was understood by all that Abie did not have to read or translate. Maurice was the best at translating and at learning new words.

Though Abraham continued to discard the traditions, he felt a resentment when his father did because he felt that something was being discarded that linked everyone to their mother. These nascent feelings of resentment for this slight to her memory were coupled with a sense he had that he was a disappointment to his father because he would never achieve what his father envisioned he should be. He was the eldest son, and by the established school standards, he was illiterate. His struggle to read Hebrew and Yiddish was even more of a struggle than his effort to learn to read English. When it came time for him to become a bar mitzvah, Jonah did not press him and Leah understood what was in Abie's heart. So both of his parents helped him memorize the needed prayers and portion, and as soon as that day was over, he followed his father's lead and did not return to the synagogue. Abie also knew that now that his mother was gone, his father would not allow Maurice, Harry, or Sammy to spend their time learning about their religion because that time could be better spent on secular studies. Abie knew that more than anything, Jonah Chernov wanted his children to be Americans, to get out of poverty, and he also wanted them to accept the idea that all organized religions were the superstitious ramblings of old men who wanted power over the minds and purses of the faithful.

Abie didn't care much about religion or its intent, but he did know that he could never fulfill his father's dream. Actually, he felt more at home and respected on the streets and among the other kids whose parents didn't seem to have high academic expectations for their sons than he did at home. On the street, he was respected for his smarts and his bravery and no one judged him or cared if he could read or not.

After a moment, he shook himself back to the reality that Harry and Sammy were in one school, and he was in another, and couldn't protect them on their way home. Reporting it to the police would accomplish nothing so if anything was to change, he would have to make it happen. When attacked, the boys had been playing in the old carriage mews that ran behind the houses between Blake and Sutter. It was open at both ends, the north end being closer to where the Irish kids lived and the school, and was everybody's shortcut into both neighborhoods and the shopping area.

The image of the boys in the alley coalesced into a fantasy where his brave Merry Men would leap out from behind the garbage cans and boxes that were the thick trees of Sherwood Forest, and he would heroically swoop down from his hiding place in the trees, dropping onto the attackers and kicking them to the ground. Yes, he would station his loyal outlaws in the trees with bows and arrows, and others would be camouflaged and hiding behind trees at both ends of the pathway so when the Sheriff and his men came through Sherwood, they would be trapped and given such a beating that they wouldn't think of coming back again.

He smiled to himself. His plan was not something adults would do or could do, but he and his friends could get away with it the same way the Irish kids were getting away with it. He and his friends wouldn't sit and debate over tea and get nothing done. He knew his friends would be up for it, and he figured that Joey, who also had no love for the Irish, would want to help. Now all he had to do was to borrow his father's hat and coat, get a cane, and make some excuse to take Harry and Sam out late Friday afternoon. He had two days to put the plan together.

The Sabbath sun hung low in the autumn sky, and the reddish sandstone finials and faces carved on the two and three story buildings that lined Blake Avenue became crimson and gold. The pushcarts were gone and only the permanent stalls stood empty in the gutter, for the immigrants who had moved from the Lower East Side once the Brooklyn Bridge was finished, recreated what they knew on this less than fashionable street. Each of the stores beneath the apartments had already closed two hours before. Abe, wearing his father's old coat and hat, followed by Yitz, Dovid, Meyer, Acky, Boris, and Mashe, with Harry and Sammy in tow, moved quickly and quietly to the alleyway, hoping not to be seen. But if anyone did see them from a window above, it would look as if an older man with a cane was taking the boys to one of the little house shuls on Sutter Avenue. Joey and five others were already there when they arrived.

In the alley, Abe explained the tactic and Joey nodded and smiled in agreement. With the other Italian kids, he moved to one end of the alley to hide behind the garbage cans and boxes. Abe had his friends do the same at the other end. All had scarves over their noses and mouths and were told to rush the Irish screaming, but that they weren't to say anything that would identify them to the cops. Myer and Acky climbed to opposite fire escapes and were each handed up two heavy metal garbage cans and instructed that when the Irish kids came under the fire escapes, the cans were to be thrown down on them. The crash would frighten and confuse them and they wouldn't know what the hell was going on. "We'll have the element of surprise," said Abe, "and the second you hear that crash, you jump out, rush them, and beat the shit out of them." Abe clenched his fist and thrust it into the air for emphasis. Then he told Harry and Sammy to hide behind some crates, and to stay hidden and out of danger.

When all was in place, Abe looked up at Myer and Acky on the fire escapes and they became imaginary archers hidden in the trees. He walked past others crouching behind crates and cans that he imagined as dense foliage. At the other end of the alley, he stood with his head down and watched the old men shuffle past him, responding to any "a gutten Shabbos," with a nod. These men knew to avoid the alley knowing it had become a dangerous place even if it saved them time. Five minutes passed and Abe could see about six or seven kids in the distance wearing knickers and caps pulled over one eye, strutting like Chanticleers down the street towards him. The Sheriff's men had arrived, he thought to himself, and he smiled at the prospect of his victory over injustice. He waited a moment until he was sure the Irish kids saw him. Hunched over on his cane, he imitated the steps of the old men and slowly shuffled into the alley as they ran towards him. He moved quickly so he would be positioned a little beyond the fire escapes when they caught up.

"Hey, you Christ killing kike, were y'a go'in?" one shouted.

When he saw that they were in position, Abe turned around and straightened himself up to his full height. They stopped short, surprised. At the same moment the four garbage cans came crashing down on the heads of the Irish boys, hitting and flattening three of them were they stood. They lay on the ground groaning and Abe's foot was the first one to find its way into the ribs of a red faced kid. Simultaneously, the other Jewish and Italian kids came screaming out of their hiding places, their fists clenched. The Irish were overwhelmed despite their efforts to get away, and they were beaten down onto the dirt where they lay in a heap, moaning in pain. "This is for beating up old men and little kids. And before you go whining home, I'm going to give you a special present that you won't be able to tell anyone about because it's just too good to share," Abe said through his mask, and he unbuttoned his pants and peed onto the squirming pile of punks.

"Now," he continued smiling, "You go home to your priest and say that it must have been God's will that you got your asses kicked. He'll understand!" Harry and Sam watched from their hiding places, their eyes wide, amazed, and grateful for what their big brother had done.

Rachelann waved her arms over the Sabbath candles to gather in the light as her mother taught her to do, covered her eyes, and said the blessings. Before she sat, Jonah said, "We have been given light so we may see what is before us. We light candles, bring light to a world where there is darkness. This is our reason for being." The statement had nothing to do with the actual Hebrew, but in Jonah's mind it gave a rational reason for lighting the candles, and offered no gratitude to God. God did not deserve his gratitude. Jonah insisted on this translation after his wife had died.

Leah's chair at the head of the table was always empty, but her influence was a constant presence. Rachelann took her seat next to Abe who sat between her and Maurice. Sammy, his face still swollen from the beating, sat at their father's right and next to him was Fanny and Harry who also had a purple ring under one eye and a split chin that needed stitches.

"Make the kiddish, Abie," Jonah said. Abe rose and recited the ancient benediction, and again, Jonah rendered his own translation: "The earth has provided us with grapes, and we have fermented wine. Drink and let the wine warm your bodies and lift your spirits. L'Chaim, to life." Though Jonah had taken God out of his translations, he did not demand that the children do the same. So when he made a similar blessing over the bread, the younger children, following Rachelann and Abe, mouthed it quietly in Hebrew. As his father did before him, he did have each of his children stand in front of him for a blessing, but no longer was it the priestly benediction that began with "May the Lord bless you and protect you..." His blessing was that they become good and honest people, study hard, and make the world a better place. All understood that *A Woman of Valor* would not be read because their mother was not there to hear it, and in its place, there was a silent moment of remembrance.

Though Jonah's issue with God continued, the thought of not having a Sabbath dinner, or a Passover seder, or any holiday celebration that brought them all together, was out of the question, for he knew too well that the consistency of ritual was the only thing that assured anyone in any family some degree of stability. He knew that in every Jewish home in Brownsville, the exact same blessings were being said and probably, the exact same foods were being served. He knew that all over this blessed country that opened its doors to him, and all over the cursed country he had left, every Jewish family was doing exactly what he was doing. His children were and would be moving into their own worlds as they grew older, but for this time, the consistency of Jewish rituals brought them together and would keep bringing them together. No matter what happened in the world, there would always be sundown on Friday and no matter where they found themselves, Sabbath would begin. In Jonah's mind, there was a cognitive disconnect that enabled him to insist on such celebrations while ignoring the fact that all these weekly, monthly, and yearly events had God at their core. So at the Chernov Sabbath table there were always tears of memory for the missing wife and mother, but there were also ironies, paradoxes and always the ghost of Jonah's father who years ago would stand each one of his children before him, put his hands on their heads, and bless them from his heart and from the strength of his faith. Jonah focused on Reuven's image blessing him and he tried to channel the goodness of that man's life into his own, but he could never quite achieve what he imagined it should have been and he knew he never would. Jonah Chernov had chosen to evolve into something new that his father and his father's faith could not understand. Whenever his mother presented herself in his memory he quickly dismissed her, for he could not imagine his mother without conjuring up some unpleasant memory that continued to subtract from his life even though she was thousands of miles away in Vienna with his sister Ruth. The past, he mused, never left, and for good or for ill, it continues to inform the present. Leah's death, his guilt at having left her with such anger between them, the thought of her dying alone at the bottom of the cellar steps, the latent feelings for Marta that once again blossomed into a passion he had not felt in years, their secret meetings during this year of mourning, their love making, and the thought that he was losing his children's love, all fused in him like something concocted in hellish crucible. Tears welled up in his eyes and he quickly wiped them with his napkin before his children noticed.

Rachelann took the big silver ladle given to her parents when they married in Krivoser, and doled out the soup and the noodles that she and Fanny had made that morning.

"Papa," Harry said through puffy lips. "My teacher said that we have a new president named Theodore Roosevelt. What's a president do?"

"He's the man who heads the government in this country," Jonah replied. "It's like if all the people in this country were in one big family, he'd be the Papa. Do you understand?"

Harry nodded and lowered his head. "Then what's a government?"

Jonah smiled.

"Don't you know anything," Maurice interrupted. "A government makes the laws that tell you what you can do and what you can't do. It's like Papa telling you that you can't stay up late or that you can't play in the gutter."

"So Papa is the president and also the government?" Harry replied, his face turned quizzically to his older brother. Maurice frowned, having thought he had settled the matter, and with little will to explain the concept of checks and balances to a twelve year old.

Jonah beamed. "Well, Maurice," he said. "You decided to answer him and now you have more questions. I think you should finish what you started." Fanny giggled and shook Sammy to pay attention.

Maurice thought a more simplified answer would do. "We learned in school that the president is the head of the government and can suggest that rules be written, but that these rules have to be approved by other people who are voted in by the people who live in the country."

"So if Papa is the president of the family, does that mean we are the people who live in the country?"

"Yes," Maurice said. "You finally understand."

Rachelann, Jonah, and Abe, who were pretending not to care, smiled. Though two years younger than he was, Maurice was at the top of his class in all of his subjects, and Abe was enormously proud of his younger brother. He knew how proud his father was of Maurice, and there were times when he was envious of that pride, but such feelings were fleeting and did not get in the way of the affection he felt for him. Like Biblical Joseph's eldest son Manasah, Abe also knew that it would be the younger and not the older brother who would be the first son to fulfill their father's dream and it did not sadden him at all. He loved Maurice.

"Then doesn't that mean that if Papa makes a rule, we can tell him it's a good rule or a bad rule and either follow it or not?"

Maurice sank in his chair and shook his head. Everybody was laughing so hard, that the table shook and sloshed whatever soup was left in the bowls.

"Would you like to explain now what a democracy is little brother?" laughed Rachelann as she stood to clear the empty bowls.

"What's a democracy?" said Sammy softly, and Jonah's face glowed with pride.

CHAPTER 2

After Leah's death, and with some money his sister Zeena loaned him, Jonah expanded the candy store by putting in shelves that held staples that he knew people needed on a regular basis. Mostly, he stocked things that now came in boxes like Uneeda Crackers, and staples like rice, flour, sugar, and salt. Of course there were the candies; the little bottles of sugar water encased in wax, the strips of colored sugar dots on long white paper, the little metal corrugated cups with the hard strawberry sweet in them and the little spoons that went with them, and the children's favorite, bubble gum. In the winter, there was some competition from the man who sold hot chickpeas off a rolling cart and the knish man, but Jonah knew that everyone had to make a living. He had also installed a kinescope machine that for a penny, one turned a crank, looked through the eye piece, and watched pictures move. It was like bringing the movies into the store, and was a big draw for both children and adults. It was a poor person's entertainment even though the nickelodeon a few blocks away was only a nickel. Most people could spare a penny, but not every person who came into the store could spare a nickel. It was Maurice who had first seen this wonder outside another candy store and thought it might be a good idea to get one, and it was.

Though Jonah and many others of the community considered themselves free thinking Jews who did not attend shul on the Sabbath or keep all the laws, he nevertheless kept the store closed on the Sabbath so as not to offend the part of the community that was observant. He did this for two reasons. First, it was not in his nature to deliberately offend and rub devout noses into what would be viewed as offensive behavior, and secondly, the business man in him knew that to keep the store open would lose him customers and make him something of an outcast in the neighborhood. So Sabbath was spent indoors doing inventory, stocking shelves, and cleaning up for the business week which for his community began on Sunday. The boys would be out with their friends, probably sitting on the synagogue steps, the older ones smoking and laughing, while their fathers were inside at prayers tormenting God with questions as to why their own sons had thrown off their religion in this new land. This seemed to be what was happening. After their bar mitzvahs, most of Abe's friends also stopped attending services. It was part of what he called "being assimilated," but it seemed to him that the Jewish boys were abandoning their faith in greater numbers than other groups who lived in the area. He imagined Rachelann and Fanny in the women's gallery or walking with their friends.

The bell above the door tinkled and a surprised Jonah looked up. No one came into the store on Saturday. Two men stood backlit against the glass door, and the shadows they cast along the floor and up the counter touched something dark in him. He froze for a moment, caught in a distant memory, and then remembered where he was. He moved around the counter towards them, recognized them as police officers from the neighborhood and so he felt his body relax as the threat dissipated. Perhaps they had news about the thugs who beat up Harry and Sam.

"Mr. Chernov," Officer Dugan began, "We think we may have a lead on your complaint, but the boys who may be responsible were badly beaten by another group and two are in the hospital with broken ribs. There's been a lot of fighting between the Irish and Italians here so we're looking at everybody to get to the bottom of this problem. These parents are also asking us to catch the punks who did this to their kids."

"I am sorry these boys were hurt and I'm glad their parents want these hoodlums caught, but I don't understand why you are coming to me."

Officer Fitzpatrick, the shorter and rounder man interrupted. "You see, in the attack on these Irish kids, only one person spoke and he said, looking at his pad, 'Go tell your priest that it must be God's will that you got your asses kicked.' We found that very peculiar because if they were Italian, Polish, or even Irish punks, they wouldn't have said that. So we're thinking it might have been some Jewish kids. We have had some run ins with your eldest son before."

Jonah felt his face flush at the memory of the meeting he had in the kitchen, and of Abe berating him and the others for their unwillingness to do anything about the problem. Could he have been involved?

"I still don't know why you are coming to me?" he said timorously, not knowing what they knew.

"Well, since it was your sons who were initially beaten, we thought that retaliation might come from some of the local Jewish boys."

"When did this happen?" Jonah continued.

"This past Friday evening," Officer Dugan responded.

"Then it would be highly unlikely that Jewish boys would be involved because they would all be home helping prepare for the Sabbath." As he spoke, Jonah searched his memory for when his boys were finally in the house, but he couldn't honestly say that he saw them all before Shabbos began.

"You have an older son who has been in trouble before." Fitzpatrick said. "Can you vouch for his whereabouts?"

"Certainly, I can," Jonah said without hesitation. "He was here with me."

The officers looked at him and then at one another. "Have a good day, Mr. Chernov, and if you hear of anything, please let us know."

"Of course," said Jonah as he moved to the door to open it for them. "And a good day to you, and thank you for trying to find who hurt my boys."

Jonah closed the door, locked it, and took a deep breath as he steadied himself against the door. He slowly released his breath feeling relief that they were gone and anger at what he imagined his Abie had done. For a moment he was transported back to Krivoser where the police would come into the shop to harass or extort his father, and he was angry at what Abie might have done to focus police on him and his family again.

"Two policemen came here asking me about you this morning," Jonah said before Abe's other foot was over the threshold. "Is this how you were brought up? To be a hoodlum? To hang out with kids who are going nowhere? To be violent?" The questions that weren't really questions in Jonah's mind, sprayed his son like bullets from a Gatling gun, and the young man was pinned where he stood, seemingly cowered by the rapidity of the accusations. "I lied for you," he continued, his face flushing. "I told them that you were here for Shabbos. And do you know why I knew you were involved in that attack?" he continued quickly. It was a rhetorical question. "Because the cop said something about one of the kids telling the Irish kids to tell their priests that the beating was 'God's will.' Now who would have said that if not you? The cops concluded that if the kid said 'go tell your priest,' that kid had to be Jewish, and I concluded that since you had heard me say what the priest said to me, you were the one who said it and was involved in the beating." He paused, waiting for a reply.

The only response that Abraham Chernov had to his father's accusations could be discerned by a slight sucking in of his lower lip and his eyes looking to the left. He knew that when confronted in the street like he had been, he had to either pick up a weapon or talk himself out of the situation. Normally, he would have been calm, but this was not in the street and this was his father coming at him again for something the elder Chernov viewed as a serious infraction of decency. But Abe viewed his own behavior as heroic. In this instance, he would not avoid the confrontation and he would not go on the defensive. Over the past months since his mother's death and his father's distance, he had built up what he considered righteous anger and righteous resentment for his personal loss, for his treatment at school, for his feelings of constantly disappointing his father, and for that dreadful suspicion that his father was involved with another woman while he should have still been mourning his mother.

"I did what I did," he said matching his father's intensity "because you and your friends have absolutely no idea what it is like to live on these streets and to be in an undeclared war every day you walk out of the house. You were going to the Irish cops to complain about Irish kids beating up Jewish kids. A lot of good that would have done. The only law and order here comes from the real fear that one group of kids will kick the hell out of them, or make an alliance and take over the neighborhood. We laugh at the cops because we know they don't give a damn about us and are out there only to kick us around and take protection money. You think they came here because you complained? They came because the priest probably visited those punks and they told him what I said. Then the priest went to the cops, and you can bet that Irish cops listen to a Catholic priest sooner than they'll listen to a Jewish candy store owner. What they saw was that their own had been beaten up and it may have been a Jew that was involved. That must bother the hell out of them."

Jonah was surprised at his son's response, having thought a dutiful son such as he would have lowered his eyes in shame. But this was no longer the Abie he knew, and within this father there was suddenly a conflicted mixture of pride in his son having acted and sudden loss. When did Abie change? he thought, and why did he not see it?

"Maybe I don't know what's going on, and maybe I am foolish to believe that the police will do something to protect my children," Jonah rejoined, "but I do know that going somewhere with the intent to hurt someone is not what we do. It is not what Jewish people do. The Talmud may teach that 'If a man comes to slay you, slay him first,' but no one was slain here. You had no right to deliberately go out to hurt people. That is not our way."

"Then you'll be kicked around all your life, Papa," Abe countered. "The only way they won't come to 'slay you' is to make sure they're too afraid to do that. Being on top and feared is the only place where you can be safe, and you get on top by being stronger and smarter than everyone else. Those punks will think twice before attacking my brothers and other Jewish kids again because they got a taste of fear. You have fear on your side, and you have control."

Jonah looked as his son as if he were a stranger. When Jonah was Abie's age, he was working with his father every day in the shop, learning his trade, listening to Reuben quote the Torah and Talmud, accepting without doubt what was said as God's word, and dutifully learning the languages Reuben insisted he learn if and when the opportunity came when his son would be able to attend school. But life changed quickly His father was murdered and Jonah hadn't been a tailor in years. He never got the chance to go to school as he dreamed he would do, and he no longer believed in the God his faith taught. He wanted a better life for his children, the promise of America that could only come through education. But this son seemed disinterested in any trade, and following his example as far as God was concerned, Abie was now seemingly twisting the meaning of sacred text to justify his behavior. This was not what Jonah had intended. Because of Abie's problem with the written word, Jonah could not envision Abie as becoming more than a worker at a machine.

"Then if you go after people like that," Jonah continued, "they will come after you and you'll be looking over your shoulder all your life. Don't think I don't know the friends you have and how you spend hours in the poolroom and playing cards. People talk and I don't like what they say. Don't think I don't know about the dice games. You should better be in the library with your brothers and sisters at least trying to learn."

Abe's cheeks flushed at the comparison and he swallowed his father's disappointment like hot water that scalded his throat and burned as it seeped into his innards.

"So you think you know all about me, Papa," he shot back. "What about what I know about you? What about you going into New York every Wednesday afternoon to that big house on Fifth Avenue? What about that woman who takes your hand and leads you in? What happens after that?"

Jonah blanched. How had he learned about his visits to Marta and did his other children know? Had Abie been following him? And for how long?

"At least what I do I do in the open where everybody sees. Yes, I play pool and I'm really good at it. And yes, I play cards and dice and I'm really good at those too. And a lot of the money I make I give to Rachelann so she can run the house. Do you think what your store brings in supports this family? Do you think only you support this family? You only see the food on the table and that we are doing what you expect us to do. But that's not how it is. That's not how the world works. Who is she?" Abe said suddenly.

"She's a friend from the old country," Jonah said feeling suddenly trapped and looking for some way to exit. "She's someone I used to know in Paris." As he spoke, his mind was racing as to what to reveal and what not to reveal about his clandestine love affair with Marta.

"And were you seeing her while Mama was alive?" Abe challenged.

"Certainly not! Never!" Jonah replied so emphatically, that Abraham knew he was telling the truth. "I met her again after your mother died and we've renewed our friendship. That is all. She raised your cousin Elizabeth from the time she was an infant. Ask your Aunt Zeena the next time you see her.

Her name is Marta Birkov, and I go there because she has some friends who come over to learn to speak French. I help with that." He began to regain his composure. "And just what business is it of yours where I go on Wednesday afternoons and who I meet? What is it your business who my friends are? I don't follow you to the poolhall to see what you do there, and I don't expect you to follow me. I'm the Papa here, not you."

Abe weighed his father's admission and decided not to proceed. He would wait, but he knew this would continue to be a point of contention between the two, and his father knew this also. Jonah would have to speak to Marta. Perhaps it was time for everyone to get together and reveal the secrets. Perhaps that would be the only way to move ahead and not have to keep looking over one's shoulder. Perhaps the truth would right the balances. Yes, he would speak to Marta their next Wednesday together. But more immediately, he had to find a path for Abe that would take him out of the poolhalls and card games, and not bring him into conflict with the police. Perhaps Zeena knew someone who would take him on.

The only time Abraham Chernov felt free were those times when he cut school and took himself down to Delancy Street on the Lower East Side. There he watched men and boys kneeling on the sidewalks throwing dice against the sides of buildings. Years of tossing dice against the bricks of a Brownsville gave him plenty of practice so he felt confident. He knelt down, tossed the dice, and lost. He tried it again and lost. And then he realized that he had been set up like all the others were set up by people who knew what they were doing far better than he. So he stopped playing and just watched. For weeks he would come back and just watch. By just watching, Abe eventually came to see who the set up guys were and who were the bosses who paid them. But there was a third party, the one who bankrolled the game. It was a machine that moved from street corner to street corner, fleecing men of their take home pay, and boys of their paper route money. They were nothing more than marks who didn't know shit from Shinola. At first, he didn't either, even though he thought he did. So when Abe finally felt that he had learned what was needed, he waited for a certain roll, threw down his money, and won. He won several times during that game, and then walked away, fully believing that if you aren't greedy, if you are thoughtful, and if you plan, you can be a winner. Something was to be learned every day. Here, Abe Chernov was a winner because he knew what he was doing and he was the one in control. He was no sucker and never would be. It was a promise he made to himself.

CHAPTER 3

1905 New Year's Day

Jonah approached Marta's home on Fifth Avenue. The wind, like a broom, swept remnants of cracked ochre leaves, seared at their edges, down the avenue and along the stone walls that bounded Central Park on the east. In comparison to some of the other homes he passed on his walk, Marta's house had no expansive grounds or castle-like appearance. From a distance he could see its four stories, the top story, a slanted facade made of copper which had oxidized into a pale green much like the Statue of Liberty. The entry level floor, with its protective wrought iron door, was of white stone blocks with columns supporting the first story rounded balcony. The first and second story facades were of curved red brick with rounded arched windows on the second story and square windows on the third. The fourth story was set back, allowing for a balcony with a stone balustrade where he and Marta would sit looking at the park and children playing there. It was not the grandest house on the street, but far grander than any home Jonah had ever been in before.

He loved the autumn afternoons with Marta on the little balcony off her bedroom and their moments together in the elegant room that Ezra had dismantled and shipped from the Duchamp mansion in Paris to New York. From time to time it did occur to him that he was sitting in Ezra's chair in front of Ezra's fireplace, but he caught himself realizing that none of these things were really Ezra's. Ezra was the thief, not him. All had been stolen from the man Marta told him had disappeared from a wind and rain swept deck one frightful night of her Atlantic crossing. Marta concluded that Ezra murdered him and threw him overboard, and Jonah did not disagree. Ezra was capable of anything to get what he wanted. Jonah felt a sense of triumph sitting in the same plush velvet chair that Ezra had sat on while Ezra was now sitting in jail on a stone slab waiting to be executed.

Jonah knocked softly and waited quietly, watching as the leaves swirled around his feet like tiny water spouts. The twenty or so years that he and Marta had spent apart, the years of missing her, the years of swallowed anger and resentment towards his mother and his wife, faded like winter breath whenever he was with her. Now, each time he saw Marta, each time he held her, it was as if he were seeing her and holding her as he did when he first came to love her in the little apartment they shared in Montmartre. In her arms, he could almost forget his life without her.

Though the years of anger and dissembling dissolved when he was with her, he remained painfully aware that at some moment in Paris, living with his mother and Leah, he had concluded that if he could block out the rancor and the verbal abuse, he might be able to survive the life in which he found himself. But in learning not to hear them and in learning to discount whatever vitriol and pain might have broken through, in learning to survive as best he could under the conditions of his life, he came to believe that if he could stop feeling, he couldn't be hurt quite as much. And this he did. But in finding Marta again and being reminded of how happy he once was, it became clear to him that when he turned off his feelings to protect himself, he had also turned off other feelings, even those he needed in order to fully love. Sarah and Leah taught him hard lessons, and he learned to respond without really feeling.

In time, he became used to not feeling, often thinking that if he didn't feel, he didn't have to see himself as inadequate or powerless. Not feeling helped him not feel the pain.

The years he lived in Paris and the years he lived in Brooklyn, were years he spent believing that he had no recourse to the life he had chosen with Leah. In many ways, he felt broken, always living from hand to mouth, and abandoned by the God in which he once believed. In the months since Leah's death, he slowly became aware that by believing that he was helpless and hopeless and could offer his family no real comfort, he had separated himself from his children out of shame. Suddenly, he understood why he had missed seeing his children changing and growing away from him. Again, it was his fault as it was his fault that the marriage failed. He was present, but not really there.

He had created strong brick walls around himself for protection. He could even remember laying the foundation when he was a child being castigated by his mother. He realized now, now that he was forty-two, that he, and probably most people, do not move very far away from who they were as children, even though they become adults and parents. But the bricks in his wall were transparent, and he could see the world as it moved before him. He could see Marta on the other side and he wanted her more than he wanted anything else in life. In the months of their clandestine meetings, he had risked physical and emotional intimacy with her, and even though he knew her heart, the encounters were always tinged with trepidation. Loving, for him, and truly opening himself to another was still a risk, and it might always be a risk. Trusting any woman with his inner self was a chance, and might always be a gamble. But the solidity of this wall was also a measurement of how much he wanted her, and the life they would have if he was willing to free himself from his fear, his past, and breach it.

Marta's smiling face appeared behind the beveled pane of the inner door, opened the next, and extended both hands to him. In her eyes, light seemed to dance only for him, and her smiling lips caressed his even before they met. The blond and silver streaked hair swept up carelessly up on her head, washed away the intensity of his thoughts as he waited for the door to open.

She pressed her lips softly against his as her arms enveloped him in an earnest embrace, and he responded by raising his arms and pressing himself against her.

"Look at us," she laughed. "Like teenagers. Give me your hat and coat, and come in out of the cold and sit. Do you want tea, coffee, or hot chocolate? I've made all three." Suddenly, she stopped and laughed, recognizing the rapidity with which she was giving directions and making offers. "Look, at me. I'm as silly as a schoolgirl trying to impress a new beau. You just come, catch your breath, and sit down by the fire to warm yourself. It's getting cold, and I fear that we're in for an early snow."

Jonah allowed himself to be led to the velvet chair near the fireplace, and again he found his eyes tracing the two carved caryatids with their heads and up raised hands supporting the marble entablature. A welcoming fire in the hearth sent out a comforting warmth that embraced him. The Empire clock with its black and gold sphinxes on the mantle suddenly chimed one in the afternoon even though the grey skies made it seem that it was early evening.

"Coffee, tea, or chocolate to warm your insides," she said playfully.

"I think I'll be different today and take coffee. Marta, I think there is something different about you today," he said suddenly studying her face." She smiled slightly, blushed, and placed a napkin on her lap without responding.

A silver service with the Duchamp crest on each of the pieces sat in front of Marta on a table opposite the fire, and she lifted a Meisen cup and saucer in her left hand and the Baroque coffee pot in the other, looking at him for guidance. "I know you take sugar with your tea, and I think you do take two with your coffee. Am I right?" With small silver tongs, she lifted two cubes of sugar, and stirred them till they dissolved. He took a napkin and placed it on his knee with one hand as he accepted the coffee cup and saucer with the other. He was delighted that she had become a fine lady who lived in this wonderful house and was someone who never had coffee or tea served to her in an old memorial glass. She offered him some cakes, but he declined.

"Something has happened this past week that I need to tell you about," he said in a voice tinged with unease. She lifted her own cup to her lips and leaned in intently. He told her of the incident with Abe, the police, and the confrontation between them in the store.

"He knows I come to see you every Wednesday. He's followed me here, but I don't think he believes that I am teaching a group of society ladies French. I think it might be time that we tell the children about us."

Marta put her cup to her lips and averted her eyes from his. In her fantasy since they met again, she had always imagined them living happily together, but she had skipped over the reality that there were other lives involved and other forces with which they had to contend. For one, she had never told Armand that Jonah was his biological father, and the half-brother of all of the children Jonah had with Leah. Zeena had told Elizabeth that her father was not Ezra and that she was her biological mother, but nothing else. All the secrets would have to be revealed, and the thought of how the children would react to it frightened her. Marta lowered the shaking cup from her lips and set it down. Her outward composure, the dissembling composure she learned to use to survive living with Ezra, belied the anxiety and heat she felt racing up her body and into her cheeks. She listened to Jonah as if he spoke through a veil, and her mind tried to envision and orchestrate what would be the best way to go. Now, with what she had to tell Jonah, the situation would be made even more complex than it already was.

"We must handle this very carefully," she said, seeing that he was becoming agitated as he spoke, envisioning the family gathering. "I think both of us tried to pretend that his day would never come, but it has." She studied his face to be sure that he had heard her and he had not faded into his own dark reverie of what might happen at such a meeting. She recalled their meeting a year before when she told Jonah about Armand and how his eyes filled with tears at the thought that he and Marta had created a child together. How proud he was when she added brief memories of the boy's life and his studies at the university.

"Armand knows of your visits to me, but knows only that you are an old friend from Europe." She paused. "Jonah," she continued, "before we decide when and how we are to talk to all the children, there is something you must know." She took another sip of tea and gathered her thoughts. "You have not seen Armand since that terrible night so many months ago when he saved me from Ezra's madness. I know how much you ache to sit with Armand, to talk with him, and embrace him as your own. I also have not said anything because he and Elizabeth had so much to deal with what with Ezra going to prison, and with them having to be called as witnesses against the man they believed was their father. But there is something more that you must know before we proceed to tell the children everything." She shifted her position. "Come sit next to me and hold my hand."

Jonah smiled at the invitation and moved to her side. He took her hand in his and brought it to his lips, kissing it gently. He turned to her and smiled. Again, the years faded and they were back in the shadow of Sacre Cour in the little apartment with the mismatched furniture. Oddly enough, she was also transported back to Paris, and in her imagination they were sharing a pastry and she was about to tell him that she was pregnant with Armand. It was a moment that was denied to her and to him because of the circumstances, but in her fantasy, they both laughed at the news and fell into each others arms with unbounded joy and kisses. It was a perfect moment of two young lovers sharing the happiest news imaginable.

"What is it?" he said softly.

Her hand quivered in front of her mouth and she smiled nervously. "Years ago, a lifetime ago, I was not able to tell you that we were going to have a child together because that very same day you told me you had found your family. You were in such pain and so very torn that I could not bear to add to it. I know you chose me, and that has sustained me all of these years." She paused and pressed his hands. "It seems that we have been given a second chance. I do not know if there is a power in the universe that rectifies and sets right mistakes, but today I'm going to tell you what I could not tell you so long ago."

"Are you saying that you're going to have a baby?" His words were spaced as if he was processing the revelation. But we're middle-aged people. Who has babies in their forties?" He started to laugh, stood, and faced her, his hands taking hers and pulling her up to him. "Oh, my God," he said. "We're going to have a baby." His brain filled with the memory of the joy he had the first time they had made love again after their years of separation. "This is so wonderful. This is so right. This is so incredibly crazy." He was as giddy with the excitement of a child on a swing, but his expression suddenly changed when he thought of how his children would respond. How would everyone respond?

"This is a very complex situation Jonah," she continued, putting her hands to the sides of his cheeks and cradling his face, "and we must handle this slowly and delicately."

"Ordinarily I would put this talk about marriage off for another year because such a subject for your children so soon after their mother's death would cause them pain and anger." She paused. "They would also resent me. It will be difficult enough when they learn that they have an older half brother. Can you imagine what they will feel when they learn that they have a brother or sister on the way? Jonah, even I'm confused trying to keep who's who in this insanity, so can you imagine how overwhelming this might be to young ones? But how long should we wait? Certainly I think we should be married before the baby is born."

Jonah took the last sip of his drink, and studied the delicate flowers on the inside of the empty cup in his hands. "Abraham is insistent on knowing who you are, and I was not exactly calm when he confronted me. I did not handle it well. I get upset with them too easily. Sometimes my own children overwhelm me, but I'd like them to meet you, and Armand. I'd like them to see this world and perhaps get themselves a vision of this life because it will be their life once we do marry."

As Jonah spoke, Marta was calculating how many months before the birth, and she was determined that the new life growing within her would not be born into illegitimacy regardless of how Jonah's children felt. Marriage would have to come within the next several months. She was terribly conflicted for Jonah's sake. Does she risk the animosity of his children, or the legitimacy of their child?

"Marta, I want to get married sooner than later. Children grow up and move away. They'll be angry if we marry in a month or in a year. No matter what we do, they will be angry with me and resent you. Why should we have to wait to begin our lives again together? How many years do we have left?"

She considered his words. Had she not been pregnant, she would have pressed for a longer space. But now there were other concerns.

"Jonah, you may be willing to face years of rancor and alienation from your own children, but I do not want that for you and I don't want if for myself or for our baby. No, this has to be carefully thought out, but I'll tell you what we can do. You and your sister will be celebrating your birthdays in two weeks. Let me make a party for the two of you. I know that your children adore her and they've met their cousin, David. I'm sure Elizabeth and Nathaniel will come, and everyone can meet as young people who can first become friends before they become family. We can see how they respond to one another and decide what to do." She paused, confident that her plan would be accepted and lifted the cup of tea to her lips.

"I agree with all my heart," he said, "and I need to say something to you that goes beyond consideration for our children." He paused and took a breath. "At certain times in our lives we become aware that our time is running out. Suddenly, there are fewer and fewer choices. All my life I have felt as though I was standing on a precipice, and the rocks and sand holding it up were giving way little by little. I know that I must have the courage to go forward while I still can. I must do it for myself. They will move into their own lives and I will be left, so there are choices I have to make for myself. There is no one to blame but myself if I choose not to move. Marta, my dearest Marta, my soul has been in darkness for so long that I thought it was dead until I found you again. Perhaps I had to die before I was worthy to live again."

CHAPTER 4

Marta, Elizabeth, and Armand, stepped out of the carriage in front of the Plaza Hotel where they were to meet Zeena. The epauletted doorman, his large black umbrella open to keep the flakes of snow off those alighting from the cab, moved quickly and carefully down the red carpeted steps to the newly arrived passengers and opened the door, offering his hand to the black gloved lady in the fur trimmed coat. Marta stepped onto the lightly dusted pavement and smiled her appreciation. Elizabeth followed, as Armand handed the driver his fee through the small window.

"I love this place," Elizabeth said remembering the first time she accepted Zeena's invitation here so they could get to know one another. Over the past year, they had established a standing appointment at the Palm Court for lunch the first Sunday in each month. She, Nathaniel, and Zeena had become very close. The massive gold standing candelabra on either side of the entrance lighted their way.

They entered the marble lobby and saw Zeena standing near a huge floral display of white flowers that stood in marked contrast to the regal woman wearing a mink hat in the Russian style and a full length mink coat. The multi-tiered crystal chandelier above her lit a smiling face and extended hands that belied the anxiety she felt. She was counting on the friendship that had been established among them to stand in the face of what she and Marta had to reveal. As she kissed Elizabeth on both cheeks, David approached with Nathaniel. They, too, had become good friends. Elizabeth's eyes smiled her surprise and delight at seeing them.

Marta and Zeena had decided that everyone should be told the truth about how everyone was related at the same time, believing that the friendships and affections that had developed since they all met would be a bridge over these very murky waters. When Zeena told Elizabeth that she was her biological mother the week following her graduation concert at The Dakota, Marta was also there for support and approval. One woman bore her and the other raised her, and Elizabeth would never have to choose between them. She had two mothers and though it took some time for her to fathom the moment, she was delighted and embraced them both. Life is full of wonderful surprises and great sadness, she mused, and such events seem to tumble over one another like children playing leap frog. She was suddenly Jewish and engaged to the love of her life, the man whom she called father was not her real father and in prison, and one of the most famous actresses in the world was her biological mother. Of course, learning about Ezra was difficult for her, for she did love this man and could not understand why her two mothers despised him so. It saddened her tremendously that after finding out that they were not his children, Ezra refused to see her and Armand. That was a pain they both shared and carried.

Zeena glanced up at the white and gold clock above the door and noted the time. The miniature trio adorning the clock, the Greek fates of antiquity, were holding a thread that symbolically stood for a person's life. One allotted the thread, one would spin the story, and one would eventually cut it. Today she mused that that thread held the story of this family, and whether it would be either strengthened or damaged depended upon how she played her part.

"I've asked the management to allow us to use a corner of the Edwardian Room," Zeena said, interrupting the greeting and pleasantries, "because what Marta and I are about today needs some privacy and not the distraction of music and other people."

The group stopped and looked at her wondering what she could possibly mean. She raised her hand to a gentleman in a morning coat who made a deferential motion for them to follow him as he moved though the archway, turning past the court, and then a left down a long corridor of marble pilasters with gold Corinthian tops.

Unlike the French neo-classical softness of the Palm Court, the Edwardian Room was decidedly masculine in its spirit with its dark mahogany walls. Immediately confronting them was a large roaring fireplace above which was a panel holding a raised coat of arms under a carved rounded cornice. Above this was a landscape painted in golds, oranges, and yellows of some ancient fortress atop a rocky mountain. Dominating the room was a multi-tiered, ornate bronze chandelier whose dim lights bathed the room in a quiet dignity and elegance that fully reflected an age of wealth, privilege, and entitlement enjoyed by a very few. A round table for six was set in a corner with crystal and silver on a white tablecloth.

Elizabeth, Nathaniel, Armand, and David looked at one another and then at Marta and Zeena and then back again.

"Since this is a very special gathering, I've taken the liberty of ordering all your favorite entrees, but we are going to start not with the appetizer, but with dessert." A chuckle of delight moved around the table as three waiters brought in trays of cakes, parfaits, and cookies. In front of Elizabeth and Nathaniel was placed a sealed tray of delectable confectionaries with a seal assuring the taster that the delights were kosher. Tea and coffee was poured and the giddiness of the young people at the sight of the creamy custards and chocolate sauce oozing out of delicate pastries or over fruits that had been imported.

Zeena lightly struck a demitasse spoon against her water goblet. "My dearest ones," she began, "ours is a unique family brought together by odd circumstances and strange coincidences. I, an actress crossing the ocean, meets a young man on the ship who turns out to be my very own nephew." She smiled warmly at David. "And not long after that, a young lady appears at my door you all know as Elizabeth, my very own daughter." She also bathed Elizabeth in a smile. "And Elizabeth, finding out that I was her mother, immediately became, in the eyes of the Jewish People, a Jewess, and that led to Nathaniel's parents blessing their union." Nathaniel squeezed Elizabeth's hand at his side where his silent affection would not be noticed. Elizabeth smiled without taking her eyes off her mother. "But in finding out that I was her mother, I also had to reveal that the Marquis Duchamp was also not her father and that saddened her. So you see that when people unlock their secrets, they at the same time may unlock sadness as well as surprises and happiness. But secrets told also unlock anger and resentment at the lies that were told to protect the secrets, and that is why Marta and I brought you all here today. Before we begin telling you what we must tell you if we are all to move on in truth, I first ask you to have some of the desserts in front of you so the sweetness on you tongue may hopefully counteract the bitterness you may taste from our story."

The young people looked at one another curiously, wondering what would follow. Each took a favorite sweet, smiled at the taste, and waited.

Marta's gloved hand shook as she lowered the napkin from her lips. Clearing her mouth with a sip of black coffee, she looked at Armand, smiled briefly and said, "Armand, after that terrible evening in Zeena's home, I made you aware that the man who raised you, the man you called 'mon pere,' the man the world knew as the Marquis Duchamp, was not your biological father." He nodded his assent. "But the man who was, I mean who is, a man I loved in Paris, the man I conceived you with in love, is very much alive." She paused for a reaction, to see Armand's eyes narrow slightly and cock his head to one side more in surprise than in shock. "His name is Jonah Chernov, and you saw him at Elizabeth's recital, but I didn't introduce you then. You've seen him since at our home because he visits me on Wednesday afternoons." Again she paused, waiting for him to scour his memory for his mother's afternoon guest. "I would have told you, but I wanted Zeena here because this Jonah Chernov," she held her breath and let it out with the words "is also Zeena's brother and her twin. Yes, Zeena, in addition to being my friend, is also your aunt."

Armand put his fingers to his mouth, tracing with his pointer and thumb around his reddish blonde mustache and back to his pursed lips. He was more confused than angry at this latest deception. He also felt a curious relief in the reaffirmation that Ezra was not his biological father. From the time he was very young, he had a vague feeling that Ezra did not understand him or even like him very much. He, despite his accomplishments, had always felt that he was a disappointment to the man who raised him.

"Then are you saying that Elizabeth is not my real sister but my first cousin, and that I am half Jewish?"

"Yes," she said simply after a small pause, "that's exactly what I am saying." Her response was measured and given softly, so that she could be sure that he fully comprehended the magnitude of the revelation. "I want you also to know that this man, Jonah Chernov, is a kind and sensitive man, skilled in languages, a lover of art and music, and very intelligent." She paused again letting this new information seep in. "You are very much like him, and I am so very happy for that, my dearest Armand. I need you and Elizabeth to also know that I am very much in love with him and always have been."

Everyone smiled at Marta's very personal admission while trying to process out what Armand had been told and how he would respond. They waited in an uncomfortable silence.

Armand now played with a small tuft of hairs that grew under his lip and lifted a cream filled pastry to his lips. His newly discovered Aunt Zeena was right. The sweet pastry helped. "I'm not sure what I can say," he began, trying not to allow his confusion to be revealed as he sensed that at the edges of his confusion were feelings of anger with hints of betrayal. "Suddenly, you tell me I have a new father that I've yet to meet, and not too long ago you told me that the man I believed to be my father was not my father at all. And all this, Madame, comes very soon upon you telling me that you are my real mother. I was glad about that because you are the only mother I have ever known, and you were the only mother I have ever loved, and I would have continued loving you whether you were my mother or not. We know each other only as a mother and child can know each other. But learning that I have a father that I've never met before is different, and I'm not sure how to respond. I don't know this man. The father I thought I knew I did not know at all, and now that I know who he was and what he did, I'm glad he is not my father. He did not give me life, though the life I had with him will always be with me." He thought for a moment and continued. "I don't know if I need a new father now. I'm an adult and I'm in college." As he spoke, Armand searched his brain for something to hang on to so he would not go spinning off or chide his mother for the duplicity that he suddenly realized had been infused into his life. "You have been both father and mother to me, and I feel no loss or emptiness."

He paused and looked at the rest of them as they looked at him. "Certainly, I'm curious," he said, recovering himself from the awkwardness of the silence, "and there is something in me that makes me curious as to how a son and a father who've never met might share certain qualities." He suddenly became the anthropologist of the textbooks he studied, hoping that with a more impersonal appraisal of the situation he might find some immediate protection, but he quickly realized that his default into something clinical was a way of separating himself from the conflicts of this new reality. Unconsciously, he was moving himself from a jumble of difficult feelings to the safety of a protective intellect. Still, he did not want to seem insensitive, seeing how much his mother loved this new stranger that would be part of his life. He knew he would have to meet Jonah Chernov and eventually, embrace him. "I will meet him,

Madame. I will talk with him. I will come to know him and he must come to know me for your sake," he continued rescuing Marta from the sadness he saw creeping into her eyes.

Marta felt tears forming in the corners of her eyes. She rarely cried, and when she did, it was in the quiet of her room and never in front of her children. Now she felt herself welling up for fear that his statement of love for her was the mere kindness of the moment, and that he really wanted to push himself away from the table in a rage and leave the restaurant. A single tear rolled down each cheek. He had never seen her cry before, and he instinctively reached out to the woman who always been there to comfort him and sing to him and tuck him into bed. His hand touched hers and she placed her cheek on it and wept.

"I was afraid you would hate me," she said, lifting her head, trying to control her sobs. "I would die if you hated me."

"I could never hate you," he said tenderly. "But why couldn't you tell me what I've always felt? Yours was the first face I saw when I awoke and the last face I saw when I went to bed. You carried me when I needed to be carried, and held me when I needed to be held. You scolded me when I needed to be scolded, and you taught me right from wrong. Madame or mother, you are one and the same. How can I ever feel anything but love for you."

Armand said truthfully what he knew had to be said to comfort this woman, but his soul and brain were at war with each other. His feelings were weaving themselves into complex patterns never woven before. When this story was fully told, what a tapestry of this family would be revealed? If Marta Birkov was his mother, and Jonah Chernov was his real father, who was he really? Was he still Armand Duchamp? So much more had to be learned and discussed. But not at this time.

"And one other thing." He paused, hoping that what he would say next would end the current drama and move the moment to some lighter tone. Everyone's attention was fixed. He took a breath. "Now that Elizabeth is my cousin and not my sister, do I still have to be nice to her?"

Everyone laughed as he had intended.

"You'll have to be even nicer to me now, my little cousin, because as your big sister, I felt an obligation to keep all your secrets, but as your cousin, I might no longer feel obliged to do that."

The laughter continued at Elizabeth's quick return, and the erstwhile brother and sister each knew that nothing had really changed between them or would ever change for that matter. Marta's quiet tears attested to her relief. Now it was up to Zeena to reveal what she would reveal.

The liveried waiters poured tea and coffee. Armand, lost in his thoughts, focused on the plate in front of him, looking as if he had been called on in class and had not given the correct answer. David and Elizabeth anticipated what would follow. The lives of the people at the table were changing over coffee, tea, and pastries.

"I know that this is difficult for you, Armand," said Zeena fixing her gaze directly on him, "but I for one am delighted that I have a nephew who is a spectacular young man with the world at his feet, and one who now knows that I am his adoring aunt." Armand smiled at his newly acquired dramatic relative, and found solace in an eclair.

"Now what is to be revealed must be revealed," Zeena continued with an uncharacteristic hint of nervousness in her voice but with a hint of drama that all had come to expect. "And I must start with my own dearest child."

Elizabeth felt herself contract at what might be said, and took Nathaniel's hand again. Elizabeth, while constantly enjoying her mother's company, her ebullient style, her dramatic mannerisms, and the lavish gifts that were always a surprise, was not fully comfortable with other kinds of surprises, especially when they could be very personal. She attributed this reticence in her nature as the effect of her Presbyterian upbringing. Elizabeth looked at Armand and he looked back with an expression that told her it was her turn in the hopper.

"Must this be done now, here, in front of everyone?" she said softly, hoping to dissuade her mother from her intent.

"I know this is going to be uncomfortable for you, my dear, but we are all family, and if what has to be said is not said so everyone can hear, then the secrets that have ruled our lives will be pushed into another generation and those who keep the secrets may just never move on or come to truly understand themselves." Like Marta, Zeena also paused to measure her daughter's silent response to the latter truth. "Believe me, I know what secrets and lies can do to a life, so I think it best to just rip off the proverbial bandage." Zeena cleared her throat. "Elizabeth," she began. "You know I am your biological mother, and like Armand, you also know that the man who called himself the Marquis Duchamp was not your biological father. Yes, at one point, many years ago, he was my husband, but I came to our marriage bed pregnant with you."

Elizabeth closed her eyes, her fearful mind swirling with the unknown ramifications that her mother's story would impose on her life. The hand that was not squeezing Nathaniel's under the table, covered her mouth in anticipation of the answer to the question she had asked but was told that she would have a response at a later time. This was the time.

"I gave birth to you in Russia some time before your aunt Dora and uncle Jonathan were married and had David, but I'm fuzzy on the time so I cannot give you details. It is enough for you to know that you were born before your aunt and uncle were married."

David, who was listening intently for any reason as to why he was being made privy to these revelations of family secrets, sat up when he heard the names of his parents. He put the pastry down. Why were they being included as a time reference? he thought.

Zeena waited for the information to seep in before continuing. Every eye focused on her in anticipation of what was to come next. "You see, my dear, I was being forced into a marriage by my mother with the man you all knew as the marquis, but who Marta and I knew as Ezra Bendak. My distaste for him drove me to do something I would never have done, but have never regretted." She exhaled and leaned back in her seat holding the armrests to bolster her resolve to relive those traumatic moments. "It was during a holiday called Purim, and a time when Jewish men are invited to drink to excess. As was the custom for girls, I veiled myself as Queen Esther, lured the young man I loved into the barn where he was living, and I seduced him. He was so drunk that he had no idea of what was happening. I did this because I was desperate not to have Ezra Bendak be the first man to have me."

She paused and thought of a little Yiddish expression her father often used when she or her siblings were disappointed and when things hadn't gone their way: 'Menshen tracht un Gut lacht; Man plans and God laughs.'

"But the universe plays its little jokes on us," she said wistfully, "and the first time I was with a man I truly loved, I conceived you." Tears began to fill Zeena's eyes at a memory that was so clear and so mixed with such love and such pain. Marta reached out and put her hand on Zeena's in a comforting gesture.

"I assure you Elizabeth that this man, your father, never knew in his drunkenness that he had been with me, and I stress that point because it is most important, especially for David to know this. The ring you wear around your neck that Marta gave you, I took off that man's finger that night and put it on my own. To me, it was a symbol of our betrothal, and our marriage." Before either of them could interject the question Zeena knew was coming she continued. "I quickly married Ezra because it was the only way to protect myself, my child, my family, and your true father from Ezra's malice. If he knew the truth, there was no telling what he would have done."

"Will you now tell me who that man was?" Elizabeth said hesitantly, alternatively wanting to know and not wanting to know.

Zeena looked at Elizabeth, then to David, and back to Elizabeth. "The man I loved so long ago, the man who did not love me but loved my younger sister, Dora, the man I married in my foolish heart when I conceived you, was your uncle Jonathan, David's father."

Before Elizabeth could respond, Zeena looked at David and said, "David, what I did I did long before he married your mother. I was a foolish, selfish child running from a life I hated. I was desperate to win something for myself, some memory to cherish before all my dreams collapsed. Your father never loved me. He only loved your mother. I hope you can forgive me."

David lowered his eyes. "It was a long time ago, Aunt Zeena," he said softly, "and I know that my parents love one another very much. What you did has nothing to do with me," he said, trying in some way to separate himself from this disquieting truth. "This is something for you to work out with my parents. From where I sit, I think what my father and mother do not know will not hurt them. This will hurt them if they find out." The image of David's parents happily living in Switzerland came to mind as he measured the distance between Geneva and this recent revelation. "For me, I am grateful to you Aunt Zeena for all you have done for me, and I am very happy that you and my father gave Elizabeth to the world. I think it ironic that Armand and Elizabeth, who were brother and sister, discover they are cousins, and Elizabeth and I who believed we were cousins, discover we are brother and sister." The sudden reversal of roles amused him.

"Please, David, do not hate me for the foolish acts of a foolish young girl," Zeena said imploringly while wiping the tears off her cheeks.

"I don't hate you, Aunt Zeena, and never shall. The fact that Elizabeth and I share a father is strange, but it not horrific. It's not going to separate me from my family and the people I love. Again, I only ask that my parents never learn of it. Will you agree to that, Elizabeth?" he said turning to her. Then he added, "We are still all family, and that's what counts, but you have to know Aunt Zeena, that while the truth may be liberating to you, what does your truth do for us?" My life does not really change with this revelation, but Elizabeth's life does, and from the look on her face, not for the better. Did she really need to know this now or did you tell her so you don't have to carry this truth by yourself?"

"I shall never tell your parents and I'm sure Elizabeth will not either," Zeena replied acquiescing to his request. "Thank you," she mouthed silently, registering David's pointed barb about telling the truth.

Elizabeth barely heard David's response, for she was too much absorbed in the newness and shock of her mother's revelation. The feelings that Zeena's story generated were feelings that had never entered the protected world in which she had lived her life. Despite her outward nature and her romantic and occasionally unrestrained notions, hers was very much the sedate existence of privilege, preparing her for neither the drama and tragedies of life nor life's traumatic and sudden disclosures. At this moment, she felt as if she were struggling for air, alternately pulled up and down in a swift current of betrayal and anger, self-pity and loss.

"I do not know what to say to you, mother," she said slowly. "In fact, I don't know what to say to any of you." She sat up in the chair, and made a helpless gesture in the air with her open hands like a helpless child asking to be lifted up. "Suddenly, I do not know who I am, and I feel as if I am floating like a leaf that will never land. You say I was conceived in a barn?" she continued looking at Zeena. "You tell me I was conceived by a terrified girl who was not married?" She stopped and a sudden realization came over her. "That makes me illegitimate, doesn't it? Why did I have to know this?" Her questions poured out of her, questions that were embedded with accusations and judgements. "The man I thought was my father is in prison for murder, and all I thought I knew about my life and my world was a lie? Where do I go with this? How do I move into the next moment?" She started to sob and fell into Nathaniel's arms.

Nathaniel held her and comforted her while condemning Zeena with his eyes for telling a truth he felt his fiancee did not need to know. "Did you have a ring of intention from Ezra Bendak before you seduced David's father?" he said suddenly, not caring about the tone of his voice and surprising everyone at his uncharacteristic intensity.

"What does that have to do with anything?" Zeena replied.

"It may have everything to do with it." His expression demanded a response.

"No, Ezra never gave me a ring except at the ceremony," she said with some caution. "Why do you ask?"

"I ask," he said, "because a betrothal ring before the wedding binds you to the man you will marry. That's our law. If you had no ring, there was no binding, and the child of your union outside of that marriage is not considered illegitimate." Zeena relaxed and her eyes widened. Elizabeth lifted her head and through her tears looked at him hopefully. "Only the child of a married woman with a man not her husband, or the child conceived by a betrothed woman by a man that is not the man she will marry, is considered a mamzer or bastard in our faith." The authority in his voice remained and continued to reprimand his future mother-in-law. "Elizabeth is the child of two unwed Jewish people and she is just as legitimate in the eyes of Jewish law as you or I," he said flatly. He turned. "Elizabeth, my dear, dear, Elizabeth," he continued, taking her face in his hands tenderly. "There is no shame to you because of how you were conceived, and this shall never be spoken of again." He looked around the table silently demanding their assent. Everyone looked at one another and nodded. "Everything else we can work through. You are no different from the girl I loved when you walked in here. You are who you are. You are what you have been. You are what you always will be. You will be my wife. If the name Duchamp is a fraud to you, the name Seligman is not, and soon you will be Elizabeth Rebecca Seligman. Your history may have changed, but other people lived it, not you. Now dry your eyes and smile. If you like, we can talk about it with the rabbi tomorrow."

There was some movement at the doors to the dining room as they opened for the luncheon crowd. Everyone at the table looked and took some relief in the idea that this family meeting could not continue. Fashionably dressed men and women were led to tables around them, chattering and laughing as their chairs were held for them by the liveried footmen in attendance. The head waiter came over to Zeena and bowed slightly. "Shall we clear the table of the desserts, Madame, and bring the entrees, or would you just like aperitifs brought to the table.

Zeena looked at her family. "I think the entrees," she said with a flamboyant gesture, "I'm famished and can certainly use a bottle of your best Pino Noir."

Later that evening, Elizabeth and Armand stood at the entry to the study. "Madam," said Armand. Marta looked up from the monthly accounts to see her children standing in the doorway. The candles on the candelabra on either side of the large mirror above the hearth, flickered with the slight breeze that was created as they entered. The small room was warmed from the glowing embers behind the carved iron grate.

"Come, sit." and she motioned them to the tufted leather couch near her desk. The gas lamps bathed the room in a soft gold.

"You have to know, Madame, how difficult it was for us to hear what we heard today." Armand held Elizabeth's hand for reassurance. "Now that we are alone, is there anything else we need to know?"

"I don't want any more surprises," said Elizabeth. "I've had quite enough."

"Then you must sit down. I am so very weary of the secrets. I think telling secrets lift burdens, but may become burdens for others. However, there is one other secret that you must know, and I'll keep that to myself until tomorrow."

CHAPTER 5

The night after the revelation over luncheon at the Plaza, Elizabeth, Armand, and Marta dined alone. She had cooked their favorite dishes, and as she placed them on the table, Armand initially wondered if there were some special occasion that he had forgotten. But he soon realized that Madame was about to tell them what they needed to know so there would be no more surprises, and she prepared these dishes to cushion whatever blow was coming.

She fingered the crystal goblet and studied the deep claret wine she had poured for herself. She invited her children to pour their own. "To new beginnings and the truths that come with them," she said as she raised her glass to her lips.

Armand followed. "To new beginnings and the truths that come with them," he parroted. There was a brief silence as each savored the delicate whispers of nuts and fruits on their tongues. "What new beginnings are we talking about Madame?" Elizabeth said, trying not to sound anxious. Both still referred to her as Madame. Armand, even though she had revealed to him that she was his mother, could not as yet use the word. Habits are not easily broken.

Marta put her hand to her mouth and traced her lips and throat with her fingers. Then she tapped them lightly on the table. Armand looked at her quizzically and ladled a large helping of Beef Bourguignonne. "Are we going to talk, Madame, about what needs to be talked about?" he said trying to smile. He put a cube of the sauce soaked beef into his mouth. "Oh, this is marvelous," he said momentarily forgetting the gravity of the moment.

"Life happens" she began, "and there are things we do to survive that must be kept secret for the protection of those we love." This was her preamble, her setting the ground rules that made it clear that what she did she did with good intentions. She would hold nothing back. "I have kept the truth from you for good reason,' she reiterated, "and I do not regret my decision because it gave you both a privileged life." She wondered if they understood what she had just said. She wondered if they could he even imagine the life of squalor they might have led had Ezra not believed from the beginning that Armand was his son? "The man you called, 'mon pere' is out of the picture and cannot hurt us, and there is more to this ever changing story that I want you to know." She took another sip of wine to bolster herself, and Armand put down his fork and looked at her intently. Elizabeth had not touched her food, but sat uncharacteristically quiet with her hands in her lap.

"I met Jonah Chernov on a train to Paris from St. Petersburg, and he asked me if I would help him take care of his sister's child. That was you, my dearest Elizabeth. He believed Zeena was dead. Jonah was married to a woman named, Leah who died about a year ago. For the entire time we were in Paris, he searched for his family. At that time, he had his own child, a daughter he had never met." Elizabeth raised her eyes at the mention of her mother's name and looked at Marta. "During these months together, we fell in love. Ezra had been married to Zeena and believed the little girl I was caring for was his. He wanted you, Elizabeth, as a reminder of your mother. When Ezra found us and demanded you, Jonah and I were going to take you and leave together, leave everyone, and run away. But Ezra found him and had him beaten so badly that he was hospitalized and nearly died. Jonah had his family, and I had the choice of finding him, or staying with you. I stayed with you. By the time Jonah got out of the hospital, we were already in New York. I had no options. I could not let Ezra take you from me, Elizabeth. I had made you my own." She paused to see if Elizabeth would respond which she did by nodding her head and smiling. "Armand," she said turning towards him, "I was a month pregnant with you when we left, and after Ezra took me to his bed and I began to feel you growing within me, he concluded that he was your father. I allowed him to think this for your protection. He probably would have murdered me and you if he knew the truth."

"You're telling me that I'm a bastard." he said.

"No!" she said emphatically, cutting him off. "I'm telling you that life is complicated and you are never to say that again. You are no different today then you were yesterday. I carried you under my heart and I carried my secret to protect you. You are here, and you are safe, and you have the world at your feet. There is nothing illegitimate about you. You are what you think and you are how you behave. That is all there is. Now you know my secret, and I urge you to keep it to yourself because the world is filled with fools."

Armand, measuring the wisdom of her warning as well as the woman herself, responded softly. "All our lives we looked at you as if you were our mother. You looked after this household the way a mother would, and you cooked for us the way a mother would. Why didn't Ezra marry you if he believed you were my mother? Why didn't you want to make me legitimate? Why didn't you tell us who you really were?"

"To him and to the world, you were his legitimate son. He concocted a story that your mother had died in childbirth. Legitimate was not any part of his life. Yes, I wanted him to marry me, and I even tried to give him his own children to further ensure our security, but he did not marry me because I was not what he called his 'social equal.' I laughed at this because the reality was that he wasn't a Marquis either. His whole life was illegitimate. He was a thief, a fraud, a liar, and possibly a murderer. He stole his title and everything you see around you. If there was any truth in his life, it was that he loved Zeena. It was an obsession, and to marry me would have meant that the fantasy would be broken. I could never tell you the truth about me being your mother because he threatened to throw me into the street if I did. I could not risk losing you and Elizabeth."

Armand's look became dark as he absorbed this new revelation of the Marquis Duchamp whom he was coming to loath. His relief at not being the real child of this man more than compensated him for being born out of wedlock.

As he listened to the story, he detected under the gravitas of the subject, the giddiness of a child sharing a secret with a friend. It was a paradox he could not fathom. "But there is something more that you must know. Your real father and I have been seeing each other once a week for several months, and we've been intimate."

Armand blushed slightly, but knew that adults were intimate even though he did not want to think of Madam, his mother, being intimate with a man, even if the man was his father. "You really don't have to tell me this," he said with an embarrassed smile on his face. Elizabeth took another sip of wine.

"But I must tell you both this news," she said, her eyes suddenly bright, because all your life I have kept secrets from you, and I will not any longer. Elizabeth asked that there be no more surprises." She hesitated and said, "You are going to have a brother or sister. Armand, your father, Jonah Chernov and I are having a child."

"What?" Elizabeth said incredulously. "But you're ..." and she was about to say "old" but stopped.

Armand seemed to deflate in his chair. It was all too much to comprehend: a new father, a new sibling, and half brothers and sisters filling spaces that had never been filled before. He looked at Elizabeth who sat like a stone wondering how this new revelation would play out with the Seligmans and with Nathaniel. Would they be as accepting of this news as they were when they were told her story?

"Then we are happy for you, Madam," Armand said seeing that he was getting no clue from his sister who was lost in her own confusion. "Why would we not be happy to see you finally happy? And whenever you decide to marry my father, I shall be proud to escort you down the aisle."

CHAPTER 6

Old Doc Appleman looked up from the ground compound he was carefully sprinkling onto a glassine rectangle that he was about to meticulously fold and place in a box next to others for one of his customers. "Why, it is good to see you again, Mr. Chernov," he said solicitously. "Now, whose birthday is it this time?"

Mrs. Appleman, a pleasant little woman with white hair and glasses, came out from behind the soda counter smiling, imagining which tables and how many chairs would be needed for the Chernov family. She smiled at them wistfully, thinking of Leah.

"It's no one's birthday," Jonah said smiling. I just wanted to bring the family in for a special treat."

Special treats were rare in the Chernov household, so the young children just considered it as good fortune, but Rachelann and Abe new differently. There was something their father wanted to say to them and he was going to make it as palatable as he could. Mrs. Appleman began to move the round wooden tables with iron rims into the center of the room. Abe helped without being asked to do so. The tables were small but heavy, and the twisted iron legs made a scraping sound across the bare wooden floor. Maurice and Harry also helped and moved the matching chairs. Fanny and Sammy walked over to the window and ogled the large glass containers, each suspended by three metal chains that held some red and blue magical liquids. After a flurry of the little ones deciding who would sit next to whom, Abe and Rachelann took their places.

"Vanilla, chocolate, strawberry, my little dears?" Mrs. Appleman chirped cheerfully as she waited with her pad for a response. Jonah ordered a two cents plain with a little cherry syrup on top and the children each chimed in with requests ranging from ice cream, to a lime ricky, to a strawberry phosphate, and to an egg cream.

"There are eight of us," said Harry, "and if we all order something that cost a nickel, then the bill would be forty cents, but since papa ordered a seltzer for two cents, the bill will come to thirty-eight cents. And since it's nice to leave a tip, say a nickel, then the total cost would be forty-three cents."

"And if you changed your mind and decided you didn't want anything, what would the bill be then?" Jonah inquired.

"Then it would be back to thirty-eight cents," he smiled.

"And if we decided to split the bill and everyone had to pay, do you know what would it cost each of us?" his father continued, fully confident in his son's maths skills.

"That's easy," Harry replied with a hint of superiority, "five point three seven five cents. But if you round up, to six cents, then you could leave a nicer tip."

"How does he do that?" Maurice said. "He's only eight. I'm twelve and I can't even do that."

"That one will go far, Mr. Chernov," said Mrs. Appleman as she returned with the tray of orders and started handing out the treats. "To be good in math is to be able to do anything in the world. By the way," she said, changing the subject. "We're using a new chocolate syrup called Fox's U-bet in the egg cream. I hope you like it. I put some of it on the ice cream for the children for no extra cost."

The younger children attacked the sweets like bear cubs on a pot of honey while the older ones savored the tastes. Jonah took a sip of the seltzer to clear his throat and tapped his glass with a spoon. All looked at him. "I have something to tell you."

Rachelann and Abe looked at one another and then back to their father.

"We've been sent an invitation to visit an old friend of mine from the old country. She was a very good friend and I met her again at your Aunt Zeena's apartment. She is also a good friend of your Aunt Zeena."

"Does she live in the city like Aunt Zeena, Papa?" Fannie asked, "and is she a famous actress, also?"

"Yes, she lives in the city, and no, she is not an actress. She's just a plain person like us only she lives in a big house across the street from a big park."

"You mean like Central Park with the Zoo?" Maurice interjected.

"Can we go to the zoo, Papa?" Sammy pleaded.

"Will we take the new subway?" Harry asked. "Can we please take the subway?"

"Yes," Jonah continued, trying not to lose his focus. "We'll do all these things in time. But first I want you to meet her and her children. She has a son named Armand and a daughter named Elizabeth." He looked at Rachelann and at Abe. "I think you could become good friends."

"People become friends after knowing each other over a period of time." Rachelann said. "Do you think we will be seeing these people more than just for this visit?" She was not comfortable with her father's intimation. What was this woman to him, and why would he think that she and her siblings would become friends with her children? She looked a Abe.

Jonah stiffened slightly and took a sip of his seltzer. "This woman is a very dear friend that I knew in Paris. It's a very long and complicated story and perhaps one day I shall tell it to you, but certainly not now. And yes, I hope this will be the first of many visits."

"Then you knew her when you and Mama lived in Paris?" Rachelann said.

"I didn't know you lived in Paris," said Harry.

"There's lots of things you don't know," Maurice shot back still smarting from Harry's math lesson.

"Where's Paris, Papa? Can we go there, too?" Fannie asked.

"Yes, I did know her in Paris, but I don't want to go into that now," Jonah responded, ignoring the children's questions.

Abe picked up on his sister's challenge. "Then who really is this woman, and what is she to you? And yes, why do you want us to meet her?"

The younger children lowered their eyes feeling somewhat rejected and focused on the desserts as Jonah threw a cautionary look at his eldest son.

"Because Mama and I had been separated when we left Russia, and I had this little baby girl whose life I had to save. That little girl is your Aunt Zeena's daughter, Elizabeth. This woman, and her name is Marta Birkov, was Elizabeth's wet nurse and it was this woman who kept your cousin alive. I owed her a great deal."

"What's a wet nurse," Sammy asked innocently.

"Not now, Sammy," said Jonah.

"You're now telling us we have an older cousin?"

Jonah wanted to say that not only do you have an older female cousin, but you have an older half-brother and another on the way. But too much was coming at them at the moment and he decided that now was not a good time. Telling them of Armand's existence needed more thought.

"This woman and I had to live together for the child's sake, and when I found your mother, Marta left with Elizabeth for America and I went to live with your mother. I did not see her again until I met her at a party at Aunt Zeena's home and that was long after your mother passed away." He emphasized this to deflect any comments that he might have been seeing Marta while Leah was still alive. Rachelann seemed somewhat relieved.

"So what is your relationship with her now, and why do we have to meet her and her children?" Abe reiterated.

"Because she is a very good friend and I intend to continue seeing her. I'm letting you know this so you don't have to be suspicious of me leaving the shop on Wednesdays, and so you won't feel compelled to follow me. Now you'll know exactly where I am going and who I am seeing."

Jonah could feel his voice shaking, and to quiet himself, he kept reminding himself that he was the Papa and in control. He was definitely becoming exasperated by the tone of the conversation and the challenges coming at him. He was fearful of raising his voice defensively in public. This was definitely not the moment to tell them about Armand or about the new baby.

"I'm not going," Abe said flatly.

"Yes, you are going, and you will be respectful," Jonah shot back without thinking.

"Stop this now," Rachelann interjected in a dark whisper. "Not everybody has to know our business."

The bell above the door tinkled its welcome to another neighborhood family. Mrs. Appleman, eager to remove herself from the drama she could not ignore, moved to the door with a welcoming smile. There was a sigh of relief around the Chernov tables for what everyone knew was only a temporary respite from the issue before the family.

"Finish your desserts and don't forget that you still have homework to do." At least they now knew about Marta and Elizabeth, but telling them about Armand and the baby would be a challenge.

CHAPTER 7

Abraham and Rachelann, like petulant children awakened too early from sleep, walked reluctantly behind their excited brothers and sister. A cold wind whipped around their legs, but it didn't deter Harry, Sam, Maurice, and Fanny from playing an improvised game of tag around their father as they made their way to the trolley that would take them to the Brooklyn piers. The younger children saw a trip to Manhattan as a rare adventure not experienced before because in one magical day they would ride on a trolley, a new subway, and see buildings taller than any buildings they had ever seen. Abe and Rachelann thought only about what might be a radical change and challenge to their lives.

"I am not happy about this," Abe said suddenly. His dark eyes focused on the sidewalk. "Momma is gone only a little more than a year, and now we have to meet this woman and her family. It's just not right."

"We don't know exactly what's going on between them," Rachelann said in a reassuring whisper, "but she is making a birthday party for Papa and Aunt Zeena and we've been invited. Beyond that, we don't know anything until we get there and see."

"I know exactly what's going on there," he responded somewhat annoyed that his sister did not leap to the conclusion he had made. "And I'll bet you that before too long he's going to tell us that we're going to have a new mother."

"We'll never have a new mother," his sister said indignantly, lowering her head in deference to her mother's image as she considered her brother's prophesy. Papa remarried? Where did that leave her? She had a place in this family as the nurturer and organizer and was content to be that, but what would her place be with a new wife? The family would be uprooted. Was this why her father suddenly began to speak to her about her future? Was this the reason why he had spoken to her one evening when the children were asleep about the need for finding someone to love and to share a life? He was easing her into the idea that he wanted to remarry and have a life with this woman, a life that excluded her. She felt her shoulders sag as she exhaled and hesitated in her stride. This is something she had not considered before. Suddenly, it became clear. The party was not just a party, but the first meeting of two families that her father wanted to become one family. That was not going to happen. Abe was right to be suspicious, but now was neither the time to discuss the matter nor what should be done about it.

The trolley screeched to a stop, showering the top of the cab with sparks from the electric cables above. One by one, the Chernov family stepped up followed by their father who counted out the copper coins into the hand of the collector. Each of the children ran to take seats by a window so they would have an unobstructed view of whatever was to be seen. Jonah, Rachelann and Abe sat side by side on the rear seat in silence. The silence became uncomfortable for Jonah.

"I think you will like this family even though they are very different from ours," Jonah said, trying to control what he could only define as anxious enthusiasm. But the tone of his voice did not go unnoticed. "Marta's son, this Armand I spoke of, goes to Columbia University, and Elizabeth, her daughter, is a violinist and soon to be married." Again, silence. "Armand is a few years older than you are, Abe, and his sister is less than a year younger than you, Rachelann. He looked at his daughter hopefully, but was met with stone. "Elizabeth, that's her name, is going to marry a young man whose father owns the Seligman Department Store in Manhattan. I'm sure we'll be invited to the wedding."

"And what will I wear to such a wedding?" she said, looking down at the plain brown skirt of what she considered her best outfit. Her comment was sudden, out of character, and did not hide her resentment.

"You will have a beautiful dress," her father replied reassuringly without giving any consideration to the reality of the cost of outfitting his family for such an occasion.

"Will I have a new dress too, Papa?" said Fanny, hearing the end of her sister's comments and her father's reply.

"Of course you will," he replied and caught her in his arms as the trolley lurched and stopped for other passengers.

Uncomfortable minutes passed, and Jonah moved to his younger children, pointing out to them landmarks of this section of Brooklyn everyone referred to as the Downtown. The children's excitement grew as they finally reached the entrance ramp on the bridge and the wheels eased themselves onto the flat boards that made up the bridge ramp. The children were on their knees at the windows, trying to peer over the iron railings at the rooftops and then at the water below. "It's like seeing the way a bird sees, Papa," said Sammy, as he pressed his nose against the cold window pane. Even Abe found it difficult to contain his excitement, and the anger in him gave way to the realization and exhilaration that he was hundreds of feet above the East River looking down at miniaturized schooners, steamboats, and dozens of barges and ferries far below. On those other occasions, when he had followed his father into the city, he had always followed him on the ferry, which was cheaper.

The sky, which had been overcast for the past hour or so, suddenly began to splinter with streaks of blue, and the rays of a hidden sun found the gray openings and etched the rims of the clouds with silver. Harry and Maurice, followed by Sam and Fanny, ran up to the front of the trolley to get a closer look at the first of the two massive towers that suspended the countless cables that held the roadway above the river below. "Those are Gothic arches," Maurice said proudly, but Fanny was far more interested in the big white and grey birds that hovered eye level with the trolley, only to swoop down on the garbage scows below. Where Maurice saw things to name and Fanny delighted in the birds, Sammy saw triangles, thousands of triangles that ran the entire length of the bridge on both sides. Above his head, connecting these structures were massive iron girders also supported by smaller girders. "Why so many triangles?" he said, but no one could answer his question. He would have to ask his teacher. To build such a thing was wonderful, and a flicker of a dream inserted itself in his brain. How was such a thing built, and who built it? His teacher would know.

About two blocks away from where they got off, they could see the outline of a bronze and glass kiosk with a green spherical lamp that let passengers know that this Lexington Avenue Line station was open. Jonah knew the Beaux Arts style of the kiosk from his time in Paris, and it conjured up those ornate buildings and those warm spring nights when he and Marta would take the baby into the city for a concert in the park. He was briefly lost in the memory when Sammy pulled at him to move faster.

They descended the steps, each in his own wonder and anticipation of this new engineering miracle that had only opened to the public a month or two before, and each child knew that he would be the first of their friends to ride a subway. Eager hands slid over the brass handrail that guided them down under the street where they found themselves in a large white tiled space, punctuated by iron beams that supported the city street above them. Like children at a carnival ride, each waited in line to drop a coin into the turnstile and proceed onto the platform. Maurice saw them first. Dividing the tile walls were small, white sail boat sculptures pulling away from a background of royal blue tiles. These plaques were surrounded by wide, pale green borders. His mouth opened slightly, for he had seen such a type of sculpture in a book about the Renaissance, but he never expected to see such art like that in a subway. He tried to memorize the images so he could describe them to his teacher, and wondered if other stations had walls such as this one.

Sammy also saw the tiles, thousands of tiles, perfect white squares that seemed to him like little boxes stacked from floor to ceiling. He knew he could not count them, so he concentrated on the ornate cornice that stopped them. And then his eyes focused on a large series of rectangles created by sea green tiles surrounding the stations's name: Canal Street. Triangles on the bridge and now squares, ovals, darts, and rectangles on the subway. The whole world could be seen as a series of shapes. He felt as if he had come to a great awareness, a secret of looking at the world that only he knew.

Each felt the vibration under his feet, heard a faint rumble that got louder and louder, and felt a gust of cold air that swept around their legs. Fanny grabbed onto her father's waist and peered out at the long boxes that rolled into the station, spewing sparks from the tracks as it came to a halt in front of them. People, laughing and jabbering, stepped out and moved past them. Anxiously, Rachelann moved away from the warmth of the pot belly coal stove, gathering the children like a mother hen gathering her chicks. She pretended not to be frightened to enter the mouth of this vibrating beast. Abe, who saw himself as the defender of the family, fought to contain his imagination and his sense of control, but succumbed to the mechanical wonder. His fantasy pushed him to see himself as a knight errant, bent on another improbable adventure. Suddenly, the train became a dragon retching fire and sparks, and the door was the dragon's mouth eager to swallow him and all the helpless people on the platform. He was a Jonah in the whale, and once inside this new Monstro, he would find the heart of the creature and dispatch it. But he would not do this until he reached the besieged kiosk on 77th street.

The children had never been to the Upper East Side of Manhattan, and everything was a wonder in their eyes. The ornate wrought iron fences that protected the stone homes cast fantastic shadows on the cobblestone walks. Wooden shutters kept unwelcome eyes from prying, but occasionally the shutters were open, revealing wonderful chandeliers and great mirrors with gilt frames above marble fireplaces. Well dressed people with well dressed children in tow followed the peel of the church bells that drew them to their Sunday services. Rachelann felt disquieted and terribly out of place at the appearance of such wealth. She had not seen this inequality before, but now she was acutely aware of it, seeing the privately owned hansom cabs emerge from the mews shared by these homes. Suddenly, the inequities between people became very real. She did not belong here. None of them belonged here.

Jonah walked in silence holding Fanny's hand. He had seen what the children were seeing months before, and now he could only see a future he could not divine. In his fantasy, he imagined everyone as happy as he had been, greeting one another with open arms and immediate affection, but since Abraham had discovered his secret, Jonah knew that his son and eldest daughter saw his relationship with Marta as a betrayal to their mother's memory. And what would they say when they learned that they had an elder brother? And God, what would they say when they were told that another child was on the way? He had not as yet told them anything. He seemed never to find the right moment, but the truth was that he was afraid to tell them because he imagined that Rachelann and Abe would demand that he choose between them and his life with Marta and his children with her. He felt like a coward, but why? Was he fearful of his own children and their judgements on him? Was he afraid that they walk away? Certainly they were old enough to go out into the world and make a life for themselves without him. They might even coerce the younger ones into going with them. Was that what he was afraid of? But he was the Papa. He was not to be judged. Back in Russia there would be no conversation. Things were done because you had to survive, and children did what they were told and obeyed their parent's wishes. But here in America, as wonderful a land as this was, the old ways were slowly being eroded by opportunities for the young and new found freedoms. Children were becoming more and more independent from their parent's wishes. He was seeing this deviance in the behavior of the children of his friends and in the behavior of his own children. Both opportunity, independence, and freedom were wonderful blessings, but blessings with a price.

He should have found the time to tell them everything. Then they might have absorbed it, did their best or worse with the information, but at least they would have dealt with it and he would have known how to proceed. Now, only a block from Marta's home, her family waiting, he was compelled to tell them without preparing them, and whatever followed was his fault for acting like a frightened child. And what would Marta say to him? He had promised that he would tell them and he did not. She would be angry. He had never felt anger from her, and he didn't know how he would deal with that.

They were approaching Central Park and as they turned onto Fifth Avenue a brisk wind enveloped them in a dance with autumn leaves. Jonah heaved a deep sigh and stopped.

"Children," he called, "Come here out of the wind. I have something I need to tell you." They all stopped and turned. Looking at one another quizzically, they returned to him. Rachelann and Abraham moved more slowly than the others. "Remember" he began, "that when it was time for you to go to the doctor, Mama and I wouldn't tell you because if we had told you a week before you would have been upset for the whole week?" He paused as the younger ones nodded. "We thought it was best not to upset you. When you realized where you were going, the upset lasted only for a little while and then it was quickly over." He paused for understanding and acceptance of the rational. "We only wanted to protect you."

"Are we going to see a doctor, now?" said Sam.

Jonah smiled. "No, Sammy, we're not going to see a doctor. We are still going to see my friend Marta. But I need to tell you all that Marta is more than just my friend." He took a breath. "Back in Europe, back in a terrible time, Mama and I thought we had lost each other. I had a responsibility to take care of your cousin Elizabeth, and Marta was helping me do it. Mama and I thought we would never find one another again, and before we did, I was living with Marta as a man lives with a woman." Abe and Rachelann looked at one another and moved in closer. "Marta became pregnant with a child, but I never knew about him because I found your mother and went back to her as was the proper thing to do."

"But if you weren't married," interjected Harry, "how could you have a baby? Don't you have to be married to have a baby?"

"Don't be an idiot," Maurice whispered to his younger brother. "I'll tell you later."

"Are you saying," interrupted Abe, "that this Armand you've been talking about is our older brother? Is that what you're saying to us? That you had a child with this woman and we are about to meet him and her?" His voice was shaking, and Rachelann put a hand on his shoulder to calm him. "Well, isn't that just wonderful."

"I didn't know we had another brother," said Maurice, calculating his age.

"Are there any others," inquired Rachelann, her voice dripping with sarcasm. "Was this little baby girl my cousin like you said or was she really my sister? Is there anything else we should know before we meet your secret family?"

"No, you do not have a sister. The little girl is your cousin; your Aunt Zeena's child. You'll also meet her today, and yes," Jonah continued, hurling her sarcasm back at her with a shriveling glare. "I intend to marry Marta."

"Are we going to have a new Mama?" said Fanny.

"No," Abe said. "You'll only have one Mama. In fact, this woman will never be a Mama to us."

"She doesn't expect to replace your Mama," Jonah shot back beginning not to care if they accepted his decision or not. "She will not replace your Mama, but she will become my wife."

There was a deadly silence, and only the wind and leaves, now enveloping them, seemed to bring some false sense of animation to the Chernov family. Jonah had made a decision. Ultimately, all of these children would grow up and leave him, and he would be left alone if he acquiesced to his children's demands. He could not imagine life without Marta, or never seeing Armand again. And what of the new life that grew within her. He was confident that his younger children would join him, but he was not sure that his older children would. He looked directly at Rachelann and Abe, and the look was a challenge to them. Fanny took her father's hand. "I have a Mama that I can remember. It would be nice to have a Mama to hug me again," she said innocently.

Quiet tears rolled down Jonah's cheeks as he took his daughter's hand and began moving towards the avenue. "Harry, Maurice, Sam?" Sam, who was holding Abe's hand looked up to him for guidance. When Abe did not move, Sam pulled at him and he began to walk forward, numb as to what would follow. Rachelann, tears on her cheeks, followed.

Jonah did not look behind. He had made a choice like so many other choices he had made in his forty odd years that would enable him to survive on some level. Children leaving their parents was the way of the world. But parents were left behind, sometimes together, sometimes alone, and why should he be alone and without love? His children also would move forward into the world as they were meant to do, and he would do so, too. Why should he deny himself love and happiness because his children were loyal to their mother? They should be loyal to Leah's memory, but why should they resent him finding a life with another at his age?

CHAPTER 8

Fanny's eyes, like a hummingbird hovering and darting from flower to flower, moved from ceiling to floor to walls when she stepped over the marbled threshold of the entry to Marta's home. Everywhere her eyes alighted, she sucked in each sight before settling on the nectar of another. First, she stared at the shining glass triangles dangling in the hallway, reflecting the hearth's inviting fire that warmed this single room. Her eyes next fell on the table under the chandelier, a table made of pieces of colored stones so carefully worked that the images of flowers and birds were seamlessly meshed. She traced the gold leaf painted legs of the table to the carpet upon which it stood, a carpet of richly patterned wool of odd shapes, edged by men on horseback who rode around the edges, encasing a field of flowers in shades of blues, greens, ochre, and cream. And finally, her eyes drank in a floor made up of checkered wooden inlays that ran into all the other rooms touching this entry foyer. No oilcloth floors here. No dangling single bulbs over an old table. No coal stove to heat the rooms. It was a room out of story books and how she would love to live in such a house! Her reverie was interrupted by a tall woman who approached her slowly. Marta, in a simple light blue dress with embroidered flowers on the bodice, approached Jonah and his children with smiling eyes and extended arms. She bent down and took Fanny's hands. "You must be Fanny. What a pretty little girl you are." Fanny melted. "Welcome to our home," she continued, looking at the Chernov children. "We are so very glad to have you visit." Without a thought, Fanny threw her arms around Marta's waist, and allowed herself to be hugged. It was such a long time since she had been hugged by a lady.

A housemaid silently appeared and waited patiently with her arms extended for their coats. She and Abraham quickly exchanged glances, and in that fleeting moment, seeing her eyes, he felt himself move to a place where there was no anger. Her eyes were green. He had never seen anyone with green eyes, and he tried to conjure some image so he could remember them. He finally settled on the pale green of early spring leaves. To Abraham she was suddenly the prettiest woman he had ever seen, and embarrassed, he immediately averted his eyes. "Why was this woman looking at him like that?" he thought.

"Virginia," said Marta, "When you are finished with the coats, I'd like you to help me bring in some tea and cocoa to warm my guests."

"Her name was Virginia," he thought, and he wondered how much older she was than he. He had heard that name before in school. It was an Irish name.

The music they heard coming from the parlor abruptly stopped, and not far behind Marta was Zeena, with Elizabeth and Nathaniel in tow. Zeena first kissed her brother, wishing him the happiest of birthdays. Jonah returned the greeting as she kissed her nephews and nieces.

Lastly, a young man appeared who Rachelann and Abe immediately knew was Armand, their half-brother. How could they not know. Save for their coloring and the shape of their faces, Armand and Abe could have been fraternal twins; the same wiry frame, the same height, and the same demeanor that spoke of an eagerness to get started. Armand surveyed the noisy and hectic scene before him, wondering how to proceed. Introductions were being made, and he decided to wait until his mother turned to him and beckoned for him to approach, which he did with his usual self assurance. He first extended his hand to Jonah, and the hand shake lingered, each man seemingly reluctant to end it first.

"Are you our new brother?" Sammy said, responding to Armand by hesitantly offering his hand to Armand's outstretched palm. "Yes I am," Armand replied. "And may I say that you have a very strong handshake. A handshake is a good first impression, and you my little man, make a good one." In turn Armand shook the hands of Harry, Maurice, and Abe, and knew immediately that Abe's handshake was not hesitant, as were his brother's, and a little too firm to be polite. There was an implied challenge in the handshake, and Armand smiled at his newly found younger half-brother and seemed willingly to accept it. Armand smiled at Rachelann, and she, nodding her recognition of him, forced a hesitant smile.

"Allow me to introduce you to your cousin Elizabeth, and her fiancé, Nathaniel Seligman" said Marta. "They were making the music you heard when you came in. Perhaps they might continue if you'd like that after lunch."

Fanny hesitated as she stood at the threshold of the sitting room off to one side of the foyer, and her eyes beheld beautiful murals that depicted tall trees in the foreground and little people, some lounging on the grass watching the sheep and goats graze, as others danced and played musical instruments. She wished she could hear the music. On another wall there were people riding horses near a great river, and another wall depicted boats on that same river, sailing past a clean and beautiful city. She wondered what it would be like to live in such a city. Marta, with a gesture of her hand, invited the child to a chair so she might feel the full warmth of the fire which quietly danced in the alabaster hearth.

Marta sat on a sofa behind a table with a silver service on it, and inquired of her newly arrived guests if they'd prefer coffee, tea, or hot chocolate. As each responded, Virginia would carry the cups, but she seemed to hesitate when she approached Abe. When their eyes met for a second time, she lingered just a little too long. No one except Abe noticed, being completely taken by the one lock of her strawberry blond hair that had become dislodged from her cap and fell onto her shoulder. "Th th thank you," Abe said, very aware that he had uncharacteristically stuttered. She smiled.

Marta asked the children how their trip was, and the three younger brothers regaled her with what they had seen. Maurice spoke of the things he could name, and Sammy spoke of the shapes he had seen, while Harry mentioned all the squares and triangles that could not be counted. Fanny said nothing but smiled and focused on the strange woman-like bird with gold claws and outstretched wings that was affixed to the table against the wall.

Marta was delighted at how bright and aware they all were. Rachelann sat sipping her tea, resentfully comparing her mother's simple brass samovar to the finely crafted French silver service that had been placed before Marta. The comparison firmly established the vast divide between this world and hers. Abe sipped his coffee, trying not to be obvious about his attraction to the pretty serving girl.

After they had finished their refreshments, Marta whispered something to Virginia and Virginia disappeared. A moment later she returned and announced that lunch would be served.

They rose and walked past the warmth of the fireplace in the foyer to the dining room were the stained glass windows depicting each season Ezra had commissioned from the Lenett Studios, shimmered in the winter sun. The hues they cast fell on the damask covered table, creating something of a canvas where the images shifted with the changing light. Twelve chairs covered in a material the likes of which Leah's children had never before seen, stood waiting for them. Maurice realized that here there was no rough wooden bench or odd spindle-back chairs brought in from another room. These chairs all matched, and extras stood on either side of the sideboard so even more people could be seated. He ran his finger over the smooth dark oak and the carved sea shell cut into the back's recess.

"Sit where you like, children." Marta said, and turning to Jonah she smiled and said, since both you and Zeena are celebrating your birthdays, I think it only fitting that you each sit in a place of honor at each end of the table. I insist."

Rachelann sat down between Abe and Sammy. Before her was an oblong centerpiece with a raised crest exactly as the one incised on the tea set. In its center, two highly polished cherubs rested against a cornucopia filled with flowers, and at their little silver feet, fresh fruits intermingled with blooms. She wondered where this woman had gotten out-of-season fruits and flowers. A pair of matching multi-armed candelabra, also with little cherubs, stood at either end. The cost of such a thing, she thought, could feed a family for a lifetime. Sammy reached for a fruit, and his sister pulled his hand back with a sharp reminder that he was to show these people that they, too, had good manners.

"I hope you are all quite hungry," Marta said smiling, "and make sure you leave some room for the birthday cake." The younger boys shook their heads in a silent promise as did Fanny. "And by the way, everything is strictly kosher. It was all catered from Nathaniel's mother's caterer." Rachelann, who thought she would use the idea of non-kosher food as a means of expressing her disapproval and rejecting what was happening, now had no excuse to decline Marta's generosity. The woman was certainly making an effort.

Abe looked at the plates and the array of neatly laid out silverware before him. There were multiple forks and multiple spoons and he immediately concluded that each had its own special use. But since he had no clue as to which was the appropriate one to use for whatever was to be placed before him, he glanced over at his sister hoping she might know. Their eyes met with the same unspoken question, and Abe immediately saw that she was as clueless as he.

Virginia passed behind the family, ladling soup from a tureen into the bowls of his siblings. As she passed Abe, she whispered, "Work from the outside in." Abe went to the farthest spoon on his right and picked it up. Rachelann followed and stopped Sammy from using the teaspoon. Abe smiled to himself. Virginia did take notice of him.

The luncheon progressed. Zeena was animated as she spoke of the new Lycium Theater that had just opened; the ornate stone Renaissance columns that supported the cornice, and the elegant oak doors and interior that would set the standard for all theaters to follow. She spoke of the new play she was rehearsing and how all of them would be invited. Elizabeth spoke about the wedding plans as Nathaniel sat silently, smiling at her every word. Naturally, all of her new cousins would be invited, and Marta suggested that they all would go to Seligman's for wedding attire. It would be her gift to her new family. The younger boys responded to questions about what they were learning at school, and about their first trip on the new subway. Armand spoke about ice boat sailing on the river with his friends at Colombia. Rachelann, being Rachelann, spoke about the possibility that she would get involved in the growing movement against little children working in the factories, and of the brutal sweatshops, but her father suggested that such a topic might be held for another occasion. Rachelann withdrew, concluding that this new group of people were not interested in making the changes in the world that she wanted to see happen. Abe sat quietly, feeling inadequate. He had nothing to brag about at school, and he was sure they would not be interested in the fight he had last week or how much money he had won at cards or in the poolhall. Fanny said little but fingered the damask napkin on her lap and quietly ran her fingers over the tapestry on the chair in which she sat. In the splendor of the table and the room in which this ample and delicious lunch was served, Fanny silently confirmed that if it were true that her daddy was marrying this nice lady, this is where she wanted to live, no matter what anyone said to her.

After the special cake was brought in to celebrate Jonah and Zeena's fortieth birthdays. Toasts were made to their continued good health and Marta's gifts to her forthcoming husband

and sister-in-law were given and admired by all. The family all returned to the drawing room to listen to Nathaniel and Elizabeth celebrate their uncle and mother with a Mozart piece for violin and piano.

Throughout lunch, Armand had noticed that Abe seemed disconnected from what was going on and suggested that they leave the others. "My room is quieter," he suggested, "and I thought we might talk and get to know each other a little better."

Abe was somewhat conflicted. While he was vaguely uncomfortable with what would be this new family and wanted some space from them, he was also curious about them and the lives they lived. He knew that Rachelann did not like them at all because of what she perceived as the inequity between their way of life and the lives of those she knew and read about. But Abe did not share his sister's sense of obligation to improve the lot of the downtrodden. In his mind, he was part of the downtrodden, and who was lifting him up? If truth could speak, it would say that Abe was fascinated and drawn to this carefree, lavish life style where everything seemed perfect and everything was in place where it should be. He could get used to such a life, but he did not want this particular one. No, he did not covet what these people had, but he did imagine that he could have just as good. He only didn't know how he could make that happen yet.

They ascended a circular staircase to the third floor where Armand's bedroom was. Armand opened a paneled oak door and invited his brother to enter. Abe sensed that the room was very much like the young man; organized, masculine, and forthright. There were books neatly arranged on shelves and interspersed between them were trophies attesting to Armand's skill as a crewman and as a baseball player. Small certificates of achievement that Abe could not easily read, dotted the walls. In the center of the room between two heavily curtained windows was a double brass bed. Abe smiled to himself, imagining how he, Maurice, Harry, and Sam all shared two beds in a room that now seemed no more than a large closet. Standing in the corner near the entrance was a large mirrored chifforobe, and next to it a tall, slender stand that held a basin. Above the basin was a shelf for Armand's shaving equipment, and at eye level was an oval mirror. Abe had started to shave a year ago, and he did it in the kitchen sink because there was a mirror there and light from the window.

"Make yourself comfortable Abe," Armand began as he moved to his desk and took a meerschaum pipe out of a rack. "Smoke?" he said inviting Abe to join him. But Abe had never smoked a pipe, only cigarettes, and feared he would have made a fool of himself if he had done it incorrectly or started choking. He felt very much as he had felt at the table confronting the place settings. He took a seat on the bed and watched this older version of himself stuff the bowl, light it and move to the window to open it. "My mother doesn't like me smoking in here because she says the smoke sticks to the curtains," and with some effort, lifted the large window that overlooked the rear garden and roof tops. Chilled air rushed in, briefly whipping the flames in the fireplace. "She's right of course, but I find smoking relaxing when I'm working, and besides, I don't mind the smell of the curtains." Armand pulled out the desk chair, turned it around, and sat down. "You didn't say very much at the table," he said trying to ease himself into a conversation. "Your brothers jabbered away about school, but you said little." Abe lowered his eyes. "Your dad, I mean our dad," he said correcting himself, "told me that you had some learning difficulties and that were thinking about quitting school." He paused. Abe made no reply. "I ordinarily wouldn't say anything because it's really not my concern, but you are my younger brother, and your father seems really worried about you." He waited again. "He said you hang out with some bad kids who are going nowhere. So is it true? Do you really want to quit and cut off a path in your life that needs an education? I'd really like to help you if I can."

Abraham Chernov felt heat rise from his neck to his cheeks at the question, and at all the information his father shared about him with this stranger. But what he was feeling physically wasn't so much from a response to the questions or the information, but what seemed to him a complete betrayal on the part of his father. His problems at school and with reading were not something that he ever wanted discussed with strangers or with anyone for that matter. Brother or not, this person was still a stranger. Abe never liked being the topic of conversation, especially where his inadequacies were concerned, and mingling with the flush on his face was this new resentment towards his father and his brother for the embarrassment he now felt. He took a hard look at Armand. Here was a guy who had grown up with everything a kid could want. Armand was smart, accomplished, self-assured, well dressed, and on his way to a great life. He seemingly lacked for nothing. And here he was, a poor street kid with little to offer, save what Joey called moxie, a good eye for the game of pool, a skill with cards, good at memorizing numbers, and a questionable future that probably would involve the police.

"I do okay for myself," he said, feigning calm and desperately trying not to reveal the depth of the anger that was starting to percolate in his chest. "Some people just aren't cut out for sitting in a classroom, and as far as my friends are concerned, you take your friends from where you live." As he responded, he saw himself sitting alone on the stoop in front of the stores, smoking and flipping a coin, or sitting with Joey and the guys in the candy store. He thought about the midnight forays into the backyard of the dairy behind the house to steal empty bottles and return them to stores for the deposit, and of the fights with the Micks and the Pollacks he and Joey didn't like. It was true, he didn't have much going for himself or where he might be going, but he knew he could never make it in school. Teachers had always told him he was bad and stupid. They told him who he was and in a way, what they expected him to be. And since he couldn't be noticed for being smart like his brothers, at least he could be noticed for being bad. Abe Chernov would not be ignored. Abe Chernov would never be invisible. Besides, in all the years he had been going to school, not one teacher had ever given enough of a crap about a bad kid to wonder what might be wrong with him.

"I'm pretty good at cards, and with numbers," Abe said suddenly, as if to put something out there about himself that would make him distinctive and of value.

"Really?" Armand said, swiveling the chair to face the desk and hoping that he had made some connection. Abe watched him as Armand took out a fresh deck of cards, opened the seal, and handed them to Abe. "Shuffle."

Abe smiled curiously, wondering what this was about and shuffled the cards. "Poker?" Armand suggested. "Poker," Abe said. "Open or closed?"

"Open," Armand replied, interested in what he might learn about his new found brother, and if the kid really had some skill with cards and numbers.

They played eight hands. Armand won the first two, but Abe won the next six. "How the hell did you do that?" Armand said.

Abe said nothing, knowing full well he had something for which his older brother admired him, much the way Abe admired Maurice and Harry. He wanted to be admired. Now the playing field was a little more even. "Can't tell you," he said. "Can't give away my secrets."

"I have an idea," Armand said suddenly brightening. "I'm in a poker game with some classmates who get together for a weekly friendly game. How would you like to join us? They're an arrogant bunch and I'd really like to see if you can take them down a peg."

"I don't have any money," Abe said flatly.

"Not a problem. I'll spot you. If you lose, I lose my money and they stay arrogant. If you win, you can keep all the money. Consider it a gift. What do you say?"

Abe knew nothing of college boys, but he knew a lot about poker. "Ok," he said feeling nervous and a need to deliver on his boast.

"But you can't go in there looking like you're from the Bowery" Armand said, and immediately regretted the statement. "I'm sorry I said that. I didn't mean it that way."

"It's OK," Abe replied. "We don't have much, but I'm not ashamed of how I look."

"Clothes make the man," Armand said going over to the chifforobe, and bringing out a pair of grey woolen slacks, a tweed jacket, a high collared shirt, a vest and a tie. Abe tried very hard not to show his excitement at the thought of putting on a pair of long pants and taking off the knickers and black socks that he was wearing. Armand laid the clothes out on the bed and left. Abe was glad because his underwear and socks had holes in them. He quickly dressed and stood before the mirror, transformed except for his bare feet.

Armand returned with a pair of shoes. "I'm thinking we are about the same size in everything, so perhaps you also have a wide foot. The shoes you are wearing just won't do."

Abe took the socks that Armand extended to him and put them on. Armand was also right about the shoes. They fit perfectly.

Armand stood Abe in from of the mirror. If you like what you see, little brother, you can keep the outfit. Abe swallowed hard at the offer. He did not want to like this person, but Armand's largesse was more than he had anticipated. Perhaps this halfbrother's interest in him was sincere and not perfunctory. Certainly, he posed no threat to Armand. Perhaps Rachelann was wrong about these people.

"I like having a new little brother," Armand said smiling at the similar twin reflections in the mirror. And won't it be nice that we may have another little half-brother in a few months?

Abe suddenly felt himself freeze, and his jaw first tightened and then involuntarily drop. Armand watched Abe's visage morph into something quite different from the one he saw seconds ago.

"Oops," he said. "I thought you knew about that. I thought everybody knew."

Everyone turned as Armand and Abraham entered the room. Marta and Jonah stood.

"How do you like the transformation?" Armand said, putting aside what he knew had to be festering in Abe's soul. Now, both dressed smartly and similarly, they looked as if they had stepped out of a men's fashion catalogue. "Abe and I are going out to meet some of my classmates. We'll be back before dark. I promise."

Jonah looked at Marta thinking that Armand had made some headway with Abe and that Abe would finally be meeting young men who would accept him and turn him away from the streets. But Abe looked at his father with no expression at all because all the fantasy and adventure of what might befall him for the rest of the evening faded with a new betrayal. Three betrayals in one day; the betrayal of his mother with this woman, the revelation to strangers of his learning problems, and now this new child. How could his father have hidden so much?

CHAPTER 9

The following morning the younger children sat around the kitchen table jabbering about what they had seen the day before. Rachelann was busying herself at the stove, glad to be back where she had some feeling of importance, as Abe, still dressed in Armand's suit, quietly opened the door to the kitchen and came in looking as if he had slept in his clothing. He had.

"Are you just getting home now?" Rachelann said with a hint of authority and more than a hint of judgement. Her eyes darted to the door and then back to her brother who wavered as he stood there. "Did you sleep in your clothes?"

"I guess I did," he replied. "Is it very late at night or very early in the morning?" The boys began to laugh.

"It is still pretty early this morning," chirped Harry. "You're lucky Papa is getting something in the cellar and he isn't seeing you now."

Abe walked over to the stove and poured himself a cup of coffee from the porcelain pot. "I made a few dollars last night," he said proudly, taking a wad of bills out of his pocket and giving each of his brothers and Fanny a dollar bill. Their eyes widened. "Our new brother has some very rich friends who don't play poker very well." He gave Rachelann five of the bills for herself and for running the house. "Now put it away, because if Papa sees it, they'll be a lot of questions and he might take it away." They quickly complied as Rachelann just looked at Abe with a hundred questions of her own.

"Now, I'd advise you to go change your clothes before Papa comes up and sees you like this and begins asking questions," his sister warned.

"I really don't care if he sees me like this and I don't care what questions he asks because last night I learned something really important about myself and about the upper classes. And I don't mind telling you and Papa what I learned about his newest son and his friends."

"I think you need to splash some ice cold water on your face to clear your head before you tell us anything. Get out of that suit and get into your regular clothes. We brought your good clothes back with us last night and they're in the chifforobe. And hurry up."

Abe staggered through the parlor and into the room he shared with his three brothers. As the bedroom door closed, the basement door opened and Jonah came in carrying several boxes. Maurice went to help.

"Isn't it time Abe got up?" he said taking out his pocket watch and glancing at it.

"There are deliveries to make before school." The boys looked at each other, smiled and tried not to laugh. Jonah had his back to them at the sink, washing his hands.

"I heard him moving around not long ago, Papa," said Rachelann tossing a warning look at the boys. "I'll go get him."

In a moment, they were back, Abe dressed with his face and hair still wet. Everyone was seated and they began to eat, with Abe taking long sips of black coffee.

"There's something I want to talk to you about," Jonah began as he sat in his place. "It's about yesterday." He took a sip of coffee and cleared his throat. "Marta and your Papa are going to be married in the very near future, and I want you to think of what will happen to this family as a kind of journey for us all to what I know will be a better place."

"Like a Promised Land?" Maurice interjected, thinking about the Bible story and the Exodus from Egypt that he had recently read to his younger siblings.

Jonah thought for a moment and agreed. "That's a good way of looking at it. Think of it as we're all going out of Egypt to a new and a better place. Think of it as an opportunity to see new places and to meet new people like the people you met yesterday."

"So what you're saying," said Abe, lifting his head and looking directly at his father, "is that Brownsville is like Egypt and the East Side of Manhattan is like the Promised Land?"

"In a way it is, because living in Marta's home, we'll be able to see to it that you'll have better opportunities than I can give you here."

"So you're marrying this woman for our sake, Papa?" Abe continued. The response caught Jonah up short and his brow furrowed. He had no idea that Abe would be on the attack.

"How dare you think that I could do such a thing," he said angrily. "I love this woman with all my heart, and I would never take advantage of her for what she has." He paused. "And she loves me, too." Then he thought of what they must be feeling about his not loving their mother any more, and he felt compelled to pull back his words. But Abe shot back at him.

"So why doesn't she move here and share your life, Papa?"

"Why are you being so foolish and asking such foolish questions?" Jonah was becoming annoyed. "Would you give up a home such as she has and come to this? I don't have to ask her to prove to you or to anyone else that she loves me. I know the depth of her love. I know her story. I know the path of her journey and she knows mine. Children," he said taking his eyes from his eldest son, "all of you have dreams, things that you want to happen in your lives. All children have dreams, and so do adults. But even if you know what you want out of life, that doesn't mean the road to get there will be a straight road or safe. I know. I also had dreams, but the road I was on to that dream got torn up, twisted, and pockmarked with holes. Things just happen in life, things you cannot control. They all help you to pave that road and you're compelled to walk on it because there may not be another. Believe me, children, I don't want your journey to be like my journey."

"Did you ever reach your dream, Papa?" said Sam innocently.

Jonah expelled a deep breath as a succession of memories seemed to rise up to mock him. First came his vision of himself as a tailor, happily working next to his father and going home to a happy life with Leah. Then there was Reuben's dream for him, a dream that had the barriers torn down that would allow his son to go to the university and become a linguist or a scholar. These early dreams were destroyed by Ukrainian peasants with pitchforks and axes, acting for the Russian Czar, and a burning field. His next dream was to work with Herzl, to speak to Jews all over Europe about the dream of a Jewish homeland in Palestine. That dream was dashed by Leah's demands and his responsibility to his wife and to his children. And of course there was the long forgotten dream of finding love with Marta Birkov, of two souls becoming like one, but that dream died at the hands of thugs sent by Ezra. His road was strewn with brutality, death, and disappointments. If he could make the road for his children less challenging, he would do it because he could feel somewhat redeemed for not having been able to provide them with what he desperately wanted them to have. What did Abe know of love and of using people? He would marry Marta Birkov if she had a pushcart on Blake Avenue.

"I know you are all afraid of this new path because you don't know what lays ahead," he began, "and I want you to know that the unknown is always frightening. I am afraid, also. When we left Paris to come here, your mother and I were afraid because we didn't know what we would do or what life would be like for us. We put our foot out like our ancestors did at the sea and bravely took a step. Because you were children, you looked at the journey as a new adventure and that is how I want you to view my marriage to Marta. Fear is normal when we are beginning new things. Fear is normal when things are going to change.

Whenever we take a new step, we have to step out with courage and a belief that what we are doing is right and what we are doing will bring us closer to our dream. Think of this as an adventure where you will be discovering a new world and a new you. Look at this as the beginning of the rest of our story. For something to be better, a person may have to give up something that they already have to make room for the new thing. I am asking you to give up what you have here for something that I think is better for you out there."

Jonah sat quietly, wondering if his children understood. I know what I want to do with the rest of my life, he thought. Finally, I have a choice to make my life and the lives of my children better, and this time, everyone can win. At last I can help them leap over what could be a generation of waiting so they can have now what others might not have for another fifty years. Now my children can have the education denied me. Now they can dream their dreams and make them real. And I can still have a dream come true. Marta is offering this, and I know in my mind and in my heart that this choice is right for all of us.

"It's time you left for school, and you come right home for lunch," Rachelann said, breaking the silence. "And don't take the shortcut even if you're late. I'd rather you be late than chased or in a fight."

The three of them sat in silence for a moment, sipping their coffee.

"You want to know where your oldest son took me last night, Papa?" said Abe hoping Armand might be diminished with the story he was about to tell. "We went to a room at the Astor Hotel where Armand and his fraternity brothers had this amazing card game that went well into the morning." He tried to judge his father's reaction, but could divine nothing from Jonah's face. "And there was a lot of booze, the good stuff, and nobody stopped me from drinking. There were girls there, not nice girls, Papa. Girls that were paid for whatever went on in the other room. I saw them handed the cash. I played cards all night and won enough to pay Armand back the money he spotted me and take a few bucks home. I really think I can learn a lot from Armand and his friends."

"Why are you telling me this, Abe?" Jonah asked, feeling his face flush.

"Why? Because these rich boys, these college boys like your eldest son, are no better than me and the guys who hang out at Rose's. Only these guys look better and speak better and smell better, but underneath it all, they're still sleazy. Sleazy is sleazy, no matter how you dress it up, Papa. And you think these are the people who are going to make my life better if I hang out with them? Sure, I might hang out with them Papa, but not so I can be more like them. I'll hang out with them because they are rich and easy marks. I'll hang out with them so I can take their money. And I'll tell you something else, Papa. The kids I hang around with here are better people and more honest than these guys will ever be. At least my friends aren't arrogant bigots. Here, at least I know that if I'm gonna be called a kike, it's going to be to my face. With Armand's friends, it's a little more subtle. They were telling jokes about micks, and wops, and kikes. They were telling jokes about me, though they didn't know I was a kike. And Armand didn't say anything to them. Do you think he was embarrassed about his half-brother, Papa? Do you think he's told anybody that his father is a Jew? You know how I felt, Papa? I felt like I was the other, the one not invited even if no one said anything. I could feel it. You know what it feels like Papa, to know you're there and yet feel invisible? To be mocked to your face. You know what that's like? And you want me to become part of that world?"

When his father gave no reaction, Abe threw his last dagger. "And Armand, my elder, well educated and classy half-brother, was so impressed with my skills as a gambler that he made me a proposition. You know what he suggested, Papa? He suggested that we become partners. He'd supply the marks, I'd clean them out, and we'd split the profits."

CHAPTER 10

1906

Abe stood in front of the house on Fifth Avenue with his foot resting on an iron boot scraper in the shape of a griffin. He smoked nervously. Across the street, new spring leaves, a pale chartreuse, filtered the afternoon sun as if through a sieve, and the shadows each cast on the leaves below trembled in the light breeze. It was indeed, a beautiful day for a wedding.

"Papa wants you to come in now," said a voice through the open door. Maurice stood near his brother and put a hand on Abe's shoulder. "Abe, his getting married is going to happen whether you like it or not."

Abe turned to him, tears in his eyes. "It just ain't right."

For the past few months, the family had shuttled back and forth between these two very different worlds and as they did, the children became divided. Maurice, Sam, and Fanny, as young as they were, came to see the potential of what this new life could offer them. Certainly, the new clothing that they wore only on the weekends made them feel better about themselves, and they liked the feeling. Certainly, the delicious food that was always plentiful eased the old fear of not having enough. But what especially turned the younger brothers was the thought that by living here, they would not have to deal with the Polish, Irish or Italian kids in school and the fear of being mocked or attacked. Fanny, for the most part, just loved being in a place that seemed to her like a castle in a fairytale, and she especially loved sleeping on the day bed in Elizabeth's room that had red velvet curtains trimmed in gold that came down from the ceiling and draped the sides. In it, she felt safe and warm.

On the other hand, Rachelann, Abe, and Harry felt only resentment. As far as the two elder children were concerned, a marriage only a little more than a year after their mother died was disrespectful of their mother. More than once, in a variety of ways, they had spoken of their displeasure, but their father made it clear that he wanted to be married before the child was born.

Abe turned towards his brother and went through the open door. On the center table stood a large vase filled with yellow hothouse roses, jonquils, white tulips, and pink and white peonies. His eyes followed these same flowers as they were threaded through the banister leading to the upper floors. In the large sitting room, the tufted velvet couches and chairs were arranged facing the fireplace, above which stood a large mirror that caught the faces of Aunt Zeena, Madame Chalfont, her companion, his cousin Elizabeth, her fiance, Nathaniel, and several people he had met over the past weeks in Marta's home. But the faces in the mirror that surprised him were the faces of people from Brownsville, faces of people who knew his mother. These people should have told his father he was wrong to marry this woman so soon after his wife's death; a woman who was pregnant; a woman who wasn't even Jewish. The fact that Marta was not Jewish had not been thought of before, and Abe was surprised that it came to him now, so he added it to the list of indignities he harbored as another rationalization for his anger.

The pale blue chiffon dress with appliques in silver silk covering the bodice and waist, hung straight down from Marta's breasts, concealing the child that had been growing in her for the past several months. Armand, wearing a brown vested suit with a Windsor collar and paisley tie, accompanied his mother, nodding and smiling at their guests as they stepped on the petals that fell from Fanny's hands. Fanny, dressed appropriately in white layered organza with a large blue bow atop her auburn hair and matching one around her waist, delighted in the glow of smiling faces as she pretended that she was a very important person like her Aunt Zeena, and these were her admirers. Jonah, attired in a new light brown herringbone vested suit, stood next to the judge, his eyes riveted on his beautiful wife to be. As he was focusing on Marta, he was simultaneously fighting off images of when he nervously stood in front of the synagogue doors so many years ago, watching Leah move towards him wearing a wreath of wild flowers that held her veil in place.

Abe and Rachelann sat in the last row. "There's not even a chuppah," Abe said, twisting in the rented chair. "And I don't see any wine."

"What did you expect," whispered his sister. "She's not Jewish, so why would you expect a Jewish wedding? Certainly, no rabbi would marry them with her being God knows what and pregnant."

Abe did not know why he expected anything more than what he saw unfolding before him. Religion, and worship, these meant little to him, but something in him told him that this was not the way it should be. He didn't even understand what the "it" was, but he had a vague feeling that something important was being eroded that had nothing to do with faith. It did have something to do with connections, and that was all he could identify. Something that was important to his mother and even important to his father was being devalued. He shifted uncomfortably as the judge continued, and Abe started again to feel an all too familiar heat rise in his body, flush his face, and flare out his nostrils. It was the anger at another betrayal, a final betrayal to the few vestiges of his mother's memory, and his father was once again to blame. For his own selfish reasons, his father was spitting in the face of tradition and giving his brothers and sisters permission to do the same. Still, he did not know what it was or why he should even care.

"I gotta get out of here," he said, already leaving his seat. His sister moved to stop him, but he was out of reach. He stood in the foyer, leaning against the wall, and feeling his gorge rise, he raced up the stairs to Armand's bedroom and the adjoining bathroom where he sank to his knees and retched into the commode. Nothing like this had ever happened to him before. It was rage. Plain and simple. That was the only way he could explain it. His whole world was collapsing around him, and his insides were churning like meat in a grinder at the thought of it. All of it was suddenly real, and the changes that he was being asked to make, the people he would be asked to befriend and even love, were abhorrent to him. This was not the life he wanted. This was not the life he knew or would be comfortable with. He would have to move carefully if he were to be free.

He pulled the chain, and watched the water swirl. Then, grabbing a towel from the holder, he opened the faucet, filled the basin, and plunged his face into it. It was a shock, but it was what he needed to cool his rage, and clean his face. Among Armand's toiletries was a bottle of mouthwash that he took, swished around in his mouth, and spit out into the sink. His eyes were still red, but he wasn't sure if it was from crying or from the strain of retching. He put the towel to his face again, and glared at himself in the mirror. As he studied the sadness he saw, the image of the housemaid, Virginia, appeared behind him, reflected in the mirror.

"You're not feelin' well, Master Abe?" she said, genuinely concerned. "I saw you race up the stairs like there were a dozen Banshees from Hell come screamin' after yee."

Abe did not know what a Banshee was and he was not in the mood to start a conversation with Virginia, even though he had ached to be alone with her at other times. "I'll be okay, thanks for asking," he responded, somewhat embarrassed that she had seen him in this way.

"Then you'll be tellin' me you're not upset with what's goin' on down there, with your Da getting married and havin' a baby with my mistress?" Abe said nothing. "We'll to be sure,

I'd damn well be upset myself. You can't be blamed for what you're feeling."

Abe wondered if she really understood what he was feeling. He wondered if she were someone like his sister or Joey that he could trust and talk to. But he was too upset and too embarrassed to find out now. "What do you know about it?" he said sharply, moving past her into the bedroom.

"Oh, I know what's been goin' on around here for months now. You know that rich people look at servants as if they're furniture, but we see and we hear plenty."

"I wouldn't know because I never had a servant and I'm not rich."

"But when you move in with your Da and your brothers and sisters, you'll be plenty rich, and we can talk to each other every day if you like."

His immediate response was to tell her that he had no intention of moving in, but before he spoke, the last part of her sentence repeated itself like a lilting echo. What did she mean by that?

"I like you, Master Abie," she said. "Sure you don't mind me callin' you Master Abie, now do you?" As she spoke, she moved slowly towards him, almost gliding. As she approached, she took the cap off her head, and a mass of reddish gold curls covered the white blouse she wore, much like strands of copper and gold chains set out on white velvet. Abe backed up slowly until the back of his thighs were against the bed. When their faces were close enough, she raised her hands to his face, and pulled it down toward her lips. Abe did not resist, and his anger at his father now was mixing with his curiosity about why she would be doing this. He began to breathe heavily. He felt himself growing and pressing against his pants, and he was at once both embarrassed and mesmerized. She moved against him with the certainty of someone who knew exactly what she was doing. Her lips were full and soft against his own, and he felt his own lips slacken as they gave way to hers. His eyes closed and he focused on the warmth of her mouth and the sweet smell that came up from her body. His eyes fluttered and opened in surprise when she pushed her tongue against his teeth, silently demanding that they open to her. They did, and his own tongue, reciprocating, naturally glided over hers and relished this new way of kissing. But the throbbing in his trousers and her movement against him was causing a heat to grow in him that would not be denied. Their hands began to explore one another with increasing passion, and she suddenly pushed him onto the bed, and began opening the buttons on his trousers and pulling at his undergarments.

"The door," he said before her mouth would cover his lips again.

"It's locked," she said, pulling up her skirts and climbed on top of him.

Abe felt Virginia take him and place him against her moist opening, push herself down upon him and move up and down until he easily slid into this secret place, a place he had never known before or felt before. His urgency became wonderful and almost unbearable. Her urgency seem as great as his, and she fell upon him, pounding against him for a while until she insisted that he lay on top of her. He did, and for the first time he opened his eyes to see what was a mandala of silken threads framing her radiant face. Her green eyes were glazed over as if they were seeing a hidden, magical world. He could not take his eyes off of her until he felt something deep within that grew and grew and took on an insistence of its own that would not be denied. His eyes closed and he felt his face contort in a pleasurable pain. Certainly, he had felt the sensation before, but never, never like this. Her own body began to push and grind until she gasped, raised herself against him, cried out, and collapsed. Abe had no idea what had just happened to her, and he was concerned that he had done something wrong. He withdrew from her, and suddenly knew another pain, one caused by an extreme sensitivity, but it soon passed. He lay next to her panting for breath.

"Now wasn't that nice, Master Abe. Now don't ya feel just a wee bit better?"

"Yes, that was very nice," he said smiling, as he looked down and saw himself exposed.

"Now you'll not be embarrassed in front of me," she said intuiting his feelings. Abe put his penis back into his pants and struggled with the bottons. "Actually, I've never been with a young man who had one that looked like yours. It's kind of interesting."

Abe certainly knew what had happened, and yet did not know what had happened at all. He had been with a woman for the first time, which was totally unexpected and wonderful, but it was during his father's wedding with his whole family downstairs. And where was his righteous anger now? Now he was even more confused.

"Oh, I must look a sight," Virginia said getting up from the bed, straightening her skirts and moving to the mirror in the bathroom. "Now you fix yourself up Master Abe and take yourself downstairs to the party because I have some fixing up myself to do." She paused. "Now if there is anything to talk about, we can talk about it the next time you visit. This was your first time? It was fun, don't ya think?"

Abe walked down the stairs, lost in the sensation of having made love for the first time. As he reflected on it, he couldn't believe it happened. He had to tell Joey. He had to tell somebody. He knew it was he who had been seduced, but that didn't matter. It had happened, and he felt, and he grasped for the word, more, more, manly. Was this what a man felt? There was nothing against which he could measure it. Abe was almost at the bottom of the stairs when his revery was interrupted by an angry voice. It was his father. Would his father see the flush he still felt on his face, or hear his heart still pounding. At that moment Jonah looked up and saw Virginia quickly turn and disappear down the corridor.

"Where have you been," Jonah said sharply. "There was a line where people congratulated us and you weren't there. Your absence embarrassed Marta and me. Your absence embarrassed your brothers and your sisters. Rachelann said you were sick and had to leave. I don't believe her. Where were you?"

Abe's liquid revery of the moments just past turned to vapor in the heat of his father's castigation. The frustration and fear that he had put aside momentarily came roiling back over him like a storm churning up mud and debris from a river.

"You're embarrassed? You're angry?" he responded. "I was sick. I threw up because I was sick to my stomach. I'm still sick, but what I'm sick of is all of this. I'm sick of how you never told us about this woman until I shamed you into telling us. I'm sick of how you started seeing her before Mama was even dead a year. I'm sick of how you went to bed with her and are having a baby with her. I'm sick of being the son you will never point to with pride."

Abe was heaving and Jonah was about to respond to his son's disrespect. But Abe just continued.

"And I'm angry, too, Papa. I'm angry that you told Armand of my problems in school before we even met, and I'm angry that you're forcing our family to move away from all our friends. I'm angry that you now have a son in college, and that you love him more than you love me. I can see how you look at him. I can see the pride in your face. You never look at me that way!" He took a breath. "And I'm angry that all the traditions that Mama loved, that we kept so she'd always be with us, will disappear once the family comes to live here. It's already happening if you look at your wedding. There was nothing there that was part of us, part of Mama, and I didn't want to be part of it."

He stood on the step looking down at his father and tears, for the second time that day, rolled down his cheeks. Jonah felt as if he had been beaten by sticks, and his first inclination was to indignantly refute each and every accusation as he had done in the past when defending himself against accusations made by his mother or wife. But he thought of his father at that moment and how Reuven would have responded. Recalling what his father had taught him, that when a son is unruly, he should be held even closer, Jonah reached out to Abe and embraced him, rubbing his back and softly saying, "Sha, sha, Abie, sha."

He led Abe into the sitting room, sat him down, and poured two glasses of Port. "I cannot respond now, even though I want to. They will be looking for me, but I do want you to know a few things. First is that I loved your mother, even if we didn't have the best of relationships. That happens. Maybe one day you'll understand, but you must know that each of you was conceived in love and continue to be loved, as this new child was conceived in love and will be loved. I honor your mother's memory, but she is gone and I am alive. I have a right to be happy as you have a right to be happy. You, your sisters and brothers will grow up and leave me. Why should I be alone? I have found someone who wants me and loves me. I hope one day that you all find such a person. Now, as far as keeping the traditions, if you keep them to keep your mother close, that is good. For me, I keep them as a reminder that I am part of a people who gave the Torah to the world, and with it, light and justice. The world is sometimes a dark place and sometimes only the law will keep people from doing dark things. My problem is not with tradition or with the law. My problem is with God. Marta knows my traditions and she has agreed to honor them once I move in. Abe, you're old enough to know what you have to do. I can't force you to live here. Now, you think about what I've said, dry your eyes, and come in for something to eat."

CHAPTER 11

After the wedding, Abe moved between the apartment in the back of the store where he and Rachelann decided to live, and the house on Fifth Avenue. When Abe stopped his sporadic visits, his father became frantic and went back to the store and the apartment, hoping that Rachelann would know where her brother was. With a deep breath of resignation, and no small hint of annoyance at Abe for pushing more of the responsibility for the store and upkeep on her, she told her father that there was a poolhall named McGraw's near the Herald Building on the Bowery. Jonah knew where it was, and wearily turned to retrace his step to the Lower East Side.

Amid the smoke filled billiard parlor, the dim lights, the brash girls serving liquor, a thoroughly uncomfortable father scanned the patrons for his son. Abe was across the room, a cigarette dangling from his lips, moving around the table setting up a shot. As ill at ease as he was, Abe seemed relaxed and unrepentant. Sensing a presence, he looked up and saw his father. He froze for a moment, then whispered something to the man he was playing, and laying his cue stick on the felt, motioned to John McGraw. McGraw nodded, and a moment later, Abe and his father were sitting on a worn leather couch in the office.

Jonah's opening statement had nothing of the calm understanding that his voice had the afternoon of the wedding.

Now, his voice revealed the honest fear of a father, fearful that his son had been injured or dead and the shame of finding his son in such a place when he should have been with the family, celebrating his sister's birthday. Jonah did not know where to begin.

"Is this what I wanted for you, Abe? Is this what Mama would have wanted for you?" he said, his voice quaking with tears. "My own son, my son, a gambler, a pool player? Someone who lives on his wits, who takes his living and his life from the streets. Was this what we dreamed for you in America?" The older Chernov was overwhelmed with a dark sense of failure. If this was what Abe had chosen, had he failed as a father to teach his son a better way? He thought of his own father and what Reuven had taught him, but he had changed it, made it into something different that his son was rejecting. Had he put his own needs before his children's needs, and in doing so, had he given this son silent permission to turn away from a decent way of life?

"And would you be prouder of me Papa if I sat at a sewing machine like you did in Europe and lived from hand to mouth until I died, never having lived?" He was defending his choice. Abe took out a cigarette, and spoke through the smoke. "Your dream for me in America?" he repeated. "I'll tell you what I learned what your American Dream really is. You want to know?" he said rhetorically. "In America, if you got money, you got respect. If you got lots of money, you got the ears of alotta important people. America tells you what kinda man you are if you got money. First off, money buys you respect and lots of money buys you power. I see it down here every day. I got a lot of ideas, Papa, and I don't need any lousy diploma to be what I wanna be. And I'm gonna get what I want by doing exactly what I'm doing now, here. And believe me, Papa, I'm good at it. And because I'm good at it, I'm making money, I'm getting noticed, and I'm getting respect." With that, Abe took out a wad of folded bills from his front pocket. "This is what America respects, Papa, and in America, the more of this, the more of a man you are. That's what it means to be an American if you really want to know."

Jonah sat back feeling himself go limp. He looked sadly at his son and shook his head.

"America divides the world between the suckers and the ones who get over on the suckers," Abe continued, "and I ain't no sucker, Papa. I ain't no sucker." He repeated it again to emphasize the reason for his choice. When I walk into this pool hall or down the street, people here are noticing me and starting to respect me for what I can do with a pool cue or with cards. I don't disappoint them like I disappoint you, Papa. And they like me because they know I look out for number one, and they respect me for that. There's a code down here, and the code says that if you don't look out for yourself, no one else will. Hell, if a guy is dumb, someone is going to get the best of him, so why not me? If I don't, I'm as dumb as he is."

"So I'm a sucker and everybody else who isn't a gambler is a sucker? Is that it, Abe? Everybody but you is a sucker?" Jonah was inflating with rage at the selfishness and shallowness of his son. This he had never learned in his home, and whatever Abe had learned about how to treat other people, he had dismissed.

"This is the code you're choosing to live by? This is how you're going to treat people? You're losing your soul, Abie. I thought we gave you at least something of value, but I was wrong. People aren't things to be fooled and cheated. You are losing yourself by your own choosing."

"This wasn't only my choosing, Papa, because this dream of yours is a myth, and if it is real, it's real for somebody else. You told me that in America we would be free to be anything we wanted to be. Well I can't be what I might have wanted to be because they can't teach me how to read. They said there's something wrong with my head. So am I supposed to paint ceilings or sweep dirt? And you told me here, everybody would get along. So tell me there ain't real Jew hatred here like there was in Russia. Tell me that those men who won't be tricked or bullied aren't found in alleys with their heads bashed in with their pockets turned out so the next pack of haters could see that this Jew or Italian had already been picked over? Tell me that we're not called parasites, the lowest of scum? I can't fight back by becoming a lawyer like Armand. Do you think Armand would have gotten into Colombia and Harvard if his last name was Chernov and not du Champ? Notice, he didn't change it, but I don't blame him. He knows what the game is and he knows how to play it. Armand has a lot to lose by telling his friends that his father is a Jew. Marta's house isn't mine, Papa, and it isn't yours either. You were lucky, Papa, lucky to have a new wife who took you and the family out of Brownsville. But look at those you left. What road out do they have? Sure, there are no Cossacks riding in, brandishing swords and cutting throats, but how long will it take for these people to get out of their poverty and the slums? I'm not waiting around. If America tells me I'm free, then I'm free to do what ever the hell I want to do. And I'm free to live any way I choose. I'll bet you I make more money in a day than you see in a week. You ever play pool with an alderman, Papa, or cards with the mayor or political bosses? I do, and that gets me both respect and connections. I got connections, Papa, and with connections, you don't have to be afraid. If I get picked up by the cops for something, I make one phone call and I'm back on the street. Remember that day in the kitchen when all the sheep around the table shuddered at the thought of having to give up some time to stand outside to protect the kids to and from school? Decent and honest men like them I don't want to be. They sat on their asses pretending there was no problem so I did something about it. Those Micks never came near Harry or Sammy again. A little while ago I was willing to fight anyone in Brooklyn because I had nothing to lose. I'm learning that there are ways of getting what you want without getting your hands dirty."

"But you don't have to do that Abie," Jonah pleaded. "I have enough money now to set you up in business so you can earn an honest living. Come back home, Abie."

Abe said nothing, so Jonah continued.

"You have a choice that your friends don't have. Yes, I was lucky to find Marta again, and I was lucky that even though I had nothing, she didn't want me for things. She wanted me for me. She loves me, and that is something you cannot fully understand until you learn to love another person. That's how it should be between people. That's what love is. I understand that you don't see any of this as belonging to you, but try to see what your brothers and sisters see."

Jonah stopped for a moment and waited for some reply, but again, there was none. Then he said, "Is it that by accepting this life we're offering you you will be betraying your mother's memory? Is that what this is all about, Abie?" There was another pause, and tears gathered in the corners of Abe's eyes and rolled down his cheeks. "Yes, at first, you had the life of the streets, but you also had to balance that with the life your Mama and I tried to teach you in the house. If you don't want to live with me and Marta, I can't force you. But I beg you, don't give up what we taught you. The life you are choosing is not a life that a Jewish boy chooses. It cannot end well. Such a life never does."

"Papa," Abe said. "I don't want to be like the kind of Jew who came over on the boat with you. Your dream, their dream, may be true for the people who have been here for generations and are Christian, but that's not how your dreams of America works for me and my friends. Jews are still afraid here because there are plenty of people who came over on that same boat with us that brought their old hates from Europe with them, and still blame us for every evil in the world. Oh sure, we're free here to be tailors, butchers, peddlers, or store owners, but little else. We're also free to starve and be looked down upon like we are dirt. And those bitches in school, a place we were told would be the great leveler and our best bet to bring ourselves up, never told me I could overcome my problems and become something if I kept at it, But they did tell me I was worthless and good for shoveling coal or digging ditches."

Abe's handsome face, his dark brown eyes, his sleek auburn hair shinny from the macassar his barber combed into it, stood looking at his father as if the man were in some way being pulled away by an unseen force. They were indeed separating. Abe would recreate himself out of the energy he felt kneeling in a dice game on some corner, or out of the vigor he felt in the card games hastily begun on the stoops of some street. There was the power he felt strutting down the street in his wing-tip shoes, tipping his expensive fedora to pretty ladies on his way to McGraw's. Abe would become a man like no other man on the teeming streets of New York City.

Abe and Jonah Chernov had reached an uneasy truce, and neither knew where this new relationship would take father and son. Now, feeling independent and finally free from the deprecating remarks of teachers, Abe emancipated himself and baptized himself in the waters of the street, the poolhalls, the bars, and the restaurants of Manhattan. These became as familiar to him as the streets of Brownsville, but with a difference. Brownsville was tawdry and a link to a world he was seeing for what it was. One day, he knew, he would separate himself from it.

New York was different, and he loved it with a passion. It had a vibration all its own, and in some ways he felt that his whole self was in synchronization with it. Abe walked everywhere and the city caressed him like a lover, especially Broadway, because it pulsated with the same energy and kinetic potential that pulsated in his own body. He was bombarded on all sides by signs that beaconed or teased, and by the screech of the metal trolley wheels on metal grooves. He knew that the overhead sparks that cascaded out of the wires touching the guide wheels were sending surges of energy to the motors, and in some magical way, the city was doing the same to him. The dissident honking of car horns that warned horse and wagon drivers to move out of the way always made him smile, as did the bright flapping awnings in reds, yellow, blues, and greens, shading huge windows that offered goods and services. To him, the city was a giant mechanical machine made up by thousands of shapes, hundreds of colors, and a myriad of sounds. It pulsated with a vibrance he could feel, and he was part of it, a moving part that seemed to appreciate it as few others could. No, he was not passing through the city as he surmised most did without truly looking at it, without feeling it or breathing it in. He felt its power, loved its power, and it empowered him.

On one of his strolls, his eye caught the image of a dapper young man reflected in the window of Captain Jim Churchill's Restaurant on 46th Street and Broadway and he was pleased with what he saw.

It had been a good morning at the poolhall, with plenty of rubes to hustle. In fact, it had been such a good week at cards and pool, that he pocketed enough cash to go into one of the better men's shops on Pitkin Avenue and purchase the new three piece suit, shirt, collar, and tie which he sported that day. This would be his New York City image. The Brownsville image would be quite different.

As he scanned the reflection of the young man, flush from the poolparlor down the street, his eyes focused beyond the glass to the other well dressed men sitting at the white marbled tables having lunch. His fantasy took hold that he was a well to do businessman, an owner of a factory who had decided to step inside for a quick lunch. So he entered a new adventure and waited near the door for several minutes before a large woman in black, sporting a white lace shawl, approached. She did not smile and gestured him to a table for two at which an older man had already been seated. Abe briefly smiled at the dour woman and the corners of her mouth raised slightly though begrudgingly. If I had a restaurant like this, he thought, I would hire only pleasant people to greet customers. The man at the table looked up, grumbled, and removed his coat and walking stick from Abe's seat only to put them on the back of his own. Abe sat down, scanned the menu, and decided on the pot roast.

Kosher meat no longer was considered. A pretty blond waitress came up, took his order, and disappeared. As he waited, seeing that his luncheon partner had his face buried in a paper, he began to look around. At each table of four, two of the chairs were taken up by hats, coats, and walking sticks. With a quick calculation, he saw that at least a quarter of the seats were given over to outer garments. "What a waste," he whispered. The man with whom he sat looked up from his newspaper, and then away. Abe sat for a moment. At the new Astor Hotel where Armand had taken him for the card game with the boys from Colombia, Abe noticed that there was a room for checking these items. If he could rent a space in a place like this so people wouldn't have to put their coats on chairs, there would be more people who could sit and eat without others being inconvenienced. He looked back at the vestibule and envisioned a portion of it for such a venture. Why not? Abe thought. He glanced down at his new shoes and the white cuffs of his new shirt. He looked accomplished and well off. No one could dismiss someone in such a suit, and the worst the man could say was no. So why not?

After finishing his lunch, he beckoned the waitress to come over, and as he did, he took out a quarter and put it on the table. Her eyes widened. A nickel tip was the most she usually received. Abe knew exactly what her response would be because you had to spread some money around if you wanted to get things done. Everything was a gamble and everything an investment. That was a lesson he had learned from older gamblers; that life itself was a gamble and that you sometimes had to bet on yourself to make things happen.

"I'd like to see the man in charge," Abe said slowly, holding her eyes with his while deepening his voce to feign some authority. The young lady picked up the coin, smiled playfully at the darkly handsome young man, her eyes flirting with unspoken promises. Despite himself, Abe felt himself blush, but her response reinforced his conclusion that money, even a quarter, could get you something more than a smile from a pretty girl if you pursued it.

"You want to see Mr. Churchill?" she continued somewhat coyly. "He's the owner. His office is over there, and if you like, I'll show you. By the way, I'm Sally."

Abe followed, thinking that this is the kind of girl who should take hats and greet people, and if this quixotic idea of his worked, that is exactly what she would do for him.

Sally knocked on the door and a deep rumble that sounded like, "come in," came though the open transept. She opened the door, entered, and curtsied in deference to the large man with the white moustache sitting behind the desk. "This young man would like to speak with you, Captain Churchill," she said, again smiling at Abe. She curtsied and backed out of the room.

Captain Churchill looked up briefly, assessed Abe's attire which indicated someone of means and someone who might have something worthwhile to say, and placed the pen back in its holder. "And what can I do for you today?" he said, swiveling in the slatted oak desk chair. "Was something wrong with the food?"

"No sir," Abe responded. "The food was quite good, and the service from that young lady was excellent." Abe cleared his throat and thought it best to get right to the pooint with a man who was obviously very busy. "I have a business proposition I'd like you to consider that would free up seats in your restaurant so you would be able to seat many more people and not inconvenience your guests at the same time."

Captain Churchill leaned forward and clasped his fingers together and nodded his head indicating interest. Abe smiled to himself because he knew he had the man hooked. "And it won't cost you a dime." he added quickly to keep the momentum of interest. "In fact, you'll make a profit." Captain Churchill motioned for Abe to sit in one of the chairs.

"And what is your proposal?"

"If you would agree to it sir, I'd like to open up a coat and hat concession in your vestibule. This would free you from having to answer to people who hold you responsible for lost coats, hats, or canes. And with no outerwear on the seats, the patrons already there won't be annoyed that they have to move their belongings. You can seat more people and make a better profit." Abe paused and waited for a response, trying not to show his excitement.

"So you want to open up a business in my vestibule" Churchill mused. "I had thought of that a while ago, but didn't want the expense. You're saying that you'll carry the expense?" He paused again, but I think I want some rent for the space."

Abraham was caught off guard. He hadn't considered that possibility. Of course this man wanted some of the take. That's what businessmen did. That's what made them businessmen. "Certainly," Abe said quickly. "Would an eighth of my weekly profit be acceptable?"

An eighth is better than nothing, the Captain thought, figuring that whatever an eighth was would still be pure profit, and he would not have any responsibility. Besides, how much could there be in tips? The Captain stood and moved around the desks towards Abe and extended his hand. "You're a smart kid," he said. "It's a deal. By the way boy, what's your name?"

Abe got on the trolley going towards the Brooklyn Bridge. He had created a skeleton of an enterprise, and now he had to hang some flesh on it. That meant he had to invest in himself in the way of a uniform, coat racks, hangers and check stubs. What the hell did he get himself into? Churchhill had said yes, and now it was up to him to follow through and make this happen. He remembered a cold chill of regret wash over him as he and Mr. Churchill shook hands on it. It was a spur of the moment idea based on one of his dumb fantasies, but that handshake made it real. Now he had to pony up the money or be branded a fool or worse, a liar. His reputation, or at least the one he was trying to create for himself, was at stake. This man had actually bought into the idea, and this was a real New York City businessman, so there had to be some merit in it as well as profit.

So as the tram rumbled over the East River, Abe decided that the entire enterprise would run on tips, and since it was only logical that men would tip girls more than they'd tip boys, he would have to hire a girl who was pretty and friendly, like Sally, the one in the restaurant. She would be perfect, and probably knew the regulars by name. He would ask her if she would do this, and he would ask her how much she made in tips as a waitress. He could pay her a flat salary which he would make sure was more than she would make waiting tables, and maybe a percentage of the tips. He decided that all tips would go into a box so no one would be tempted to skim off the top like he saw the hat check boys do at the Astor. With the tips in the box, he would be able to see over a period of time how much tip money came in and average it out. He was positive that Sally would be honest with him to gain his trust and to prove herself, but if she wasn't, he would have to get rid of her. This could work, he thought, and if it worked at Churchill's, he could make it works elsewhere. Over time, if he watched carefully and was fair, he could build up a reliable and honest workforce.

He tried to rein in his imagination and just focus, but that was not Abe. Suddenly, he saw himself as the owner of a chain of concessions in restaurants and hotels all over the city. Maybe all over the country. Perhaps, by the end of the year, he would have enough to put a down payment on the old dairy behind the store. That piece of property was going to come in handy once these crazy women got the government to stop selling booze. He saw that coming, and was already thinking how he could turn that into a profit.

The following day, Abe went back to Captain Churchill's and offered Sally Banks the job, but made it clear that he could not say what the pay would be until after the first couple of weeks. He also said he would front her the salary she was already making for whatever time she had to give up to help him set up the concession. She gladly accepted because she, too, saw the potential for making a lot more money than she was making slinging hash for old man Churchill. Besides, she liked Abe from the moment she saw him. At first, Abe thought that he would run the concession, and Sally would hang up the coats, but she convinced him that the patrons would find it extremely flattering if they were told, "No check needed, sir," and that's what Sally would say to the regulars. She also assured him that that personal touch of recognition and a pretty smile would open their pockets nicely. Abe, sensing that this savvy young lady knew what she was talking about, agreed to hang up the coats. As she predicted, when the concession got up and running, the tips from the regulars were far more than the tips from the occasional customer. Sally had a good business head on her shoulders.

The money was surprisingly good, better than he and Sally had imagined, and Abe, seeing the possibilities in this venture, took a chance and approached the owner of a new restaurant that had opened up on Forty-eighth Street. The same basic deal he offered Churchill, he offered this new owner. But this owner wanted more than an eighth, so they agreed on a flat one time fee that Abe could pay off.

Restaurant after restaurant bought into Abe's idea, and before long, he recognized that he had to devote himself to running this business full time, but always making time for the card table, the races, and the poolhall which remained his first love. Sally became something of his business manager, keeping the books and overseeing the day to day operation.

There were others who saw what Abe was doing, and were making their own efforts at setting up concessions in restaurants and hotels. Abe didn't much care about these others because he had more than he could handle. But one day when he and Sally were accosted by some toughs from the West Side and threatened with bodily harm, he knew he needed to do something about it. He needed help, someone completely trustworthy, and someone who could exert just the right influence when there was a conflict with those who would horn in on his enterprise.

Each evening, Abe returned to the store and apartment his father had given over to him and his sister. Initially, after Jonah's wedding to Marta and the argument that ensued, he and Rachelann decided they would live there while the younger children lived with their father. The two of them ran the store with Jonah coming in two days a week to relieve them. Now, with the concession business taking up much of his time, Abe happily turned the running of the store over to his sister who was not happy about the situation at all.

And so it was, Abe, in what he called his Brownsville uniform, huddled under the canopy of another candy store that seemed to be the only store still open on Saratoga Avenue. The New Lots train above him rumbled to a screeching stop and tired workers plodded down the stairs. Some turned to go home and some turned into the store for a cup of coffee or some conversation with a friend or with the owner, Rosey Gold. Mrs. Gold, the gruff immigrant owner, had been a casual friend of his mother's from their shetle days, and though his mother did not care for Mrs. Gold's gruff ways, they shared a bond of mutual understanding and hardship. There were times in the past when he was feeling particularly down with no one to talk to, that he would sneak out of the house at night, come here, and talk to Mrs. Gold. Here, there were never any expectations or judgements, and though surrounded by rough men and wannabe gangsters, he felt comfortable and protected. She never betrayed his late night prowls to his parents, so this had always been a safe place, free from prying eyes. Mrs. Gold understood. So this was where he and Joey, along with other kids, met along with other street toughs who gathered and planned, shook hands, or agreed to fight. Rose Gold, who had no children of her own, considered the boys who hung around her store till all hours of the night, her boys. It was rumored that she even bailed kids out of jail when their parents couldn't or wouldn't raise the money. "You're not like these other kids, Abie," he remembered her saying. "You're going someplace. You're smart and you're good looking, like your father. You're not like the rest of these bums who stand outside at all hours of the night, spitting and smoking and waiting for something to happen. You're the kind who makes things happen, Abie."

So here he stood in the warm and inviting glow of the light emanating from the shop, waiting for Joey to appear.

"I'm making a lot of money, Joey," he began, knowing that such an opening would peak his friend's interest immediately. "And I'm going to need your help if I'm going to make more."

Joey DiAngelo leaned in. "Is this about that hat and coat check thing you got started? I don't see myself as bowing and scraping to swells for dimes and quarters."

"I'm ain't asking you to do that. I need some help in keeping other people from muscling in on my business, and I see this as an opportunity for you to make some really good money if you can handle it."

"Handle it, you gotta be fuckin' kiddin'. Of course I can handle it."

"But you don't even know what it is." Abe said.

"I don't care what it is, buddy. I can handle it."

"Okay. I need some muscle to help me keep what I have and grow the business, and if you help me keep the business going and growing, you and me stand a good chance of cleaning up."

Joey leaned in and looked around furtively. "How much we talkin' about?"

"Possibly hundreds a week." Abe paused. "I need you and some of the guys to go to certain owners of certain restaurants and make them aware that my coat and hat concessions will give them the best deal in town and that any other company is not going to work out so well for them."

"You mean protection? We go in, bust up a few chairs, maybe a face, maybe a mirror..."

"No, not like that. This is a legit business, and I want to keep it that way," interrupted Abe. "No one pays you to get me the concession. I pay you a fee for being my representative.

No one gets hurt, and no furniture is broken. You'll be like my agent. Where I think there is going to be some competition, I send you in first. You talk to the owners real nice, telling them that I would like to talk to them. In the conversation, you give them the impression that any other concession group wouldn't be as good or as profitable as mine. I want you to take Mendy and Al with you so maybe the people you're talkin' to might be slightly intimidated, but they say nothing. Hell, I get scared when I look at them and we're friends. Then you leave them my card, and I come in later and cut the deal. I pay you from the money I'll make when they sign with me. You understand what I'm sayin'? Like you'll work on commission. The more concessions I open because you first spoke to the management there, the more money you make. I'll front you your first week's pay," and Abe slid five folded twenty dollar bills over to Joey's fingers.

"So who gets hurt?"

"Nobody, except the guys who want to open up concessions where I want to open up concessions. Then we introduce them to Mendy, Al, and a bat."

CHAPTER 12

1911

Rachelann, holding the teapot she had just filled, put two scoops of shredded tea into it so it would brew.

"What do I do there?" she said, cutting two slices of cake, and pushing a plate towards Abe. "Marta and the cook are in charge of the kitchen, and that Virginia girl takes care of the house. There's even someone who comes in just to do the laundry. How many fancy teas can I help serve Papa's fancy pupils? And am I to become Aaron's nurse maid, joining the governesses in the park, and pretending that he's not my half brother? Is that going to be my life? So I move between there and here, smile at whoever comes in, and pretend I don't feel what I feel. I did this because Papa asked me to do him a favor and try, and I did. Since their wedding I've been shuttling between that house and this place. I'm just tired of it, and I want to stop having to be in both places. Either I'm taking care of Aaron, or you, or the store, or bringing Harry back whenever he runs back here. Everyone seems to have settled into a life except me."

Abe poured a shot of whiskey into his glass and offered the bottle to his sister, but she declined with a disapproving look.

"So what's wrong with having servants?' he said matter-of-factly. He had heard her complaint before. "Name me one person you know who wouldn't be happy to change places with you? There you can be a lady with no responsibilities until you get married, and here you have a store to run with responsibilities you hate. Why don't you just learn to enjoy that life like Fanny and the boys do, or don't you think you deserve a life of ease? Ain't that what people come to America for?"

Rachelann looked at her brother incredulously. "You were offered that life and you walked away from it for the same reasons I'm walking away. Those fine ladies just sit around, and the world isn't made better by people just sitting around being pampered." His suggestion incensed her. "If you can tell me 'just to enjoy it,' you haven't any idea of who I am. After Mama died, I knew exactly what I had to do. Do you think I loved washing everyone's clothes, cooking for everyone, and working in the store? That wasn't what I envisioned I'd be doing. I wanted to go to school, but I accepted what I had to become because there was no one else to do it. Mama and Papa always told us to 'make the world a better place,' but I've only been able to make the world a better place for you and everyone else. Unlike you, I didn't have the luxury of choice. Now I want more." She saw Abe move uncomfortably, but also saw that he was trying to understand. "I don't feel as if I have any real value."

Rachelann stood suddenly and walked to the sink in silence. Then she turned. "I know what it's like to be a housewife, without even being a wife, and I don't want to spend my life in that drudgery."

"So why not let Papa and Marta introduce you to a nice rich Jewish boy from Manhattan. Maybe one of those fancy ladies he teaches has a son?" He drained his glass of tea and whiskey and held the cup up to her for her to pour him more. "That way you can have servants to do the hard work, and you can go out into the world and make it a better place."

"Pour it yourself," she scowled and sat down again facing him. "You haven't understood a word I've said. You're just like Papa. I come to you with a problem, and all you think I need is for some man to give me advice on what I should do with my life and how to solve the problem. Are all men so thick, or is it only the Chernov men? You don't know what's inside me. I doubt if you know what's inside any woman."

"I do okay with women," he smiled, missing the point she was making. In the space that followed, he wondered if anybody really knew anybody else. Abe responded after seconds of reflection on his own inner life, his hidden doubts, and his own secrets. "So tell me what's inside of you," he said pensively. "Tell me what it is you really want. Do you even know?" He paused for her to consider his invitation.

"I know that I don't want to help Papa run his school, or chat with Marta's friends over lunch. I don't want to be Aaron's governess, I don't want to run a grocery or candy store, and I certainly don't want to associate with the people you know."

"Now is that a nice way to talk to your younger brother who only wants to help?"

Rachelann paused. "I'm sorry. It just came out."

"I'm an honest businessman who has a hat and coat check business in restaurants and hotels. So maybe I dabble in other things, but who's being hurt? Everyone is very well paid, and everyone is very happy. I do believe I'm making the world a much better place in my own way. I'm assuming you asked Papa what you should do with the rest of your life?"

She ignored what she thought might be sarcasm in his question. "Yes, I did, and he said that if I liked, I could help him teach languages to those rich ladies and their over privileged brats who come to the house. But I don't want to do that; that's not being on my own. I don't want to be under Papa's gaze. I don't want him to do anything for me. I want do see if I can make my way by myself. And I don't want to be under your gaze either. I want to be independent and create my own life, the way you did. I want to see what the world is like."

"The world is a pretty rotten place, Rachelann, where you have to fight for every inch of space you want to call your own. You want to see the world as it really is? Go to work in one of those sweatshops for pennies, and then bring home extra work at night so everybody can make a few more pennies. Go share a bed with two other girls in a tenement, and have to divide the pittance you make with the people you board with and the family you send money to back in Europe. The men and women who work for me don't have to live in that kind of poverty. Go out there and see what the world is really like and that will make you sick. What you have between your two worlds, my dear sister, is a damn sight better than what anyone else has!"

Rachelann bit her lip. He still did not understand. None of them did. "I can no longer be beholden to you, Marta, or Papa. No, Abe, I need to get a job on my own so I can be with the people I really want to help. Everybody is doing something that is giving them a purpose and satisfaction. I want that for myself. Elizabeth and Nathaniel once took me down to a settlement house on the Lower East Side. Those are the people you're talking about. I saw how they live. I saw the depravation and suffering and how they were barely surviving. But in those people's eyes, I also saw hope and faith in a better tomorrow. I can do something there. I can teach them English at night. And I can write about them so people who have real money will know about them and help. I can get a job at one of the Jewish newspapers like *The Forward*."

"And where will you be living while you're saving the world. When everyone was here, you took money from me, but now you won't. So you live on what the store brings in, and you're too proud to take money from Marta and Papa. How will you live while you're writing these wonderful stories that are gonna save the world? You think a newspaper will hire you just because you say you want a job? You gotta have something to write about."

"A month ago, I went to a lecture by a lady from the government named Frances Perkins. She was talking about the terrible conditions in the garment industry. Papa still has friends who work there and I've heard them talk around this very table about that terrible way of earning a living; the heat, the lack of air, the hours, the stench in the toilets, and the children who work there for pennies. I can talk to them, or even better, get a job working in a factory and see for myself. That will be a story that they will notice. After they see it, they will want to hire me to write other stories."

"I still think it would be better if you took money from me or taught for Papa."

"Why, Abie, because I'm an unmarried girl who needs a man to take care of her?" She picked up the newspaper. "I'm going to bed."

The following morning, Rachelann woke up just before sunrise, leaving oatmeal and coffee on the stove for her brother before wrapping herself in her winter coat and stepping into the unseasonably chilly late March air. She walked to the trolley along with other men and women who seemed to be trudging reluctantly to their work, but she kept her eyes directly ahead of her on the sliver of crimson sky that burned the horizon. Daylight grew steadily, much the way embers of a hearth grow when a billow pushes puffs of air onto them, and she could not help but smile at what she hoped would be a day of bright promise. It would be a beautiful day; it would be her day. Whatever she wanted out of life was not in Brownsville but in Manhattan. She stood at the trolley, watching the plodding horses come to a halt. They seemed as reluctant as her nameless companions. She sat and again scanned the want ads of yesterday's *Forward*, focusing in on the one that seemed certain to give her the experience she would need to write. The ad spoke of a machine operator's job in the The Asch Building at Washington Place. Its location was foreign to her, but she nevertheless was confident that someone in the city would be able to help her find it. Certainly she knew how to work a sewing machine. Both parents had taught her that. Now she would put that skill to use to tell the stories of young girls who were all but enslaved and trying to break out of poverty or help their families. She felt somewhat like a fraud; her father and siblings were living in a mansion, her brother wealthy from his own devices and vices. At any time she could disappear into wealth. Unlike most, there was a safety net under her. She dismissed that reality, though it still hinted vaguely at hypocrisy.

"Excuse me sir," she said when she got off the trolley at the base of the Brooklyn Bridge. "I'm trying to get to a village near a Washington Square Park. I don't know where it is, but they have work. I'm trying to find the Asch Building. Do you know where it is?" The first man did not know and neither did a second. But a third man said she had to take the crosstown trolley to Broadway, and from there she could ask directions.

Hesitantly, she paid her coins for the cross town trolley and took a seat. She watched people scurrying about their businesses, and wondered at the diversity of lives being lived in the city. So many thousands of people and so many thousands of lives, some touching, but most never touching and unaware of the others. She wondered how such different people from so many different countries and with so many different beliefs could come together and make this country work. She guessed that their unifying purpose, like hers and her family, was just to survive and to go to bed on a full stomach, and not be afraid that someone would break down the door and drag them away. She also wondered if ambition to be independent and make the world better was also an objective. In any case, she thought, people are just people and most people just want to be happy, safe, and content simply to be assured that there would be a tomorrow and that they would see it on a full stomach. That was it. Yes, it suddenly became clear to her what would give her life meaning. She wanted to make people feel safe and unafraid.

At the next stop, she was told to cross the street and take that trolley to the park and a place called Greenwich Village. This she did, and feeling that she had finally thought and verbalized something important, even if it was just to herself, she fell into a contented sleep. But that sleep was suddenly shaken by a clanging bell being rung by the conductor announcing the last stop and how she had to get off because the horse was lame and he had to return it to the stable.

The clanging bell startled her awake, and she immediately saw that she had missed her stop. "But when will the next trolley be here?' she pleaded to the conductor. "I have a perspective job, and I have to get there." She glanced down at the watch fob on her coat. "It's on Washington Place, and I'm so very late."

"Nothing I can do about that, lassie," the conductor replied. "But the next conductor will be bringing the horses in about an hour or so, so ye can wait here or you can begin to walk."

Rachelann looked around somewhat in a daze and in a panic. She could not believe how foolish she had been. "Where am I?" she said.

"Well, you're in Bowling Green, lassie, my last stop, and over there is Broadway." The conductor pointed and Rachelann followed his hand with her eyes. I'd be advising you to walk north past the Trinity Church and a bit further on is St. Paul's Chapel. You just keep going up past Chambers, past Canal, past Houston Street and then ye be com'in to the park ye be after. Make a right turn and then a left and then ye be where ye want to be. Of course," he continued, "since it'll take time for you to walk, I think ye should be walk'in with an eye to a trolley that may be coming up on ye."

On any other occasion, Rachelann Chernov would have relished the sun, the chill in the air, and the sights and sounds of the open area in which she now found herself. She walked down Broadway past the great red stone church with the neatly planted tombstones behind the great black iron fence. On any other day, she would have smiled at the familiar Lower East Side crowds haggling with pushcart peddlers and store merchants, just as they did on Blake Avenue in Brooklyn. She would have slowed her pace to drink in this place they called Greenwich Village with its tree lined streets, the arch at the entrance to the pretty park and the beautiful federal houses that lined it on all sides.

She moved quickly, occasionally looking over her shoulder to see if a trolley was coming, and eventually, gave up on the thought. Soon, she was at the park and turning onto Washington Square Place. She realized that the time for the interview had passed, but she thought that perhaps the time was open ended, and jobs would still be available. She looked up from her watch to see a tall building in the near distance. This was it. As she hurried towards it, she was surprised to see smoke issuing out of windows on the upper floors, and she stopped suddenly, trying to understand what was happening. Why were they tossing bolts of material out of the windows? Just like the factory owners to try to save their cloth, she thought, just when workers were in danger. Now, the bolts of cloth were hitting the ground with more frequency. As she approached, she looked up saw a bolt coming directly at her. She was about to scream when she felt her body hurled out of its way and felt the weight of a man on top of her. Pain radiated thoughout her shoulder and side when she hit the sidewalk. Initially, she thought to berate the brute until she turned her head to see the grey eyes of a dead girl staring out at her, blood oozing from where her crushed skull hit the sidewalk. Rachelann screamed. The bolts of material were not bolts but young women hurling themselves out of the windows, preferring a sudden death on concrete than the slow torment of being burned alive. She continued screaming uncontrollably, and felt herself being pulled up by both arms and dragged across the street to a place of safety. Thud, a life snuffed out, and then another. The horrifying sounds of screaming girls, suddenly silent, suddenly dead on the pavement became unbearable. Her language was lost. She could only scream herself. One after the other, horror after horror lived in seconds, and lives, souls, dwelling within bones and flesh dashed into oblivion in the time that it takes to fall eighty feet. Thud, another world destroyed. Thud, dreams and love suddenly gone. Mothers and fathers inconsolable. Children bereft of a parent. All lost in the seconds it takes to fall to earth. Nothing, she thought, in the world makes such a sound as that.

Rachelann clutched the arm of the man who held her up. Girls appeared at the window, flames from the lower floors licking their tortured faces. Rachelann, looking up, pleaded silently with the shape in the widow that she not jump, that some miracle of God would intervene. But the girl looked to heaven and leaped into the lower flames, her arms seeming to flail for balance or perhaps believing that she could fly up to the sky. Then, the horrible sound and the blood, the twisted limbs, and the scorched clothing. The man tried to turn her head away, but he could not. "Hasn't anyone called the fire department?" she screamed, and then in the distance, she heard the clanging bells of fire engines coming from different directions. "Don't jump," she yelled into the air. "Help is coming."

Girls continued to fight their way to the windows, either for air or for the chance of not being burned alive. No one can know. Still, they kept climbing onto the window sills, heads bobbing behind them, screaming and choking smoke as they fought for clean air. Suddenly, the flames on the lower floors exploded the windows and sent flares of fire into the paths of the falling girls; the scorching fire inflicting even more pain as they fell to their deaths.

Firemen rushed with nets and held them up, but the force of a body falling so far and so fast broke the net. Bodies kept falling through. The firemen raised the tallest ladder they had, but it went only to the sixth floor. Rachelann saw one girl jump towards it and miss. Suddenly, before all the other faces disappeared from the windows in an explosion of flame from within, one young man, still wearing a hat and coat, lifted a young woman to the burning sill, kissed her tenderly, and, holding her in his arms, jumped with his love into eternity. The thud on the concrete was just as devastating; the sound of lives, dreams, love, and hope, extinguished.

The stranger pulled Rachelann away from the horror, and led her down the street. Out of the corner of her eye she could see the side of the building, and there, amid anguished screams, were still more women burning alive as they fought to get out of the windows. Suddenly, one freed herself from the others, opening a space, and one by one, like burning dolls, screaming their anguish, hair aflame like dry kindling, threw themselves to earth, piling one upon the other like carelessly tossed branches. No longer could Rachelann absorb the physical and emotional revulsion she felt, and passed out into the arms of her companion as the water from the fire hoses mixed with the blood on the sidewalk and trickled into the gutter. The next rain would wash it all away. Already, a policeman was tagging numbers to the wrists of the dead girls.

His name was Alexander Berkman, and he was an anarchist who had come to the corner of the Asch Building to speak to anyone who would listen to him rant about the inhumanity that man foisted upon others; the slavery that causes the poor to struggle for the crumbs that capitalists toss on the floor from their economic feasts. He was a leader in the Pioneers of Liberty, the first Jewish anarchist group in America, and affiliated with the International Working People's Association. He was there to foment a strike against the sweatshop when the fire broke out.

"Let me take you home," he said softly. "Where do you live?"

Rachelann immediately thought of the house on Fifth Avenue, and was embarrassed by the wealth it represented. "I live in Brownsville, in Brooklyn," she replied, "but I don't want to go back there right now. I need air. I need to walk." She looked back at the twisted bodies, and her gorge rose when she suddenly realized that she could have been one of the burning girls at the window had she not fallen asleep and had to walk to the factory. "Blessed be the name of the Lord," she said softly. "I was going for a job there. I could be dead. God saved me."

Alexander Berkman snorted. "I don't know you young lady, but I have to wonder that if 'your God' was the one who saved you, then logic would demand that 'your God,' for some reason, did not want to save all the others." He looked up at the burning tower that was now silent.

He continued leading her towards the park and sat her down on a bench facing the fountain.

"Why would you seek out a job in such a hell?" he asked. "Are you destitute?"

"No, I'm not. I just wanted to see for myself what it was like so I could write of it first hand so the world would know about what happens in such a place. Then, perhaps, I can make things better."

Berkman recognized a kindred spirit, and he also recognized that he was drawn to the pretty young woman who appeared to be in her twenties with no wedding ring on her finger. "If you are interested in writing," he continued, "a friend of mine puts out a newspaper entitled, *Mother Earth*, and I am an editor there. Perhaps you would like to meet her and my friends."

Rachelann nodded and briefly considered her good fortune of meeting a man who would help her begin her career, but she immediately berated herself for even allowing such a thought to enter her mind when the tragedy she had witnessed was only two blocks away. She nodded her head and felt calm and safe enough to cry. An arm caressed her shoulder, and she allowed herself to be pulled to this stranger's chest.

"What you have just witnessed," he said softly to her ear, "is the result of the rich and powerful, the wolves, who created a world where the sheep are easily slaughtered. This is one of the very deep truths of our lives, young lady." Rachelann lifted her head and looked into his intense brown eyes. She saw in them a passion and a rightness to a cause that she had never seen before, and it at once intrigued her and frightened her at the same time. He shouldn't be talking like this now, but she seemed to sense that this was his only way of dealing with what they had both just witnessed. He pulled her to her feet. "We live in a world where the Devil, in the shape of Capitalists, have polluted and debased the poor who struggle against the economic slavery into which they've been forced. I and my friends are the voices that cry out against injustice. You can be one of those voices."

Alexander Berkman pulled Rachelann's face to his and kissed her passionately. She struggled against his body, but he was too strong and too insistent. A man had never kissed her in this way, and certainly not a stranger. Yet the sensation of his lips on her lips, the pressure of him, the warm sensation that flowed from his lips to hers and into her face and down her body, all became a new awareness and one she simultaneously welcomed and rejected.

"You should not have done that," she said, being released and pulling away. "I'm not a whore that you can handle like cheap goods. I don't even know your name and you do not know mine."

"Then what is your name young lady? Mine is Alexander Berkman, but you may call me Alex."

"I shall call you Mr. Berkman if you don't mind. I'm always respectful to my elders, and don't you ever do that to me again." She waited to see if she had crushed him with her reference to his age. "And you may call me Miss Chernov."

"I would still like you to meet my friends if you are still interested in writing for our newspaper." He extended his arm to her and though Rachelann hesitated, she took it.

Together, they retraced Rachelann's steps down Broadway, moving through new streets like Essex, Rivington, and Eldredge. The people did not yet know about the fatal fire that killed so many, and she could not help but wonder if some of the people she passed going about their lives would arrive home only to discover that one they loved would never be coming home again. At the thought, she felt faint. What she had seen this day, she would never forget, and she feared that she would relive the horror night after night in her dreams. Berkman urged her on, eager to get to his friends and tell them what had just happened, and how they might use the tragedy to further their ends.

Finally, they reached Orchard Street where she found herself in front of a four story red brick tenement with a black iron staircase. Below the staircase were two stores, and above these were two other stores, flanking the entrance door that led into the tenement. The interior was dark, illuminated by a single gas jet fixture that descended from the ceiling. Initially, the only thing illuminated was the molded tin ceiling and the cobwebs. As her eyes accustomed themselves to the dark, she could see that once, when the building was new, the owner must have endeavored to enliven the space, with small paintings that might have been scenes from a park. They were too sooty to tell. Beckman took her arm and led her up the stairs. In the distance, another gas jet on the wall guided their way. On the top floor, Beckman rapped three times and one more time before a short, dark haired girl in her teens he greeted as Rebecca, peered through the opened door. Her youthful face glowed with a smile when she saw Beckman, and Rachelann wondered if this was his daughter. When Berkman introduced her to Rachelann as a member of his association, there was suddenly pain in the girl's eyes and something Rachelann could not define.

They entered, and Rachelann found herself in the kitchen of a three room flat that ran from the front of the building to a light well in the rear. The kitchen was bare, save for a wooden table with several mismatched wooden chairs, a sink piled with mismatched plates, and a cast iron stove, much like the one she cooked on in Brooklyn. On the stove sat a large copper oval for boiling water, and next to it, a flat iron sitting on its coal heater. Both men and women's undergarments were hanging above a washboard, sitting in a tin vat. A window that allowed light in from the front room was also bare. She wondered why no pretense of making this room more presentable was made. When Rachelann was ushered into the front room, she encountered the same spartan decor. The late winter light cast shadows through tattered curtains onto a thread bare couch and a sewing machine that stood in front of the window. There was no rug on the peeling painted floor. On the mantle were a clock and two oil lamps. Nothing hung on the walls to indicate people made this their home, yet facing the fireplace were covered hassocks upon which sat a woman that she was later introduced to named Emma Goldman. Making up the rest of the circle was a man named Fedya Aronstam, Berkman's cousin, and a woman named Helene Minkin, Emma's friend. The teenager sat away from the group, sulking.

None of the women moved to welcome Rachelann when she was introduced, and Berkman seemed to ignore the rudeness. Only Fedya stood, shook her hand, and held out a bag of sweets.

"Sweets?" Berkman said incredulously. "Sweets?" he repeated. "You dare spend what little we have on your own selfish pleasures when you know that every cent we earn must go to the Cause!" Rachelann was suddenly aware of why this apartment was so spare. Beckman continued, "Luxury is a crime and a weakness. Did not Rakhmetov himself teach this to us?"

Rachelann had never heard of Rakhmetov, and she began to be suspect of Berkman for railing against some candy when he should be telling the story of the fire.

"Man does not live by bread alone," his cousin replied. "Sometimes men need a piece of candy."

"I'll not argue with you now, cousin, but we will come to some understanding sooner than later. I have more important things to tell you." He turned to Emma. "There was a fire today at a factory. A crowd was gathering around me when I looked up and saw smoke belching out of the windows on the upper floors, and then women and men crashing to the ground."

Emma Goldman immediately stood at the news, her expressionless face showing the resolve of a woman possessed. She moved quickly to the small desk in the corner. The others stood also, their faces turning pale at Berkman's account of what had happened only hours before. "How many dead?" Goldman blurted, her brain already creating the headlines. "We must put out a special edition; tell me everything you remember." She started to write.

Rachelann looked at them both, and she could not fathom their responses. This Emma Goldman seemed not to reflect on the tragedy at all, nor did she allow it touch her in any way. Her initial rigidity could just have well been caused by ice filling her veins. And Berkman related the tail factually, as if he and she were using the tragedy for some hidden purpose.

"How many dead? What was the name of the factory and where was it?" she demanded.

"It's off Washington Square and I stopped counting when we were almost killed."

"It was the Triangle Shirtwaist Company on Washington Place in the Asch Building," Rachelann interjected.

"Who is this woman?" Emma shouted, acknowledging the stranger, "and why is she here?"

"I rescued her from being hit by a falling body, and I stayed with her as a gentleman would till she stopped screaming. She wants to be a writer and save the world, so I thought she might be a kindred spirit and able to tell the story from a more personal point of view. You know I tend to be too cynical and hostile." His eyes encouraged Rachelann over to the desk so Emma could get a better look at her.

"But it's so soon," she protested. "It's so horrible even to think about it let alone write it. I don't know if I ca..." She was interrupted by the woman at the desk.

"Look here, whatever your name is; if you say you're a writer, then you write. That's what you do. If an editor sent you to cover a story about an old woman being eaten by a tiger in Long Acre Square, and it turned out to be your grandmother, you'd still have to write it because that's what a reporter's job is. Now, if you want me to see what you can do, you'll sit here while Alexander writes the story from his point of view. I'm sure it will be heavy on the responsibility of the owners of the factory, and how little the city government has done to protect its citizens. Her glance at Alexander Berkman made her wish crystal clear, but she need not have given it. Both knew exactly what had to be done. "Now you, oh, what is your name?"

"Rachelann."

"Good, Rachelann, I want an eye witness point of view. I want our readers to see exactly what you saw and feel exactly what you felt. I want them to be there because if you can make them see what you saw, they will be willing and eager to help us do what has to be done to get justice for the workers. You make me cry, and I'll give you a job."

Rachelann sat by the dimming light and wrote her story as she recalled it. The letters under the wooden stylus squirmed like little worms through her own tears. She did not want to relive a moment of the tragedy, but she had to. She asked that the oil lamp be lit so she might be able to see better, but Berkman at first reaffirmed his belief in frugality for the Cause, and then, reconsidering, relented. She wrote of each thud and how it still pounded in her ears, and she wrote of how the water from the hoses mixed with blood of young people on the street. She wrote of the screams of people as they came towards her, and of the sudden silences. She also wrote about what she had thought, about the lives suddenly cut short and the countless generations that would never be born. "To save a life is to have saved an entire world." She recalled her father saying that, but now she knew what it really meant.

Rachelann was shaken from her sleep by the thud of a piece of wood being tossed onto the embers of the fireplace, and by the unceremonious clank of the iron door on the stove. She slowly opened her eyes to see little dabs of sunlight on the empty writing desk upon which her head still rested. A slight breeze moved the tattered lace, and the intricate patterned reflections danced like minute leaves of filtered light on her bare arm. As she slept, someone had turned off the lamp. Someone had also taken the pages she had written.

"Coffee is almost ready," said Fedya from the kitchen. "We have some rolls and jam. Nothing ever fancy here." He watched the pretty girl with the unkempt upsweep of auburn hair stand, rub her eyes, and move towards him. "I brought up some cold water so if you want to wash the sleep from your eyes, it's near the tub," he continued. "Alex is still in bed, and Emma took your story and his to the printer very early this morning. It should be out on the streets by noon."

Slowly, the reality of yesterday returned to her, and all became clear as to where she was and the tragedy she had witnessed. She remembered writing about it and nothing more. Everything seemed so distant. Her hands cupped the cold water and she splashed it on her face and neck. Fedya handed her a threadbare towel and she dabbed herself dry. "I must leave," she said suddenly. "I have never been away from home." Then she realized that her father probably thought she was at the little apartment in Brooklyn, and her brother probably thought she was in the house on Fifth Avenue. She was in no need to hurry. She only had to decide where she wanted to go. "I would like a roll with jam." Fedya moved towards her holding a steaming tin cup, and offered her milk and a bowl of sugar cubes. At the same moment, Alexander Berkman staggered out of one of the two tiny back bedrooms, followed by Rebecca. Fedya gave him a disapproving look as Rebecca plodded past them, out the door, and down the hall to the communal toilet. "Emma would kill you and throw Rebecca into the street if she ever knew what the two of you were doing in her absence. For God's sakes, Alex, she's young enough to be your daughter."

"The girl is old enough to know what she wants, and she wants me in her bed. Wouldn't you love such young softness next to you, dear cousin? Can I help it if I'm irresistible?" He smiled, looking at Rachelann; a smile that let her know that if she had an inkling to invite him into her bed, he would not resist. Fedya was incensed at his silent suggestion, and Rachelann felt her stomach lurch.

"Feyda," she said quickly to change the subject. "I was about to ask you about this Cause you spoke of last night."

He poured a cup of coffee for himself and sat across the table from her. Berkman poured his own and sat next to him, anticipating an opportunity to gather perhaps another acolyte to his way of thinking.

"The object of the Cause," he began, "is to help all people to secure liberty." His eyes looked at her intently, wanting her to understand his passion. He also wanted her to like him, and wanted her to think he had something of value to offer. "But to do this in the purest way, you have to let go of any personal obsessions that could get in your way, and any established authority."

"But to get rid of the established society, you create chaos in the streets." She recalled her father quoting the Talmud saying, 'that without government, people would eat one another.' When she first heard that, she was too young to fully understand it, but now she did. She was among anarchists.

"But the government must have the workers as their primary concern and not just the fat cats who get the thieves elected." He took a breath. "We must learn to live in peace and harmony with our fellow man; to cultivate respect for one another and brotherhood."

"Once again Feyda," Berkman interrupted, "you are superficial. For there to be any benefit from society, the workers have to cooperate. People must change their attitudes towards one another, and establish a whole new set of values, relationships, and practices. Each person has to be free and equal to every other person."

"These are wonderful thoughts," Rachelann interrupted. She had heard such talk around the table in the Brownsville apartment when her father still lived there and had society meetings in the parlor. She did not think of her father as a socialist. After all, he owned his own small business, but most in the Krivoser Society worked for others, and they laughingly referred to each other as Parlor Pinks. 'Comes the revolution!'

was an expression she often heard. "I'm not sure your Cause is something that can be put into practice," she said earnestly. "You are asking that people change their very basic natures, but I tell you that unless you provide for every need your workers have, they will not cooperate unless forced to do so. Survival is survival. Without people to direct and be in charge, there will be chaos. And once people become in charge, there will be corruption. That is the way of the world. It may be a glorious concept in theory, but not in practice. You need a whole different kind of human being, and such people do not exist."

"They don't exist yet, my dear," Berkman responded. "Certainly, such a spirit is not born overnight, but we are trying it here among our little group," Berkman said. "In this apartment, we are experimenting with a collective life so we can show others how it can be done. We hold things in common. We share our food, our costs, and our..."

"And your women?" Rachelann said as Rebecca returned from the toilet and moved sleepily to the back of the apartment. "It sounds like a wonderful idea if you're a man, but does this sharing extend to a woman's sexual appetites as well?"

"True freedom applies to both men and women, and if a woman wants more than one man, she is entitled to her pleasure." Berkman squirmed in his seat, knowing full well that if Emma or Rebecca wanted other men, he would be enraged. "This new spirit, as I said before, will not come to us overnight, but we must look at it as a newly planted flower that needs to be nourished by sunlight, water, and earth. With care, it will grow into a new existence for humanity."

Berkman had taken over the conversation, much to Feyda's annoyance. "Rachelann," Feyda interrupted, "I understand the problems you pose, but it is a very complex issue. We are trying to create a social revolution where much more than conditions will be reorganized. Our aim is to bring people together as one; the farmers, the factory workers, the teachers, the doctors, all with the goal of uniting everyone who works for someone and making a better life for them. That's ultimately what the Cause is all about." Feyda's eyes pleaded for understanding. They might just as well have said, "understand me. Value me."

"I have no difficulty with bringing people together to make a better world for the poor," Fedya said. "The idea that the world needs mending was part of my religious upbringing, and I still hold fast to that idea so we are in agreement." Her eyes were kind.

"Religion has nothing to do with it." Berkman countered fiercely. 'Religion is the opiate of the masses.' Haven't you read Marx?"

"My father probably knows more about Karl Marx's ideas than you do, but I also know that the very essence of Marx's idea of raising the poor and the downtrodden, is founded on Torah law. Where do you think Marx got his ideas about how the worker should be treated? His two grandfathers were rabbis. He learned as a child that 'the poor will never depart from the land,' and at the same time, he learned those commandments meant to protect the worker. Though he may have denounced his Judaism, he didn't denounce the core ideas of the social foundation that the Torah offers. No ideas exist in a vacuum. They have to come from somewhere. Everything that you said that was good, I learned from my father, and he learned it from his father. Whatever is decent in this world can be traced back into that single source that you seem to reject."

Alexander Berkmam was clearly annoyed and at the same time intrigued by this woman's assertiveness, knowledge, and conclusions. Rachelann reminded him of his Emma, both formidable, and both potent, yet young and very pretty.

As Feyda was offering the steaming water to Rachelann to refreshen her cup, the door opened and Emma Goldman stepped in with an arm load of papers fresh from the press. "We worked half the night, and the papers will be on the street and handed out in a matter of hours. Rachelann, I read your story to some of the women cleaning the office, and they cried. You have a job if you want it."

"I need some sleep," said Emma Goldman, looking at Alexander and then at Rebecca who had just entered. "And you can get some rest also."

Before Rachelann could protest, she was ushered down the hall by the dark haired, stocky woman in her thirties and pointed to a small bedroom that was no larger than a closet. The two narrow beds crammed into the space made walking difficult. A tattered curtain hung by two nails above an iron bed that had been painted blue but was chipped, revealing the original white paint beneath. A threadbare towel hung over the top. There were no linens on the blue and white striped mattress and pillow, and there was a vague odor of urine from an open chamber pot under the bed. The sight and the odor caused her to become nauseous. Rachelann looked at the bed, and though she was desperately tired, she could not bring herself to lie down on it. She thought of her own room that she shared with Fanny at the apartment, and though modest, with its two wooden beds and a mismatched dresser and chest, it was clean and neat. She thought of the bedroom that was hers in the house on Fifth Avenue with its brocaded bedspread in periwinkle blue with matching curtains. She thought of the decorative yellow and gold ceramic commode set, and the mantle with the white and gold figurines. The door to the other bedroom closed and she heard the creek and strain of a wooden bed being stressed by what had to be the body of Emma Goldman falling on to it. Footsteps behind her caused her to turn, and there was Alexander Berkman smiling at her before he followed Goldman into the room.

Perhaps I don't have to live in such a place with such people to fully experience what others in this situation feel and how they live, she thought. I have seen it, and I believe it. She knew as she thought it, that this was a rationalization for the growing contempt she felt for these people despite her sympathetic feelings for their beliefs. Surely, she could write about the desperation and degradation without having to live it daily. She also knew that this was not the life she wanted for herself. Abe may have been right. It is natural for people to want to better themselves, so why step down when everyone who was forced to live in the squalor she saw would be so happy to step up. And though she felt angry with herself for seeming to give up her ideals so easily when confronted with this ugly reality, she could still write and do what she felt had to be done while moving between the two life styles that she had. She had alternatives to this.

Feyda returned from the toilet reading a Yiddish news paper. "The tragedy is on the front page," he said. "But there is nothing written from an eye witness point of view like yours. I read the paper Emma brought home. You did a wonderful job, and I did cry a little. You have a good way with words."

Rachelann picked up one of the papers Emma had brought home with her, and saw her story on the front page. She scanned it, and she felt unlike she had ever felt before. She was proud of herself in a way that was so different from being proud for having fixed a good meal or having kept the apartment orderly. This feeling was a feeling of having accomplished something good. But she was caught up short when she realized that her name was not printed as the author. Though she was pleased that her words would be read by many people, she would not be getting the recognition that was rightfully hers. This was an entirely new thought to her, and she realized that under her anger was an even deeper feeling of having been erased.

Her dark brown eyes were hard as she picked up her coat and hat.

"Where are you going?" said Fayda. "You look so tired. At least have some coffee and something to eat." He did not want her to leave because he liked her. He also immediately surmised that the dark expression on her face was the result of having seen her name omitted from the paper, and he referred to that. "You are angry," was the only thing he said.

"Yes," she replied. "Don't you believe that workers should be honestly paid for what they do and recognized for what they do? I worked all night on that story. That was my work, and I could at least have been paid for it by being recognized for my effort."

"You are right," he said sitting and putting her coffee in front of her. But this is Emma's paper, and Emma does whatever she wants. More often than not, she doesn't give credit to others even when they deserve it like you do. Besides, maybe it's for the best. The story was really excellent, but Emma, Alex, and I are under constant scrutiny because of our beliefs, and your name appearing in her publication would bring you under scrutiny, also. You may not want that in your life." He paused. "Perhaps you might want to take your original pages and go over to *The Forward* or maybe an English paper and give it to them. You may be the only person to be there when the tragedy began. Others only saw the aftermath. You saw it from the beginning. You will make them cry."

Rachelann finished her coffee and stood. Feyda helped her on with her coat. "You're a good man, Feyda, and I like you. I would also like to see you again, but for my own reasons, I don't want to tell you where I live. I will contact you." She started for the door, holding her hand written pages. "But before I go, I do want you to know that this is not how I want to live," and she waved her hand around the room. "Though I agree with your ideas, I don't think tearing things down without a vision of how to build them up is going to do anything to make the world better. You are a revolutionary," she continued, "and basically I think a good man at heart. But there are people in your movement and fomenting problems in Russia that I don't believe are good men in their hearts, and they will ultimately enslave the workers much the way Capitalists do here." She studied his eyes for understanding. "Revolutionaries want things to change immediately, but the world changes slowly and only law that is mutually agreed upon will last. People like Alexander and Emma do not invite mutuality. Nothing good lasts from a revolution unless honest people agree to work together to make things happen. Like Moses, we are 'strangers in a strange land,' but from what I've learned about this country, such an agreed on system is in place and has been working. I would not see this country torn down no matter how flawed it is, and as bad as it is, it is still better than any other place in this world. This is my country now, and I shall not see it hurt. I can do work like yours, but I will do it slowly and without violence."

His voice dropped to a whisper. "Then I would like you to meet me away from Alex and Emma. You are right that their's is a violent vision that calls not just for civil disobedience, but for bringing about their changes through the overthrow of the government. My cousin has wrongfully committed himself to violent action to inspire revolutionary change, and he wants to bring all anarchists under one umbrella. You may not know this, but he has already spent years in prison for trying to assassinate Henry Frick, that damn industrialist." Fedya did not tell her that he himself barely escaped with his life when he realized that the police were also looking for him. "I believe in individual freedom," he continued, "and I don't want to see any organized group impose its will on people like me or you."

"Then we shall see one another soon." she said, moving herself to the door, thinking that perhaps she did not really want to see him or any of them again. Still, she was attracted to this man with his dark, unkempt hair and passionate blue eyes.

Rachelann smiled at him and left the apartment. She desperately needed to sleep, and the closest home she had was on Fifth Avenue.

She found the trolley that took her uptown to her father and stepmother's home. For a split second, she imagined that the knocker's brass lion's face was mocking her hypocrisy for going to a place of extreme comfort when she should have been on her way to Brownsville. Virginia, in a white lace cap, a white apron edged with lace, and a black ankle length dress under it, opened the door slightly, and then wider when she recognized her employer's daughter. She curtseyed slightly when Rachelann entered, and Rachelann was even more annoyed at herself because of an undeserved respect.

Still, she could not help herself relish the caress of warm air coming from the fireplace in the foyer, and she knew that a soft eider down mattress, comforter, and pillow were awaiting her exhausted body.

"Rachelann," said Jonah as he and Marta were coming out of the morning room holding the newspaper.

"You look exhausted my dear," said Marta, scanning the noticeable wayward strands of hair sticking out of a hat carelessly placed on her head. "You look as if you haven't slept all night?"

"Have you seen the papers about the tragedy and the fire?" Jonah interrupted.

Rachelann suddenly stopped, looked at the paper's banner headline: "More than 140 Die As Fire Sweeps Through Three Stories of Factory Building in Washington Place." Under it was a photo of a line of bodies with men and women searching for loved ones. Rachelann burst into tears. At that moment, and for a reason unknown to her, she had allowed herself to fully apprehended what she had seen and how close she had come to her own death. She swayed and caught hold of the table. Marta and Jonah bolstered the weeping girl between themselves, and walked her back into the morning room.

"Virginia, bring smelling salts and a cold compress," Marta said. They sat her down on the couch in front of the fireplace and draped an afghan around her shoulders. It was as if the entire experience, the screams, the thuds, the acrid smoke, had suddenly coalesced into a new reality that she could experience fully now that she felt safe.

"Sha, sha, madeleh, quiet, quiet, my little girl," Jonah said reassuringly, and placed a snifter of brandy into her shaking hands. "This will help." Virginia returned with the smelling salts, but Rachelann motioned them away.

As she felt the warmth of the fire on her face, and the amber liquid warm her insides, she relaxed, and staring into the flickering hearth, told them what had happened, how she came to be there, and where she had spent the night. Then, taking the papers she had written from her purse, she handed them to

Marta who read them with great interest before handing them to Jonah.

"This is a remarkable account my dear," Marta said, looking at Jonah. "We did not know you had such a talent. None of the papers have written such a deeply moving account of the tragedy."

Jonah's eyes had tears in them as he finished the story and looked at his daughter. He was enormously proud of his eldest child, and for the first time saw her as more than just the stability in their family when Leah had died. She had suddenly become a new source of pride, and the thought of almost having lost her was too unbearable to consider.

Together they escorted Rachelann to the periwinkle bedroom, and Marta and Virginia helped Rachelann undress and get into bed. The mattress, comforter, and pillow enveloped her like her mother's soothing arms, and she was asleep before she could even think of the prayer she said every evening.

"This must be published," Jonah said excitedly as they descended the stairs, "and I know just who might be willing to help Rachelann." He turned to Marta. "If I'm not mistaken, Mrs. Reid is due tomorrow for a French lesson, and if I give this to her and ask her to show it to her husband, I'm sure she will do it. But first we must make a copy and keep the original." He became animated with his idea. "Wouldn't it be wonderful if Rachelann's piece could be printed in the *Tribune*! And perhaps they will ask her to write other things." He turned to Marta and lowered his voice. "I would be so very happy if I could help her. She has done so much for the family, and now I'd like to do something for her. It is what a father should do." He paused mid-step. "I never thought of Rachelann having a dream of her own. Doesn't everyone deserve a dream." He thought for a moment of his own dreams and disappointments because circumstances in his life would not permit him to follow his. "She has never complained about doing for me, and now I can do for her. But we can't tell her unless it happens. I don't want to raise her hopes and then have them dashed."

Marta smiled in agreement. "But Jonah, don't tell her to give the story to her husband. Tell her that because she is part of a newspaper family, you would like her to just edit it. I know her well enough to know that she will take great pleasure in thinking she has discovered a new talent, and even greater pleasure to see her find in print." She kissed Jonah on the cheek and went back into the morning room to copy the pages.

Rachelann slept fitfully, occasionally waking up to push away the dream images that came to her. When she awoke the next morning, her body and shoulder did not ache, but the waking images of the day before would not abate. There was a sadness in her that she had not felt since her mother died, and she wondered if sadness piled upon sadness would in some way inform the rest of her life. Jonah and Marta called Dr. Scholnick, Jonah's family doctor. They were concerned about what seemed to be a deepening depression. Rachelann had known and trusted the doctor since she had come to America. The diminutive, mustachioed man, the ever present cigarette dangling from his lips, arrived late in the evening and administered a sedative. "She is not sick, at least not in the physical way," he said, "but I fear the experience at the fire is causing her emotional turmoil. Bed rest can help, but I think she may need something more. I think she needs to pour her energy into something that will let her feel she is doing something that is having an effect. Right now she is feeling very helpless." Dr. Scholnick's cigarette ash dropped on the floor and this eyes apologized over his black rimmed glasses. "I've seen this reaction before, mostly with people who have recently experienced death or an accident. Such patients cannot bury the memories, so the best thing is for her to face them, as she involves herself in something important. Listen to her, and have her tell her story. That will help her accept it." He crushed the cigarette out in an ashtray, and immediately lit another.

Mrs. Whitlaw Reid, not a publicity shy lady of fashion, adjusted the 'Merry Widow hat' created exclusively for her by Lucile, before being ushered into the morning room where tea, coffee, and chocolate had been set for the ladies who weekly came to the *Chernov Institute for Language*. With its exaggerated wide brim supporting a mass of feathers and flowers, Mrs. Reid, as well as several other fashionably dressed ladies with similar hats, gave the room the appearance of an animated Edwardian arboretum. The styles were changing, even though the more matronly women were still having their ladies maid stuff them into full bodied corsets that were quickly going out of style. Such women were still clinging to the wasp waist dresses of a few years past that emphasized their bosoms while allowing themselves to feel the luxury of frilly crinolined lace overskirts, and the fantasy of fading youth. For most of them, their wasp waists had departed may years ago. The younger women, still balancing large feathered hats, did so to balance the newer hobbled skirts and tubed frocks that while inhibiting walking, gave a more natural shape that created an elegant silhouette. Marta fancied neither of these styles, having abandoned the stifling corset as soon as she became aware of the fashion designs of Paul Poiret who encouraged individuality and personal style rather than following slavishly current trends, especially those that were not flattering. Though now middle-aged, Marta's shape was still youthful, and she appeared in a columnar dress covered by a vibrantly embroidered Japanese silk kimino. Fanny had told her that kimonos were becoming stylish as dress wear at home when entertaining. Fanny, though young, had become the fashion authority in the house.

"My dear Madam Chernov," Mrs. Reid began, "I was so flattered that your husband chose me to edit this wonderful piece of writing, and I was so very moved by the writing that I insisted that my dear Whitelaw read it immediately, though your husband had the good taste not to asked me to impose upon him at all. Naturally, I would not be so presumptuous as to tell my husband what he should print in his paper, but I did say that such description by an eye witness was unique, and he had printed nothing as engaging as this piece." She took a breath, a sip of tea, and a strawberry scone. Marta handed a cup of tea to another lady, and smiling, turned again to Mrs Reid. "And what did your husband say after reading the article?"

"He was very impressed with the point of view and passion of the piece, and said that he would consider printing it, but he could not possibly reveal to his readers that it was written by a woman. Only women who write for the society pages have their names attached to their work, and he said that this is too graphic and indelicate for the society page. But he did say it could go on the opinion page, if your stepdaughter's first initial only was used." She paused. "You know that it takes years of being tested as a reporter that wins you a byline."

Marta thought better of telling her what she thought of her and her husband, and the *Tribune*'s protocol, so she merely smiled without showing her teeth. "I'm confident that my stepdaughter would be willing to see her article in print, even though her full name would not be there.

"Oh, where is my head today? I almost forgot. Tell your stepdaughter that if she is interested in writing for *The Tribune*, she is to see a Mr. Collins at the editor's desk at her convenience. And here is my husband's business card with a note to Mr. Collins about your stepdaughter's skills. Do give it to Miss Chernov with my compliments."

Marta turned to another lady, trying not to reveal the joy she felt at the success of her manipulation. The lady in the oversized hat retired to a seat next to another matron and began talking about the tragedy. Soon others joined, and there was genuine concern and sadness expressed. Then a younger woman who was there to learn bits and pieces of conversation in preparation for her Grand Tour honeymoon, said that she had read in the paper that The American Red Cross and something called The Joint Relief Committee were planning to raise funds for the survivors and families of the victims. The ladies agreed that this was a good idea, and they talked about the possibilities of involvement. Just then, the large oak pocket doors with the Lenett stained glass windows opened, and Jonah invited the ladies into the library.

For the next week, every paper in the city railed against the inhumane conditions in the sweatshops, the curse of child labor, the shoddy construction of fire escapes, and the greed that made these conditions possible. Each and every day, *The New York Sun, The Evening Post, The Daily Graphic*, as well as *The Times* and *The Tribune*, having devoted thousands upon thousands of words to the tragic event, created a ground swell in the hearts of the citizenry that became an eruption in legislative initiatives.

On the third day after the fire, Jonah found Rachelann's commentary on the editorial page of *The Tribune* and went quickly into the morning room where Marta was writing an acceptance to an invitation to Sabbath dinner at the Seligman's. "Look, they printed it. Now we can tell Rachelann."

Together they went upstairs and knocked softly. "She'll be so excited," Jonah said expectantly. In his heart, he wanted her to know that he loved her and supported her dream. A soft voice said they might enter. Rachelann was sitting in the widowseat with her legs propped under her, reading a book. She forced a smile.

An animated Jonah began. "I have something wonderful to show you," and he handed her commentary in print with her very own byline, R. Chernov.

"How did this happen?" she said, her brow furrowing and her eyes confused. "How did this newspaper get my story?" This was not the response neither Jonah nor Marta had expected.

Jonah looked at his daughter and then at his wife. "I teach the wife of the publisher and she is my friend. I gave it to her to read, and she gave it to her husband. The paper wants to interview you and possibly invite you to write for them." He looked at her quizzically. "I thought this was your dream.

Rachelann, this is a wonderful opportunity. Isn't this what you wanted?"

"But it's my dream, my dream, not your dream, Papa. I needed to do this on my own just to see if I could do it on my own. You had no right to get involved in this. You had no right to show it to anyone without my permission. You and Abe always think you can tell me what to do. Why do men always think they have to solve everyone's problems?"

"Now Rachelann," Marta interrupted. "Your father had the best intentions. He saw an opportunity to help and ..." She was interrupted.

"This is between me and my father," Rachelann shouted, "and you have no right to get involved in my affairs either. You're not my mother."

"But I am your father," Jonah replied, "and I'll not have you raising your voice to my wife. What I did, any parent would do. You think it's easy getting through this world without help. Parents help their children to the best of their ability. I have a contact and I used that contact to help you. That's what a good parent does. There's an editor named Mr. Collins at the paper who is willing to speak to you and it's an open ended invitation. Don't you want to write for a newspaper? How many others out there would love to be able to just walk in to *The Tribune* off the streets and get an interview?" Jonah felt a very old feeling rise up in him, the same unpleasant feeling he had when he had done something that he thought was good, but was still berated by his mother and Leah for it not being enough or too much. He reaffirmed in his mind that there were some women that just could not be pleased, and his daughter was now one of them. In this case, he had tried too much, and his daughter was angry with him for becoming too involved in her life without her permission. It was a new age.

"You call up this Mr. Collins and you tell him that I don't need his help," Rachelann demanded.

Rachelann walked to the closet and threw her clothing on the bed. They saw that she was resolved to leave. "You're not well enough to leave," her father said. "Who will take care of you?"

"I can take care of myself. That's the point. I can take care of myself. I can get a job on my own, and I can get my work published on my own. I can even see a doctor on my own if I think I need one. I am not helpless!"

"Then don't see this Mr. Collins. Just walk up and down Herald Square and into the offices of different newspapers in the city without an appointment and see what happens. Have you ever read a news article by a woman? I got you in the door, and getting into the door is sometimes the hardest thing to do. Thousands of people out there have talent, but I have lived long enough and seen enough to know that in most instances, it's who you know that counts." Jonah's jaw clinched. "I'm not sorry for doing what I did, and when you see that no one is falling to their knees, begging you to write for them, you'll see that I was right. Collins' office will be the only one where you will walk in and say that you are expected. You mark my words that eventually, you'll end up on a bench waiting to see Mr. Collins."

"You call and you tell Mr. Collins that I'm not interested," she said as she closed her case.

I will do no such thing, Jonah thought. The foolish child doesn't realize that if I called back this favor, there would be no way on earth there would be another opportunity like this one. "You don't throw away opportunities like this, because another my not come along." Her father tossed the card into her suitcase and left the room muttering.

Marta became a barricade between her stepdaughter and the sad man she loved who had just walked out. "That wonderful man has suffered greatly in his life," she began, "and had to give up his own very real dreams to come here with your mother and make a life for her and their children. A mind like that, a soul like that in a candy store! Yes, he may not understand what women want or know, but he understands more than most, and he deserves better than what you've just given him." She stopped abruptly. "And if you ever want to be welcome in this house again, you come back with an apology on your lips!"

Each day, Rachelann's applications for positions were perfunctorily accepted by the stern guardians of each editor's office, and each told her that the proper procedure was to apply through the personnel department. No one seemed interested in interviewing her. She even attached the piece the Tribune published to her applications, but still no one was seemed interested. On two occasion she was told that her letter of intent should be directed to the society desk, homemaking, or advertisements where the women worked. Newspaper reporting, she came to see, was indeed the dominion of men, and this also angered her. At least with her brief encounter with the anarchists, she felt something of an equal.

Though vowing not to do it, she ultimately stood in front of Mr. Maurice Collins whose tall starched collar braced his neck as if it were in traction. He looked over his wire framed glasses and motioned for her to sit. She did, keeping her own back as straight as his, and trying to convey the idea that talking to editors was a common occurrence. Within, she was conflicted and angry, having to admit to herself that her father was right, despite how she felt. The little card that this little man fingered impatiently as he studied her over his wire rimmed glasses, was the only thing that opened any door to her in her week of trying to gain entry to the newspaper profession.

"Mr. Reid, for some reason known only to himself, told me that if and when you came into this office, I was to assign you something to write on the aftermath of the fire. I read the piece you wrote and while it has merit, do not imagine that I am pleased to be given this order. I am complying, but never think I like this imposition, and understand that I have the option of firing you if I don't like what you write. What power persuaded this man to give you his personal card with the note on the back I'll never know, but it must have been formidable for him to break with *Tribune* protocol."

Rachelann's eyes laughed, knowing full well the power behind the request, and she found herself musing on the influence an assertive woman can have on her husband. "I hope to prove myself," she said.

"Then I want you to cover a woman named Rose Schneiderman who is speaking at the Metropolitan Opera House on April second. I also want you to know that I am not inclined to give a woman a reporter's job. Reporting is man's work." He cleared his throat. "This woman is a socialist and a union activist who will be speaking at a memorial meeting and whose audience will be dominated by women socialists from The Woman's Trade Union League. You can bet she will use this platform to fire up and organize factory workers."

"And you don't think factory workers should be organized?" Her voice was more assertive than she had intended.

"What you or I think is of no importance when there is news to be reported. That's the first rule and I expect you to keep whatever bias you may have out of the report. I edit news and facts, not opinion. You just write what you see and hear and bring it back. Then I'll judge what's to be done with you."

Rachelann had never been in the opera house, believing it to be the exclusive province of the rich and for the exclusive enjoyment of the of the privileged few. She was always vaguely annoyed when her father enthusiastically spoke about one performance or another that he and Marta had attended. She was therefore surprised to see that high up, almost in the rafters of the building, were wooden seats reserved for the poorer people who could not afford the cushioned seats in the other parts of the theater. This consideration of the poor impressed and softened her. She was also very impressed by the intricately carved proscenium arch highlighted in gold leaf that formed an inverted U in front of the massive red velvet curtain. She could not seat herself in the press section because Mr. Collins did not give her a pass for that section, but seated herself in a sea of women dressed in grey and brown who were framed in tufted mahogany seats. The light from the great gilt and crystal gas chandelier above her enveloped the assembled crowd in a haze of amber light that shimmered on them and on the damask walls like twilight shimmers on a still lake in autumn.

The faces were somber. All conversations were muted, and these came to an abrupt stop when Rose Schneiderman stepped up onto the podium. She was a tall, thin woman with angular features, wearing a simple black hat adorned with egret feathers.

"I would be a traitor to these poor burned bodies...," Rose Schneiderman began. Rachelann wrote as quickly as she could, jotting down a key word here or a phrase there. But the overall message at the beginning was that the paltry amount of money donated by the public would not ameliorate the situation because those who protested the conditions that caused the deaths of the women were threatened by the police. "But every time the workers come out in the only way they know to protest against conditions which are unbearable, the strong hand of the law is allowed to press down heavily upon us." She said that she could not talk fellowship because too much blood had been spilled, and that it was up to the working people to save themselves by creating a strong working class movement. The applause and cheers were as loud as if Caruso and Melba had just finished a duet. For some reason, her mind wandered to Fedya.

The hall emptied, but Rachelann waited, hoping to get something from the speaker that was not in the speech that would make her lead paragraph unique. She did when Rose Schneiderman, speaking to the small group of women around her said that The Woman's Trade Union Leagues's leadership will seek to have Max Blanck and Issac Harris on first and second degree manslaughter charges. Rachelann found out something that no other reporter knew, and she knew that she found it out from Rose Schneiderman because Rachelann was a woman. An adoring crowd followed the speaker into the lobby, and as Rachelann turned to go, she saw Fedya standing near the door.

Mr. Collins read the headline Rachelann proposed, looked at her over his glasses, and passed it to another member of his staff to verify the fact that there was indeed going to be a trial. When the fact checker had returned with verification, Collins was obviously pleased, and the story ran on the front page but without a byline. The following day, Rachelann was directed to the personnel office to fill out papers for a job. When she returned to Collins' office, she was told that Mr. Reid was so pleased that he asked that she be assigned to continue the coverage of the aftermath of the fire and the trial, exclusively. She was grateful for the job and angry at the discount, but realized that to play the game, she had to be in the game. If having to be anonymous was the initial ante for entering the game, so be it. In time, she would win.

On her own initiative, she made an appointment to interview a noted social worker named Frances Perkins who was now heading the Committee on Public Safety. The task of this organization was to identify specific problems in the workplace, and to propose new legislation regarding the length of the work week and overall working conditions. Rachelann initiated a meeting with Al Smith, the Majority Leader of the New York State Assembly, and maneuvered her way into an interview with Robert F. Wagner, the Majority Leader of the New York State Senate, reporting that this collaboration between politicians and reformers was happening under the aegis of none other than Charles F. Murphy, the Chief of Tammany Hall, who decided that it would be politically astute if he were on the "side of the angels." Her success did earn her a desk at the Tribune, but a desk in the vicinity of the women who wrote about society and cooking. The discount and the chauvinism that kept her from the recognition she felt she deserved, irked her to the point that she resolved that the fledgling women's movement and their efforts to get the right to vote would become a secret cause of her own. And from her vantage place where she saw herself as straddling two worlds, she would see what she could do to foment some rebellion of her own by writing under a nom de plume and masquerading sedition as society news and turning it into news that had to be on the front pages, too.

CHAPTER 13

1917

Abe leaned back on the slatted chair and took another sip of coffee. "Now there's something else that I want you to put into that brain of yours for consideration." Abe whispered. "You want to be really rich, Joey, don't cha?"

"You still thinkin 'bout that damn kraut's old dairy?" Joey smirked, knowing exactly what Abe was going to say.

"Yeh, I am," Abe paused, giving Joey time to acclimate himself to listening again to an idea he had rejected months before. "You remember what I told you about this Prohibition? It's coming, Joey. My dad and his wife were talking about it and it's going to happen. You ever hear of that, Joey?"

Joey DiAngelo leaned forward, and folded his hands on the scarred table, leaning into his friend's hair-brained scheme. Abe knew that it took time for Joey to process information, and leaned in to lessen the space between them. His voice dropped to a whisper, knowing that Joey would be engaged by the secrecy.

Abe continued, "There's this organization called the Temperance Society, mostly made up of old Protestant ladies and rich old Protestant white guys who are teaming up to get the government to stop selling liquor in the country. My sister said they want to keep foreigners like us sober so our fathers won't beat up their wives and kids. You ever see your dad hit your mom, Joey?"

"Once," Joey said, "and she hit him up the side of his head with the iron frying pan she was holding. He bled all over the fuck'in kitchen. I shit my pants laughing, and then he beat the hell out of me for laughing at him. Italian women don't take that shit, or at least my mother don't."

Abe laughed.

"Anyway," Abe continued, "this new law seems to be a big deal, and though they're sure it's coming, my college boy brother says that it can't happen yet because the states have to vote on it, and the government will need to find the money they'll lose from the tax on booze that they now get. He says there's going to be something called an income tax."

"What money?" Joey inquired.

"Joey," said Abe, looking at him incredulously. "The money that now comes from the tax that comes from the booze the liquor stores sell is going away, and the government will have to find a new way to replace the booze tax. It's going to be called an income tax. But whatever tax they pass, and whatever law they pass, it's not going to make people stop wanting a drink." Abe searched Joey's face for a glimmer of understanding. "Don't you read the papers?" he said, refusing to believe that his best friend was just so ignorant of what was going on in the world. "As stupid as that law will be," he continued, "the schumks in Washington really believe that Americans are going to obey it, but I know and you know that people who want to drink are going to drink, and if they want to drink, they'll find a way to do it. And that's where we can make some big money."

Joey smiled his dark smile that showed no teeth. He knew that even if he didn't yet see the full picture, he also knew that Abie's ideas were good, and were ideas that were going to line his pockets. Abe's ideas always did. "So whadaya got?" Joey asked.

"I got this. Let me explain it again. Most of the money the government takes in comes from a tax on booze. They ain't gonna say people can't sell or buy booze until they can raise the money in some other way. That gives us time to set up something where we can get into the business as soon as the government stops liquor from being sold."

"Into the business of what?" Joey asked.

"Into the business of making and selling booze," Abe said. He felt himself growing impatient, and he conjured an insulting imprecation, but knew not to utter it, for Abe also knew from his years of friendship with Joey that if you made some illusion or reference to Joey's lack of intelligence or ethnicity, you could get hurt. Very hurt. He had seen Joey hurt a lot of people for real or imagined slights. Besides, Joey knew his own limitations, but just didn't like his limitations pointed out.

"You remember Hegamann's dairy, right? The old kraut with the dogs who lived across the alley from my father's store? You remember how we use to sneak into his yard where he stored the milk and cream bottles, steal a few at a time and bring them in for deposits?"

Joey's eyes began to laugh at old memories when he, Abe, and Harry would wait till it was dark and slip through the broken wooden slats and come out with two bottles a piece and return them the next day for the deposit. Each taking more than two would have made the old man suspicious. He started to laugh, and soon they both were laughing at those first hesitant forays made years ago. Their success gave them permission to get involved in other activities that also got them some easy money.

"I want to try something," Abe continued. "Meet me at my house after it gets dark and bring some white paint. I bought a case of cream bottles."

"What do you mean, you bought bottles? I could have lifted them from a grocery store."

"We don't have to do that anymore, Joey. Besides, we're going to need a lot of them to get started, and if bottles start disappearing, somebody would get wise. Besides, I have money now and we don't have to steal. This ain't gonna be penny ante shit."

Later that evening, Joey watched as Abe brought up a case of bottles from the basement, put them on the counter. He watched as Abe carefully painted the outside of the bottle, explaining that if they painted the inside, the paint might chip off and change the taste of the liquor. Then Abe handed Joey a brush and told him not to paint the neck of the bottle. Abe smiled broadly and said, "We're going into business."

As the bottles dried, Abie took a bottle of whisky from the kitchen, and began to fill the bottles up to the painted rim. "We're gonna sell bottles of booze as if they were bottles of cream." he said delighted with his scheme. "I'm seeing a need here, and we're going to fill it."

"Yah," Joey said, fully understanding Abe's vision. "After that law passes, people will be climbing over one another to get their hands on some good booze and we're going to supply it for them, right, Abie, right?"

Without waiting for the question he knew was coming, Abe continued, "We're getting jobs as dairy delivery men. We'll have white outfits and we'll get to know the customers. Hegamann delivers to lots of people around here, and we know a lot of those people. All we do is make it known that they can have a steady stream of good booze delivered to them daily, weekly, or any time they like. It will be like a business within a business. We bring them what they order from the dairy, and we have on the wagon a little something extra. They pay us a good price for booze, and we collect for Hegamann what he gets for a bottle of cream."

"And if we're caught," Joey continued, "we're only two milkmen working for Hegamann's Dairy; his bottles, his dairy, his booze. We know nothing about it. Our customers won't rat us out, cause they're breaking the law, too."

"I like the way you think," Abe said, and they smiled at one another.

"First we buy cheap liquor now and store it in my basement so we have some product to sell as soon as the liquor stores close," Abe said, seeing it all laid out before him like a map.

Joey interrupted. "But after you can't buy booze any more, where do we get it so we can resell it?"

"There are at least three ways to do that," Abe said. "One way is to buy it from Canada. I've made friends with guys in the restaurants and in the hotels where I got my concessions who have connections. For an upfront fee, they'll connect us. Or, we can buy it from someone making it illegally here, and believe me, there are going to be a lot of people doing that. Can you imagine the numbers of people who will be tossed out of work. They'll go into cellar businesses. The third way is to make it ourselves and that's going to take a big operation, but ultimately that will be the cheapest way to go."

"How big an operation?" Joey asked.

"I don't know much about making booze, but I know your dad and my dad make enough wine to last the year and to give some away. But that's small stuff. To really make this work big time, we're going to need a place that has big vats and big stills."

"Like the dairy?" Joey suggested now fully seeing what Abe had been envisioning. "Exactly," Abe replied. "Just like a dairy." There was a pause. Abe and Joey again smiled a familiar smile that said they were again both on the same page. "We have to do something that will let us get Hegamann's dairy without Hegamann becoming any the wiser."

"Look," Joey said. "We don't know when this law is gonna happen, but you say it will. So maybe we can expand the concession business, make a lot more money and buy the dairy."

Abe's eyes widened. "You're right," he said. "We can build up enough cash for at least a down payment, keep it as a dairy making milk and cream so we have a great cover, and put in a still in another part of the plant for the booze. We can even open up a shop where customers can buy directly. You're a genius, Joey. A fuck'in genius."

Joey smiled at the compliment, not completely sure that what Abe envisioned was what he had in mind. But still, he like being called a genius.

"But I'm not sure we'll have enough money when the time is right," Abe said. "I don't know how much a dairy costs or if the old man wants to sell." Abe realized that he was really getting ahead of himself and that his fantasy could explode when reality stepped in. He had to give this more thought.

Joey saw his friend's body suddenly sink. "What's up, Abe?"

"I just realized something. What bank would give two street thugs a mortgage? Getting the dairy is a great idea, but I don't think it's gonna work. What if Hegamann doesn't want to sell? And even if he does sell, then we got no patsy to blame things on if the cops come down on us."

Joey looked at Abe and his eyes narrowed as if he were seeing something far away. "You leave that to me, Abe. You just handle the business end of this, and let me handle this end as soon as that dumb law is passed. I'm thinking that when the time comes, there may not be any need for a bank if the old man sells to us directly for cash, along with some payout plan if we ain't got enough."

"But why would he do that?"

"Because maybe nobody but us would be interested in a dairy that had a serious fire."

CHAPTER 14

1918

Joey didn't want the entire dairy to go up in flames, so after dousing the wooden rear of the dairy with gasoline around midnight, he waited till sun up as the dairymen were loading up their wagons before throwing a bottle of gasoline with a burning rag attached. He counted on plenty of men being around to save the front of the building, while only the rear, the part of the building where the new stills would go, would be destroyed. Abe insisted that rebuilding a legitimate business with an illegitimate purpose would not be noticed by the cops. The building licences needed would be issued with no questions asked, especially if there was some grease for someone's palm. After all, it was only a dairy, and it would still bottle milk. The regular workers would still deliver daily to their regular costumers. There would be a second delivery, a weekly delivery made by Abe and Joey's friends dressed as dairymen who would have some of the same clientele and maybe a few new ones.

The conflagration was immediate, beginning at the base of the structure, creeping up slowly like silent fingers. The rear window exploded from the heat, and flames from the burning casement fell into the office and onto the paper strewn desk beneath it. When the smoke began to seep under the office door and through the dairy to the front loading docks, the workers raced with full milk pails to the rear. Then, the empty buckets were filled from the water pump in the backyard, and a bucket brigade was started. Though a heroic effort was made, the fire was not brought under control until the firemen arrived with their pumps and hoses. As anticipated, the fire destroyed the rear where the offices were, but not the concrete sections that held the milk vats and bottling parts. The business would continue, and by building a separation between the front and the rear, the stills could be installed and no one would be the wiser. It would appear that just honest workmen were rebuilding and extending the old dairy. Joey stood quietly behind the wooden fence and watched. Old man Hegamann and his daughter rushed out of their house in their nightclothes, jabbering in German, and screaming at the workers for using milk and not water.

Two days after the fire, Abe sat warming his hands with a cup of fresh coffee that Rosey had just made. It was late and the candy store was almost empty. He looked at the pictures of the burning dairy and felt vaguely disquieted by what had happened, even though he knew he was as responsible for the fire as was Joey. Joey came in and slumped himself into the booth.

"You should know what I did because we're partners," Abe began.

Joey took out a pack of cigarettes and tossed them on the table.

"I figured it would look kind of fishy if we suddenly appear at Hegamann's door with an offer to buy his dairy."

"So what did you do?" Joey asked, lighting a cigarette and proffering one to his friend.

"Well, I got us a couple of lawyers who have an office in the city. I met them at one of the card games that Armand set up. When I told them that I wanted to expand my concession business and needed some legal advice, they offered to help.

"Why didn't you ask your brother?" Joey said, "It would have been cheaper."

"I don't want more of my family involved in this. My father is angry enough, and I don't need Armand letting something slip to my father. Anyhow, I'll talk to Armand when I really need him. These two lawyers, a Joseph Pambino and a Joseph Bernstein are really smart and slick. They agreed to take us as clients for something called a retainer fee. I asked Armand what that was, and he said it was like up front money, so now they work for us."

Joey smiled at the idea that he had lawyers working for him.

"For a couple of hundred dollars," Abe continued, "we got incorporated into a new business that I told them to call 'The White Mountain Dairy.' You and me, Joey, are a corporation. The corporation owns the dairy, so Pambino and Bernstein will go to Hegamann with the offer; not us."

Joey's eyes narrowed. "Now wait a minute," he interrupted. "How the hell can a corporation talk to Hegamann, and what do you mean we don't own it? Who the hell owns it if we don't?"

"Joey, the corporation is kind of a front, and we're what's called silent partners. That's so if anything goes wrong, we're protected. We own it, but nobody will know that we own it. My brother explained it to me and said it was all legit. That's how it's done uptown. That's how high class people get away with all the shit they get away with and still keep their money and stay out of jail. They become corporations so they can't be touched. Hegamann will never see us. We'll have nothing to do with it. The old kraut gets cash up front in his hand, and no bank is involved. Hegamann's lawyer, if he wants one, will deal with our lawyers." Abe lit a cigarette and leaned back. "I'll be honest, Joey. I don't fully get it, but I trust these guys and you gotta respect my brother for what he knows. They advised me that this was the way to go." He paused.

"These guys remind me of us if we had brains." Abe laughed at a future that might have been his because he knew he had the brain, but just couldn't read all that well. Joey laughed too, but for a different reason.

"Yeh, you and me cudda been lawyers and hung out a sign Wop and Kike, Attorneys at Law,"

Abe laughed. "So maybe in a month, when the time is right, they'll make the offer to Hegamann, and I figure that now we can get a really good price. I mean, who wants a half burned down dairy?" Abe blew a satisfying smoke ring, took a sip from the coffee cup, and leaned back. "The next thing we gotta do is line up someone who knows something about distilling liquor."

"My old man has a still in the cellar, so I started watching him." Joey became somewhat animated. "The first thing he does is he takes grain and mixes it with hot water and stirs it like crazy. He said that that makes the sugars in the grain dissolves. Then he adds yeast like my mother uses in making bread, and that turns the stuff to alcohol. That gets boiled in a vat, and the alcohol boils off into a steam. But you can't drink steam, so the old man said you needed to cool it so it becomes a liquid. He has this copper coil and he passes it through cold water and what drips out of the end is booze. But he said y'a gotta watch the temperature because if it get too high and the water starts to boil in the vat, you get weak booze." Then his excitement changed to one of concern. "Where we gonna get this stuff?"

"From all the distilleries going out of business," Abe said reassuringly. "I think we can pick up what we need along with maybe a guy or two who know something about doing what your pop does, but on a bigger scale. Professional distillers are gonna need jobs. I've looked into this. I have contacts in the hotel who know wholesalers, not just here, but in Canada. We'll need hundreds of pounds of sugar, and hundreds of pounds of yeast. We're going to need grains shipped in and lots of water. That's why I'm going to buy the building I live in and expand the current store into that The White Mountain Dairy. And the corporation will own that, too. And next to the store that's now empty, will be a store that sells live fish. No one will questions large deliveries of sugar to a market. No one will question lots of water used by a fish store. We'll have different distributors so no one place will appear to be delivering too much. And deliveries will be staggered. And when we start remodeling, we're even going to cut a tunnel from the store to the dairy so stuff that shouldn't be delivered to a milk dairy will get there." Abe sat back and took another sip of his coffee.

CHAPTER 15

1919

"C'mon Sir Barton, C'mon Sir Barton," Abe screamed, shaking his racing form and moving his body imitating the undulating horse straining cross the finish line. The calculations of timing, the factoring in of the weather and track conditions, the lineage of the horse and jockey's history, had all paid off. Those who laughed at Abe and Harry for their approach to horseracing, scratched their collective heads and were forced to accept the idea that the Chernov boys had pushed gambling on "the sport of kings," into another dimension. After all, they had just won big money by betting on the first horse to win the Triple Crown. To professional gamblers, winning was the only thing that counted, and Sir Barton, having already won the Kentucky Derby, and the Preekness, now finished first in the Belmont Stakes. 1919 was turning out to be the best year of Abe Chernov's life.

Harry, whose memory was such that he was able keep all of Abe's winnings and IOUs in his head, had statistically figured out that Sir Barton would be the big winner of the Triple Crown, and once he had decided that, he had convinced his brother to bet a sizable amount of money on this horse. Though Abe was always cautious about how he bet his money, he never had any doubts as to his brother's acumen when it came to odds or spreads in any race or game of chance. Harry always came through. The money Abe had saved from his concessions combined with Harry's skills, had now made both of them their first fortune.

Jonah blamed Abe for luring Harry from a college education to the world of high class dining, supper clubs, fast women, race tracks, all night poker games, and the underbelly of New York City. He refused to accept the fact that Harry, prodigy that he was, loved the celebrity and benefits of this particular world. So Harry's choice to align himself with his older brother became another bone of contention between Abe and his father. To Jonah, who firmly believed that anyone who could conquer math could conquer the world, Harry's taking leave of formal education was tantamount to another betrayal of what the Chernov family should have valued as good citizenship and as good Jews. It was Jonah's intent that each of his children would make a meaningful contribution to the world. Armand, already a lawyer with an important New York firm, had been recruited by an expanding U.S. Justice Department anticipating a need to bolster and reinforce the soon to be implemented Volstead Act. To Armand, Washington would be a challenge and an opportunity to change the pervasive culture of corruption. Maurice was already working on his doctoral degree in economics with a minor in art history. And Sammy, having followed his childhood dream of learning everything he could learn about fine art, how things worked, and how things were built, was excelling in his studies in 20th Century Art and architecture. Rachelann, was writing for a newspaper, and Fanny was becoming a fashion designer. Aaron, now fourteen and very bright, was questioning everything, especially his teachers and challenging the hypocrisy of the world around him. Sometimes, Jonah thought his youngest son was too bright and too confrontational for his own good. But Abe and Harry were the thorns. In Jonah's dream, Harry, would have become a physicist, or a mathematician like Einstein, and not taken his older brother's path to immediate gratification. Maurice and Sam saw the long term benefits from a slower and more legitimate route, but not Abe and Harry. As far as Jonah was concerned, one son had corrupted another son, and that was unforgivable.

As Abe waved and kissed the winning ticket, Harry had already calculated the amount each would have. Harry fixed his imagination on a Cord and a chorus girl from the Zeigfield Follies, but Abe's money was destined for weightier things. With his half, together with the money he had already put away, he could now not only buy the dairy for cash, he could also buy the building in which he grew up, with the candy store and the adjoining stores. People were going to want to go out and have a drink and some fun. The store would still be a grocery store and a front. The apartment in the back where he grew up and the basement would become a nice little retreat from a law most people would come to hate and willingly break. Maybe Fanny would be interested in taking care of the cash register at his after hours night spot. It would be very fancy, and she could design it if she liked. Booze would be served in teacups along with light refreshments, and the waitresses might do double duty as both servers and entertainers. Of course there would be a small bandstand. And like the concession, Abe envisioned such retreats all over his city. Now he had all the money he needed to make the dream come true.

CHAPTER 16

1919

Mr. Harris and Mr. Reid were standing as Rachelann entered the elegant oak paneled room on the top floor of the Tribune Building. Mr. Reid, his blue eyes bulging in anger, pulled the cigar from his mouth, roughly stamping it out with one hand and grabbing a shaft of papers with the other. These he waved menacingly at the woman who stood placidly in front of the two men. At a nod from the publisher, Mr. Harris sat, and cleaned his pince-nez in an effort to do something with his shaking hands. The news editor had never before been called to such a meeting where one of the reporters under his supervision had been accused of what amounted to perfidy in the publisher's mind.

"You dare try to maneuver into my paper this socialist garbage, and call for an abolishment of 'wage slavery.' What is that? Who is enslaved? Show me one person who works for me who doesn't go home at night to his family and a meal? You call people who have jobs, slaves? And you expect me to print that rubbish?"

Rachelann Chernov, her auburn hair pulled back tightly in a bun, sat down though she wasn't invited to do so. She did not fear this man as did her editor. She straightened her back and unabashedly looked directly at her employer. "You are missing my point," she said, believing that the question was not rhetorical. "I am not accusing you as an employer. You pay an honest wage, but there are many who do not, and I am speaking to them. What I am saying is that I believe that all workers should enjoy an American standard of living. This simply means that they come to a place that is not vermin infested, and they are able to eat wholesome food that is not days old, and that they have warm clothing that is not in tatters, and that there is enough money so their children can see doctors when they are sick and perhaps be able to put something away so their children can get an education. Isn't this what America is all about?" She was as diplomatic in her response as she felt she could be, but she could not and would not back down from her truth, despite this man's position and his importance. She felt she had the right to write and defend her principles. Was freedom of speech not protected? This man was defending the effects of extreme Capitalism, and she was advocating for the downtrodden. It was a battle she had been fighting since the fire.

"I, Miss Chernov, am the publisher, and my thoughts, not your thoughts become the foundations for the editorials. This thing that you have written is laced with your bias and you have slanted the writing to intimate that what you are writing speaks for the voice of *The Tribune*. I am the voice of *The Tribune*, not you, and this paper is about anything that I want it to be about, and it is not about to create more class conflict than there already is. This piece borders on sedition, and invites, no, encourages, the labor unionists not only to organize, but to strike. It is diametrically opposed, Miss Chernov, to the values of the companies that advertise in our paper and keep us all in our jobs." He paused for breath and then continued immediately. "You write that they should form unions, urge their members to get into politics, urge them vote with their own economic issues in mind! What the hell do you think you are doing?"

"It is your right, Mr. Reid," Rachelann said standing up. "But let me ask you this? Whose economic issues should be on the worker's minds, Mr. Reid? Yours?" She had nothing left to lose. "Should they be more concerned about the Captains of Industry who have their mansions on Fifth Avenue that were built with the wealth garnered on the backs of immigrant labor? These workers as you call them, should they be more concerned about the welfare of the bosses who own the sweatshops so the bosses can have their American Dream while the worker goes begging? Not everyone can own a business, Mr. Reid, and not everyone can own mines and railroads like your friends do, but everyone can and should make more than two dollars a week for putting in sometimes sixty hours, and not everyone should have to take work home to insure that there is enough money to feed their children. Go into the squalor as I have and smell the stench of dirty bodies. See the faces of famished children. Listen to the labored breath of consumptive parents. When will people like yourself and your friends say, 'I have enough!' When will they see the depth of despair of their workers and offer them hope?"

Mr. Harris sank further into his chair, fearing that he would become the brunt of Reid's next outburst. He was amazed that someone would speak to the editor this way, and though he was fearful of the outcome, he could not help but admire the woman with whom he had worked for the past eight years. Over those years he had learned that this woman was more competent, more punctual, more sober in her judgements, and more honest in attempts to right the wrongs of the world than any of the male counterparts who worked around her and were paid more than she. Still, her bylines were still R. Chernov at the insistence of Mr. Reid who also admired her work ethic, but did not permit the world to know that a woman was his star reporter.

"You have a choice, Miss Chernov. You can either rewrite this incendiary piece or pack up your things and get out!"

"Mr. Reid," interrupted Mr. Harris timorously. "if I may speak to Miss Chernov alone. She is a very popular writer, and I do think the paper will suffer if she is gone. She has many followers."

"No, you may not speak to her alone," Reid fumed, "because I want an answer now!"

There were tears in her eyes as she gathered up the small mementos of her professional life at the paper, but her anger with Reid was put aside, and she focused on the picture framed face of an elderly friend, Samuel Gompers, one of her inspirations and mentors. On more than one occasion, he had asked her if she would bring her writing talents to the New York Office of the American Federation of Labor.

Rachelann Chernov and Samuel Gompers had met several years before at a Socialist gathering that she was covering. He was not there because he was a Socialist, but because he believed it was important to keep his finger on the pulse of the working man and woman, no matter what their political ideologies. Meeting there, she learned of his work to establish an umbrella organization where a central labor office could coordinate the actions of different unions in large urban industrial cities. From him, Rachelann learned about contracts being achieved through collective bargaining between labor and management. From him she first heard about the skills needed to successfully bring combatants to the table. And from him she came to believe that despite the cumbrous hours that negotiations took, Gomper's ideas of a sure progress for the workers could only be sustained with face to face deliberations. These ideas were subjects of interviews she had with him and that had been published.

At an early meeting, she remembered him telling her that an important man in his career told him to keep in touch with the Socialist movement, to listen to what they had to say, understand them, but never join the Party. Not only did she take his counsel, but she also applied that same wisdom to the Communist Party and any anarchists association, much to the consternation of her anarchist friends. She found this elderly gentleman stimulating, and he was charmed by her devotion to the worker and her assertiveness. "Come and write for us," he said at one of the Saturday evenings at the Socialist Hall.

Today, she would take him up on his offer. She would go from *The Tribune* to the AF of L, and never miss a beat. He and his organization had been an inspiration to her for years, especially their belief in the right of the worker to a decent life. Though her past associations with Berkman and Goldman had pushed her further to the left of Gompers, Rachelann was always one to work within the lines of pushing the labor movement forward without it spilling into radicalism and open revolt. She was not interested in supplanting Capitalism with a worker's commonwealth as Feyda seemed to be, and she was certainly not interested in tearing down the government as were Berkman and Goldman. Rachelann wanted what was due the worker without destroying the society in which that worker and his or her family lived. Capitalism needed to be reigned in, not obliterated.

"This is a rough draft," she said, handing the proposed leaflet over. Leaflet writing was not what she thought she would be doing, considering her talents, but the most immediate need was for one to be written. "THE GENERAL STRIKE DECLARED! TO ALL WORKERS IN THE WAIST AND DRESSMAKING INDUSTRY AND GREATER N.Y. AND VICINITY.

Sisters and Brothers: Today, January 21st, 1919 10 A.M. Prompt. YOU ARE DIRECTED TO STOP WORK AND GO DOWN ON STRIKE. You are hereby requested to leave your employment as orderly and quietly as possible. Do not make any disturbance. Pack up your tools and everything that belongs to you promptly at 10 AM and leave your shop to join the ranks of the strikers. Avoid arguments and enter into no discussion with your employer or any of his representatives. If the employers refuse to permit you to use the elevators, walk down the stairs. Let the workers of each shop, headed by its shop chairman, march in an orderly manner to the meeting hall to which you were directed. Do not wait for any committee to take you down. Let this circular be your committee.

"Then I'll list all the meeting halls and which shops should go where," she continued. "It will be signed by the General Executive Board. I.O. L.W. U. Strike Committee, Amalgamated Ladies'Garment Cutters' Union, Local,10 Ladies' Waist and Dressmaker's Union, Local 25, and Buttonhole Makers' Union, Local 58. Did I leave anyone out?"

All shop workers in the dressmaking and waist industry from Madison Avenue, Broadway, and all from 20th to 38th Streets and those from 25th to 42nd Streets boisterously milled around until they were asked to be silent. The speaker who had been tasked with addressing them had fallen ill, and the organizers who knew of Rachelann's past and present involvement, impressed upon her the need to speak. It was with some reluctance that she stepped up to the podium and introduced herself as R. Chernov, formerly of the *New York Tribune*. It was the first time she had revealed herself publically, and applause broke out immediately, not only because they recognized her as a behind the scenes stalwart force for the labor and suffrage movement, but because she was a women who had gone beyond where most of them were able to go. An outline of the speech to be delivered had been thrust into her hands as she walked from the wings. When she saw the name Clara Lemlich in the opening paragraph, she knew how to start and where to go. It would come naturally.

"Ten years ago," she began, "the great leader, Clara Lemlich stood at a podium much like this one and declared that there would be a general strike of shirtwaist workers, and that if she ever betrayed the cause of worker rights, her right hand should loose its cunning. That strike lasted four months, and in the end, those brave people earned for you better pay, equal treatment for workers who were in the union and not in the union, and shorter hours." She paused. "Today, some of you here walked out with her, and you can remember when a 65 hour work week was normal, and that kind of week could expand to 75 hours in season." There were whispers and nods of personal recollections by those who lived through those days. "I can see where some of you remember that you had to supply your own needles, thread, and even sewing machines. But the strike of 1910 earned us advances," she paused, "but not enough!" And she repeated again, "but not enough!" There was a thunderous burst of applause and the audience sprang to its feet chanting, "Not enough! Not enough!"

"That strike," she continued, "forced a collaboration between Tammany Hall and reformers because the politicians realized that while the owners had money to contribute, they didn't have the hundreds of thousands of votes that we control. We have the power through the ballot box, and though we cannot exercise that right yet..." The mostly Jewish female audience recognized the veiled reference to the second most pressing problem that they faced; the vote. Though they did not have it yet, a husband and father could be urged to vote for those politicians who would aid his wife or daughter in their efforts to better their working conditions and their families' lives. This every woman there knew. "The pressure we put upon the legislators because of the influence we wield in the market place and in the house, has forced them to create commissions that have forced those changes that prevent hazards and loss of life. Fire hazzards are being eliminated. Sanitary eating and toilet facilities are being installed, and diseases that come from the dust and smoke are being addressed. Because of you, the most progressive labor laws that have ever existed, are being written. Yes, because of you!" Another thunderous round of applause broke out from the crowd as Rachelann gathered her thoughts. "Yet once again we are forced to come together to threaten another general strike, because though progress has been made, it is still not enough. So we ask you, Governor Sulzer, where are the safer entries and exits that were promised? Where are the fireproofing and the fire extinguishers that were promised? Where are the mandated reductions of the time women and children can work that were promised? We demand to know!" The audience began to chant, "Where? Where?"

Rachelann stepped back slightly and waited for some semblance of quiet before she continued. "Earlier," she said, "I spoke of Clara Lemlich and of her courage and leadership. I would like to speak of another great person whom you all know, Mr. Gompers, and I would like to recite for you his dream of tomorrow. 'What does labor want? We want more schoolhouses and less jails. More books and less guns. More learning and less vice. More leisure and less greed. More justice and less revenge, and more opportunities to cultivate our better natures.'"

Rachelann took her spectacles off and let them dangle from the fine lanyard and pin to which they were attached. She was tired, and she wanted some respite from the emotions of the past week. As she briefly scanned the front rows and those standing to the side, she saw Feyda standing inconspicuously next to a column. She could not help but smile. She had not seen him in a very long time.

She took a deep breath and went on. "Those of you who have studied for your citizenship know the Gettysburg Address. In it President Lincoln refers to a nation 'of the people, by the people, and for the people.' The visions of the American Labor Movement are not unlike the visions set down by that wonderful president. Like him, we also envision a time when ignorance will be uprooted, and our children will have the opportunity to leave the factory and workshop and go to school and to play in the schoolyard. Our vision is to make homes happier and make life worth living. We believe in the dignity of the working people, and we are for the working people. We wish to govern ourselves, with policies determined by ourselves, and not by factory owners."

Feyda Aronstam waited patiently until the last of the appreciative well wishers had gone before moving into the light. He stood there smiling at her, and he could see a slight blush on her cheek. "Before it is forbidden, would you accompany me for a drink?"

She smiled at his allusion to the soon to be instituted Prohibition legislation, knowing full well that he would never dream of abiding by anything the government would institute. Beyond that, she just smiled because he was there. She did not miss Alexander or Emma, or the stifling tenement the three of them shared, she did miss his gentle eyes, his sudden kindnesses, and a look that she received from few other men.

"I see you've been busy doing the people's work. That is a good thing. It is the best thing a person can do," he said, half smiling. "To make the world better for the workers is the most noble of callings."

"Ah," she sighed. "Always ready to indoctrinate someone in the great 'Cause.' I would have hoped you would have had something more to say to me after so long an absence."

Now it was his time to feel a flush on his cheeks. He hadn't intended to preach but to compliment. But what did she want when she said, "more." Had she not read the affection in his eyes, but only heard the words on his lips? "I have followed your articles each time they appeared," he said, searching for the hidden meaning of 'more.' And I am sorry to hear that you will no longer be writing for the newspaper."

She smiled, thanking him for his support. "That's still not what I expected you to say," she reiterated.

He was confused by her response. Dare he hope that she could still care for him? "Perhaps we might go somewhere and talk, and perhaps have some supper," he suggested somewhat sheepishly. She was tempted to ask him if she would have to pay for them both, since Berkman had always kept this man penniless, but she did not. She would not insult him by asking. He was who he was. Her truth was that whatever anger lingered, it was anger rooted in the fact that Alexander Berkman and

Emma Goldman had so dominated this man, that he had lost himself and that he could never get away and become the independent man she needed him to be. Feyda's Cause was noble, but nobility did not feed children or put a decent roof over a family's head. She knew that had she accepted him and his invitation into a common law relationship living communally in that tenement, it would have been she who would have to work to support them all while he and the others would continue to exist on air and the high sounding ideals that was the harbinger of their revolution. When she had given him the ultimatum between her, a legitimate relationship and job, or staying with his cousin and Emma, she realized his reluctance to answer told her that he was not ready for such a commitment or such a life. Perhaps she was a little angry with him, too. She still cared deeply for him.

"There is a nice deli around the corner where we can share a brisket and potato plate," she said, and they serve beer."

"I can afford to buy you your own plate of brisket and a beer," he said, reaching into his pocket and taking out a silver dollar. "Things have changed since we last saw one another."

"You said 'things have changed' since we last met. I was wondering if you had changed and separated yourself from Alexander and Emma. Is that what you meant?"

"I mean things have gotten worse for everyone here, what with the flu killing so many people, and the revolution in Russia putting all immigrants, especially Russians, under the relentless scrutiny of the government. Now with the labor unions and the strikes that sometimes turn violent..." As he spoke, he wistfully studied the effervescence rising through the amber liquid before he took a sip. His dark moustache was all foam when he reset the glass on the table, and she laughed, motioning with her hand to her own upper lip. He smiled back at her, his dark eyes laughing, and wiped his mouth.

"We thought that the people here would rise up with us and support us," he continued, his voice shaking, "but all we did was engender anger. The Italian Galleanists and their bombs have brought down a hell on all of us that no one wanted, and the government has lumped us all together. I barely escaped a raid against the Union of Russian Workers two days ago. People who were just near the union hall who said they were Russian were beaten and arrested. The night school I've been going to was targeted just because we were in a space that we shared with the Union. Anyone perceived to be on the radical Left is being deported. None of us are safe."

"I'm safe, and so is my family," she retorted angrily. "Feyda, you and I are Russian immigrants, and while I and my family may lean to the Left, we've become citizens and you my dear are still an anarchist." Rachelann immediately understood his fear, but also understood that the choice to align himself with Goldman and Berkman was his choice and no one else's. She had chosen not to do that, and she was trying to distance herself from him emotionally. It was difficult because she still had strong feelings for him. "When you came here, there were choices you could have made to make life better for yourself and others. But your country is your 'Cause.' In fact, you don't want a country because with a country, you'd have to become responsible for yourself and the people around you. What you live for is another revolution because your hatred for the Tzar and his government continues to control you. An old hate controls you, my dear Feyda. And Alex and Emma control you. Russia is not America, and the Russian Government is not like the American Government. It never was and it never will be. Other immigrants may be perceived as having too much loyalty to their nation of origin and their cultures, but Jewish immigrants, you and I, have too much loyalty to hatred for how we were treated on the other side of the world. We brought that hatred and distrust with us. The difference between us is that you want to make things right by destroying the government, and I want to make things right by working with this system to make it better. President Wilson himself said that a hyphenated American cannot be a truly loyal American if he or she has one foot here and one foot there. I believe him. Getting rid of our hatred and suspicion for what was, is what we have to overcome to be American. I am doing that and there can be nothing between us unless you do that too."

"And you agree with Wilson?"

"I know what it is to be a creature of passion, Feyda. I also had become so focused and loyal to a single ideal that I couldn't see anyone else's point of view, and because of that, I almost lost my family. Such focus and loyalty can also enslave a person. I have written and interviewed labor agitators and anarchists, and while I do believe that strikes are needed, I now see that ultimately negotiation is the only way to bring about lasting changes. You and Berkman and Goldman would see all governments torn down. And then what do you have after you tear everything down? You have what the French had after their Revolution. What they had is happening now in Russia, a reign of terror and betrayal. You will see that after they exile and murder the nobility, they will go after the Jews. After the Jews, anyone who does not agree with them. The anarchist who destroyed the old Russia to become the new Russia will become a government that will also destroy dissenters as the old Russia did. That is the way of the world. And let me finish with something my father said to me when I also spouted your anarchist ideas. He said, 'Without government, men would eat one another.'" She stopped abruptly, and the silent pain she had carried for years exploded.

"I left you, Feyda, not because I no longer loved you, but because I could not stomach Alex and Emma's treatment of you and your willingness to be abused by them for the 'Cause.' Your great 'Cause' that keeps you destitute, living in squalor, stalking the streets like some ghost that cannot find his grave so he can rest. That's why I left you. You allowed people who were so much less than you to walk all over you, and I would not allow myself to love someone who would allow that and who would always have me second to his 'Cause.' I could not allow myself to give up my dream of having a family where I wasn't terrified that my husband would not come home at night because he was sacrificed to the 'Cause,' or that my children would starve."

He lowered his head, and she saw his tears roll down his cheeks and disappear into his beard. "Rachelann, I don't know what to do." He took the napkin and wiped his eyes and nose. "Rachelann," he repeated looking at her shimmering in the watery aura that surrounded her, "I'm in too deeply and I don't know how to get out of it. I've been going to school at night so I could learn a trade. I'm trying to break from them, but their hold on me is strong." He paused for a more fearful truth. "Now those who continue to meet secretly have chosen me to plant a bomb and threatened my life if I refuse. They already suspect that I am disloyal because I'm going to school and I've gotten a small job. They say that if I do as they say, they will trust me again. But if I don't, they've said that they will kill me. I fear for my life, and I could think of no one but you to tell. I have no one else to trust. I have no place to go that is safe."

She pulled back at the word, 'bomb' and looked around to see if anyone was listening.

"You will never go back there again!"

"Well, Papa, that seems to be what the job is all about." Armand poured himself a brandy and walked back to the couch where Jonah sat. "They told me I was to prosecute anarchists and subversives for the Justice Department's Bureau of Investigation, but some of the people I've met like this J. Edgar Hoover person and this Mitchell Palmer, talk as if they never heard of the Constitution. Palmer has pressured the Department of Labor to back off its insistence on telling people that they have the right to an attorney until a case against the defendant is established. This they say will 'protect government interests.' I myself have seen Hoover bypass people in Labor who disagreed with him and got those same warrants from those who did."

"You seem very conflicted," Jonah said, silently proud that his son recognized corrupt officials when he saw them, but knew better than to ask him what he was going to do about it? This belonged to his son, and if his son asked him for his opinion, he would give it. So he looked sympathetically at Armand and nodded his understanding.

"And they expect me to be the lead prosecutor fully knowing that these people are being brought into a court room already having their rights abused. Hover and Palmer don't want a prosecutor; they want a persecutor. Hoover got Labor to agree to let him move against the Communist Party, and he's pushed this mandate to allow him expand to any organization that hints of being red or even pink. I can see Hoover expanding this mandate all over the country with Palmer acting as his sword of justice. And Papa, because Palmer raids organizations, anyone found in or near one, members and non-members alike, visitors, students, and even full American citizens who should not have been arrested and cannot be deported, are taken in and subjected to the most brutal conditions."

Jonah thought of many of the friends from Krivoser, the 'Parlor Pinks' as they were known, who, though not affiliated with the Communist Party, were certainly sympathetic to the social values they advocated. These were good people, good Americans who would never dream of lending their hands to anything that would violently overthrow the country that took them in and gave them back their lives.

"So what are you going to do about it?" said Aaron. Jonah looked up and smiled at his youngest son who was quietly standing by the door. At fourteen, Aaron had a generous mop of straight brown hair that fell just above his eyes, and over the tops of his ears. He wore it like a crown, and though his friends slicked theirs back with Macassar, as was the fashion, Aaron was independent of mind and tended towards his own style. His features, like his father's, were soft but as yet undefined as to what they would become, and like his older brother, his eyes were bright blue and alert. Armand looked up and smiled.

"So what are you going to do about it?" Aaron repeated in his distinctively resonant voice that was laden with teenage challenge.

Armand's smile at his intense younger brother was more like a smirk because he knew that Aaron was relentless when he was in pursuit of an answer or a point to be made, and would not let up until he had an answer. Still, Armand was conflicted. The appointment he had recently received was a long time in coming, and he knew that this was his opportunity to begin the long desired career he had wanted with the Federal Government. But his brother's challenge spoke to a different level, and he did not want to disappoint this young idealist by seeming to close an eye to something he knew was unjust. So the question had to be addressed honestly and for the first time, he would have to verbalize that which he had not verbalized before.

"I am going to stay," Armand said with an expulsion of breath that contained both resignation and relief, "and let me tell you why. The people being brought up on charges of sedition may or may not be guilty, but evidence is being manipulated to make as many of them look guilty as possible. If I resign, I take myself out of the battle for justice and there will be little I can do to protect their rights. But as an officer of the court and a member of the Justice Department, I can at least see to it that whatever evidence there is against them is not fabricated, and whoever is brought in as a witness, has not been coerced in any way. People who would dismiss the law by going around the law, can often be stopped by exposing them with other laws. I can do that only if I stay."

"Okay." Aaron said, his face lit with admiration. "So what's next?"

Rachelann and Fedya arrived at the townhouse and were surprised and relieved that Armand's car was parked in front. They had walked the blocks from the subway, taking turns to furtively look around to see if anyone was following them. As they approached Fifth Avenue, she felt confident that they were alone. She led him to the delivery door in the great house and let themselves in with a key. "You work here?" Fedya said.

"No," she replied, wondering how he was going to respond to her when he found out that her father and stepmother did.

"Then your mother is a cook here? No?" he continued.

"No, my stepmother cooks here, but she is not the cook." She realized she was stalling for time. Would he think that she was a rich girl pretending to be poor because she was bored and using him and his ideals as play things? That was never the case.

There was a fire warming the kitchen and he immediately moved towards it to warm his hands. Rachelann took off her coat and put a pot of water up on the stove. Before the tea was ready, she took a bottle of schnaps from the cupboard and two glasses. He studied the etched delicacy. "I want to talk to you before we go upstairs."

His eyes looked at the ceiling. What did she have to do with life upstairs in such a fine house, a house of Capitalists? She read his concern and confusion in his eyes.

"Fedya, my father and stepmother live in this house, but when you met me, I lived in Brownsville in the back of a grocery store. It's a complicated story, and one day I shall tell it to you. For now, just know that the people upstairs are Russian; Jewish and not Jewish, and very loyal to the United States Government. They are good people and will help you, but I have to tell you that if you cannot accept me and my family for what they have and who they are, I think it best that you leave now."

"I have no place to go where I will not be in danger and hunted. Whatever is upstairs will not kill me."

"Then pour the schnaps into your tea and get warm, and we'll go upstairs."

Rachelann led Feyda up the first flight of stairs from the kitchen and servant's quarters to the second flight that led to the hidden door that led to the foyer. The marble fireplace blazed with warmth and invitation, and the crystals in the center chandelier reflected a welcoming amber and red. Feyda stopped, and while his core railed against the opulence and the wealth that had created it, he nevertheless was fascinated by being in its presence. He was grateful that behind these walls, he felt a curious safety he had never felt before.

Rachelann ushered a reluctant Feyda into the library where she found her father, Marta, and her two half brothers sipping brandy and hot chocolate. They were startled when they saw Rachelann and a disheveled man next to her that Jonah surmised immediately as Rachelann's once romantic interest. He also knew of his ideology and of his friends. He stood but did not extend his hand.

"Papa, you remember I spoke about Feyda? This is my stepmother, Marta Chernov, and these are my two handsome half brothers, Armand and Aaron. Everyone, this is Feyda. Feyda has a problem and a need to be in a safe place until he can work it out."

Feyda was nervously kneading his hat in his hands while looking at the walls of books on either side of the great mantle. He sat where Rachelann had put him, and began to tell his story to attentive listeners. When he finished, he sat silently, waiting for some response.

"That's an amazing story," Aaron said, fully involved in the adventure of the tale, but too young to fully comprehend the dangerous ramifications of it.

"And you bring this anarchist here to endanger us?" Jonah said, standing. "What if you were followed?"

"I bring here a man who is afraid for his life and for the lives of others who need our help.

And I made sure we were not followed," Rachelann responded sharply. "Now if you can't give him shelter until this bomb business goes away, we'll be off."

"And where will you go, back to Brownsville where the police and government agents are watching every Russian Jew in the streets? You both will be picked up." Her father paused for a moment. "Not for him do I agree to help you, but for you."

"Feyda," Armand said, facing the man in the chair opposite him. "If you will consider doing what I am about to ask you to do, I think I will be able to rid you of anyone who wishes to harm you and get you pardoned for your past associations." Feyda leaned forward. Armand continued. "I want you to return to the tenement or wherever you meet with your group and agree to plant that bomb. Once they tell you the target and time, you will tell Rachelann, who will then tell me. If you agree to this now, tomorrow I will go to the people I work with and tell them that I have convinced one of the key figures in the anarchist movement to become my informant. In exchange for providing information that will lead to the capture of other ringleaders in this movement, I promise that you will be exonerated and given a full pardon. That will be the key condition, so when you are captured along with them, your capture will remove all suspicion from you. I will arrange it so that all of you are separated from one another so no one will ever see you again. You go free to live your life without this past clinging to you, and they go to jail or get deported."

"But these are relatives and friends," he protested. "How would I live with myself after such a betrayal?"

"And you think by sending you off to plant a bomb and possibly getting yourself killed, they are not betraying you?" interrupted Rachelann. "You are expendable to them. They wouldn't send Berkman. No, he's too important to the 'Cause.' But they will sacrifice you in a heartbeat. You should have no loyalty to them for how you've been treated." She paused. "And let me tell you something else, Fedya Aronstam. If you don't accept Armand's offer, there will be absolutely no chance that you and I will ever be together. You choose. It's either them and your Cause or me!"

The following week, Feyda brought the bomb to a prearranged warehouse where the full charge was exchanged for something that would explode, but not cause injury or damage. In that way, when the anarchists read in the paper the next day that a bomb went off but proved to be poorly made, the bomb maker would be held responsible and no one would suspect Feyda. Rachelann kept the pardon signed by Hoover himself in a box in her room and waited to hear from Armand. The day after the dud harmlessly exploded, the anarchists, along with Fedya, were gathered in the tenement apartment to plan their next attack. New York City Policemen, supported by Federal Agents, stormed up the stairs and captured the entire cell. All of them were led in handcuffs, beaten and bloodied, to the paddy wagon and then to jail. Like Armand said, none were put together, and Armand, good to his word, had Fedya freed. Alexander Berkman and Emma Goldman were deported back to Russia. Armand was the prosecuting attorney.

Though Fedya was freed, his name was not taken off the list of those suspected of subversion. One evening, Rachelann looked out of the window to see two men standing in the shadows across from the house. Armand looked into the matter, and though the pardon was real enough, there were those who saw that it got lost in the system. So Armand reluctantly had to tell both Fedya and Rachelann that they were on a list of suspects, and a case was being built against him for his association with the anarchists, and against his half sister for her tangential involvement years ago. Her recent work as a labor rabble rouser and suffragette merely stoked the fire of those bent on getting rid of anyone who spoke out and demanded changing the status quo. He knew that such allegations against her so bent the Constitution that any charge could not hold, but her situation was tenuous at best because of the mindless paranoia that was seeping into the brains of the bureaucrats in the Department of State and in the Department of Justice.

Jonah and Marta listened carefully to Armand, and realized that getting Rachelann and Fedya out of the country was the best possible plan. Jonah insisted that they must be married quickly, and also insisted that they had to have papers that erased their identities so they could travel and not be accosted. They agreed that Armand must be able to honestly deny any knowledge of where they were so he might be protected, and that Abe would have to become involved. Jonah hated the idea of relying on Abe's underworld connections for forged papers, but his daughter's well being was in the balance, and as a father, he had to weigh his sense of his integrity against her life. Naturally, the only option he could live with was that of protecting his child. Any parent would make that sacrifice and take that risk, though his involvement made him culpable before the law. He would get in touch with Abe immediately.

The following evening found Abe reaching out to accept a drink from his father, and settled into a chair facing the elder Chernov. His dark eyes were intense, and there was a rigidity in his manner that seemed a protective barrier he created in anticipation of whatever new or old condemnation of his life and business was to come his way. There was an uncomfortable silence until Jonah spoke.

"So, how are Virginia and Leo?" Jonah asked.

"Perhaps you might visit their apartment one day and see for yourself," Abe responded, looking directly at him, "or is seeing them only at weddings and funerals less problematic for you?"

Jonah had anticipated a polite and superficial exchange before getting to the matter he wanted to discuss, but he realized from the answer and tone of his son's response that the ancient resentments and animosities still were foremost in Abe's mind, and these needed to be verbalized before Abe would be able to listen. Jonah was annoyed and tried to be honest and soften his voice, but he felt heat rising to his cheeks.

"I see them where my wife and I are invited and are made to feel welcome," he said softly, "and I don't accept invitations from my children that do not include my wife. I'm sure that if you were married, you would not either." He paused, weighing the value of picking at a wound that seemed not to heal. "I'm sorry," he said immediately. "I should not have said that, and that's not why I asked you to come."

Abe dismissed the apology. "You barely know your grandson," he continued, unable to let it go.

"That is not my fault or Marta's fault," Jonah countered, his voice slightly higher, but still controlled. "Marta and I love Leo the same way we love Aaron, and they were growing up like twins when they were young. But Virginia got it into her head that she didn't like the way she was being treated here, and became so contemptuous of us that any sort of relationship became impossible. She took our kindness, and after deciding that what we were willing to give a servant impregnated by my son was not enough, it was she who decided that she did not want us in her life. That meant Leo would not be in our life either." He shifted in his seat and took a larger sip of the brandy. "Being pregnant with your child," he continued, "did not make her family. We could have thrown her out when you told us she was pregnant, or we could have offered her money to go away as other people do with servants who take the sons of their employers to their beds, hoping to better their station in life. We were kind enough to keep her on. Who else would have hired an unmarried pregnant servant girl?"

"You did not accept her, and you treated the mother of your grandchild as a servant."

"She was a servant, and she had no status other than that. You and she should have been grateful for that." Jonah put out his hand and counted off on his fingers. "One, she was well fed. Two, she was paid regularly. Three, we also paid for her doctor visits, and four, when her time came due, your son, my first grandchild, was born upstairs in the room where he was conceived. Dr. Scholnick was there, helping her from her first kvetch to her last."

"You threatened to throw us both out of the house if I married her. My business was just starting, and I had little. Should I forget that, Papa?"

"Yes, I did not want you to marry," Jonah snapped back. "You were barely out of your teens, still a child yourself, and children have no business making children or raising them. Besides, she's ten years older than you are. She was a woman who seduced a boy. How should I feel about that? So for protecting my son from the burden of being a teenage husband, both you and she carry this anger toward me and my wife? Virginia conveniently forgets that after Leo was born, it was I who told you to marry her for the child's sake, but by then you weren't interested in getting married because your business had taken off and started you living the high life. Marriage and a child would have tied you down. Did you tell her that we had given you permission, or did you continue to let her believe that I was standing in the way of making her an honest woman? I could understand why she thought she should be treated better than a servant, but as soon as she knew she was carrying your child, she started making demands on us and how she felt she should be treated. So you moved her back to her people on the West Side. It was you who took our grandson away from us, to deprive him of our love and the opportunities we offered freely because you and she didn't like my response to you marrying a woman about whom we knew nothing, one who was years older, let alone having a child out of wedlock. I should not object to a woman who seduces a son upstairs while his father was being married downstairs?" Jonah felt that something inside him was clawing its way out of his gut, and the something was the frustrations he had felt over the years for his inability to make

Abe a better man. "Was a father to think that such a woman was a worthy bride for his eldest son? If Virginia wanted to be welcomed as more than who she was, she might have been a bit more conciliatory and congenial. Had she tried in the slightest and not held us in such contempt, I might have rethought my feelings for her, but to take my grandson into the church and have him baptized as a Catholic was beyond toleration. And to do this behind your back, and our backs, was just more of her actions that confirmed the type of person she was." The scabs were torn off, and the wounds, left by half forgotten memories, seeped blood again.

"You were never going to accept her because she wasn't Jewish."

"Is that what you think? Is that what is also sticking in your craw all these years?" Jonah's voice was incredulous. "Who do you think I am? Did you forget that I married someone who wasn't Jewish? How could I marry out and condemn you for wanting to marry out? I'd be a hypocrite to deny you marriage to the person you loved. Marta is not Jewish, and according to tradition, Armand and Aaron aren't either. But that never stopped me from loving them unreservedly. There are no religious conditions on my love for my children or grandchildren. They are my flesh. Leo is my flesh. You are my flesh. I'm no hypocrite," he repeated. "I would have loved my Catholic grandson the same way if you and Virginia allowed me any sort of relationship. It was you who agreed to how he was to be raised, and it was you who agreed to deprive him of his grandparents, and it was you who agreed to deprive him of a heritage because you rejected it yourself. Your wounds are still festering because I reject the life you've chosen, a life with crooks, and gamblers, whores, and now with illegal booze. You still refuse to let go of your anger at me for marrying Marta a year after your mother died. I'm not ashamed to say that I love Marta. I'm not ashamed to say that I was entitled to be loved back, to marry and to give our unborn child a legal name. I loved Marta and married her because I loved her. You still haven't married Virginia. I'll bet you haven't because you don't love her and you know it. A person should marry for love, but sometimes a person needs to marry for honor, if only to protect his child. I objected to the marriage when you were young, but you're a grown man now, and you still haven't made her your wife. By not marrying Virginia, you dishonor yourself and our name."

"The agreement I have with Virginia is our business, and not carrying my name protects them and keeps them out of the spotlight." Abe's black eyes blazed and his eyebrows furrowed in anger. But this truth that his father hurled at him was, nevertheless, a truth. He didn't love Virginia, and he didn't want to marry her. Moreover, he did spitefully separate his father from his son for all the reasons his father mentioned. But the one emotion that impeded the relationship over these years was the feeling by Abe of the older man's profound disappointment in him. No matter what good he did or how much money he had, he felt he could still not please this man.

"And what about protecting everyone else whose last name is Chernov," Jonah fumed. "That's Abe Chernov's father. You think he's in on the graft and the brothels? How could a man who runs a language school afford such a house?' I've heard such snickering, and others report other allegations. Out there, there are people who think I have no integrity because of lies that are told about me being involved in my son's various business enterprises. You think this house hasn't been under surveillance? You think we have never had the police knock on the door of this house?"

"Fine, it's all my fault. It's always my fault." Abe felt small again, and he only felt it when he was in this house. Elsewhere, he was revered, admired, and feared. But here, he felt like a scolded child.

Both father and son looked at each other with the regrets of past decisions made and words hurled in frustration and anger. Tears rolled down Jonah's cheeks, and Abe's were moist. Each wanted to hold the other and just weep away their history, but neither could do that because the realities would remain after such an embrace, and each knew it. Abe stood up abruptly and walked to the side board and poured himself a double whisky. He gulped it down and wanted to escape. "Why am I here?" he said.

Jonah had taken a breath and calmed himself, desperately wanting to continue talking about their relationship, resolve it, for as difficult as the talk was, it was still talk and not silence. The disappointments and feelings of betrayal each felt for the other could only be dispelled through confrontations such as this, but Rachelann's situation was pressing. "I need to talk to you about your sister."

"The rabble rousing anarchist or the or the well attired princess?"

"Rachelann," Jonah replied, stifling a smile at Abe's assessment. "She and Fedya are in serious trouble and must leave the country." He studied Abe's face for a response, but his jaw remained tight. "They need new identities because Armand says they are secretly being investigated for subversive activities. This Hoover person reneged on Feyda's pardon even though Feyda willingly turned state's evidence, bringing down his anarchist cell, and sending friends back to Russia."

Abe ran his hand through his slicked down hair and leaned his head back on the antimacassar and laughed derisively. "And you say you're not a hypocrite. Here you despise me for what I do and who I know, and now you come to me and ask me to use who I know to help my sister."

"I'd do the same for you if I had to," he responded, the inconsistency not being lost on him as well. "This could involve jail for Rachelann because of her past associations, or deportation for Fedya. There is more at stake here than my consistency. When it comes to my family, I'm more willing to do what is good rather than what is right. Life can't be reduced to black and white, Abie. There are too many variables, and being inconsistent is sometimes needed to survive."

"So let Fedya go. You and Armand know enough people in high places that would build a fence around her. I don't think the government will be willing to take on both the labor movement and the suffragettes if they go against my sister. She's too well known. I don't see a problem."

"Well, the problem is that she loves him and she is pregnant by him. They're being married here quietly by a rabbi tomorrow, but they also need to be married in a municipal court under assumed names as soon as possible. They need papers to get a marriage license. They need new identities quickly so they can get out of the country. They want to go to Palestine."

"I know people who can do this. Let it be my wedding present to the happy couple." He laughed. "I'll make sure they have very American names."

"The wedding is tomorrow at three. Come if you like, and bring Virginia and Leo. This animosity must end. I leave it to you."

When Rachelan and Fedya said they wanted a judge to marry them because Fedya did not believe in God, Jonah made it clear that if his daughter was to marry a Jewish man, believer or not, she would do it properly and modestly in the presence of a rabbi. She immediately pointed out that he and Marta were married by a judge. Jonah countered with the fact that Marta was not Jewish, and that it had nothing to do with this matter. Though she found this yet another inconsistency in the man's way of thinking, she saw that he was so emphatic in his insistence that she acquiesced. Though she knew that her father had a long standing argument with God, tradition was foundational.

Jonah and Marta knew of a young rabbi named Mordecai Kaplan, who had gained some notoriety in their community for his radical religious and political views. Rabbi Kaplan had recently officiated at services at the newly opened Jewish Center in Manhattan. They met him right before he was invited to leave by the synagogue board for the very same reasons that attracted Jonah and Marta to one of his services. Jonah found Kaplan's ideas, ideas that suggested that God was not a personal God, and that God was the power that enables a human to fulfill him or herself, unique, provocative, and interesting enough to pursue a relationship with this young man.

Mordecai Kaplan was young enough to be one of Jonah's sons, and two years after joining him, at The Society for the Advancement of Judaism which Kaplan had formed, Jonah and Marta were invited to witness the very first bat mitzvah ever held, with Rabbi Kaplan's daughter Judith, reading from the Torah.

That Sabbath, Jonah heard the rabbi insist that our continued existence as a people had more to do with our feelings of Peoplehood than it did because of a belief in God. This was indeed a radical idea that made Kaplan a pariah in the religious community, but it did resonate with Jonah. "Our concept of God has changed over the centuries," the rabbi taught, "but our experience of being one with other Jews had not." Jonah saw truth in this. He knew that God was one, and now he also believed that the Jewish people were one, unified, inseparable. That explained so much of why he behaved as he did. He had always felt this way but never verbalized it. God was there, but just out there. It was the people who factored into his life. But what really resonated with Jonah was that here was a scholarly man, a man who grew up in the same Orthodox tradition as he, who had also given himself permission to think of God not as he was taught by the tradition, but in an entirely new way. In fact, Jonah could sit at this rabbi's service and not feel the least bit guilty about not believing in the God of the Torah. Yes, he could believe in God, but now another had confirmed that he didn't have to believe as he had been taught. His dilemma was over. Now he was being taught that Judaism was a religious civilization that was held together by tradition, language, and the culture of a distinct people. Yes, much of this civilization rested on God's existence, but Jonah finally understood that the tradition, language, and culture could also flourish without believing in the God of the Torah. God did exist, but now he could see God as the power in the cosmos that gave human life the direction that enabled humanity to become self-fulfilled. This Jewish Civilization could exist just as well with this concept of God as with any other. That was it. He felt as if a great weight had been lifted off his shoulders.

After the ceremony, standing before those of his children and grandchildren who were present at this hastily arranged marriage of his eldest daughter, he looked at the supper table and raised his kiddish cup. "Endless, Existence, fountain of all life. The earth has given us its bounty, and from this wealth. We have crushed grapes and we have fermented wine. We are grateful to you, Source of all life for the wine that warms our bodies, gladdens our hearts, and sustains our spirits." Similar blessings over the bread followed. In Jonah's theology, all man could do was to be grateful for what has been created and expect nothing else. No miracles, no interventions, no disappointments, no rage at being disappointed.

In March of 1920, the American Civil Liberties Union, received anonymous papers attesting to illegal practices of the United States Department of Justice, detailing the unlawful practice of entrapment, of secret detainments, of denial of rights, of unlawful seizures without search warrants, and the use of provocateurs when arresting radicals and those suspected of supporting un-American ideologies.

That May, a detailed report was submitted to the new Acting Secretary of Labor, Louis Freeland Post, who cancelled more than 2,000 warrants as being illegal. The report made official what was charged anonymously, and Palmer was given a hearing. In June, Massachusetts District Court Judge George Anderson wrote, "a mob is a mob, whether made up of Government officials acting under instructions from the Department of Justice, or of criminals and loafers and the vicious classes." Palmer's teeth had been filed down. Armand read the newspapers accounts of the report and the court's decisions and smiled contentedly.

"Did you have anything to do with that report, like being that anonymous person?" Aaron asked him at dinner one evening.

"To do such a thing would have been an act of disloyalty to my superiors," he said, and continued eating his soup. Aaron's eyes danced with admiration for his big brother.

CHAPTER 17

June 25, 1920

Dearest Family,

    First off, Fedya and I want to especially thank Abe and his friends for their help, and we also want to thank you, Papa and Marta, for the clothing and money that allowed us to move through the crowds as if we were rich people. It seems that rich people are not scrutinized the way poor people are. Those clothes are now packed away because they are really out of place here, but perhaps one day we shall need them again.

    We sailed from New York to Liverpool as Mr. and Mrs. Edward Davidson. Fedya decided not to grow his beard back, and I like him like that. He doesn't look quiet so fierce or foreign now. Life continues to grow within me, and we are looking forward to beginning our lives as a family in Palestine.

    Because we appeared to be Christian Americans as we traveled, I felt kind of free and invisible. I imagine that's how you feel when you run the world and you write the history books.

    We are fortunate that the war is over and immigration has resumed, although the devastation is readily apparent. It will take years for Europe to heal, and I'm not sure it ever will. You can see the desperation and resentment on the faces you pass.

I'm glad we are Americans. I'm glad you and Mama did what you could to bring us all to safety.

From England we took the boat to France, and then the train south to the coast. I remember the train when we left France so long ago, and how excited and frightened I was. We were not questioned very much at any borders, and because we said we were on our honeymoon, we were accorded great courtesies, especially when we landed and stayed for a time in Sicily before sailing to Palestine. The Sicilians were particularly kind, and I was wondering if that had something to do with Abe's friends or was it just because Italians are really nice people. Again, thank you, dear brother. Finally, after weeks over land and sea, we reached Haifa where we were greeted as tourists. Sadly, that was not the case for other Jews trying to get into the country. We are eternally grateful for the money you gave us because so many of the people have so very little, and money does get you whatever you need.

The British are very suspicious of Jews and you can see that they don't like us entering because they fear the reprisals of the Arabs and for good reason. There is a man named Hassan al-Banna who is appealing to the Arabs here with the message that it is the nature of Islam to dominate, and not be dominated, and that Islam should impose its law on all nations, even to the entire world. He's Egyptian and his goal is to restore the old Caliphate and unify the Muslim world into a global Islamic empire. His speeches terrify the Arabs with the horrors of hell for anyone who does not want to return to the purest behaviors demanded by the Koran. He calls for a final holy war against Jews and the rest of the world. The British are also viewed as "the rest of the world" and the Arabs have become even more hostile since Britain issued the Balfour Declaration, establishing a national home for the Jewish people in Palestine. You'd think the British authority here would be more supportive of their own country's vision for us, but they are not. In fact, the British are turning a blind eye to al-Banna's activities. Al-Banna's men have been stealing weapons, secretly training fighters, and forming secret assassination squads that have supporters in the army and in the police department. Even in the short time we've been here we have learned this and can see the handwriting on the wall. The Arabs are bringing pogroms like the ones in Russia and Poland into Palestine. I'm not sure if the newspapers are covering this in America, but Arab marauders recently attacked the Tel Hai Settlement killing a man named Joseph Trumpeldor and seven of his comrades who had decided to be the first armed Jewish resistance fighters. After this terrible loss, a defense force they call the Hagana was formed to defend Jewish life and property. Fedya is a volunteer. I worry whenever he goes off, and I'm very proud of him at the same time. Arab riots have broken out all over, and most recently forty-five Jews were murdered at a hostel for new immigrants in Jaffa. You'd think the British would respond to protect us, but Sir Herbert Samuel, the high commissioner who, by the way is Jewish and usually supportive, responded by suspending Jewish immigration to appease Arab grievances. Arabs show their grievances by murdering innocent people. We show our grievances by writing petitions to the government. It's who we are, and it's who they are. But enough of that.

Fedya and I are happy to have met so many Russians, Poles, Americans, and Frenchmen who have also come here with the dream of revitalizing our ancient land once more. We were thinking of moving onto one of the agricultural kibbutzim, but Feyda and I think that our experience in organizations can be better used elsewhere. My dear husband has found employment with the Histadrut, the labor union, and because of his socialist and now Zionist ideas, it's a good fit. Here, such ideas are honored, and he does not have to fear brutalization or prison as he did in America. Fedya has come intellectually and spiritually home. As for myself, we've set ourselves up in a little apartment in Jerusalem, and I'm very happy. We are busy learning Hebrew, which was established as a common tongue because there are just so many people from so many parts of the world here, and this is a good way of unifying the people, though each day I find myself also speaking English, French, and Russian with neighbors or in the markets. We and people like us are quickly becoming Jewish Palestinians like we became Americans, but ethnically, everyone seems to cling to our historic roots as a source of tradition, comfort, and remembering who we are.

The people we are meeting are not particularly religious, and I can see in the future a conflict between the secular people who are the people who come to work and build, and those who are here because this is where they want to be when the Messiah comes to bring redemption. But the bulk of those who are coming now, the Zionist youth, believe that redemption comes only from working the land. I personally believe that it is just as important to do all I can to ease the way for other Jews to find refuge. It seems that knowing so many languages fluently, and being an American, also has its advantages. Having our own land is the only way we might have some degree of safety. Your friend, Herzl, was right Papa. People come here because they want to establish for themselves the just and egalitarian society the European Enlightenment promised, but in reality, denied to us. People just want to be safe and unafraid.

With Love,
Rachelann and Fedya

CHAPTER 18

1920

Right after Abe and Joey spoke in Rosey's candy store, and before the Volstead Act imposed Prohibition on a disparaging public, they and their friends had begun hijacking the final deliveries to liquor stores, bars, and hotels and storing the stolen bottles in the candy store basement. So, by the time the 18th Amendment became law, there were stacks of wooden crates piled up that were just waiting to be poured from the familiar liquor bottles into pint cream and quart milk bottles painted white. Abe, Harry, and Joey laughed over the wording of the law, because while it read that while the act forbade the manufacture or sale of intoxicating liquor, it never specifically prohibited the use of intoxicating liquor.

Abe and Harry's winnings at the track, plus money that Abe had saved from the concession business, was more than enough to entice old man Hegamann and his daughter to sell his burned out dairy to an unknown buyer without asking too many questions. Joey was right and the fire caused just enough damage to the back of the dairy to push Hegemann into a panic. Though the entire back of the dairy was destroyed, the front part, the part where the milk and cream were bottled, was intact and could continue functioning as a dairy which was exactly what Abe, Sam, and Joey wanted. A legitimate business could be run in the store out front which would now be known as the White Mountain Dairy. The money garnered through delivering the liquor could be laundered there and also in the candy store, the fish market next to it, and the concessions.

Joey had contracted with Italian day laborers to rebuild the back of the dairy and increase its size to handle large stills and holding tanks. They hired men who had worked for legitimate distilleries who were looking for places where they could ply the only craft they knew and continue to feed their families. Each was suddenly very loyal to their new employers. Abe and Joey congratulated themselves on providing good American and immigrant craftsmen with jobs, and had a good laugh over it. But they also laughed at the stupidity of a government that would take a legitimate industry that employed thousands of people, put them out of work, and turn such a lucrative venture over to crooks who would make enormous profits by taking the business underground. Abe loved the idea of giving these workers jobs, and the act was spurred not only by a profit motive, but by an imagination that took him back to that old childhood fantasy where he would swoop in and save the people from the dragon. To him, the government had become a dragon; he the hero.

Mostly, it was a cash and carry venture, and the books were kept in Harry's head. Where legitimate documents such as deeds were needed, it was Armand who advised Abe privately, while Bernstein and Pambino set up the White Mountain Dairy Corporation as a holding company where the three became silent partners in order to be protected in case the operation went south. To protect himself and his career, Armand never met Abe or Harry in public because for Armand to move up in his chosen career path and in the political hierarchy, it would be best for people not to know that Abe Chernov was his half-brother. He had separated himself and his name from Ezra's by going to Harvard Law School and setting up a law practice in Boston. Now that he was back in New York with the Department of Justice, it was best that his relationship to

Abe and Harry Chernov be kept within the family and out of public scrutiny.

The boys who grew up with Abe, Harry, and Joey gathered one night in the candy store and were invited into an enterprise that they knew would help them earn some real money. They were pleased to initially take on the jobs vacated by some of Hegemann's drivers when the dairy closed down for renovations after the fire. The old gang, loyal to Abe and Joey, canvassed the neighborhood to urge the renewal of service for old customers, and impress upon new ones the benefits of the expanded services of the White Mountain Dairy. Few resisted. The stolen liquor they had warehoused in the basement was ready to be poured into pints and quarts once the law took effect, and they were able to make deliveries within a day of the White Mountain Dairy opening its doors for business. Yes, the regular milk and cream bottles rattled and clanged against the steel cradles in which they were carried early in the morning, and in addition to the daily delivery, there might be another bottle that brought a smile to whoever opened the metal containers on the doorstep.

Abe immediately knew that others would have similar ideas, and this was proven true when three thugs arrived from Detroit looking for someone to invest in an idea of speed boating liquor across Lake Michigan from Canada to Detroit. Abe, hearing of the plan and liking it, agreed to pay for the enterprise under the condition that the three would come to work for him. But Harry convinced him that if the liquor was delivered to Detroit, there were too many risks of it being hijacked by others getting into the business. So Abe had the idea that if the liquor could be brought in from England, and off loaded onto speedboats near the coast of Long Island, they would be in a better place to oversee the storage and distribution around the city to the bars, hotels, and brothels. The Detroit trio complained, but Mendy and Al convinced them that they should take their complaints quietly back to Michigan.

Profits from the imports suddenly made the dairy seem a small change operation, but Abe, Harry, and Joey saw it as a public service for the community. And because the three felt a strong commitment, they created an organization called the East New York Benevolent Society, where all the different people from all the different smaller societies could reach out to them for low interest loans for education, weddings, or medical expenses.

Other opportunities presented themselves as the Volstead Act tightened its grip. Speakeasies, private clubs that were hidden from the eyes of the police, started to spring up all over the city, and because Abe could ease his way in both back alleys and boardrooms, everyone knew that he was the go to guy if they wanted a steady supply of good imported liquor for these secret enterprises. The boys selected places in Manhattan and Brooklyn, some in the most elegant parts of town and some in the seediest. Generally, the underpaid and understaffed police were well paid to glance the other way, and they did. On those occasions when there was a raid, Abe was always informed which club was targeted a day or two before the police came down on it. Naturally, there was no trace of anything illegal, and the tea cups that usually held gin, whiskey, or scotch, actually held tea when the cops arrived.

Though Abe was never brought into a courtroom, colleagues less astute and connected were, and on such occasions, they called upon Abe and his resources for help. In many instances, Abe and Joey paid Pambino and Bernstein quietly for their defense of friends, but when Joey was hauled before a judge, and the business threatened, Abe went to Armand with a hypothetical, and using that hypothetical, Armand suggested that Abe's associate refuse to speak because the Fifth Amendment of the Constitution declared that he did not have to incriminate himself. Abe brought this idea to Pambino and Bernstein and this ploy, though never having been tried in a court of law before, worked. Joey got off, and Pambino and Bernstein became the go to lawyers for the underworld. The success of taking the Fifth gave gangsters of all stripes a legal recourse that was eventually supported by the Supreme Court.

Abe, Harry, and Joey had another good laugh, and Armand, privately, smiled.

Sally, Abe's first hire, took over the concession business and was compensated very well for her skills. She also took it upon herself to let regular customers know that she knew of young ladies who would be interested in making the acquaintance of nice men if such men were so inclined. She even had cards printed with a particular phone number where the connections could be made. Eventually, she suggested to Abe and Joey that they consider opening up brothels in addition to the speakeasies. She would be in charge of these and someone else could run the concession. She had amassed a sizable clientele from all walks of life, and all were satisfied and repeat customers. But, unlike Harry, who carried everything in his head, Sally kept a detailed client book that she knew would keep her out of prison if it ever came to that. She was now a full member of the team.

In every precinct of New York City where the team set up either a speakeasy or a brothel, the beat cops and the supervisors on their payroll who appeared at the doors out of uniform were treated like royalty.

The people who resented the restrictions the government imposed on their freedom became increasingly sympathetic to the bootleggers and any other group that seemed a proxy army fighting against a stupid law. Part of that reaction manifested itself in the loosening morality of the general population, much to the consternation of the stalwart ladies who got the vote and used that vote to pressure the passage of the Prohibition Amendment.

As a symbol of the general population's response, the cocktail was invented and became the choice drink of the day among the social elite, while illicit gin and whisky remained the choice of the general population. Cocktail parties became a popular happening in the best of homes, while a bottle of schnapps was standard in many American living rooms. In hidden away speakeasies that the general public frequented when they could, the music was hot and the women were easy. In the nightclubs in Manhattan where the Jazz Age fully bloomed, flappers with rouged knees, bobbed hair, and stockings rolled down, stood on tables and would shimmy shake the night away in beaded dresses that they lifted well above their knees. Woman could smoke in public, drink with impunity, and vote. And while lesser known jazz musicians wailed in sound baffled cellars that were out of earshot of those who might complain, Count Basie and Duke Ellington backed up Billie Holiday and Lena Horn in Harlem. Impresarios like Florenz Ziegfeld treated the elite and not so elite to the likes of Fanny Brice, Jimmy Durante, and Eddie Cantor. Jerome Kern transformed Broadway for all time with a racially mixed cast in *Show Boat* that starred Paul Robson. Sleek Art Deco adorned fast rising skyscrapers, and the steel spire of the Chrysler Building looked down from its own place in the heavens benevolently on sophisticated ladies and the dandies on their arms.

This New York belonged to the Chernovs. Abe and Harry, their illicit businesses thriving, moved with effortless ease among the well healed elite as well as the underbelly of society. The city also belonged to Jonah and Marta, with season seats at the Metropolitan Opera, at Carnegie Hall, opening nights on Broadway, and dinner parties at their home for friends. Zeena continued to be a diva in the legitimate theater, and Elizabeth and Nathaniel, married with children, continued to concertize privately while expanding Seligman's into one of the great department store chains in the country. Maurice was a professor of economics, rising in stature at Colombia, David was something of a Broadway impresario, Armand was a lawyer with the Department of Justice, and Sam was becoming a painter of note. Aaron was excelling in high school with an eye towards Harvard, and Fanny continued to flit from flower to flower like a desperate hummingbird, but always in the fashion of the moment and always exquisitely quaffed.

CHAPTER 19

1921- Jerusalem

"Do not imagine, Mr. Davidson, that we do not know that the Jews are gun-running and secretly arming themselves against Arab attack. And, do not imagine that we are not aware of this Hagana as you call it. Illegal guns are coming into Palestine, and we are resolved to find out the extent to which this Hagana has met with success." The British commander lit a cigarette and smugly smiled at the sad eyed man before him who put his hands in his lap so his interrogator would not see them shaking. "That's what we'd like you to tell us." Feyda looked down at the cup of tea placed before him, but did not touch it. How British of the British to offer tea at an interrogation, he mused.

"I know nothing of what you speak," he said hesitantly, "but since you raised this issue, and if your information is correct, kindly tell me what else are the Jews supposed to do?" Fedya regarded the British as biased oppressors who may have been supportive on paper, but in reality had caved into every Arab demand that was made of them for fear of violent reprisals and loss of face.

The commander dismissed the question with an imperious wave of his hand. "We are told that machine guns have reached your larger colonies. Is that true?"

"Let me answer your question by first making you aware of something," Feyda said, and feeling more confident, took a sip of the tea. "We Jews saw little need for protecting ourselves because we thought the British Government in Palestine would do that for us. We are now painfully aware that your Home Office demanded that the process of developing a Jewish homeland be slowed down and that no appearance of bias to the Jews was to be shown. Because your Home Office would not allow the British troops to protect us as they should have because you did not want to appear as taking sides against the Arabs, the riot last year in Jerusalem that you did not stop saw Jews massacred. What more proof did we need that Jews would receive not only inadequate protection from your military administration, but little sympathy. Most recently, the outbreak of hostilities in Jaffa garnered again a tepid response to protect Jewish lives and property from the Arab marauders. The British forced us to conclude that we can only depend on ourselves."

"Then you are telling me that there is an organized gun-running operation going on?"

"I am telling you nothing of the sort," Fedya responded, his voice rising. "I'm a labor organizer with the Histadrut from a kibbutz that grows oranges and pomelows and I now reside in Jerusalem with my wife and family. What would I know of gun-running?"

"We have it on good authority that you also dabble in the import and export business. Is that true?"

"It is true that I do have an interest in exporting fruits and vegetables grown here to other nations, but that has nothing to do with gun-running, I assure you. Besides, wouldn't that be against the law?" Fedya smiled. "What I will tell you is this. The Arabs have shown over and over again an unwillingness to live side by side with us, and they resolve to murder every Jew in Palestine. Even the Egyptian Expeditionary Force Commanders and your own General Lawrence have stated so much." He paused.

"Let me ask you this. If massacres of British troups were being planned by the Arabs, and the Jews, who were charged to protect you, were not going to protect you, would you not break your own law to protect your own?" Fedya waited and continued when he did not get a response. "I have nothing to do with guns, but I do see what is happening around me and what is not. We have as much right to be here as they have, but while they want to kill us, we want to live in peace, and the British are not willing to come to our aid and protect us. That's the long and the short of it. I think you will appreciate a statement in one of our holy books that says, 'If a man comes to slay you, slay him first.' Does Britain deny us the right to protect ourselves?"

The commander sat down facing Fedya and changed his tactic. "I sympathize with your people," he began feigning sincerity, "and you must know that the British support of Zionist aspirations are steadfast. I have read the Balfour Declaration, and I know that his Majesty's Government views with favor the establishment of a National Homeland for the Jewish People in Palestine, and I know that we will not abandon that dream in the face of Arab threats or terror." He paused, thinking he had disarmed the ignorant Jew in front of him with his support and charm. "But you and your people must also understand that there is a step by step process involved here. We believe that the only way to stop Arab violence against your people is to slow down Zionist progress. And, to make the Arabs less fearful of you, we need to stem the flow of guns into Palestine."

"Nothing will make the Arabs less fearful except our complete destruction. You know that as well as I," Fedya shot back. "Our dream needs momentum, and if it is slowed or stopped to appease the Arabs, our dream will die. If the Jews are secretly arming themselves, they do so because Zionist aspirations do not involve killing Arabs, but Arab aspirations do involve killing Jews. I say that again so you will fully appreciate our predicament and our process. We must protect ourselves because the world has shown us that they will not and we have only ourselves. It has been three years since the Great

War ended, and the Jewish People are no closer to the national homeland promised than we were before the war began. You and the allies divided up the Ottoman Empire, and you are creating nations arbitrarily without any consideration given to who will be living side by side in these random borders. Already, the land mass you designated to the Jewish People has shrunk under Arab pressure. Not only did you give the Transjordan which is seventy-eight percent of Palestine to Emir Abdullah, you are beginning to place a quota on Jewish immigration. So how could we trust that you will protect us against the Arabs and help us create a nation for ourselves? You will not face the Arab obstructionists, and we are dedicated to overcome them. Our dream will not and cannot die. It is our future, and what will save us as a people. It appears that while you gave us this dream, you will not stand by us and help us fight for that dream. Your way of dealing with the situation will destroy us, and that's why we must fight this enemy ourselves." He paused. "And if that means that we must arm ourselves to protect our lives and our dream, so be it."

"I may or may not sympathize with you Jews on this question," the commander said, reverting back to his original tone and stance. "My opinion on the Jew/Arab matter is of no importance. But I am charged with investigating the illegal Zionist gun-running into Palestine."

"And what of the illegal guns that are arming the Arabs?" Fedya countered. "Do you have an opinion on that?"

"Certainly, we cannot ignore what either of you people are doing because to ignore it is to acknowledge our ignorance of it and our inability to stop it. Of course, we can put a stop to it with British bayonets, but that would turn both of your capacity for violence towards us. We do not wish to give you both a common enemy, so it is my personal belief that we should go after the weaker of the two. If we found these hidden caches of arms on either side, it doesn't change the reasons for the hostility. Personally, I would turn a blind eye to the entire matter and let you people blast one another to hell. But, this illegal gun-running is a slur on my administration of this protectorate, on the War Office, and on the British Commonwealth. I cannot let that happen."

The commander stood. "You are free to go, Mr. Davidson, but know that we are watching you."

Rachelann lit the Sabbath lights as her mother and as her mother's mother did before her. Fedya, smiling at his beloved wife's face, radiant in the twin flickering candles, joyfully anticipating the time when she would give birth to their second child due in few months. For Fedya, Zionism had replaced Judaism, as Socialism had replaced Judaism when he was younger. But he had no difficulty allowing the traditions of Judaism to be celebrated in his home. Rachelann appreciated his support, and loved him even more for it.

Fedya had not told her that he had been interrogated by the miliary because he did not want to alarm her or cause her undo stress. But, he thought it important that she know that the British were embarking on a crusade to stop the flow of guns to the Resistance. As a member of the Histradut, the union that sponsored the Hagana, someone had to find Eliyahu Golomb so this leader could be told of the British pressure to come. Rachelann listened intently to him, and knowing that their apartment might be watched and Fedya might be followed, she suggested that he dress up as an Orthodox priest and search for Golomb. The following day, Rachelann purchased black material to make him a frock and hat, as well as a wooden cross to hang around his neck. He wore his own clothes under the disguise. Confident that he would never be stopped, he exited though the back door of the apartment building and made his way to the union office where he waited for a trusted colleague to tell him where Golomb could be found.

CHAPTER 20

July 8, 1921

Dearest Family,

    Forgive me my anger in writing this letter, but I am enraged at the British who are daily proving to us that they are Jew-haters at their core despite what they say. Most recently, they've issued something called the White Paper which places the first official quota on Jewish immigration. On top of that, they have elevated a rabid Jew-hater named al-Husseini to the position of Grand Mufti of Jerusalem, despite his role for inciting the anti-Jewish riots that were going on when we arrived two years ago. Jews, here in Jerusalem and in Jaffa, were attacked, raped, and murdered in those pogroms.

    Dear family, what Israel is most in need of are guns to help us fight back. The British, in addition to putting quotas on Jews, are also trying to stop the flow of arms to Jews, while turning a blind eye to the surrounding Arab nations arming the followers of al-Husseini. We have friends in other countries, but money is desperately needed to buy guns, and means of avoiding the blockade are also needed. If there is anything you can do, or any people you know who are willing to help us, I beg you to contact them.

    Though there is much grief, there is also joy. Our little Liora, is growing stronger each day, and she has reddish hair just like her grandmother, for whom she is named. We were glad to read that President Harding signed Congress' joint resolution, giving formal American approval to the establishment in Palestine of a national home for the Jewish people, though the Congress made it clear that it is moral support only. We are also glad that the League of Nations incorporated the Balfour Declaration into its final approval of the British mandate over Palestine. Yet with this news comes the reality that the British High Commissioner of Palestine, Sir Herbert Samuel, a Jew and someone who had been a Zionist sympathizer and who had done so much to employ new arrivals in building projects, has now appointed that same rabid Jew-hater, al-Husseini, as president of the Supreme Muslim Council. This makes him not only the key religious leader here, but now gives him the administrative and financial power to do whatever he wishes. I cannot imagine the kind of pressure Mr. Churchill, as the British Colonial Secretary, put on Samuel for him to make that appointment. England has created a monster that will turn on them as surely as he is turning on us. And speaking of Churchill, in addition to establishing quotas limiting Jewish immigration in that White Paper he issued, the British Government has also restricted the Jewish National Home to the area west of the Jordan River. Little by little, Arab pressure on England has pushed them to erode the promise of the land that was promised to us. Now we've not only lost the Trans-Jordan east of the Jordan River, but they've limited us to land west of the river. Can they take any more from us? England is not a friend to the Jews, and like the French, never will be.

I am sorry to sound so angry, but I am afraid. Please see what you can do.

Love,
Rachelann, Fedya, and Liora
PS. Our baby will be here soon.

CHAPTER 21

1923

Sadie Chernov stood behind her husband of a year, shaking her head at the canvas and making no comment other than to say, "Do me up; I'll be late."

"Where are you off to tonight?" Sam responded, seemingly more interested in the final brush strokes he was applying than to the woman who stood behind him. He swivelled around and looked at the girl from the old neighborhood he had married when she told him she was pregnant. Against the warnings about the kind of family she came out of, he did what he thought was the honorable thing to do. But in the fifth month she miscarried, and now, two people who had pretty much nothing in common save a thorough enjoyment of one another's body, lived in what one might call a marriage of convenience. Each took what each needed. They had their own friends, and their own interests. Sam's friends were artists, men and women in the forefront of the avant-guard, experimenters with far fetched possibilities on canvas and in stone or metal. Because of the social conscience that had been inculcated in his early years, he continued to view the terrible living conditions of the poor that existed in his own city. He continued his compulsion to remind the world of what existed with paintings he called "his ongoing social realism phase," much to the chagrin of his fellow artists.

Sadie's friends were what Jonah called floosies who cared for nothing other than having a good time, shopping, and drinking. Jonah had offered to pay for a divorce and even the religious dissolution of the marriage, but Sadie wouldn't hear of it. She had married into a family that took her off Pitkin Avenue, and she wasn't about to go back to it. Besides, she knew the hold she had over Sam as long as Sam didn't look elsewhere. Besides, if Sam ever ran out of money, there was always Abe and Harry to back him up.

For an artist, Sam was doing well. Now that Sadie had some money in her pocket, the girl with the naturally sandy colored hair had bleached out the softness and was now a platinum blond. Her marcelled waves were held down this evening with a rhinestone headband supporting a pale green feather. Tonight, she wore a pair of billowing multicolored harem pants, tight at the ankles and a forest green top that one might say was suggestive. She had styled herself on movie starlets of the time, and even fancied herself to be one of them. As far as Sam was concerned, he liked her brassy look, despite knowing that he was a means to an end. As long as he had the money, he didn't mind what she spent on clothes as long as he could remove them whenever he felt the need and take her to bed.

As Sam buttoned her up, he looked beyond her at the canvas he had just finished. It was new and unique; unlike anything he had done before. It was a city scape with an elevated train weaving through a skyline, but while anyone who looked at it could discern what it was, they would immediately see that the buildings seemed transparent and haphazardly arranged at fantastic angles, giving the impression that you could see multiple facets of the structures with one glance. Overlaying and underlaying these structures were suggestions of people who, like the buildings, also seemed transparent. All seemed connected organically. But the people weren't really people, but suggestions of people: vague, diaphanous, more like spirts than living beings. What struck him most from this vantage point was the dynamic forward movement that the fluid lines and brilliant colors had created. He smiled at the thought that if these images were real, the entire image would fly off the canvas.

"I think I like it," she said finally, "but do you think anyone will buy it? I mean look at the colors. Who has colors like that in a livingroom?"

Sam fought the urge to once again try to explain that you don't buy art to match your curtains, because that was not a concept she could understand. Nor would he once again explain why it was foolish to say that her six year old niece could do sketches as good as Picasso's or Miro's. "The people who understand what I'm doing here will appreciate it," he said after expelling a breath that revealed his frustration.

"Okay, tell me what you're trying to do. I'm not stupid you know," she said seeing the expression on his face and hearing the familiar sigh. "I'm only asking this because if you try to sell it, people will want to know what it means. It's like when you ask me why I bought this or that dress. You want to know what I liked about it. You know buyers like to tell their friends why the art they buy is art."

Sam made some final dabs, put his name and date at the lower right hand corner, and stood back. "Okay, this is how it works. In this painting, I'm sharing an experience with you. We're sharing something intimate, from my mind to yours. Sadie, from the time we are born till the time we die, we're flooded with images that get recorded in our brains. They never leave us, but get piled up one upon another, and the way our minds mix these memories becomes what compels our imaginations. You following me? In this painting, I'm communicating my memories of the city, the emotions I feel for it, through what can only exist from a dream state. This is a dream of what a city is for me, made up of real images woven into a tapestry by my subconscious."

"Sammy," she said. "I don't know what the hell you're talking about. The other paintings you do, I can understand. I know a person and a building when I see one. But this, I'm not so sure. Oh, God, look at the time. Sammy, honey, I need some money," she said, with a slight coquettish pout that Sam could never resist. "I'll try to be home early, but if I'm not, I'll wake you up when I do."

Sammy's Story

Sammy Chernov had moved into the big house on Fifth Avenue with his father, his sisters, and his brothers. His new stepmother and new stepbrother, Armand, were very nice to him, but he missed the hustle and bustle of Brownsville, and the kids he played with in the streets. There weren't any kids to play with on Fifth Avenue, and you couldn't draw a skully box on the sidewalk, or play marbles in the dirt, or choose up a game of tag, or stick ball, or red light green light, or Johnny on the Pony. All the kids he saw never seemed to run or jump or fall down. Kids his age seemed always to be dressed up and parading with old women he was told were called governesses. Why would anyone want a governess when you had a mother to call you in when it was time for dinner? So, when the weather was inclement, he, Maurice, and Fanny played hide and seek in the big house and there were plenty of places to hide. And when the weather was nice, he would go across the street to the big park, climb up on the surrounding stone walls and try to keep his balance walking on the rim for as long as he could. The governesses passing looked at him askance, and hurried their charges away, but Sammy could see in the faces of the kids longing to get up on the wall with him to see how long they could balance themselves. More than the park, the one thing that he loved most, a thing that Brownsville did not have, was the big art museum practically across the street from where he lived. The first time he went there he was with Maurice, and he was in awe of the men working there to change something that looked like one thing into another thing. Maurice said that they were taking away the Gothic and making it into something that sounded like bozart. He would not know it was spelled Beaux Art until he started studying architectural styles many years later. But Maurice knew stuff like that, and no one knew how he knew. Maurice taught him that the front of the building was called a facade, and designed by an architect named Hunt, but was now being completed by his son. So with or without Maurice to tell him what he needed to know, Sam would walk across the street and down the block, climb the massive steps and sit at the top just watching the people pass by, imagining who they were and wondering if they were wondering who he was. One day as he sat there, an elderly man approached him. "Little man," the stranger said, "I've noticed for some time that you come here and just sit, but you never go in. Why is that?"

"I ain't got no money," Sam replied to what he considered a foolish question.

"I don't have any money," the man said, correcting him.

"You ain't got no money either? You can sit with me if you wanna," Sam replied as he moved over even though there was no one else on the steps.

The old man laughed and extended his hand. "Then I'll take you in. It will be my treat." Sam's eyes widened, and he took the gentleman's hand and went through the massive bronze doors into a room that was the largest room Sam had ever seen. Before him was the largest staircase he had ever seen with at least a thousand steps. Sam hesitated, stalled by a wave of fear and awe washing over him.

"My name is Luigi Palma di Cesnola," said the elderly man, extending his hand to the little auburn haired boy with piercing brown eyes, "and I was once in charge of this place. So from now on, whenever you want to come in to my museum, you give the lady at the desk a card I shall give you, and you won't have to pay anything."

"You must be really important to have such a big name, Mr. Nola." The last part of the name was all Sam could remember. The elderly gentleman laughed again at the child's innocence, and extended his hand.

"Thanks Mr. Nola," Sammy replied standing up. "But can my brother come too because he really knows a lot of stuff and he can tell me about what I'm looking at. He told me that this building was a bozart, and that all buildings have a front called a facade and that means that my house has a facade and everybody's house has a facade because everybody's house has a front. I thought of that myself."

"You are a very bright little boy, and your brother sounds like a very bright little boy, too. Of course he can come in with you."

Mr. di Cesnola, reached into his pocket and produced a silver card case, and moved over to the reception desk. The dour woman at the counter looked up and immediately stood. "Good day, Mr. di Cesnola. Have you come to admire your Cypriot antiquities? We are so grateful to you for making our museum their permanent home."

"Not today, Miss Townsand," he said. "Today I'm looking at the new Roman acquisitions, but before I go off, I'm giving this budding art scholar my card which will entitle him and his brother to be admitted free of charge."

Miss Townsand, looked over her pince-nez glasses at the smudged face looking up at her expectantly. Her eyes furrowed at the child who obviously had been playing in the dirt somewhere, and she looked back at Mr. di Cesnola questioningly. The former director saw the question in her eyes. "Let's you and I do for this child what this museum was designed to do. Let's open up the world to him. The city can absorb the cost of two admissions. In fact, when you see this little man and whoever he brings with him, just smile and wave them on. This way, the cash box will even out at the end of the day and only you and I will be the wiser." She nodded her agreement to his atypical request and smiled as best she could. "Besides, my dear Mildred, who knows what will be discovered by him here, and who knows what the world will discover from his being here?"

He turned back to Sammy. "Now my fine young man, you and I are going to see our new Roman acquisitions. Tell me, do you know anything about Rome?"

"The only thing I know is that my Papa keeps telling us that it wasn't built in a day."

Luigi di Cesnola laughed heartily and pointed first to the stone sarcophagus with the carvings of nymphs and pans. "This is called a sarcophagus," he said.

"I bet my brother Maurice knew that," Sam answered.

From that day on, whether Maurice or Fanny were with him, Sam spent as much time as he could at the Met. After Miss Townsand informed him and Maurice that good little boys always kept their faces washed and their nails and shoes clean when they come to the museum, the brothers made sure that they never appeared before her without checking each other out. Certainly, Sam never looked the way he did when they first met. He asked his father for a sketch book, and to his surprise, he had it the next day. It wasn't like living in Brooklyn where you learned not to ask for anything because the money was not there. Now there was money for sketch books and colored pencils. After school, he would go to the museum and pretend he was an art student by copying pictures he liked the way the real art students did. One day, he said to himself, he would be a real art student too. While Sam sketched, Maurice just wandered and relished this remarkable new life that he had been given.

Between Marta making sure he did his homework, and Maurice constantly challenging him with new information, and Miss Townsand correcting his speech and grammar, Sammy Chernov was evolving into something that he could never have become on the streets of Brownsville in the borough of Brooklyn. As time passed, Miss Townsand found herself reluctantly developing a fondness for the Chernov boys, and in the spring, Sam and Maurice brought her flowers from the back garden. She almost cried.

CHAPTER 22

1924

Zeena was thrilled with the invitation from the Austrian director, Max Reinhardt, to perform *Das Mirakel,* a 1911 play written by Karl Vollmoller and slated as the first production to be mounted in the Josefstadt Theater which Reinhardt himself had newly renovated. Zeena had seen the revival on Broadway only a few months before receiving his letter, and recalled being moved by the legend about a nun in the Middle Ages who runs away from her convent with a knight, and is ultimately accused of witchcraft for her mystical visions. During the nun's absence, the statue of the Virgin Mary comes to life and takes the nun's place until she can be returned safely. Zeena's response to Reinhardt was immediate, though she could not decide which part would be more demanding. She and Madame Chalfonte laughed at the idea, Chalfonte musing how deep Zeena would have to go into herself to find anything that hinted of piety or virginity. She also suggested that when she got to Austria to begin rehearsals, she could easily find a convent so as to better immerse herself in the role, but finding a virgin in Austria would be a very different story. They laughed till they cried.

The trip would also be a wonderful opportunity to visit Ruth, the sister whom she hadn't seen since a lifetime ago in Krivoser. Zeena was also eager to meet the older man whom

Ruth had married, the man who cared for her, and who had given her three children. She would also schedule her European itinerary in such a way that she would also visit Dora, Jonathan, and their children in Switzerland before rehearsals began in Vienna. David could see his parents again after so many years. She envisioned a wonderful reunion, her only discomfort was the thought of seeing her mother again. How many years had it been? At least thirty had passed, a generation, and certainly time enough to have given up the gnawing feeling of fear at the thought of the confrontation and recriminations that she had played in her head over the years. These she knew would ensue. She had played characters who confronted demons, evil people, and characters with great personal tragedy in their lives. She had successfully stepped into these roles, mastered them and overcame all these fictional foes. But Sarah Chernov was something else in her mind, and though Zeena had become admired and loved on two continents, she still would be viewed by her mother as a recalcitrant and ungrateful child. People, she had learned, get stuck at certain moments in time, and she had no doubt that where she was concerned, her mother had never moved beyond blaming her for bringing the world down upon the heads of the family by running away from Ezra. To ease her imaginary conversations with Sarah, Zeena had repeatedly conjured up her mother and told her that she was a tired old woman who could not hurt her or anyone else anymore. Yet here she was in her early fifties, still feeling like a child about to be scolded for mixing the milk and meat dishes. Zeena did not want to see her mother, but could not avoid it.

Dora had never lost touch after Sarah had taken Ruth to Vienna, so her younger sister's treatment could continue with Dr. Freud. In exchange for his ongoing treatment, Sarah agreed to become the cook and housekeeper for the Freud family. Dora wrote that Freud had diagnosed Ruth with something called "hysteria" that resulted from the rapes during the pogrom when she was twelve. Her fear of all except older men became deeply rooted in something Freud called an "unconscious." Dora wrote that she had read an abstract that Freud had written on the condition and treatment of a particular female patient, and though never mentioning Ruth's name, Dora immediately knew it was about her sister. Dora also wrote that Freud's abstract also noted that from time to time, the patient could revert and become the child she was before the horror of that long ago afternoon. The danger was also there that possibility she could revert to that afternoon in the barn if confronted with sexual trauma. Still, as long as she was kept protected and in a safe environment, she could be happy and led a normal life. Freud admitted that if he pressured the patient to come face to face with the truth of her early life, she could begin to heal, but that would risk her having to live daily with a knowledge that could destroy her sanity permanently. And what good would that do? He could prove his theory and gratify his ego, but not at the potential cost of his patient's sanity and life. So the abstract concluded that some memories, for the welfare and sanity of the patient, were better suppressed. But the analyst must understand that the recording of these memories are always there, and their effects may have other ramifications and reveal themselves in other ways. All this information, Dora conveyed to Zeena in a letter sent years ago.

One day, Freud had asked a friend over for lunch who was somewhat younger than he, and Dora walked over to him and calmly, sat down. Freud was surprised at Ruth's response. For some reason, she was not afraid, and Freud asked this friend, whose name was Frederick Kreitman, to return. This he did, and when he was there, Dora smiled and laughed as any normal young woman might. Freud used this budding friendship as Ruth's link to the world outside his office and the house. Rarely, would Ruth venture out of the house, and if she did, it was into the garden. Freud surmised that Ruth's sense of safety when with Frederick was in some way inexorably linked to the security and love she had felt when she was with her father. Ruth slowly began to return to reality, and eventually, Ruth, with Frederick Kreitman holding her arm, walked out of the garden.

The Deuzendorf idled in front of the Schnelibahn Terminus as Ruth and her husband sat expectantly waiting for David and Zeena to arrive. Frederick Kreitman, whose twisted grey moustache lifted with his smile at his wife's anticipation in seeing her sister and nephew after all these years, stood a little higher in his seat, watching the crowd emerging from the railway station. It was a lovely spring day for a reunion.

He did notice a flurry of activity near the entrance and knew that his famous sister-in-law had been recognized. He watched as a very conspicuous red feathered hat bobbed up and down as his chauffeur and a man in a bowler hat cleared a path to the car.

The chauffeur opened the door and Zeena and David climbed in, David removing his hat. Zeena was about to say something about the crowd when she suddenly grew silent at the sight of her little sister; the periwinkle blue eyes of her father's and her grandmother's red hair. Suddenly she and Ruth were dancing in the yard near the barn, or walking to town holding hands and singing. Zeena, who was always in control of her emotions, began to weep and embraced Ruth tenderly. Zeena did not know what had come over her. Ruth, who had no recollections of those years, looked confused and patted her sister's shoulder in an effort to comfort her. Zeena, who remembered everything in detail, envied her sister for having erased her early life.

Zeena regained her composure, introduced herself to Frederick, and introduced David to his aunt and uncle. "I know you from your picture," Ruth said. "I saw it when I visited your parents last fall. You have a beautiful family, and I'm sorry you could not bring them with you this trip, but now that we've met, I hope you will bring them the next time."

"I certainly look forward to that," replied David. "Right now, they are all into their own lives, and couldn't break away."

The luggage was strapped to the rear of the car by the porters, who were generously tipped. The chauffeur started the motor, honked to get people out of the way, and slowly began to move.

"Frederick," Ruth said, "if we hurry, we can be at the Hoher Markat before noon and see the figures all displayed on the clock at the same time." She turned around to Zeena and David, a childlike quality of excitement in her voice. "I never tire of seeing it. It's the oldest market in Vienna, and it has such pretty things to look at. Then we can go to the Café Central for chocolate and pastry." She was like an excited child, and Zeena and David looked at each other with a questions in their eyes. Ruth had become what in those days was called, "a great beauty," and despite her years, she still was. Her shape remained slender, despite having given birth to three children, and her features were still soft and youthful. It was almost as if the child within her that revealed itself at moments of excitement, insisted on not allowing itself to age.

"All in good time, my dear," Frederick said to his wife solicitously as he patted her knee. I'm sure our guests would like to rest after their journey."

Zeena saw her sister acquiesce to her husband's suggestion and somewhat deflate, and insisted that she was famished and would love a nice cup of chocolate or coffee and a piece of Viennese pastry. She also said that she would love to see the clock.

Ruth smiled and became animated again as the car made a turn onto Schwedenplatz. It was one minute to noon, and the crowd of onlookers stood below the patina and gold colored clock in anticipation of the parade of cut out historical figures, ranging from the Emperor Marcus Aurelius to Joseph Haydn. Suddenly, there were dramatic chords from an unseen organ as the XII moved to center stage under a gold stylized representation of the sun, with rays reaching out to a statue of a child holding a butterfly on one side, and death with a sickle on the other. And then, the parade of images moving across the clock's face and royal coat of arms. Ruth stood up and began to applaud with others, turning to her older sister for acknowledgment and approval. Zeena stood, recognizing Ruth's need, and prompted David to do the same. When the organ stopped and Ruth sat, so did they.

"And now we must take you to the Café Central," Ruth said, looking to Frederick for agreement. "They have pastries there unlike any in Vienna. My favorite is the sliced fruit tart. It's candied slices of apricots, strawberries, and plums, and they stand them up on a yellow cream that sits on the most delicious cake you have ever tasted. Please let us go, dear Frederick."

Frederick smiled again and turned the car out of the square towards the Ecke Herrengasse/Strauchgase where the elegant restaurant stood. David remarked on the beautiful harmony of the Baroque building, the Corinthian columns separating the Palladian windows, and the second story life size statues overlooking the stone balcony. Entering through the grand door, they found themselves in a covered courtyard with a glass roof that enveloped the patrons in filtered sunlight. The foyer in which they stood and waited was surrounded by an interior gallery that matched the windows, but the columns were more Romanesque than Greek. In front of them was an ornate staircase to the second floor that arched over the entry passage to the dining room itself. On the wall opposite the entrance, two life sized portraits of the Emperor and Empress watched benevolently over the entitled patrons, seemingly assuring them that all was stable and good and whatever was not good would be good once again. They were seated, their orders for chocolate, tea, and coffee taken, and a cart of pastries was rolled over to them for selection.

"Try the Hefekuchen Saison or better yet the Sacher Schnitte. Such chocolate is beyond description. I'll have my usual, Rudolph," Ruth said, "and I think I would like my sister to try the Apfelkuchen."

Rudolph placed the chosen pastries in front of Frederick and Ruth's guests, as another waiter, formally dressed, placed the chosen beverages on the table. The ambiance reminded Zeena of the Palm Court of the Plaza and she felt quite comfortable and at home.

"I have something to say," Ruth began, no hint of the childish wonder she had exhibited earlier. "I wanted Frederick to drive here because there is something I need to tell you and I thought sweets would help. It's about Mama." Zeena, about to put her fork in her mouth, hesitated, and put the fork on the plate. She felt a palpable flush come to her cheeks; a feeling she had not felt for a very long time.

"I thought that when I told Mama that you and David were coming, she'd be as happy as I was, but all she did was become very quiet. Mama is never quiet, so I think something is very wrong. I just wanted to tell you this. She did seem angry that you are staying in a hotel when we have so much room. I tried to tell her that you didn't want to impose, but she just said that you didn't want to spend time with her."

Zeena did not want to tell her sister that that was the case, so she said that she would consider the change if things went well when she and Sarah met later in the day. As she sipped her coffee, Zeena had an inner dialogue with herself and with Sarah. Her initial fancy put her in a direct line of fire with Sarah's opening accusation about the years that had passed with only sporadic and half-hearted attempts on her part of making contact. If this fantasy were in fact the reality that she would face, she would have to summon up all her reserves to withstand that onslaught and remain dignified and in control. She could of course enter the room with arms wide open as if she were entering onto a stage. That might disarm Sarah and blunt her opening gambit. She had resolved not to appear tentative or guilt ridden. Why should she? The past was the past, and what she did, she did to survive. She should not have to defend her right to survive. No one should. If her mother chose to spew venom, she could ignore it and change the subject as often as she needed.

"You were so right," Zeena said to Ruth. "This pastry is delicious." Zeena paused. "Ruth and Frederick, I must tell you that my memories of Mama are not pleasant. I thought you should know that. I hope our meeting after all these years will not be something we all shall regret.

Close to five in the evening, Zeena and David found themselves standing under the dark grey canopy upon whose face was written in block gold letters, Hotel Sacher. They had just finished cocktails with the proprietor, Anna Sacher, and Zeena feared that her friend Anna's cigar smoke had settled on her new Chanel frock. For some in France, Zeena was still personna non grata in powerful circles, but Anna had no problem with that. The two women had met years before the last Dreyfus trial, and after the war, when the fashion industry was reawakened in the City of Lights, Zeena and Chalfont donned new identities and went on a buying spree. She had met the flamboyant and convivial Anna Sasher on that trip, and at once they became friends. They were kindred spirits. Anna thought Zeena had brought David, this handsome man, to her hotel as a new liaison for the duration of the run of the play. Under Anna's guidance, the Sacher had become well known as a discreet hideaway for the extra-marital trysts of the wealthy and of the nobility. She laughed when Zeena had told her that David was her nephew, but that did not stop her from letting David know that if he liked mature women, she was available. Everyone laughed.

Frederick's chauffeur pulled up, and the gold epauletted doorman clicked his heals, bowed briefly, and opened the car door. Zeena climbed in with David's assistance, and as she did so, she experienced a slight and ancient pain just above her stomach. The pain was familiar to her, but she had not experienced it in years. The pain was the physical manifestation of the thought of her meeting her mother again.

The car found its way to Wipplinger Strasse and turned onto Herrengasse near Judenplatz where Ruth, Frederick, their children, and Sarah made their home.

The house was a large Baroque beauty, painted yellow with white cornices and lintels. It was already a century old when Frederick's father, a very prosperous merchant and owner of the largest department store in Vienna, purchased it from the estate of a distant member of the royal family who had fallen on hard times. It was a small palace, a fitting home for a man whose business genius in merchandising had made him wealthy beyond his own expectations. It, along with the great Impressionist and Post- Impressionist art the elder man had collected, as well as the store, all became Frederick's when the man passed away. And for Frederick, this home was a fitting environment to display his own collections, his young wife, and his three exceptional children.

The chauffeur opened the car door and extended a hand to Ruth and then to Zeena. Ruth moved quickly up the marble steps, hoping that her mother and children were as excited about seeing Zeena and David as she was. Zeena hesitated like a child reluctant to enter a doctor's office. Ruth turned and motioned for her to follow, and she did.

The Kreitman children, anticipating the arrival of relatives from America, were standing at the door, eager to be the first to glimpse their famous aunt and cousin. Over several summers in Switzerland, they had met their Aunt Dora, Uncle Jonathan, cousins Saul and Max, but never their eldest cousin, David. The three moved away from the door as the footman opened it, and made a respectful arc. Ruth introduced Henrik, the eldest at eighteen, who stepped forward stiffly and gave a short bow. Zeena immediately laughed at his formality, took both his hands, kissed him on each cheek, and patted his face. He was immediately embarrassed at her familiarity, confused by her assertion, and ascribed them to American informality. Taking notice, Berta, their sixteen year old daughter, extended her hands first and allowed herself to be hugged. Sigmund, at fourteen, all arms and legs, stood there uncomfortably, allowing his aunt Zeena to embrace and kiss him. David followed, extending his hand to each of his cousins, as Ruth and Frederick beamed their approval. Zeena stood back and admired her niece and nephews. Their hair color was a mixture of Ruth's red and Frederick's brown, and their complections were again a mixture of their parent's tones; not fair and not dark. But their eyes were the periwinkle blue of their mother's. Each had the strong jaw line of Frederick Kreitman, and she could tell from their faces how handsome their father must have been when he was a younger man.

"Well, well, look who is here," came a flat accented voice from the parlor doorway.

Though still looking at her nephew, Zeena's smile instinctively faded, and her mind raced to the last image of her mother that she had back in Krivoser. In anticipation of this meeting, Zeena had steeled herself for all the recriminations that she had imagined would be hurled at her, and imagined how she would respond to each of them. She looked up to see a grey haired woman in her seventies, leaning on a cane, in a matronly black taffeta dress, trimmed with a large white lace collar. Sarah stood stalwartly in the parlor doorway like a dark presence charged with defending it, and though slightly bent, still appeared formidable. Had they passed on the street, Zeena might not have recognized this lady, but the voice had not changed, and the judgmental tone Zeena remembered so well was unmistakable. During the seconds it took her to recover her inner composure, she wondered if her mother would attack her right off with her accusations and vilifications, or have the good judgement to wait till they were alone. She would try not to be alone with the woman, but she knew that that was not likely. Perhaps it would be a good thing to finally lay to rest the past, and the role each of them played to bring about the old disaster.

Zeena had lived to forget her past, but like the hydra head that remained immortal and buried, her past periodically reared itself to remind her of who she was and where she came from.

"Well, well," Sarah repeated. "My famous actress daughter is here from America to visit her mother and sister. How many years has it been? Thirty or is it forty?"

David looked at Zeena and immediately recognized tension and turmoil. He walked over to his grandmother, hoping to change the tone.

"I am David, your grandson." He held out his arms to her, and she looked up at his strong features and black hair and saw his father, Jonathan, standing there. "Bubba," he continued. "I am Dora's son. Dora and Jonathan's son."

Suddenly, Sarah became aware of a new focus; a handsome man she had never met who was also her grandson. Her Dora's child. She put her left hand to her mouth and hesitantly reached up with her right hand and lightly touched his face. Tears filled her eyes, partially from the pure joy of meeting him for the first time, and partially from the pain of all the years that she did not know him or her other grandchildren. She seemed to forget Zeena and took David's arm and turned him into the salon and a settee where she sat down and patted the seat next to her so that he might sit. She was suddenly soft. Zeena was at once surprised, relieved, and grateful beyond words to David for having recognized the moment and rescued it. She would buy him something very nice, but she knew her mother, and that a confrontation was imminent.

They all followed into a sitting room whose pencil grey moldings, heightened with gouache, had touches of gold and blue. The Georges de Feure designed room with its gilded furniture covered in a beige silk embroidered cloth, was an exact replica of the wallpaper. Were it not for the gold wood, everything might have appeared to merge into one entity. There seemed not to be a straight line in the room, everything flowing into everything else like a gentle stream. Zeena noted the contrast between this light and flowing Art Nouveau style and the substantial solid oak of the Edwardian Period that graced her own apartment. She made a mental note to have Sam or Fanny acquire some art pieces from the workshops of Tiffany, Colonna, and Bing. But as elegant as the room was, it became nothing more than the environment in which one might view a life size painting over the mantle of Ruth, executed by none other than Gustav Klimpt. He depicted an exquisite young woman with long red hair and dreamy eyes, gently looking down at her admirers like a benevolent angel clad in a lavish coat that revealed only her face and hands. The coat was composed of soft edged geometric shapes in shades of gold, amber, and pale green with hints of pink, and in her hand, a dove. It seemed as if she were offing the viewer an unearthly serenity. Zeena looked at her younger sister and a tear came to her eye. Ruth smiled slightly and silently lowered her head.

Coffee, tea, chocolate, and beautiful pastries were served by the a buxom young woman in a black ankle length dress, wearing a white apron and cap which revealed a crown of blond braid. At his mother's request, Henrik sat himself at the Bosendorfer that Frederick had paid handsomely for, so his son might wrest from the keys the most subtle nuances that the great composers demanded. Frederick played. He chose the *Fantasy Impromptu* for his aunt and cousin's delight.

Henrik finished the piece to enthusiastic applause from his new relatives, and Zeena invited him to sit next to her. "I have a gift for you," she said. "I have gifts for all of you, but right now I want to give Henrik his." He watched expectantly as she asked David to fetch a leather bag from her suitcase which he promptly did, and she turned to her nephew. "Now I know," she began, "that you have studied classical music, but I also know that like most young people, you are interested in jazz." He blushed slightly. His aunt had revealed a secret that only he and his friends had discussed in undertones at the institute. "So what I have brought for you is a copy of a piece of music recently written by someone named George Gershwin. He calls it *Rhapsody in Blue*, and it is his wonderful attempt to bridge classical and jazz. I've heard it performed with the composer himself at the piano, and I think the piece will become quite famous. Wouldn't it be wonderful if you could introduce it to Vienna? I hope you like it, and I hope I shall have the pleasure of listening to you play it if you do. I also brought you a recording of it," and Henrik took both the record and the music hesitantly, and moved to the Victrola in the corner of the room. Soon, he heard the low wail of the clarinet, and he let his mind climb onto that wistful sound as it merged with the horns and strings, creating a motif that to him seemed to be the sounds of a frantic city. His eyes spoke of his gratitude, and he decided that he would play the entire piece in his head before attempting it on the piano.

David and Zeena regaled them with stories of the famous and infamous, along with pictures of New York City's new Art Deco skyscrapers. They told stories of prohibition and of their uncles Abe and Harry, who brushed elbows with movie and theatrical celebrates like Fanny Brice, or Eddie Cantor, but they did not speak of their brushes with the law, nor with the gangsters who peopled their lives. They spoke of dinners at the swank supper clubs where Clara Bow, Eva Tanguay, Billie Holiday or Lena Horn, might be singing to music played by Count Basie or Duke Ellington. David specifically spoke about jazz greats like Louie Armstrong, who, like Gershwin, was giving solo improvisations that were also bridges, but bridges to jazz from blues and ragtime.

From the other case David put at her feet, Zeena also presented Berta with Victrola records of Louis Armstrong playing with King Oliver, and opera stars like Enrico Caruso and Galagurchi. She also gave her pictures of Sophie Tucker, Al Jolson, Douglas Fairbanks, Mary Pickford, Rudolph Valentino, and May West. And especially for Sigmund, a kit that would enable him to make his very own radio receiver.

Sarah listened to the stories and the laughter intently, becoming increasingly angry with each story of Zeena's successes, Jonah's language school, Rachelann's involvement in the labor movement and women's suffrage, and on and on and on. All became twisted in the painful truth that her son, like his twin sister, had made no attempt in all the years to invite her and their Viennese family to America, or attempt in any way to include her in their lives. She had been deliberately kept from meeting and knowing these American grandchildren. Who was this Rebecca who was named after her beloved Reuben and now called Elizabeth? Who was this bastard child born in prison? Who was this Marta woman and what of this new grandson named Armand who was a prominent lawyer with the government. Who was this Aaron, named after her own father, and who was this Maurice, an economist and teacher? Who was this fashion maven, Fanny? Who was this Sammy, an artist? Her own son and daughter had deprived her of her own grandchildren, and her resentment began to expand like gas filling a balloon; a balloon would soon erupt.

After dinner, the children went to listen to the records in the parlor, the table talk turned to contemporary issues of Jewish interest and concern. "I am concerned," said David, "that President Coolidge signed an immigration act which effectively ended the era of unrestricted immigration including mass Jewish immigration to the US." Zeena turned to her brother-in-law. "I can see you are a lover of art, Frederick," she said, "Have you heard that the Ephraim Benguiat's collection of Jewish ceremonial art from the Smithsonian, was purchased by Cyrus Adler and Felix Warburg for the New York Jewish Museum? I know them well."

David's thought about America closing her gates took Frederick to a darker place that he said held frightening importance for them all. He spoke of a man named Adolph Hitler, a man neither Zeena nor David had ever heard of before. Frederick told them of a conversation with a Major Josef Hell that was communicated to him, where Hitler said that if he wins power, the annihilation of the Jews will be his first and foremost task. Hitler further assured the Major that the Jews cannot protect themselves and that no one will stand as their protector.

Frederick had been in Munich on business when a newspaper confirmed this by quoting Hitler, saying that his Nazi Party will free Europe from the power of the Jews and how the Nazis will remove the Jews from the midst of the German speaking people.

"And do you think this Hitler character has any real following?" David said.

"I am not sure of the numbers of supporters he has," Frederick replied, "but I have seen that the burdens put on Germany for creating the Great War has caused a serious economic depression. In such times, Europe has always singled out the Jews as the cause of all their troubles. I see Hitler as capable of turning on a spigot that will let loose a torrent of hatred that is barely under the surface of polite and not so polite society. I have seen street rallies here in Vienna where Hitler's name is screamed from men clutching onto lamp posts, and I have seen Orthodox Jews spat upon and cursed. We've even put the children into a private school because of what I saw as a change in the behaviors of Christian children they thought were their friends."

"What are you doing about it?" asked Zeena, looking into the future and wondering what she would do to save herself and her family if she were Austrian.

"Slowly," replied Frederick, "I've quietly opened up a Swiss bank account, and I'm quietly transferring funds into it. I've been doing that for over a year. But there is little else I can do at this time. My store is here, and hundreds of people rely on me for their livelihoods. I am cautiously optimistic that the good people of Germany and Austria will see this mad man for what he is, and reject him and his message."

"You are naive if you think the good people of Germany and Austria will do anything other than support this man," Sarah interjected suddenly, looking alternately between her son-in-law and Zeena. "You have never been through a pogrom," she continued, "where your so called good Christian neighbors come at you with scythes and pitchforks. We'll have to get out sooner or later. We will have to get out of Austria if we want to live. The Tsars wanted us out of Russia, and now Stalin is murdering the Jews left. Hitler will finish the job in the rest of Europe, and neither Pope nor ministers will raise a hand. Hitler is right when he says no one will help us. You mark my words," she continued. "They're all alike when it comes to Jews. Nothing is cheaper than the life of a Jew, and if he says this in public, you can be sure it is what he will do. You take him seriously. If he wants a Europe that is free of Jews, that's what he will get. That's what they all want."

She stopped suddenly, realizing that what she was going to say might cause Ruth to panic. She glared at Zeena, bathing her daughter in the memory of that terrible day in Krivoser so many years ago. Suddenly, to Sarah, all talk of quotas, movies, music, and Hitler all seemed to vanish. Nothing seemed more important than saying to her daughter what she had wanted to say to her for years.

Sarah stood, her hand shaking on her cane. "I want all of you to leave," she demanded. "I have something to say only to my eldest daughter." Her tone was emphatic, and each looked from one to the other asking the unasked question of what was to be done. Freud had warned Sarah not to speak of the past to Ruth, and though Sarah, if asked, would describe her blood boiling in her veins, she knew she could calm herself by confronting Zeena, as much as she knew that her instincts had to protect her Ruth. "I think you should do as Mama says," Zeena said, looking directly at her mother. She knew this had to happen, and she knew it would be nasty. Frederick stood, took Ruth's hand and led her to the door followed by David. He was not accustomed to being ordered in his own house, but he knew Sarah, and knew it best that he comply for Ruth's sake. David had expressed his concern for Zeena with a quick look, and just as quickly, Zeena assured him that she would be fine. The door closed behind them.

Sarah erupted as soon as the door closed, and erupted with the force of a river breaking through a dam. "I didn't think my actress daughter would want an audience because she'd be too ashamed of herself to want anyone to know what she did to her family." The old images she carried clawed one over the other to get out to tear at her child.

Zeena suddenly realized that the ancient wall she had created around herself so many years ago to protect herself from her mother's vitriol, reappeared with Sarah's attack, and Zeena found her defenses as strong as ever. Nothing had changed. The years had taught Sarah nothing, and the attack gave Zeena permission to feel not the slightest connection to this woman.

Zeena's response was calm and controlled. Sarah would not win this time. "I have audiences all over the world, Mama, and I certainly do not mind having an audience. But it's not because I don't want anyone to hear of what you call 'my shame.' Yes, I have done things I regret, but I have no shame. One should not be ashamed for wanting to survive. It's our most basic instinct. For your information, Mama, I'd rather not have anyone here, not for my sake, but for yours. I don't want David, Ruth, or her family to see you as you really are."

The muscles in Sarah's face seemed tightened and pulsed. "Well you should feel shame for what you did!" she spewed. "You should be ashamed for running away from your husband. What kind of woman does that? You should feel shame for getting pregnant like a common whore and going to prison, where you had a baby. Of getting involved with assassins. What kind of person does that? You should be ashamed of letting your family think you were dead. What kind of daughter does that? I cursed Ezra Bendak for what he did, and I cursed you, too, for your selfishness. I sat shiva for my father and husband and I sat shiva for you, not just because I thought you were dead, but because you betrayed us and because of how you got your father and grandfather murdered. You did that to us!"

As Sarah ranted, Zeena imagined the words dissolving in the air and forming unattached letters that slammed harmlessly against her wall as they had done in the past. But the reality was that Zeena heard every accusation, and to discount them was a childish thing to do. This was her mother's truth, and living with this particular truth had rotted away something at her mother's core that robbed the woman of all possible compassion or understanding. Sarah could take no one's perspective but her own. To accuse her own daughter of murder and betrayal was impressively vicious, even for Sarah. Zeena stared at her mother as the old woman wiped the spittle from her lips. Sarah breathed heavily and sat, exhausted from her harangue.

The room was suddenly silent, and in the silence, Zeena looked at her mother and said, "You are a tired old woman and you cannot hurt me anymore." The simplicity of the thought surprised even her. Certainly, such realizations should be accompanied by something more dramatic than silence. That simple thought was all Zeena needed to take Sarah's power away, and she suddenly felt a weight lifted off her back; a weight she had innocently and unknowingly placed there herself as a child when she had ascribed that power to her mother; a time in life when all children ascribe power to their parents. In Zeena's childhood imagination, she had concluded that since Sarah gave her life, Sarah could also take it away. In her innocence, she believed that if she did not have her mother's approval, her life could be taken. Now she knew that it was not until she tried to become independent from her mother, that her mother would never relinquish that power and let her have her own life. That was when their troubles started. Zeena wanted to become her own person, to be free, and her mother would not relinquish that magical hold she had over her children. That power had to be ripped away. She and her brother had done that by running. In their helplessness, it was all they could think of doing.

Zeena thought of walking out of the room, leaving her mother with the same questions that had tormented the woman for years, unanswered. That might be a fitting bit of retribution. But Zeena now felt unafraid, unintimidated, free, and knew that she needed to respond even though she also knew that nothing would be made right from the answers she would give. Sarah never forgot and Sarah never forgave. Sarah never changed her mind, negotiated, or listened to any voice except her own, unless she had ascribed to that voice more power than she took for herself.

"Let me start first," Zeena began, "with some news you might like. Ezra is dead. He was hanged for killing the wife of the chief of police as he was trying to murder the woman who would become Jonah's wife." She paused. "The man you forced me to marry so that you could get me out of the house and walk down the street gloating that the daughter of Sarah Chernov now lived in the largest house in town, was a murderer and a rapist. It is not I who should be ashamed but you, for being a mother who so hated her daughter that she pushed her into a marriage that you knew would be a disaster before the glass was broken. It is you who should be ashamed for creating a world for your children that was filled with fear and anxiety. You only knew fear and anxiety, and I don't think I ever heard you utter the words, please or thank you. You sacrificed me on the alter of your own needs and your own fears. Jonah tried to stop you, and Papa tried to stop you. But you wouldn't be stopped. I didn't betray you or my family. You betrayed us. Your insistence on that marriage brought on that horror. I could have borne the shame of carrying a child without being married, but you couldn't. I could even have gone quietly away to have my child, but that wouldn't have gotten you even with me and given you the status in town of being Ezra Bendack's mother-in-law."

Zeena was fully composed and fully in control. "I could not have known the consequences of what would happen by running away from Ezra, but I knew the consequences of staying with that man and living in his house. Few of us think of or consider the consequences when we see only life and death decisions in front of us. Staying in Krivoser with Ezra Bendak meant a kind of death for me, so I resolved to get away from him and from you Mama, and find some happiness. Had I known that my husband would single out our family for revenge, I might not have run. I might have sacrificed my life, as I agreed to sacrifice my happiness when you said that Ezra would ruin Papa's livelihood if I didn't accept him as my husband. I sacrificed myself for Papa, and when I could bear it no longer, I ran." Zeena paused and took a breath, fighting back her own tears at the thought of her father. "We cannot change our pasts, Mama, we can only move on. I have moved on. You haven't moved on, but you've chosen to seethe in your darkest memories. You have never been able to get beyond your own needs or your own perceptions, and whatever you think has always just tumbled from your mouth, unfiltered, no matter who is hurt."

As Zeena spoke, she watched Sarah's mouth moving, speaking with her as if imitating her words. It was like she was getting ready to jump in, already running when Zeena stopped. Zeena did not stop.

"And as far as you thinking I was dead, that was done so the Russian Government couldn't trace any letters back to Krivoser. They knew Jonah was my brother. They didn't know my real name, because if they had, everybody related to me would have been murdered in retaliation. Do you understand that, Mama? Jonah told me that that was also the reason he couldn't write. They knew I was his sister. They were watching and waiting for him to post a letter. Besides, I lived for years not remembering my past, not remembering you or anyone else. Jonah and I were protecting the family. As for me killing my father and grandfather, what can I say? I didn't plan the pogrom. I didn't lead the peasants on a rampage through Krivoser murdering Jews where they were found. That was a mob that no one could have controlled except the police, and you know as well as I that the police were part of it. They murdered my father and grandfather, you foolish old woman, not I."

"Then why didn't you or your brother write after you got to America. You knew Ruth and I were in Austria. Dora would have given you our address." Sarah's demand was emphatic.

Zeena stood thoughtfully for a moment, and a faint smile appearing on her lips. Mama, I didn't write to you because I don't like you and I don't want you in my life. It's as simple as that. I suspect Jonah may feel the same way. In fact, I know he does."

The cane Sarah held shook violently. Zeena, knowing what her mother's anger could do, walked to the door and turned. "I'm leaving now, Mama, and I don't suspect I shall be seeing you again. Keep your anger if you find comfort in it. Keep the horror of the past with you if such memories get you through your day. I want nothing of it. I remember my father blessing me on the Sabbath, and that is the memory I see whenever I think of him. I remember my grandfather looking up from his work as I brought him his lunch daily and smiling at me. Whenever I think of them, these are the memories I choose to recall, and they always bring me a smile." She paused. "And from time to time, you will come to mind, Mama, but frankly Mama, at this moment I cannot think of a pleasant moment with you in my entire life. How's that for a legacy, Mama?" Zeena reached the door.

"Don't you dare walk away from me, Zeena Chernov. I'm not finished with you."

Zeena stopped in her tracks and turned. "You may not be finished with me, Mama, but I'm sure as hell finished with you!"

CHAPTER 23

1926

"Oh, Papa," sighed Fanny, obviously exasperated. "Ignoring Prohibition is as American as playing baseball."

"No it's not!" Jonah responded emphatically, throwing down his napkin. "And what is the law should be acknowledged as the law by everyone, especially by Jews! Thirty-five bootleggers, all Jews, were jailed in Baltimore this week, and when that happens we give the world the impression that Jews are law-breakers and don't care where they get their money from as long as they get it. What one Jew does is a reflection on all of us!"

"Well, I don't believe I should be judged by what other people do," she said, "and besides, you know as well as I do, Papa, that Jews have been in the whisky business since we got to America. It has always been one of those American industries that allowed us to become part of American society. Just ask Abe and Harry."

Jonah gave a warning look to his daughter for tearing at a wound that would not heal. "But now it's against the law, and they should be out of the business!" he responded, his voice rising. "Your brothers give us all a bad name, and I don't want to talk about them."

Marta pursed her lips at the possibility of yet another flare-up at the dinner table over her stepsons.

"I find it amusing Fanny," Aaron said, attempting to draw attention to himself and away from what was gearing up to yet another ugly altercation, "that you marched proudly for the right of women to vote, and now that you have the vote, these same sisters of yours vote for a law that you vilify and openly flaunt. I see a great irony here."

"If you haven't noticed," she replied, "I, like you, am also a free thinker, so why would you imagine that I would be in lock step with everything that came out of the Suffrage Movement? Please give me the same courtesy and respect of independent thought that I have always given you." Aaron grinned at Fanny's dismissive condescension.

Jonah fell silent. Normally he would have delighted at the intellectual jousting of his children, but what was being revealed here was his own ambivalence about what he saw regarding Jews fitting into American society. He had long ago established his place as a law abiding American citizen, respected for his charitable efforts, his community leadership, and his support for the arts. But with this particular law, he nevertheless felt a sense of coercion and intolerance on the part of the government that vaguely threatened Jewish morality and culture. He was liberal in his politics and a defender of religious traditions for all, but what Jewish celebration was not ushered in with a "L'chaim, to life?" True, sacramental wine for religious purposes was allowed, but Jewish conviviality was truly enhanced with a bottle of schnaps, and schnaps was as fundamental to being Jewish as was challah on the Sabbath. So in this law, Jonah saw an infringement upon his culture, and yet, as an American, this law had to be obeyed, even though he also sensed in it a veiled attempt to Christianize America. This broader concern for the Jewish image in American Society was accompanied by a very personal concern that his own sons had chosen to involve themselves in bootlegging enterprises and God knows what else, bringing shame upon the family and shame, as he saw it, to the Jewish People. These sons took no responsibility for the image they reflected on their own people. For this, their father felt tremendous guilt and a personal shame, even though there were those in East New York who slapped him on his back and wished they had sons like Abe and Harry. It was a paradox to him, that in Brooklyn, his own sons had become something of folk heroes, but to him, their Papa in Manhattan, a source of shame accompanied by a nagging fear that something terrible would happen to them.

"You know, Papa," Aaron continued, "unlike you, most Jewish people don't support the Volstead Act, and the prohibitionists are saying the Jews are trying to undercut the law in order to regain control of the liquor industry. I'm not exactly sure if Jews ever really controlled the liquor industry, but they are making it clear that Jews who continue to be involved in any aspect of bootlegging are villains and downright unpatriotic. Papa, do you think Abe and Harry are unpatriotic?"

"That's ridiculous," Fanny interrupted. "The law itself is unpatriotic."

"So in effect, are you saying that men like Abe, Harry, and Joey are not unpatriotic?" Aaron said turning to her. Would you also agree that good American capitalists who see a market for their product and are illegally supplying the public with what it demands are patriotic? You think Joe Kennedy and his ilk are patriots?"

"Yes," Fanny said. "Supply and demand are foundational to our system," she replied with a smile.

"So what about drugs and prostitution? Would you say that those who involve themselves in those businesses are also good American patriots?"

Fanny thought for a moment. "They're certainly capitalists," she said with a smile, "but I don't see questioning their patriotism has anything to do with it even if they are breaking the law. I think that the government has the moral obligation to make sure that medicines and food supplies are safe for all, but has no right to pass laws that infringe on a person's free will to decide what is best for him or herself. If your personal behavior does not infringe on the rights of others, they should not be denied you by a government."

Marta looked at Jonah across the table and sighed with a half smile on her lips. She knew what their bedroom conversation would be that evening. "Rachelann and Fedya have been too much of an influence on her when she was young," she imagined him saying. "How did it come to this? How can one family produce such complexities? Such conflicts? What did I do that was wrong? Why isn't she married like a normal person?" And she would answer, "You wanted your children independent and educated. Having children is always a risk. You have them, but you don't know what they will become despite your best efforts. Not all of them disappoint." Marta knew that her husband, for all his forward thinking, was having feelings of discontinuity. They were both transitional figures in time, but Jonah, though denying it, still clung to the world and traditions in which he was raised. Modernity was off putting and he felt out of control. Secretly, he felt there was safety in the old ways and in tradition, and he saw it all falling away with little to anchor the future. He feared for his children and grandchildren. But she would say to him, "Come to bed and hold me. It will be alright."

Fanny, who fully embraced the freedoms of modern womanhood, penciled in the arch of her right plucked eyebrow, fluffed the reddish blond curls that fell right above it, adjusted the faux pearl headband that might have been a halo if it could rise, retraced her lips with bright red gloss, stepped back from the mirror and smiled. She was twenty-six and the world was hers. After stepping into the loose fitting black beaded dress, she aligned the shoulder straps, and placed the long strand of faux pearls that her brother Sam had given her as a birthday gift around her neck. Now she was ready. The cab would be waiting, and so would her friends.

Fanny loved her life. She loved the whirling world of being introduced to celebrities, of telephone calls, of seeing movies shown in movie houses that aped Oriental palaces, of fast automobiles, and serendipitous moments when someone would introduce her to a young writer like Steinbeck or Fitzgerald. She loved bumping into celebrities, especially movie stars and sports figures. She was ringside when Dempsey slugged it out with Firpo at the Polo Grounds on the arm of a handsome man whose name she could not recall, and she was there applauding when George Bellows first showed his painting of the fight. With friends, she cheered Babe Ruth, and she cheered on horses from private boxes at Belmont Park. She was once photographed sitting in a huge champagne glass, much to her father's consternation when she proudly showed it to him. She was a true "Metropolitanite," a term coined by Harold Ross who founded *The New Yorker*, and she could not imagine living in any city other than in Manhattan. She embraced all that was new.

Fanny chose not to remember much of life living in the back of the candy store, but she could still vividly recall the first time she walked into the big house in Manhattan and saw the crystals of the hall chandelier reflecting the fire in the foyer hearth. The thing she remembered most, the thing that made her decide that this was the home she wanted forever, was the red velvet canopied bed that she was told would be hers when Cousin Elizabeth married Nathaniel and moved away. That bed did become hers as promised, and she happily returned to it most nights. Even when Marta and Jonah suggested that the room be updated, Fanny begged them not to touch it. This was the room of a princess, and this is where she was happiest.

She, Armand, Sam, Maurice, and then Aaron, were all raised here and all moved in privileged circles. All had been enrolled in private schools, Fanny in the Todd Hunter School for Girls, and they all attended college. Her father often proudly asserted that he could not believe that in one generation a tailor turned candy store owner, turned language teacher, could have five of his eight children college graduates and in professions. Of course he credited Marta with giving him and his children the opportunity to become more than he ever dreamed they could be, and Marta always smiled at his gratitude. A woman in her situation could have had any man, and she chose him. Love and gratitude became one in his heart.

Fanny graduated from Pratt with a major in interior design, and a minor in architecture. Though Sammy had received a degree in architecture, he later discovered that his real love was painting. As children, each would design buildings or construct rooms and argue over whose was better. Fanny would always insist on furnishing them. But architecture and interior design remained the province of men as did most other professions, and getting the vote in 1920 did not break down the barriers that stood against a female's advancement despite her talent. So following the path of least resistance, and against her older sister's advice, Fanny turned to designing and writing for the fashion industry, but still conferred with Sammy whenever he needed her eye and style for the commissions that came his way. Sammy always insisted that she take part of his earnings for her efforts, but the real reward came whenever she walked into a building that her brother had helped design and saw one of her visions come to life.

Fanny was certainly not unhappy in her career. While Sammy could beam with pride over seeing one his ideas come to life in the sleek Art Deco steel, stone, and bronze skyscrapers that began to forever change the skyline of Manhattan, Fanny could see the fashionable ladies of Park Avenue dressed in her designs purchased at Saks Fifth Avenue or at Bergdorf Goodman. The people she met were the very soul of the city. Tonight, she had dressed for a party to be hosted by Horace Liveright, the publisher, who in addition to creating the *Modern Library* series, also published Ernest Hemingway and William Faulkner. Salacious allegations swirled around this paragon of the publishing industry, and she was eager to see for herself if these alleged bacchanalian revels were in fact all they were supposed to be. Besides, she had been told that Jimmy Walker, the city's new mayor would be there, but it was very hush hush. At another glittering bash she had actually met Arnie Rothstein, Frank Costello, and Waxey Gordon. Abe was there that night also, and when Waxey approached her, Abe said something in his ear that dissuaded him from further contact. But Abe was in Miami at some business meeting, and when she had seen Harry earlier in the week at his son's circumcision, he told her that he would be out on Long Island taking care of business. That was a code in the family which meant not to ask further.

So without the slightest trepidation, Fanny was once again entering the world of the underworld and the elite. Rubbing elbows in a world where paradoxes smashed up against one another randomly was her delight, and she freely admitted to herself that she was fascinated by the exuberances, the excesses, and yes, the danger of the way life was celebrated in the city by the rich. With Abe and Harry away, she would not feel restricted or inhibited in any way, and though her older brothers were an integral part of this delightful lunacy, they were still her older brothers, and tended to control her environment and give unsolicited advice regarding her behavior.

The guests were invited to meet first at a speakeasy in the West Village in lower Manhattan called Chumley's before heading uptown to someone's apartment in the sky on Park Avenue. She was well acquainted with Chumley's since her brothers were silent partners.

Chumley's was a favorite watering hole with just enough posh, seediness, and danger to draw the well heeled of high society and the well heeled of low. She knew that Abe and Harry had several precinct cops on their payroll, and whenever one cop phoned the bartender that Feds and cops would be smashing in through the Pamala Court entrance, the bartender would know to "86 Bedford" the patrons, and that meant they should scram out of the Bedford Avenue door. On one occasion, Fanny was involved in such a raid, and the customers, after draining their teacups, left amid laughter and grumblings of annoyance. The raiders found nothing except employees, quickly redressed as patrons sipping tea and listening to jazz.

The girl who took her wrap in the outer vestibule knew Fanny as her boss's younger sister and nodded. A handsome liveried young man opened the door for her and smiled a hopeful smile that she would notice him, and she flirtatiously glanced over her shoulder at him in reply. She laughed to herself at his surprise and blushed. On the small stage across a room, lit mostly by candles and low watt electric bulbs under red shades, a small band blasted out the Charleston. Flappers and their dandies crowded the dance floor, flailing their arms with abandon. Waitresses, on their way to deliver cups and saucers of whiskey sours, martinis, and Gibsons, glided seamlessly through barriers of elegant people chatting up one another on their way to their waiting friends. Every woman seemed to have a cigarette in a long holder, and every man seemed to have a cigarette between his fingers or lips. Fanny moved through the smoke and the Charleston beat, the clicking of teacups touched in toasts, the sudden shrieks of laughter, and the hum of furtive conversations. It all seemed to her like the throbbing musical accompaniment to her life; she reveled in every beat, in every laugh, in every clink, and in every note.

"We're over here, Fanny," shouted a woman with short black hair and a black egret feather sticking out of her headband. Others at the table turned, the men stood and the women waved. Sophie, the seamstress who pieced together Fanny's designs, stood with open arms, gave Fanny an air kiss on each cheek, and returned to her teacup and the lap of a man Fanny did not know. But she immediately noticed that Sophie had taken off her wedding ring and the man she was sitting on was not Al. Instinctively, Fanny sensed something dark about the man. She could tell he was tall even though he was seated, with a full head of sleeked back blond hair. But it was his eyes that frightened her; light blue, and cold as death. She recalled her father saying that you could tell a lot from a person's eyes, and she was unnerved by his. She could understand why Sophie would be attracted to this man, Al being a rather dumpy boor. But Sophie was as superficial as they came. A slight shiver ran up her spine as she faked a smile, knowing that his eyes were on her, and she was being undressed by them.

It was a table for eight. Three of the men including the one holding Sophie on his lap, she did not know at all. One woman she knew slightly, but not the starlet on Liveright's lap being fondled by his fat hands. Sophie had invited Fanny to the party, and Sophie had been invited by Liveright whose wife had used Sophie's sewing skills long before Liveright discovered other skills that Sophie possessed. The teacups were cleared and another round was set down. Sophie introduced Fanny to Horace Liveright who smiled, but did not stand. Liveright was an obese man in his fifties, a balding beady-eyed man who had a diamond stickpin inserted in a paisley cravat, and an overly large diamond ring on his pinky. Fanny was repelled by him. Sophie stood and introduced her partner for the night as Billy Shine, who nodded, but did not stand. The woman who had met Fanny before feigned a smile, and the men moved over to make room for her in the booth.

The band was now playing *Someone To Watch Over Me*. Fanny had heard it first when Gertrude Lawrence sang it standing alone on the stage of the Imperial Theater in Gershwin's *Oh Kay*, and the poignant lyrics immediately touched her. As she listened to the lyrics, she also found that she was listening to a conversation that had become more than suggestive, and had she known these people better, she might not have minded. Still, she was uncomfortable. The one man she did not know seemed to read the discomfort on her face and invited her to dance. She readily accepted. He introduced himself as Freddy Kaplan, an editor at the Boni and Liveright Publishers. He was a few inches taller than she with brown eyes and hair that was combed back without the greasy pomade that slathered Billy Shine's. He hesitated as he put his arm around her waist, looking for an appropriate distance between them that would say to her that he was more than some lothario looking for a good time, and he began to sway her slowly, dreamily to the sound. Freddy guided her knowingly, humming the song and occasionally, whispering the lyrics "Won't you tell her please to put on some speed, follow my lead, oh, how I need, someone to watch over me." She found herself moving in closer, and he took that as an invitation to move his hand in a tighter embrace. The music ended. They stood there briefly, reluctant to part. She liked him, and felt comfortable in his arms. It was something more, but she did not know what it was.

"I'd like to get out of here," Fanny said. "I'm uncomfortable. Would you call me a cab?"

"I'll take you home," he countered, a broad smile on his face. At that moment, Freddy saw Liveright beckon him over. "This place is boring me, Freddy, and we're moving the party further downtown. Call us a couple of cabs, will you?"

"I was just about to see Fanny home," he responded.

"Not if you want a job tomorrow morning, you won't," he laughed, staring him down.

"And make sure she comes with you. I like her. If she doesn't, don't bother coming to work tomorrow. Two things you've got to do for me."

Freddy looked at Fanny with an expression that alternated between anger and helplessness. His jaw was tight, but his eyes silently asked her if she would be willing to go. Fanny sensed that Horace Liveright was someone who would certainly carry out his threats, as petty as they were, so she nodded her assent, and quietly whispered, "I only ask that you stay with me until we can leave." He shook his head.

The party was already in progress when they climbed the three flights to the one bedroom apartment the starlet shared with two other wannabe Broadway babes. The room was dark, mostly lit by candles, and the shadows of the other strangers hovered ominously on the peeling oriental wallpaper. People huddled secretively in corners and against the walls; drinking, whispering, and writhing in time to the slow jazz that was played on a Victrola near the door. The room was engulfed in a haze of smoke which gave the scene a Goyaesque quality. Shadows cast on the ceiling hung heavily like black birds of prey, and each time the candles flickered with the opening door, the birds seemed to scatter in fear. This was more than Fanny wanted.

Sophie pulled her into the room and over to a table with gin filled glasses and pressed one into Fanny's hand. Sophie drank her's quickly, and moved to other bottles that were on a Chinese lacquered table with a brass Buddha and a vase with fake roses. Two standing torches and a table lamp near a couch were each veiled in scarlet and gold edged scarves which gave the room a further appearance of one of Dante's levels of Hell. A woman with almond shaped eyes, gaunt and determined, approached the two, never taking her eyes off Fanny. She ran her finger delicately up Fanny's cheek. "I've never seen you here before," she said, her voice dark and husky. "Are you here with anyone?" Fanny forced a smile and looked for Freddy. "Yes, I am. Oh, there he is. Please excuse me."

She moved into the crowed but was stopped abruptly by Billy Shine who stood a head taller than she, and who stared down at her with desire mixed with contempt. She had not noticed the scar that ran down his cheek when she first saw him, a memento from a street fight earlier in his career, and it seemed a perfect mark on such a face. His breath was rank from booze, and she began to turn away when he caught her by her arm. "Dames don't walk away from me, sweetheart," he sneered, barely moving his lips. Fanny began to tremble, not able to break his hold.

"Well, maybe this one is going to be the first," Freddy said. "Now let her go or I'll..."

"Or you'll what?" Billy said.

The people turned at the sound of an altercation and crowded in for something that might liven things up. A squat man emerged, powerfully built with dark, deep set eyes and a nose that had been broken more than once. Fanny thought she knew him as a boxer she had once seen, but she didn't care who he was as long as he was able to intervene. His breath also stank from booze, and he didn't seem like the type to walk away. "Now let the lady go or you're going to be hurt." Shine didn't respond an "or what?" sensing full well that though short, this man was a drunken brute who could indeed, hurt him. So he bit down on his teeth, his jaw twitching in rage, and walked to the other side of the room to the sound of muffled giggles. Freddy came up to Fanny and held her until she stopped shaking. "Go into the bedroom and get your wrap," he whispered calmly. I'll go downstairs and hail a cab."

Fanny opened the door to the bedroom and found some immediate comfort in the relative quiet of the room and air that did not make her eyes water. She hurriedly searched for her coat, and finding it, stopped and started to cry. She did not know why she cried, so she sat down on the pile of coats, looking at herself in the mirror opposite her. "Is this what it's all about?" she said to her reflection. "How many more parties, Fanny? How many more glasses of gin, packs of cigarettes? Who are you Fanny Chernov, and is this what you want out of life?" She stood and moved to the mirror. Her mascara had run down her cheeks, so she wiped her eyes and cheeks with her handkerchief, rouged her cheeks, and repainted her lips. As she fought a resurgence of tears, the noise grew louder and then softened. She turned, thinking Freddy had returned, but it was Billy.

"You really didn't think I'd let a bitch like you get the better of me, did you?"

He lunged towards her, grabbed her before she could move, and clamped a large hand over her mouth. He forced her onto the bed, shoved his knee between her legs and, with his free hand, pulled her dress up as far as he could, tearing at her underwear. Fanny tried to bite his hand and he laughed at the uselessness of her struggling body against his. Amid her muffled screams, she heard the noise in the other room grow louder briefly and then soften. Someone had come in. Shine tore at the buttons on his fly, and at the moment when Fanny felt that he was about to thrust himself into her, she heard a sharp groan of pain issue from his lips and his body go limp on her. She felt him being rolled off of her, and through her tears, she saw Freddy standing there with a small bronze statue in his hands whose base was red with blood. He quickly covered Fanny with one of the coats and told her to get up. Shine lay on the bed, not moving. Blood gushed out of his head wound, and Freddy frantically fought his instinct to call for a doctor or just get the hell out of there with Fanny as inconspicuously as they could. He decided on the latter. He pushed Shine's body further onto the bed, pulling the coats from under him and piling them on top so he would not be found until the people began to leave, which would not be for hours. "You go out first, Fanny. There's a cab waiting for us. Tell the driver to driver around the corner and wait. I'll come out after a short time. I don't want anyone seeing us leave this room together." Fanny left, and Freddy thrust his hand into the pile of coats to feel for Shine's pulse. The bastard was still alive.

Fanny was grappling with what had just happened; time and the world did not seem real. She tried to process it, but could not. A man tried to rape her, and now he might be dead. She had been saved by a man she barely knew. She had to get away. He had to get away. She trusted him. She could have been killed. She would do as he said. Freddy opened the door for her and she was assaulted by a blast of loud music, smoke, and ominous shadows cast by ominous people. "Oh, there you are, Fanny. I've been looking for you and for Billy. Did you see him?" Sophie asked. Fanny felt ill at the thought of what had just happened.

"No, dear, and I'm not feeling so well. I have to go."

"Did you see him in the bedroom when you got your coat?"

"No one was in there. Maybe he went to get a pack of cigarettes."

"That must be it. Ain't he the bees knees?" Sophie said dreamily.

Fanny bit down on her lip to control her anger at this stupid girl who had a man at home who was devoted to her, and yet she was here looking for a sleazy piece of scum who was lying unconscious or possibly dead under a pile of coats and jackets. She lowered her head in disgust and pushed her way out of the room.

Ten minutes later she was in a cab, softly crying onto Freddy's shoulder, shaken but no longer afraid. She whispered her address to Freddy, and the cab sped north. She closed her eyes and her quieting brain silently sang, "There's a somebody I'm longing to see, I hope that he'll turn out to be, someone who'll watch over me..."

CHAPTER 24

1928 & 1929

The older Chernov grandchildren were excused, and were asked to take the younger ones up to the playroom. They left the room amid giggles, pinches, punches, pushing, hair pulling, bickering, and threats, as each maneuvered to be first on the staircase and first to get to the toys. Sadie, Sam's wife, followed them just to make sure no one was excluded from the games, and she was followed by Maurice's wife, Gertrude, who knew well her husband's rant on the state of the stock market, and did not want to hear it again. Jonah and Marta, like a satisfied goose and gander, watched as their rambunctious grand fledglings scampered out of the dinning room.

Maurice drained the demitasse cup and replaced it on the saucer. His demeanor, always serious, was often the butt of his sibling's jokes, but he knew it was all in good fun, though their comments often made him lose his train of thought. From early on, he, like Harry, also had a gift for numbers, but where Harry used his math skills and memory for keeping double sets of books in his head so there would never be a paper trail, Maurice majored in economics and became a young associate of no less a personage than Bernard Baruch.

"What most people won't recognize," Maurice continued, "is that economic panics are just as important to the human condition as revolutions, wars, and world hunger. Novelists tend to ignore economic panics because money is not as glamorous as deaths, starvations and revolutions."

The child in Fanny giggled at her older brother's demeanor. "Tell me that this isn't going to be another warning about the seven fat cows and the seven lean cows coming up out of the Nile again. You'll spoil my dessert."

Sam, having lit a cigarette, expelled the air with, "Lighten up, Murray or you'll pop a blood vessel."

"Continue, Maurice," said Jonah, who witnessed this semi-abuse at his table for years, recalling how he and Zeena had involved themselves in this very banter and goading so many years ago. He smiled to himself at the thought. "And pay no attention to people who never move beyond the funny papers." Sam laughed and flicked an ash onto the saucer.

"We don't flick ashes into Meisen saucers in this house," said Marta, moving to place an ashtray in front of him. Sam ever so slightly rolled his eyes at the reprimand.

"Thank you, Papa. As I was saying before I was rudely interrupted by the less informed among us, was that economic conditions, panic, or financial collapses are not exciting because the man in the street mistakenly believes that the only thing lost is usually someone else's money."

"Oh, Maurice," Fanny said patting her lips with her napkin, "Money, money, money. Can't you talk about anything else?"

"I talk about money because I'm an economist, and responsible for this family's assets and investments. In fact, I'm the only one who knows what the hell is going on because I see it every day. And if you know what's good for you, you'll listen."

"Have we lost our money?" She rejoined, smiling at the taste of orange sherbert on her tongue. "So far, your investments have done us all very well. Murray, Freddy and I are content with knowing only about the bottom line." She looked around. "Don't you all just love getting rich without having to do anything?"

"Yes, getting rich is the objective," Maurice said, acknowledging his sister's comments, "but it's just that idea of people thinking that they can get rich and stay rich by doing nothing that is leading people to make insane decisions about investing. Wall Street and our own government are pushing the idea that things can only get better and that stock speculation is the path to riches. While this idea may have been true, it has run away with itself and taken on a life of its own. Margin buying has become a juggernaut that cannot sustain itself and will ultimately crash into a massive wall called reality."

Jonah interrupted. "What are you saying to us, Maurice? Have we been involved in speculation?"

"Of course we have. Everyone is involved in speculation, Papa, but I've decided to sell off everything this family bought on margin before it all falls apart." There was the usual characteristic urgency in his voice, but this evening, there was something more; a genuine fear. "It's all smoke and mirrors, Papa, and this rampant surge in buying on margin and these daily unrealistic gains in trading have people believing that it can only get better. But its all a sham. For example, people buying real estate no longer have to put up the full cash value of the property, but only the ten percent required by the binder. Yes, you can believe that the buyer of the securities on margin gets full title to the property, but he doesn't really own it because he put up only ten percent. Though he has these securities that say he owns this property, these securities are left with his broker who holds them as collateral for the other ninety percent of the loan which the speculator had to take out. So while the buyer frees himself from the burden of real ownership, from benefits, or use, the only thing they have is that paper that says they own a piece of property, and have the right to sell the binder for it and earn the difference between its original value of the property and what it's worth at the time of sale. It's like a house whose facing is stone, but whose support beams are made of cardboard. The government knows about this and won't do anything about it because ever swelling markets give the impression that the government is doing a good job. Our economy looks good on paper, but just cannot sustain itself because of what's really going on."

"But only a few months ago, President Coolidge said that no Congress has ever governed over more pleasing prospects than this one. There is peace in the world, prosperity at home, and the future is bright," Aaron asserted. "What's wrong with optimism?"

"Nothing," said Sam, who was attempting to quiet down his yammering baby with a little wine to her lips. "Coolidge and Congress are paying attention to only a very small group of people who are doing well. If you look at the world not from the privileged few who get richer and richer, but from the rest of America, you see that the farmers are unhappy with farm prices that are so low and costs so high, they can't make a living. Then there are the poor blacks and whites in the South barely existing in abject poverty. Do you know that there are slums in this country that are some of the worst in the world?"

"Thank you once again, my dear brother, for making me feel guilty about having plenty to eat and a warm place to sleep," said Fanny as she refilled her wine glass from the crystal decanter before her.

Jonah did not want to get into yet another left/right debate between his children on the social contract that did or did not exist in America, but wanted to stay on Maurice's warning.

"What have you sold?" he said, looking at Marta. After all, the bulk of their wealth was what she had secretly purloined and invested while Ezra was alive. It had grown into a small fortune.

"I've been selling off what I think are bad investments for a while now, but now I'm at the point where I'm going to sell off a lot more and I needed you all to know why." He unfolded a piece of paper that he had taken from his pocket. "The first thing I sold off were those investments in Florida near Jacksonville that this Charles Ponszi man from Boston was selling. Initially, it was a great investment for those of us who got in early, but after that hurricane hit, that Florida land boom ended and wiped out fortunes. We made a decent profit, but we also would have lost thousands if I hadn't personally gone down to Florida and saw the swamps that we owned."

"I'm not sure I like you diddling with our money without consulting us," Fanny said.

"And what would you know about money other than spending it?" Sam interjected sarcastically.

"I don't see you eating out of a tin can with your downtrodden brothers and sisters you paint on your canvass," Fanny shot back. "That deposit box of yours don't exactly make you the starving artist that you like to pretend to be."

"Will you please listen," Maurice interrupted. "All of our names are listed on every transaction, and no one is getting more or less than anyone else. So, if you agree to continue with me making these decisions, we all either rise or fall together, or you can be released from this corporation, take your money out, and you can rise or fall by yourselves. Either way, as long as I've been entrusted as executor, I'm deciding what's best for this family. What I'm seeing with the daily erratic fluctuation of the market, not only am I selling off anything we bought on margin, I'm selling off anything that does not give us dividends, and slowly divesting ourselves of our speculative holdings. I'm not trusting the banks either, so I'm putting our earnings not in bank accounts, but each of us will have a safety deposit box with the profits evenly divided among us."

"Money in a box doesn't make interest," Freddy said.

"Damn the interest," Maurice shot back. "If the banks fail, there won't be any money unless it's safely in a box. Each of you will have your own key, and you can do as you wish with your own take. You want to put it into a bank account so it can gain interest, go ahead. If you want to reinvest your own money back into the market, go ahead. But I would advise you not to spend it foolishly, because something apocalyptically bad is coming at us."

"Have you made your calculations and feelings known to your colleagues?" Armand interjected, after listening quietly to the conversation. "I know I should be more up on this than I am, but the only thing I know is that when our government agreed to an easy money plan urged by Europe, the banks and borrowers responded by putting this flood of new money into common stocks. I know my wife's family certainly did. I guess you are right when you say that people will always speculate beyond reason if they can see themselves making money when they don't have to do anything for it."

"To answer your question, Armand, my esteemed colleagues are following the dictates of those captains of industry like Mr. Mellon, Jon Rakob of General Motors, and the Du Ponts who continue to solemnly swear that prosperity is here to stay. They're businessmen. What else should they say? But I'm becoming known as the 'Cassandra of Wall Street,' and I'm getting tired of being ridiculed by people who will not see that the handwriting is on the wall. Today the *Times* reported a four and one half point gain in the industrial average, with trading well over six and one half million shares. And listen to this." He took another slip of paper out of his pocket and read, 'for cyclonic violence, yesterday's stock market has never been exceeded in the history of Wall Street.' When do you ever read in the *Times* descriptions like 'cyclonic violence' in reference to Wall Street?"

"Okay, what about this buying on margin thing you were talking about?" said Fanny with interest not evidenced before. She was looking at her husband, suddenly alert to the real possibilities of what could happen to her world if the doom Maurice was prophesying came to pass. "I have friends who talk about what they buy on margin." Her tone became serious. She was clearly unnerved. "Will these friends be in trouble?" Fanny was thinking about the money she and Freddy had invested separate from the family. They had invested with friends who had gone in together on a deal that promised enormous rewards from a market that they were assured would only rise. At least that was what the broker told them. The investment was in a piece of property, but they only had to put down ten percent of the value of this property with the understanding that this "binder," this right to buy, was what they could sell when the price of the land had risen. Then, they would make back the cost of the binder and the increased value of the land. It was all very exciting to her, though she did not really understand. What her brother had said was finally sinking in.

"Like I said before, if the asset bought on margin falls in value, your friend must come up with more money so the bank's investment and backing is protected. They may have to sell what they own, or the bank takes it over."

"And Wall Street allows this to happen?" Aaron said. "That's like setting people up to fail. I guess when you're happy, you're not looking too closely at what's going on."

"Well said, and true," Maurice answered. "Wall Street knows the dangers to the investor, but they still encourage buying on margin because it makes the market very active. But with less real money to invest, an active market can also be a dangerous one."

"And if friends wanted to get out of that deal, how would they go about doing that?"

"We're talking about your friends, Fanny, aren't we?" Sam interrupted, "because if you went off on your own not knowing what you were doing, I'd have to say that those headbands you wear cut off the circulation to your brain."

"Your going a little too far, my friend," Freddy said, standing and throwing his napkin on the plate to let his brother-in-law know that he was getting annoyed.

"Sammy," Jonah interrupted. "Perhaps you've gone a little too far with prodding your sister, and I think you owe her an apology. Whatever she might have done, takes nothing away from you or yours."

Sam put his cigarette out in the ashtray, and said, "I'm sorry." Again, he slightly deflated.

There was an uncomfortable silence as Sam lit another cigarette, and Freddy took his seat, still scowling at his brother-in-law. "Well, I think it's time that Marta and I went to see what our grandchildren are up to," Jonah said, nodding furtively at Marta. He had enough of his children for one night.

"I bought a new game for the children called, Escalado. It's a horseracing game from England where model racehorse game pieces make their way across a long fabric racetrack towards the finish line at the other end. There's this mechanical hand crank that you turn that vibrates the track in a random fashion so it seems to be a live race. I'm going upstairs to try it out. And behave yourselves." He and Marta left the room.

"Fanny, Freddy," said Maurice. "We'll speak about this matter in private. You come up to my office the first thing tomorrow, and Armand, we may need you there also for legal advice."

"I'm not sure about tomorrow," Armand replied. "I've something on my plate that you should all know about, but I didn't want to say anything in front of my parents. Hopefully, they won't find out. It's about Abe."

"Oh, God," groaned Sam. "I need a drink. Anyone else want one?" All hands around the table went up, and laughter followed. Sam brought a bottle of Canadian whiskey out of his satchel and over to the table, walking around pouring shots. "You will all forgive me for not pouring this good booze into the correct glass," he said, glancing at Fanny who had gotten up for ice cubes. He returned to his seat. "Now what dear brother do you have to say about our brother?"

"First off, Maurice, I'll be over tomorrow as soon as I can. Fanny, Freddy, you bring whatever paperwork you have, and we'll figure out something that will hopefully extricate you from this deal before it's too late."

He sat down again and took a sip. "Now, I don't know if they can pin this on Abe or not, but it would seem that certain people with whom he is closely associated have been holding up messengers from New York brokerage houses, and they've been stealing in the millions. They're all inside jobs with employees and messengers who are allowing themselves to be held up and even beaten for a share of what is stolen. When this one firm was robbed and they couldn't meet their payment to the bank for a loan, they decided to sell some securities that they were holding for collateral. But when they went to retrieve them, they discovered that the securities had themselves been stolen."

"So, what does that have to do with Abe?" Aaron asked.

"Well, Aaron, it seems that our dear half-brother, not contenting himself with just rum running, speakeasys, distribution of illegal liquor, gambling, and a variety of other nasty bits, was the one who supplied those stolen securities to that brokerage firm as collateral for one of his deals. These stolen securities are connected with Abe, and that connects Abe to this ring of thieves who stole the securities in the first place. Several of these messengers told the police that they had secretly met with certain men and a banker where they were assured that they would be able to escape without any interference from the police. Our brother was identified from a mug shot as the banker in question."

"Oh, shit!" blurted Sam. "Papa doesn't know anything about this, does he?"

"Not yet, but it won't be easy for Abe to walk away from this. His lawyers are keeping this as quiet as they can with all sorts of writs and subpoenas, but when this breaks, and it will, this is going to be big news, and Abe's face will be everywhere."

"Have you spoken to Abe recently?"

"I called him," Armand said, "but he knows that I can only quietly advise him. We can't be seen in public together."

"What did he say about it?"

"He said that he didn't know the those securities were stolen, and that he was being set up."

"Do you believe him?"

"Doesn't matter what I believe. The police have been trying to pin something on Abe for years, but nothing has stuck. This time they think they have the evidence to bring him to trial."

"Then perhaps it's time we send Papa and Marta on a long cruise, maybe around the world, so they won't be around when the police charge Abe."

"How soon do you think they'll bring Abe up on charges?" asked Fanny, her eyes welling up.

"My contacts say within the month."

"Aaron, you're graduating from college next week," Maurice said. "As a gift, the family has just decided to send you on an extended, all expenses paid vacation to Asia with your mother and father. I will tell mom and papa that I have friends who need someone to contact prospective customers for new markets. You majored in business, and you're going to law school in the fall, so they'll see this offer as an opportunity for you. I will make them feel a great need to go along just so you won't be lonely or get into trouble. As for you, I'll guarantee that the year or so that you'll be away will be well worth your while when you return to Harvard Law School or to a desk at a major corporation. Yes, you'll gather the data as cover, but your primary job will be to keep our parents away from international news reports about what's going on here. Do you think you can do that?" Maurice and Armand looked at the rest of the family who were nodding in agreement. "The fewer people in the family who know about this, the better it will be."

Jonah and Marta, were in Kyoto, Japan admiring and purchasing several Hiroshiki prints when Abe went to trial, but the news of a gangster going to trial had been pushed off the front page and radio reports with the fall of the Stock Market in October of 1929. The tabloids did more with the story, but Asia, like the rest of the world, was more concerned about how the world markets would fair in light of what was happening in the United States. The accusations against Abe were clear, and they could make the case that he was the owner of stolen securities, but they could not make the case that he actually knew about them being stolen. Harry, to his credit, had created any number of dummy corporations that stood as fences around his brother, Abe, Joey, and himself, so that there was so great a distance between these corporations and ownership leading back to the trio, that the state could not prove beyond a reasonable doubt that Abe, in fact, knew about these securities. Remembering what Armand had told him so many years ago about "taking the fifth," Abe repeatedly stood behind his Supreme Court given right. So between the State not being able to prove that Abe had a direct knowledge of the stolen securities, and the mincemeat that Bernstein and Pambino made of the credibility of their main witness, the jury remained at a stalemate until the judge finally declared a mistrial.

The Stock Market crashed during the months that Abe was on trial, and though free on bail, he was monitored day and night. He decided that only his family would be seen visiting, so the police could not say he was colluding with other members of his gang. Harry came and went without being noticed because the police viewed Harry as a legitimate businessman who owned a chain of coat check establishments in hotels and restaurants.

"It's a mess out there," Harry said. "People are jumping out of windows, and everything is up for sale. Banks are closing right and left, and people are begging in the streets and selling apples. Businesses are closing, and those still with jobs are just lucky to have work."

"How's Papa?" Abe said. "Is he following the trial?"

"As far as we know, he doesn't even know about it. We sent Aaron, Papa, and Marta off on an extended vacation where most people don't speak English, and so far so good. When he comes home, this mess will be over."

"What's going on with business? How badly are we effected?"

"Well, you know that Maurice pulled the family out of anything bought on margin and divided the profits evenly. Fanny and Freddy did some investing on their own, so they lost a bundle. For the time being, they've put their furniture in storage, and moved back into her old bedroom until they can recoop. Freddy's business went under."

"What about Virginia and Leo," Abe asked. "Are they OK?"

"They're fine." Harry said. "She doesn't know about what was in the trust for Leo, and that money will be apportioned weekly by a check to each of them."

"And what about us?"

"Well, Abe," Harry said smiling, "the crash may have improved business." Abe looked at him curiously. "With the banks closing," Harry continued, "and with those left open unwilling to make loans, even with high interest, we've sort of filled that empty space."

Abe smiled, imagining that the boys had taken a page from the Krivoser Society and opened up a loan division. The smile became a smirk. "And how much interest are you charging for the service?"

"Twenty percent," Harry said, and he pulled figures and names out of his memory and spread the air with huge dollar signs. "Sure, people would rather deal with the banks at a smaller interest, but since the banks are reluctant, we're the only option in town for those who are desperate. It's Capitalism; supply and demand. It's just like what the government did with Prohibition. They created a need, and we're filling that need. The government knew all along that prices for stocks had to stop going up. Every boom is eventually going to bust. They knew that the numbers of people buying only for short term gain had to become exhausted eventually, and they knew that people who bought on margin would have their loans called in because no one was going to want to buy their binders that became worthless. This whole mess could have been avoided if Washington had the balls to tell the Wall Street lobby to go screw themselves. Those greedy pigs in Washington, to keep their own war chests filled for the next elections, turned a blind eye to what was going on."

"Abe, we'll be making more money than we made before, and again we have the timidity and cowardice of our legislators in Washington to thank. I really must write a letter of appreciation."

CHAPTER 25

1933 & 1934

"I didn't sign up for this, Sammy." said Sadie, impatiently stamping out her cigarette while eyeing herself in the mirror. "You haven't sold a painting in God knows how long, and the kids need new outfits for school, and you dribble out little bits of it to me as you see fit from your secret bank account somewhere."

Sam heard the sequence of unrelated attacks, and without turning towards her said, "There is no secret bank account, Sadie, and you know that as well as I do. There is the safety deposit box with cash in it, and that money is to get us through, however long this damn Depression lasts. If it ends tomorrow, then you can buy new dresses, but until the end comes, I'm the one who will make sure this family has enough to live on."

"If it's our money, why the hell can't I have a key to the box?"

"You can't have a key because if you did, the money would go on your back and not for food for the table. That's why you don't have a key." Sam was getting angry.

"You cheap son-of-a-bitch," she screamed. "I work my ass off here, and you give me shit in return. Why don't you trust me?"

Sam turned from his easel. In the ten years that they had been married, their lives, like most lives caught in the

Depression, radically changed. Because Maurice had wisely sold off the families' stock holdings before the crash, there was cash in a safe deposit box that could be relied upon for as long as the lean years lasted. The money was for basic survival; rent, clothes, food, supplies, and an occasional film. Maurice had offered suggestions for budgeting, and Sam followed Maurice's suggestions to the letter. But the amount of money Sam portioned out weekly, immediately became a bone of contention between him and his wife. For Sadie, there was never enough, and the free life she had enjoyed when times were good remained the standard for what she felt happiness was supposed to be.

"You have a roof over your head, food on the table, and if you or the girls need clothing, you have that, too. When there's a special need, like winter coats, you get more. But I'll be damn to hell if I'll give you one red cent so you can buy some French perfume or imported silk scarves from Italy. You get an allowance that keeps this house and our kids more secure than most people."

"I feel like I'm on a leash."

"Then go out and get a job, and whatever you make, you can keep. Until then, we buy only what's needed."

"You'd like to see your wife selling apples on the corner?" she sneered. "Or maybe I should sell myself like some girls I know to get myself some nice things. Or better yet, maybe you should get a real job instead of painting pictures nobody wants." She wanted to hurt him as much as she perceived he was hurting her. "Or maybe you should go to work for your brothers so we wouldn't have to live in this dump any more! They're real men who know how to treat their wives." The door to the apartment slammed.

Sam sat for a few moments, not really thinking about what she had said. Yes, he heard words, but they meant little to him because they came from a person who was coming to mean less and less to him as the years passed. Sadie was from the old neighborhood, and Jonah was irate when he found out that his youngest son was seeing a girl who came out of a family that everyone knew was as common as they get. But Sadie was pregnant, and Sam married her because it was the honorable thing to do. Sadly, in the fifth month she had miscarried, but Sam was not the kind of man who would abandon his wife. Now, they had two lovely daughters, and had it not been for them, he would have moved out a long time ago. There wasn't enough money to support two apartments, and he didn't want the girls to suffer the shame of separated or divorced parents. Besides, he liked the few comforts he had in the apartment and, if it meant putting up with some ridicule, so be it. Things were always better when he gave her her allowance on Friday night, even though she always complained that there was never enough.

So today, she vilified him for painting pictures no one wanted. That was true. Those who kept their wealth after the crash found great deals in the art world offered by formerly wealthy people who had gone bust and desperately needed cash to save what they could. Modern American artists like Sam and his friends went begging when Impressionists and Post-Impressionists were for sale at bargain prices to those who could still afford fine art.

He put down the brush, capped the tubes of his precious oils, and looked at the canvas. It was good, damn good, but as good as it was, he knew it wouldn't sell at this time. Though he was confident it would, eventually, he stood, stretched, and moved to the window and looked out. The winter sky was greying with snow clouds, and close to the pane, he could feel the winter chill seeping in through the sill. The building was old. He watched drab people, in a drab street, silhouetted against drab buildings, hugging themselves against the wind as they stood around big metal trash cans of flames that lashed the cold air with a hundred vermillion tongues. The people he saw moving with the gusts or against the gusts, moved with some purpose on their way home to small comforts earned from factory jobs that they were lucky to have. Others stood aimlessly, with their hands extended towards the flames. As he watched, he thought of the Bellows painting, *Disappointments of the Ash Can*. He had first seen it in the Met when he was a child, and he loved it and others like it because they reflected his city, its vitality, the places he frequented and the people and things he saw. A truth resonated within him when he looked at them because they depicted the raw reality of the common man in the streets. While he loved the style and the content, there was always a vague discomfort that these artists had separated themselves from the real reality, the harshness and poverty of the people they depicted. As great as they were, some of these artists seemed distant, almost disinterested, interested only in the art they were creating, and not in the truth of their subjects or the world they inhabited. But Sam grew up in a home that was awash with social conscious, often sung in full voice at the dinner table about unions, worker's rights, the vote for women, and civil rights. These, he came to believe, were the proper subject matter for art, and to capture the truth, he had to live where he could see the truth. Sadie hated him for keeping her and the children in Brownsville when they could have moved to Pelhem Parkway in the Bronx or Eastern Parkway in Brooklyn.

Sadie may have been right about Sam insisting that they live in a slum, but she was wrong about his art. Still, she might have unintentionally solved a problem for him by suggesting that he do something else. Sam put a blank canvas on the easel and began to sketch the bleak scene below the apartment window and the ashtray sky. He had an idea, and the idea might just get him a job.

President Roosevelt had created the Farm Security Administration Project, a subsidiary of The New Deal Agency, and was hiring photographers to travel across America, recording the images of laborers and farmers forced into debt and living in abject poverty. Roosevelt needed these images to move the Congress to act with legislation that could alleviate the tragic destitution depicted. That's where Sam's heart was, and if he could get a job working for this agency, he could do something meaningful and have a rationale for getting away from Sadie. When away, Maurice would dole out living expenses, and whatever pittance of a salary he would make, would also be sent to Maurice to be given directly to his daughters. That would at least make things easier for them. They were young and resilient, loved by his parents who would always take them if they needed a place away from their mother.

Sam quickly brushed in brown and grey slashes of color where the people and structures of the scene below would be, so as to better capture the moment rather than rely on his memory. He then turned to a file cabinet where he kept his sketches and photographs, looking specifically for those he had taken of the gritty truth that the early photos of Riis and Hine had inspired him to take of the real streets of the Lower East Side and Brownsville. These images, he believed, were the true goal of art.

1934

The job lasted a year, and when it was over, Sam had produced a huge portfolio of black and white images depicting broken wheels laying against rusted fences, old women dragging huge, sock like bags they were filling with cotton, half naked children huddled together on broken porches, and men and women with eyes devoid of hope. He met and became good friends with Ben Shahn, Dorothea Lang, and Walker Evans. He was especially impressed with Lang's vision of the dichotomy she revealed each time she photographed destitute Americans near a sign extolling the good life. Like her, Sam saw the irony in the advertisements that seemed to mock those who had little or nothing against the prosperity of big business. Sam and the others had become the extended eyes of the millions of Americans who never really saw or tasted the very real anguish of those most effected by the destruction of the land and the collapse of the farming industry.

The project gave President Roosevelt what he needed to move the Congress to act. Sam and the other artists on the project were empowered by what they saw and what they were able to do. The group continued to meet, expanded to other artists, and lobbied Congress to create a new project for the New Deal called the Works Progress Administration which offered employment to musicians, artists, writers, actors, as well as underwriting large dramatic, media, and literary projects.

In the year that Sam was involved in the project, Sadie had met a man at one of Abe's speakeasies and entered into an affair. The man was a banker, and believing he would whisk her away to a penthouse in New York, she filed papers for divorce citing abandonment. She told Jonah and Marta that she had found work outside the state and convinced them that uprooting the girls would do them great harm. In a private note to Sam, Sadie wrote, among other things, "you don't make enough money to compensate me for living with you." Two days later, Marion and Gertrude went to live with their grandparents. Shortly after that, Maurice learned that Sadie had not paid the rent, that she had kited checks, and forged Sam's name. Furious, he retaliated. One early morning she came in from a rent party she had taken her boyfriend to, and found that everything except her clothes, suitcases, and personal items were put into storage. Both she and Sam were homeless, so she packed her belongings, took money from her lover, and went to Reno. Sam, for a brief time, moved back to the Fifth Avenue house to get reacquainted with his daughters and center himself.

Sam's early involvement with the government and his outstanding work, brought him to the notice of Edward Bruce, the head of the Farm Security Project which was under the aegis of the U.S. Treasury Department. Bruce suggested Sam's name to Henry Morgenthau, the official who had ordered the creation of the Section of Painting and Sculpture of the WPA. This time, the objective of the Section was to employ artists of merit; not just work relief. Bruce's goal was to create an agency that would foster the creation of a thoroughly American National Art that would reflect values, achievements, and aspirations of the American People. With Morganthau's approval, Bruce invited Sam to be one of the managers in charge of coordinating the art projects, the murals, the sculptures, and the lithography that would ultimately decorate the public housing projects, the schools, the post offices, and public buildings. As one of the coordinators, Sam was charged with approving content and quality which at times made him the object of vilification by those artists he did not hire. Edward Bruce saw Social Realism as a truly American style of art, and he chose Sam because of the painting of the people in the wintry scene around the fire that Sam showed Bruce at the first interview. Edward Bruce wanted someone grounded in Social Realism, and Sam's background and focus on the early twentieth century painting revealed in his portfolio and interview, gave him a leg up when being considered for the job. Sam's vision was not art for art's sake, but art for improving the world. Bruce liked that about Sam, and believed that if Sam could take that same vibrant voice and vitality of the Ashcan style and focus on current events, the social and political turmoil of the day, then that would be something special and totally American. Sam was now in a position to make this happen. While Sam and Bruce could agree on the style that would be utilized in the many public projects, they were often in conflict over the content.

"Edward, you're tying my hands," Sam said, walking away from the desk spread with miniature depictions of murals to be put up in post offices in the western states. "You're telling me that we have to bend to the will of these reactionary organizations because my artists might hint at political undertones that these conservatives don't like? These conditions and restrictions that you are suggesting will destroy the core vision of the Section.

You're insisting that they become hypocrites in order to continue eating."

"Sam, we're living in difficult times," Bruce responded, holding out both his hands as if a supplicant. "Communism, Socialism, glorified unionism, and all sorts of isms have Americans looking over their shoulders and under rocks for traitors and conspirators. We have to play this game if we want to keep our jobs."

"This isn't a game, Edward," he shot back. "We're talking here about integrity and freedom of expression. I'm told that that's granted to us in the Constitution."

"Don't be flip, Chernov. I'm still your boss."

"And as my boss, and I thought my friend, I feel compelled to tell you that we have a woefully small number of artists temporarily working for us around the country. Their creativity is being crushed by the Liberty League and the Hearst newspapers calling for oaths of allegiance by artists, teachers. They are calling for the suppression of civil liberties, discrimination against foreign born, and Negroes. These are fundamental issues that effect artists and the subject of art. By acquiescing to them, you're allowing the tail to wag the dog."

"Sam," Bruce said, "I'm a bureaucrat with a family to support in a dark time." His brows furrowed and his face began to flush. "I do what I'm told to do by the people who cut my check, and I'm not going to do anything that is going to lose me my position. I'm not an artist, but I am your supervisor and superior, and I'm telling you not to challenge me on this."

"Look, I understand that public buildings need to take public sensibilities into consideration, and Benton, Wood, Bywaters and Curry do that. But to willfully stand by silently while they destroy magnificent murals in Rockefeller Center, the Museum of Modern Art, Lincoln High School, and Rikers Island Penitentiary because they suggest other ways of thinking that the oligarchs don't find comforting, is unconscionable and totally un-American." Sam took a breath. "And you, Mr. Bruce, should have had the integrity to stand against them and their demands against freedom of expression and speech."

"Are you quite finished, Mr. Chernov? Yes?" His face was now crimson, and a large vein bulged on his left temple. "You're fired!" he shouted, "and get this garbage off my desk and clear out all the other salacious and sacrilegious garbage you've allowed to accumulate."

CHAPTER 26

1937

Shepsah Silverman stood up, believing that his formidable presence was enough to silence and bring to order the boisterous and sometimes belligerent members of the East New York Benevolent Society. It did not. "We are here to discuss procedures for moving forward," he screamed above the din, banging the gavel repeatedly. "I know there are differences of opinion, but it will be impossible to hear what they are without some semblance of decorum. Now, please sit down. Now!"

One by one, the representatives of the different lansmanshafens that made up the society, like those from the Krivoser Society, sat down at the round tables, each set with paper cups, a blue seltzer bottle, a dish of chick peas, and rugelach which the ladies auxiliary had made. Next to Silverman sat Jonah, the executive secretary, taking notes and doing his best to refrain from saying something rude to the representatives of the prustas from the Sarkienozena Society that would send them raging out of the room.

Jonah believed and insisted that if this loose amalgamation of Jewish organizations composed of old immigrants, old Communists, old Socialists, old Anarchists, and first generation Americans, could come together and speak with one voice to a government who denied them the mechanisms to confront current government policies regarding the treatment of Jews in Europe and in the Middle East, they could make a difference. He also knew that their common faith and heritage did not make up for the lack of a central organized system that would enable them to effect changes and enable them to appropriately respond to the Nazi threat. This society was the closest organized effort they could get to, and more often the meetings broke up amid recriminations and finger pointing. The real and imagined ramifications for stepping out of the place in which they perceived themselves to be, made them fearful. After all, America was rife with anti-Semitism, and their memories were long.

Jonah knew that the divisiveness among the Jews present would make any attempt to form a unified front difficult. He was aware that the older and more established German American Jewish Community, who were not part of this organization, felt that a low key approach to the Nazi menace was the best diplomatic action. But he also knew that the American Jewish Congress demanded protests, rallies, and boycotts. There was an ongoing debate about whether Jewish organizations should call for a nationwide boycott of German goods, because the Jews in Germany opposed such an effort, fearing that it would make things worse for them. The Nazis did make it worse for them by boycotting Jewish businesses when such boycotts took place here. And into this mix were the Zionists and non-Zionists who opposed each other on issues related to how to further the goals of Israel becoming a safe haven. Then there were the ultra-Orthodox Jews who were solely interested in saving Orthodox rabbis and rabbinic students. Though not represented, everyone knew about and reviled the Bergson Group who advocated a militancy that just about all rejected. In short, Jonah knew that as long as this group lacked an organized plan on how to proceed, they and other organizations like theirs, would be of little effect.

Anti-Semitism and the Depression were realities in America, and the voices of noted bigots like Charles Lindbergh, Henry

Ford, William Dudley Pelley, and Father Coughlin continued to seed the atmosphere with a hatred born of pure ignorance and ancestral misinformation. To these men, and to the people who renewed their justification for hating Jews each time they listened to them, the Jews were the cause of everything that was wrong in America. The Jews caused the Great War, the Stock Market crash, the Depression, and anything else requiring a scape goat. All this resulted in the Jewish people becoming reluctant to take to the streets or speak out for fear that they would be, at worst, beaten in the streets, lose their livelihoods, or be ridiculed by their Christian neighbors. They become ossified by what might happen. Even the Hollywood moguls, all Jews of Eastern descent and able to bring the Nazi atrocities to the public eye, were reluctant to deal with the issue for fear of losing European markets. They thought that to focus on the Jewish issue would make it seem like it was a war against the Jews and not a war against democracy or America. A war against America was far more compelling than the murder of Jews.

Jonah rose silently and waited for the people to recognize that he had something to say. People began to hush one another. He cleared his throat and his tone was somber. "Ladies and gentlemen," he said above the few remaining people who continued their own private conversation. He waited again for their attention. "The Talmud," he continued, "tells us two things I believe should guide our actions on this subject no matter what your current thinking might be regarding whatever action we take. The first is, 'Silence implies consent,' and the second is, 'He who saves a life has saved a whole world.'" He waited for the phrases to sink in. "Please, do not imagine that what is happening in Europe is something what will pass. Please, do not imagine that the pogroms that took our loved ones in Russia or in Ukraine over twenty years ago is anything like this. What happened in Russia was local. What Hitler intends is for all of Europe, and if he is successful, all the world. What I see, and what I'm asking you to see, is that this onslaught against our people is like nothing that we have ever seen before. I've read what this modern Pharaoh has written. I've read the speeches of this modern Hayman. This man is insane and this man is evil, and I believe that he will do everything that he writes and says he will do. We must believe that what he writes is what he intends to do. If we are to save those who are currently suffering in Europe, and if we are to save ourselves, we need to put aside our differences and focus on those two statements. If we remain silent despite our fears, we will appear to have no opinion, or worse, not care which would make us appear as heartless confederates, or blind to reality. No decision is also a decision. No action is also an action. If we do not act to save those we can save, we will have participated in destroying our people and our future with our own hands. We will be guilty, and history will condemn us for our silence and inaction. Our children and grandchildren, when the truth of what is going on is fully revealed, will look at us and condemn us for not doing what we could have done." He scanned the crowd. Some were leaning forward, nodding in agreement, and some were sitting there making side comments to friends while sipping tea and eating honey cake.

"This will go away, Chernov," said a man in the rear of the room. "We've seen this throughout our history. It's bad for a time and then it gets better. We're all in the same boat, and if you start rocking it by pushing the government, it could happen to us here the way it's happening there. You saw what they did to Leo Frank."

"Coward!" shouted a man at another table. "Sit down and shut up," shouted another. Silverman banged the gavel again.

Jonah swallowed hard and looked at the man through the smokey haze. "Listen to me my friend," he said, trying to control his tone. "You know as well as I, that what happed to Leo Frank did not happen because the Federal Government made it happen. A mob of angry Jew-haters pulled him from his cell and hanged him when they heard that the government wanted to give him a new trial. Honest people saw through the lies and moved heaven and earth to dismiss the verdict. If not, they wanted at least to open up a new trial. Good people who were not Jews stood up for Frank. Good people in America will stand up for us, too. Yes, in Russia, hanging Jews and pogroms were sanctioned and encouraged by a government that should have protected their people, but that's not the way it is in America. No government goons ride through our streets beating you, or breaking down your doors to steal from us or rape our women. So why are you thinking like you never came out of Russia? This is not Russia. This is not Poland or Germany." Jonah's voice became emphatic.

"We stand here at a crucial moment my friends, and wringing our hands and sheepish silence is not an option that will save our brethren in Europe. We stand at a moment where we must act for their good and for our own. You all studied to become citizens of this country. You all know that those who began this country were willing to sacrifice their 'lives, their fortunes, and their sacred honor' for it. Our own people are being massacred. What are we willing to do about it? If you were in their place, what would you have us do? I have family and friends in Europe. Most of you have family and friends in Europe. Think of your own families if you can't think of someone else's."

"So what are you suggesting we do about it, Chernov? We're nobodies with no access. What can we do?"

"I'll tell you what we can do about it, my friend. My son has access because he works out of Washington, and he knows Rabbi Wise who is the president of the American Jewish Congress. Wise has access to big people, and tonight, with your help my friends, we are going to draft a petition that I can give to my son so he can give it to Wise. And Wise will give it to someone important who can get it into the hands of someone more important. We will request that the quotas placed on immigration from Eastern Europe be raised to what they are for people coming in from Britain and Ireland. We will request that all restrictions on Jewish children be lifted, and we'll request that boats like the St. Louis with people fleeing death, never be turned away again. Finally, we will request that our government pressure Great Britain to rescind MacDonald's White Paper, limiting the number of Jews allowed to enter Palestine. When Rabbi Wise receives our petition, there will be an attached letter with a request that someone in his World Jewish Congress organize a march on Washington, and if the good rabbi isn't willing to provide people to walk with me, with us, I'm going to go to Washington and march all by myself. My name will be the first one on this petition because as an American, I have the right to petition my government. Better yet, we have a right to petition our government, and I ask that you help me do this. I am asking you to sign your names, and I am asking you to save innocent lives. I am asking you to do what's right."

Armand took the petition to Rabbi Wise, and though Wise was appreciative of the efforts and the requests, he said that he could not move on it because those Jews he dealt with in the government were still unwilling to risk their jobs on what most believed was an exaggeration of the conditions in Europe. He informed Armand that while he had no access to the president, he and his group were working tirelessly on pressing for changes in the immigration laws and forms. As far as the pressure on Britain was concerned, that seemed to be no one's priority but the Jews. But there were back doors that were being opened that he could not talk about, and the British were quietly being thwarted not only with Jews being secreted into Palestine, but also with weapons entering clandestinely.

CHAPTER 27

1938

"Why won't you listen to what I'm telling you?" Sarah stood in the middle of the room, shaking her cane at her family, genuine fear in her eyes. "This is how it starts. It started like this in Russia, and people we thought were friends were not. We are never not Jews to these people no matter what we do for them, or how we prove our loyalty. Austria is opening her arms to the Nazis, and if you think that the Austrians will stand with us against the Germans, you are fools. I lived through betrayals in Russia and in France. It won't be different here." Her voice trembled, and her prophesy of doom spouted from her like blood from a severed artery. "You didn't see for yourselves, 'Jude' scrawled in yellow paint on the windows of Jewish stores? Even big stores like yours, Frederick, are not safe if they are owned by a Jew. Go and see if it is not true. No, don't go. They'll get you. My friend warned me, and such a warning won't come again. Austria unlocked the cage door and the animals are in the streets. I've seen this before!" She sank onto a chair, seemingly exhausted from emotion.

"Mama, what are you talking about?" Frederick interjected, seeing the concern on Ruth's face. "You're frightening Ruth with all this talk. We're good Austrians. Why would anyone try to hurt us? The government won't allow it."

"Nahr!," Sarah blurted, reverting to the Yiddish word for fool. "She needs to be frightened. You need to be frightened. Everyone needs to be frightened. Who's coming for us? The Nazis, Hitler, the Austrians who hate us, that's who. Hitler wrote that we should be destroyed, and now he preaches that we should be destroyed. You should believe what people write and say! I've seen men like him before, and my friend in the convent believes it too. She told me this morning in the market that we must hide or leave Austria altogether. She received a letter from her Bishop saying that as Mother Superior, she was to forbid the sisters from leaving the convent tonight or tomorrow. She told me that she saw Austrian hooligans scrawling the word 'Jude,' on doors and windows, and that she had seen them drawing swastikas on the doors of the synagogue. This very night, the Jews are being targeted for beatings and that their stores are going to be attacked. She told me."

"This is Austria and we are Austrians," interrupted Heinrich who was clearly upset that his grandmother had insinuated that they were not safe in their own country. Sarah turned to him.

"Don't think because they like the way you play the piano you will be safe from them. I know that Herr Freud is going to England, and Herr Mahler, converted or not, is still a Jew who will have to run for his life. You have Jewish blood, and that is all there is to it. They look at us like we are vermin to be exterminated. You don't remember why we had to take you and your sister and brother out of the schools you were in when you were children? You forgot the names you were called by your good Austrian classmates?" Heinrich shrunk back. His grandmother had never spoken to him that way. No one ever had.

"Mama, you'll make yourself sick," Ruth said. "Come and have some tea."

Sarah looked at her incredulously, and for the first time in years, she would not consciously coddle her daughter or her grandchildren. "Fools," she declared. "What fools!"

"I'm going out to see about this," said Frederick, ringing for the butler to get him his hat and coat. "I'll go with you Papa," Heinrich said. "I don't believe it."

Sarah moved to the door and stood in front of it. "I said that it is too dangerous for any Jew to be on the street tonight. Why would the Sister have told me this if it wasn't true? Stay here."

Against Sarah's additional dire warnings, the father and son pushed past her and ran into the night.

Two hours later, there was a frantic banging on the front door. Herr Hoffmann, the store manager from the emporium, was gasping for breath and begging to enter. Blood from a gash on his cheek was crusting on the collar and shoulder of his jacket. The maid screamed and stepped back as Ruth ran out of the parlor, followed by Sarah and the children. "Herr Hoffmann, what has happened? Gretchen, bring strong coffee."

"Herr Kreiten and Heinrich came to the store and saw hooligans painting swastikas on doors, breaking windows, and screaming, 'Jews Get Out.' The police did nothing to stop these men, and when the three of us complained, we were shoved back and told to be quiet. Then another gang of hoodlums in brown shirts came from around the block and started throwing rocks at every window that had been marked as a Jewish owned store. Then the people on the streets, with the hoodlums, started looting what was in the windows. They became like ravenous beasts, tearing at what the other stole like they were starving children fighting over food. A man I knew called me a 'Jew lover,' and hit me with a brick. That's how I was hurt. Only after the damage was done did the police finally order them away, but in the melee that followed, Jewish men were pushed into vans and taken away. I didn't see what happened to Herr Kreiten or your son, but someone said that the police took them. By this time, there was so much chaos that you couldn't tell who was from the police and who was a Nazi. Dear Freu Kreiten, as an Austrian and as a Catholic, I'm ashamed to say that they were working together." He paused. "I am not a Jew, but what happened this night is very wrong and unworthy of Austria. I can say this from my heart. Your husband has been very good to me and to my family, and I am deeply ashamed. If I can do anything for you, please feel free to call on me."

Sarah stood, the color drained from her face. "There is something you can do for us. Stay and eat and gather your strength. Gretchen, set another place. Herr Hoffmann will be joining us for dinner."

Sarah insisted that everyone eat, even if they were not hungry. "I'm going to ask the servants to go out to look for Herr Kreiten and my grandson. You, Herr Hoffman, if you would be so good as to help them organize themselves? After that, I ask you to go to the police and inquire about them. Since you work for Herr Kreiten and are a Catholic, they will not be suspicious, and you will not be in danger. Tell them that you need to know what to do about the store and all the Austrians who work there. We would appreciate that very much."

Herr Hoffmann agreed immediately, grateful that there was some small thing he could do to help his employer, and appreciative for the chance to rest before the next ordeal.

Ruth interrupted her mother for the first time that morning. "Herr Hoffman," she said, her voice trembling, "I want you to get the windows replaced, and run the store the way you always would. So many people depend on the store for their livelihoods, and they must not be without their work. This will pass, I'm sure of it."

After a hasty dinner, Herr Hoffmann stood and offered a brisk bow. All the household staff were gathered and Sarah ordered them to follow Herr Hoffmann to the store and gather whatever information they could about Herr Keiten and Heinrich. She had asked the servants to report what they found to Herr Hoffmann, then to return to their own homes to be with their families. They left the room. "Herr Hoffmann," Sarah whispered, pulling him aside, "If you gather any news at all about my family, go to the convent door tomorrow morning and tell the nun who answers it that you have an important message for the Reverend Mother. You tell the Reverend Mother what you know, and she'll get the information to me. Herr Hoffman looked at her curiously, wondering what this old Jewish woman had to do with the head of a Catholic convent. The servants followed, resentful of the order, and appreciative of being allowed to go home.

When they were gone, Sarah motioned Berta and Sigmund closer to their mother and spoke softly. "Now, I don't want you to say a word of what I'm going to say to you to the servants. No one can be trusted except family from now on." They leaned in closer to the conspiracy. "Ruth, you and I are going upstairs and we are going to go through your jewelry. Sigmund, you bring a knife to your mother's room because we are going to have to pry stones out of their settings, and I need your strong hands. Berta, go into my room and on the mantle there is a clock that doesn't work. Open the back and take out the money I've hidden there, and bring it to me. If you have anything of value in your own jewelry case, bring it with you." The children disappeared into their tasks as Ruth helped Sarah up the steps.

"I don't know what is happening, Mama, and you're frightening me with this talk of attacks against Jews. We have never bothered anyone that they should hate us or want to hurt us. We are good loyal Austrians."

Sarah's breathing was straining from the climb. "Even basically good people have hate in them, and the civilized ones keep it to themselves," her mother said, "but there are others who need to blame others for their lives, and we are an easy target because there are few of us and we have no one to protect us. It's always been that way."

Sarah unlocked the safe hidden behind a Renoir, and took out Ruth's jewel box. Bundled together in a leather binder were Frederick's life insurance policies, deeds to their homes, a listing of art that the family owned, the ownership papers for the department store, and other real estate holdings in Vienna and in the countryside. She set these, along with a stack of cash, onto the bed, and began separating them into three piles. "Berta," she ordered, "go back to my room and get me my sewing kit and the large pair of scissors from the dressing table drawer. Sigmund, you get a large towel from the bath."

Once all was in place, she threaded four needles and cut the towel into six strips. Neatly, she carefully placed some of the cash and a few of the papers on each strip and covered it with another. Then she instructed how the sides were to be sewn so that nothing would fall out, and she attached a safety pin at the end of each. Berta and Sigmund looked to their mother for some explanation, but none came.

"Take off your shirt, Sigmund."

"Yes, and you two watch what I'm doing because you're going to have to do the same." Sarah had no time for courtesy or concerns for modesty, and she took one of the sewn towels, wrapped it around her grandson's torso, and pined it in the back tightly enough so it would not fall. Sigmund put his shirt on and was told to turn away as his mother and sister did the same.

Sarah then set him to prying out the gems that had graced the beautifully designed jewelry that Frederick had bought for Ruth on special occasions or for no occasions at all. Ruth complained that Frederick would be upset, but Sarah assured her that he would understand why they were doing this when he got home. When the mountings were empty, Sarah divided the gems into six piles and placed them into jewelry pouches. Sigmund was told to go into the bathroom and to put his pouch into his underwear and to secure it. He began to object, but the look of fear mixed with ferocity in his grandmother's eyes told him that she was not to be denied. Something was about to happen, and his grandmother was taking charge because no one else would or could. Berta and Ruth were instructed to place each of their pouches under each breast. The towel would keep the pouches from falling.

"Now, go to your rooms and pack a small valise with underwear and toiletries, but no makeup or perfumes. Then come downstairs act as if nothing has happened. I will tell the cook to keep Federick and Heinrich's dinner warm before I send her away, and no one is to say anything about what we have done. Berta, clean up these shreds, and Sigmund, you put the mountings back in the safe and make everything look like it was. Remember, not a word."

Heinrich and his father did not return for dinner, and Ruth paced up and down like a frightened child anticipating a scolding. Sarah, Berta, and Sigmund peered through openings in the curtain, listening to the shattering of glass and the screams in the distance. In the moment, Sarah was transported back to Krivoser and the peasants who had come out of the field, raped her and gouged onto her breasts Cyrillic crosses, and then forced her to watch as they ravaged Ruth. Again, she could feel the hot breath of the world's hate on her face as it once again lumbered steadily towards her and her child, heralded this time by fire and shattered glass. This time she would be ready. She had seen this coming years ago, and as chance would have it, in the years that she worked in the Freud household, she had an opportunity to befriend Sister Celestine who was assigned as a companion to accompany certain patients. Sarah had invited the sister into the kitchen for company and introduced her to Eastern European cooking. The older and younger woman became friends. Now Sister Celestine was Reverend Mother, and it was not uncommon for Sarah to find herself sitting in the parlor of the convent having tea. They were bound by friendship and by truth, so Sarah, knowing how deeply in debt the convent was, offered her friend the opportunity to receive funds desperately needed in exchange for the safety of the convent as part of their escape route if one was ever needed. Since Sarah ran a frugal household, she was able to squirrel away, over the years, a cache just for such an emergency. There were also jewels to augment the cash. She also asked that some portion of the money be used for taking in and hiding those who would be orphaned. Vowing to herself that no one else in her family would go missing, Sarah made sure that no one left the house until she said they might.

The chimes of the clock in the foyer sounded five times, and Sarah, startled, lashed out with her cane against something she sensed lurked in the darkness. Nothing was there. The others were asleep where they sat, waiting for Federick and Heinrick's return. She composed herself and shuffled over to the window. A sliver of cold grey light sat hesitantly on the horizon, seemingly afraid to bear witness to the prior evening's destruction. Federick and Heinrich had not returned, so Sarah woke up the others. She turned to Sigmund. "You need to shave your face and neck very closely. Thank God you are fair." Again, he protested, reminding his grandmother how long it had taken to grow it, but Sarah was having none of it. Turning to Ruth and Berta, she told them to go upstairs and wash every bit of rouge and eye makeup off their faces. "Look as plain as you can, and then come back down to the laundry and find something to wear that would show that you are a servant, and when you walk, slump like you're carrying a pail of water in each hand. And take nothing with you other than the things you packed last night." Each nodded in compliance.

They assembled themselves in the basement where they changed into the clothing the servants wore, and then she handed them each something to eat. "We're going to the convent. We'll be safe there with my friend, but it will be only temporary. We have to get out of Vienna while we still can."

"But we have to wait for Papa and Heinrich," Berta protested. "How can we leave them and our home? Everything we love is here."

Sarah looked at her and saw herself in her anguish and in her pleading. "I have had and I have lost," her grandmother responded, "and I am still alive. My father was murdered, my husband was murdered, and my family was torn apart by people just like the ones who were running through the streets last night. I know what is going to happen. I could have died then if I had a mind to die, but I had your mother to look after, and a granddaughter to look after. I could only do that if I chose to live. At that time I had nothing left to me, but life. Today, you have a great deal, but they are only things. If you are dead, what do the things matter? You are not these things. What you carry on you is enough for you to survive. Life is what must be protected. You have no choice. I take that choice away from you. I'm making the choices for all of you."

The sliver of vague light in the east had expanded into a swath of dull yellow that was punctuated by billows of smoke left by burning buildings. It was Sarah who first peered out of the servant's entrance from the partially opened door and scanned up and down the road that led to the carriage mews. She handed a bucket to each along with a mop or broom, motioning them to step out as she locked the door. Few people were on the streets at this early hour except for a street sweeper and some delivery men. She told them to keep their heads low and to walk with purpose. The convent was blocks away. Other people got into cars, and in the distance Sarah saw a group of men coming out of a neighbor's house, pushing the owner in front of them.

"They're rounding up Jews. Quickly, cross the street." They followed her down an old carriage mews to the next street, and again, saw others looting the belongings out of Jewish houses whose windows had been broken. They stepped over shards of glass, torn books; some in German and some in Hebrew. And then they saw the raging fire that engulfed their beloved synagogue, the charred columns, the doors ripped from their hinges, and the devils laughing as they relieved themselves on the prayer books that they had thrown into the street. In the street, a Torah scroll rolled out on the cobble stones, was covered with footprints, urine, and feces. Each of them gasped and their steps faltered, but Sarah urged them on. "Don't look at anyone, and don't say a word."

"Hey," someone yelled at them as they rushed past the ruin. "If you're going to work for Jews today, don't bother." The man began to laugh and his laugh echoed in their ears as they quickened their steps again.

"Keep your eyes to the ground," Sarah said again, "and say nothing."

As Sarah knew, four servants on their way to work in the street that early did not raise any questions as to their business there, so while booted goons detained others, they were not molested. Still, they were cautious, and even when they finally reached the small door in what seemed to be a solid brick wall surrounding the convent, they did not breathe any easier. Dangling in the wind was a rusted bell chain that Sigmund pulled. When there was no response, Sarah reached for the iron knocker in the center of the door and pounded it several times. Finally, a severe face framed in white, opened a small window in the door and studied them mistrustfully. "What is your business here?" she said sharply, suspicious of anyone who might be in the street at this moment. "Mother Celestine told us to come to clean the chapel," responded Sarah, and thrust what looked like a button through the bars in the window. The sister took it, studied it, looked at Sarah curiously, and then they heard a metal bolt scraping and the door creaking open. The sister stepped back to allow them entry. She stuck her head out of the door and looked up and down the street, quickly bolting the door again. The clanking of the bolt into the socket and the silence that followed, gave each of the refugees their first easy breath. The family was quickly moved along through the cloister, through a large oak door to an ante-room where they were motioned to sit on a wooden bench under a crucifix. Gratitude and a vague uneasiness mixed in each of them. Emotionally, they were all in a terrible state, but they were safe for the moment. Not even the brown shirted thugs would trouble the sanctity of a religious order. At least, not yet.

Their arrival was timed to morning mass when the sisters would be in the sanctuary and unaware of their Jewish guests. Mother Celestine appeared and ordered the sister to join the rest at prayers, and ushered the group up the stairs to her private retreat. Hot chocolate and buns were waiting to comfort them and ease the chill. Sarah's friend conveyed the message from the Bishop in its entirety, and told them that while they could stay in the convent, suspicions could be raised and then they would no longer be safe. No one would be safe if their whereabouts were known to anyone other than herself. Sarah thanked her, fighting her natural inclination to challenge the Bishop's order to remain silent in the face of such an injustice, but Sarah remained silent and grateful, agreeing that by Vespers, when the sister were at evening prayers, each of them would dress as a nun and move out together to the railroad station. Sigmund objected to the thought of having to dress as a woman, but Sarah's glance shut down his complaint immediately. Ruth was starting to stare into some vague future, but Berta understood immediately. The Mother Superior produced two habits and two loose fitting dresses with aprons worn by novices, and left while the family took off what they were wearing and transformed themselves into members of her religious order. Berta laughed when she saw her clean shaven brother wearing black stockings, and the white apron covering his grey dress. "You look prettier than I do, Sigmund," Berta laughed, discounting completely the hot embarrassment that decorated every part of his body that was not covered. He winced.

"You'll get used to it," Sarah said. "You're lucky you're slight," she continued. "Your build may just save your life."

Sarah had also purchased cardboard suitcases that she left at the convent on prior visits. In these, she had secreted additional changes of underwear and dried food.

Throughout the day, Mother Celestine appeared and produced fruits and cakes from her habit, and these were washed down with water. In the hours that passed, the family alternately talked quietly about what would happen when they arrived in Switzerland, and agonized over what was happening to Frederick and Heinrick. When the Vesper bell sounded, and they could hear the chants of the sisters echoing through the stone corridors, Mother Celestine returned and led them through the cloister to a wooden door hidden behind a thick bush. She pushed it open and led them into the street.

"Thank you my dear friend," whispered Sarah. "May God protect you from what is coming." Sarah took out of her pocket a ruby that had come out of her favorite brooch and pressed it into the sister's hand. "Bless you again for your kindness to my family."

"I've decided to accompany you to the station. I am known, and if I am with you, there will be no doubt and no one will stop you or molest you." She paused. "Sarah, I shall walk ahead, and you and Ruth walk behind me. I know you are concerned about Ruth, and so am I. Berta and Sigmund, the two of you follow your mother and keep your heads down." She gave them the suitcases to carry. "And what ever you do, do not make eye contact with anyone on the street."

Berta and Sigmund obeyed, and focused on the hem of their mother's garment. But the glass they stepped over, and the acrid smoke that still hovered in the air, reminded them of the horror they had witnessed and reminded them of their father and brother. The silent question that passed between them was whether they would ever see them again, and they moved closer to each other so that their hands might touch.

The station was in chaos. Throngs of people with hastily packed bags were standing in line, waiting to get whatever train was leaving Vienna for France, Italy, Switzerland, or Spain.

Sister Celestine led Sarah's family to a shrine for travelers, and told them to wait there in a circle facing away from the crowds and the uniformed guards that were stopping travelers and demanding passports or letters of transit. They stood as she said, half afraid to even look at one another. Sarah, who was always in control by virtue of her loud voice and vitriol, had never before felt such vulnerability. All control had been given over to Sister Celestine, and now she was gone. She had the money, and the jewel. Could she be trusted to keep her word? How easy it would have been to garner favor with her Bishop and the Nazis by turning over a Jewish family. She lifted her head and her heart stopped. The Mother Superior was returning with two men. No, no, she thought.

"Here are the tickets. You have a private coach to Geneva, and these porters have been paid to carry your bags and accompany us to the platform to get you situated."

Sarah's expelled her breath and nodded to the men without lifting her head.

The family followed the men to the compartment. They opened the door for them and bowed in respect. The four sat down stiffly, hesitating to breathe until the train would move. Sister Celestine stood on the platform and handed the two porters enough to garner more than one bow of appreciation.

"Berta, Sigmund," their grandmother said softly. "Here are your tickets. You must be strong because your mother cannot be strong at this time. The way she is now is how she protects herself from things that frighten her. When she is in Switzerland, in the comfort of Aunt Dora and Uncle Jonathan's home, she will come back to herself. But you must understand. I must go and send a telegram to them to meet the train. You are not to worry about me. There are things I need to do and people I need to see about your father and brother. Your focus must be on protecting your mother and yourselves. Right now, you are novices accompanying this sister to her home in Switzerland to attend the funeral of her father. That is the story you must tell, and you stay as you are until you are safe in your aunt and uncle's home. I'll contact you as soon as I can. Here is the letter that Mother Celeste gave me. You give it to the guards at the Swiss border and there will be no problem." They both nodded, "Do whatever you have to do to live," she said, and left the compartment.

On the train platform, Sarah told the sister that she had to send a telegraph to her daughter to meet the train, and that she had to find her son-in-law and grandson. It was her hope that she could buy their freedom with other precious stones, and she silently prayed that whoever held them had no ideology other than feathering their own nest. Such people could be bribed, but not idealogues. The Mother Superior argued with Sarah quietly, but Sarah was adamant in her decision not to get on that train. As long as Ruth and her children were safe, it did not matter what was to follow.

Then, out of the corner of her eye, Sarah saw a young girl standing a few feet away who was alone and weeping. She was no more than ten, and was wearing a red coat and matching hat. In her hands she clutched a small suitcase and a doll. The child looked like Dora had looked when she was that age, and Sarah, momentarily forgetting her own grief, approached and asked what was wrong. "My daddy's store was set on fire by the bad men, and now my daddy was taking me to a safe place." She wiped her nose with her hand. "He told me to stand here while he got tickets, but I saw how some men took him away. I don't know what to do." Sarah, still holding her own ticket, looked at the child and saw in her thousands of other children who would also be left alone, or sent away, or worse. She pressed the ticket into the little girl's hand. "Now listen to me. This is what you are going to do. You are going to get on this train, find the compartment where this seat is, and stay with the three nuns there who will take you to Switzerland. Do not be afraid, and you tell them that Sarah said that they should take care of you."

"But my daddy. He won't be able to find me when he comes back for me."

"You don't worry, now. I'll wait for him here and tell him that you are safe. I'll tell him where you are. What is your name?"

"Hannah Herman," she sobbed.

"Well then, Hannah Herman, it is good that we met." Sarah took Hannah's hand, took her back to the train, and lifting her onto the train, told her to go to the right and look for the compartment number. Sarah then hobbled over to the window where Berta was watching the scene and motioned for the window to be rolled down. "There's a little girl coming into the compartment. Take care of her. She has no one else."

"But what about you, Grandma?" Berta shouted over the din of the platform. "What are we to do? Mother is in another world. What are we to do without you?"

"You are a bright girl and you will know. You are three women from a religious order going to Geneva for a funeral. The little girl was entrusted to the convent and she is also going home."

A single bell clanged loudly and drowned out Sarah's last words of warning as a long low whistle began to blow. Steam billowed out of the engine further on down the platform and the train lurched and began to gain speed. Hannah pressed her face against the pane, searching for her father.

Sarah sent a telegram to Dora telling her that the overnight train from Vienna would be arriving at 9:00 in the morning and that she was to look for a nun, two novices and a little girl in a red coat.

Once Sarah changed back into her char woman clothes, she accepted the invitation to join her friend in a light supper. "Let me talk to my bishop and see if he can help you," she began, but Sarah would not accept this. "If you do that, he might ask you how you came to be involved with my family, and if he himself is fearful of any involvement with Jews, you and your convent could be in jeopardy. No, you've done enough. You've helped me save Ruth and the children. You've also helped me save that little girl. Your influence got us those tickets. I could never have given it to her if I didn't have it by your hand. Now, I must go and do what I have to do."

"May God be with you, Sarah."

"And with you, too."

They were jerked awake by the train coming into the Geneva station. Sigmund opened his eyes at the same time he felt his stomach growl. He could hear compartment doors being slid, and questions asked in German or French. Through the wall, he could hear a man pleading and then through the window he could see the same man pushed past their compartment and onto the platform. A dozen or so people stood in a roped off section, and the man was told to stand there. Guards in long leather coats walked up and down with lanterns while others made sure the people behind the rope did not move. He shook his sister awake. Hannah rubbed her eyes, and remembering what had happed the night before, began to cry. There was a knock at the door, and a similarly clad guard waited for it to be opened. "Look out the window, Sigmund," Berta ordered. "Try not to let him see your face." Ruth opened her eyes, but said nothing to her daughter or son and stared curiously at the cross that lay on her bosom. Berta was thankful that her mother said nothing. She opened the door to the imposing figure.

"May I please see your papers," he said perfunctorily, glancing down but suddenly became solicitous when he realized they were nuns. Ruth continued to say nothing, but Berta produced the letter of identification and passage from the Mother Superior that was to act in lieu of four passports. The conductor gave it a cursory scan and looked at the four people in the compartment. He directed his next question to Ruth, but when there was no response, Berta quickly said that she was returning to Geneva to bury her father, and that she had taken a vow of silence as a penance for his soul. The border guard nodded and turned back to Berta. Grandmother was right, she thought. She could do this. "And this little girl?" he said referring to the paper and looking at Hannah. This letter refers to four sisters, but no child. Berta caught her breath. "Oh," she said quickly. "She is from the orphanage in our convent. A good Catholic family in Geneva is coming to meet her with the idea of adoption. Older children are so hard to place you know, so we are very happy when someone expresses interest. There was another nun who was to come with us, but when she became ill, the child was substituted instead, and Mother Superior did not have time to change the wording. She assured us that the border guards would be understanding." The guard gave another cursory glance around the compartment.

"Sir, if you don't mind telling me, why was the man in the next compartment ushered off so forcefully and made to stand with those others?"

"Nothing for you to be concerned about, sister. The man is a Jew, as are the others. Switzerland doesn't want any Jews coming in, so they are being held until the government decides what they want to do with them. We expect them to swarm like locust, and we can't have our country overrun with Jews."

"What do you think will happen to them?" Berta asked.

"I hear we are setting up camps. We'll put them there until we decide what to do with them. I'm all for sending them back to wherever they came from."

"Bless you and your family," Berta said, silently wishing him and everyone like him, dead. Again, grandmother was right. Jews were not safe, even in Switzerland, so how would it be with her uncle and aunt? They were Swiss citizens. Where Jewish citizens in Switzerland also in peril?

Austrian thugs still scavenged the streets, looking to prey upon any Jew they could find. Sarah hobbled past them, her pail and mop protecting her from their scrutiny. But even when she opened the door to the kitchen and was inside the house, she did not feel safe. An old feeling rushed over her, a familiar vague and pervasive feeling of doom that she had carried with her from childhood. Its seed had lain dormant, but now it sprouted again. Sarah put down the pail and mop, and struggled up the stairs to the main floor. She was exhausted, but she knew she could not rest until she found her son-in-law and grandson and hopefully ransom their lives. She still had jewels enough. But as she began her struggle to ascend the stairs to the second floor, where the jewels were hidden, there was a loud banging at the door that reverberated throughout the house. A sudden fear surged adrenalin through her body and she sat down to calm herself. In a moment she pulled herself up on an unsteady cane, and slowly moved to a side window where she saw three men and a woman. Two policemen stood behind a man in a long leather coat with a swastika emblazoned on his armband. Her heart rate seemed to double and she felt faint when she recognized that Gretchen, the housemaid, was with them. The banging was incessant, and when the two policemen put their shoulders to the door, she thought it was best to open it. She had no place to go. Perhaps they knew where Federick and Heinrich were and were here to ransom them. Hesitantly, she pulled back the bar and turned the key.

"You certainly took your time, old woman," said a man with small round glasses on his nose. He was fat, and his face was wet from sweat even though the air was cool. They pushed past her. "Call the lady of the house and tell her to get down here," he commanded.

Sarah looked up the flight of stairs, knowing that her family was safe. "It's too early in the morning for the mistress to get up," she replied.

"Then I'll get her up," shouted the fat Nazi and motioned for the police to go up the stairs with the instructions that everyone there was to be brought down to him. "Old woman, do you know who I am?" he said, his eyes scanning the room like a wolf scanning a fold of sleeping sheep, coveting devouring everything he saw. "My name is Rosenberg, and I..." He was interrupted by an officer on the staircase. "There is no one here and no one has slept in the beds. They are gone."

The cold eyes narrowed and his face grew red. Sarah could see his rage and she became afraid. "I am here to clean the house," Sarah stammered. "I know nothing of where the family went. They don't take me into their personal confidence."

"She's lying," said Gretchen, moving from behind the Nazi. "She's the grandmother, and nothing happens in this house without her knowing about it. She knows where they are."

"You will lay in Hell for your treachery, Gretchen," Sarah spit the words out through clenched teeth, and for that she felt a gloved fist smash her across her face.

"You do not speak that way to a true daughter of Austria, filthy Jew," shrieked the fat man. "You will tell us where the wife and the children are, or you will never see the husband or son again."

Gretchen looked down contemptuously at the old woman at her feet, and her eyes gloated that the one who had given her orders was now taking them.

"You think these people are your friends, Gretchen? We were your friends. We were the ones who took you in when Sister said you had no place to go." Sarah was playing for time by diverting attention to the maid. "You owe your life to the kindness of Jews and this is how you repay us? Do you think these people will care about you and feed you when we are gone? Whatever God is watching you, Gretchen, He will not forgive you."

The Nazi smirked. "There is no God watching, old woman. Didn't you know that God is dead? And as long as God is dead, there is no one to judge, and we are all free to do whatever we like. You Jews ruined this world with your damn God and with your damn Jesus and your damn moral laws. The world has never forgiven you for that, and we are counting on that fact so Christians will look away from the burning synagogues, the beatings, and the broken glass. We did last night what we did because we could, and we could because we know that no one will lift a finger to help. Oh, yes, some good Christians will complain and even try to save you, but the vast silence of the others will give us the approval to do to you exactly as we wish. In fact, I do believe they will be happy to be rid of you. Believe me, your possessions are of far greater value to them than your lives." He paused till her eyes told him that she understood the truth he told.

"I will never tell you where the mother and children are," Sarah stammered, "but I know where there are jewels to buy the husband and son's freedom."

With that statement, the two policeman came forward with renewed interest. "You tell us where they are and they will be set free. I give you my word as an Austrian." the elder one said.

Sarah was tempted to spit on his shoes and call him a liar, but she thought better of it. Perhaps she could deal with him. The Nazi was a believer, and believers were not open to bribes. But perhaps the officer was.

"How do I know you will set them free? How do I know you even know where they are?"

"I know because all the Jews picked up last night are in a single location and waiting there for someone, how shall I say it, to express an interest in them. There is a price for their freedom."

The Nazi turned on him ferociously. "I am not here to barter for the lives of Jews. These people must be eradicated and Austria cleansed. To free them for money is hypocrisy and I am no hypocrite."

"Herr Rosenberg," the officer began, turning towards him and away from the woman on the floor. "Like you, I have no great love for these people, but there would be no harm is freeing a few of the wealthier ones in exchange for what they can offer. Life is hard in Austria. Money is hard to come by, and if the police can ransom a few Jews for personal benefit, we will do that if they promise to leave and never come back."

"Why let them live when we can just take it all? That is what will happen, or do you still hold with your faith that killing Jews is a bad thing. Remember, if there are no Jews to believe in God, then there is no God to judge the world. God is dead and so is his Son."

"I am not so easily willing to give up my Savior as you are, and these people are not my enemy," he said. "But the Nazis seem to be suspending our laws, and in doing so, have provided me and others like me with a way to help our families to survive. Paying to ransom a life is acceptable, and such payments have been going on for centuries. You may not fear their blood on your hands, Herr Rosenberg, but I still fear a Judgement Day."

"Killing Jews and taking what they have has been going on for centuries, too," countered the Nazi. "And that is what we intend doing."

"Then I can pay a ransom to get them back?" Sarah interrupted, wiping the blood from her lip and struggling to stand. "Then I will trust you to keep your word as an Austrian," and she reached into her pocket and pressed a loose sapphire into his hand.

He looked at it and smiled. "Yes," said the officer, and he motioned to the younger man. "Go to the station and tell the officer in charge that I told you to escort Herr Kreiten and his son back to his home." The officer clicked his heels, turned, and quickly walked to the door.

"Wait," screamed Rosenberg to the officer at the door. "You," he said turning to Gretchen. "You go upstairs to the bedrooms and bring back anything you think is of value. Such a trusted servant as yourself must know where they keep their valuables." He gave a hoarse laugh at the maid's duplicity, and she felt her face grow hot. "And now you," he said, glowering at the officer with his icy eyes. "What did she give you?" and with that, Rosenberg pulled a Lugar from a pocket and pointed it in the policeman's face. Hate flared in the officers eyes, as his hand reached out with the gem. As Rosenberg focused on it, the officer pulled his own gun, but not quickly enough. Rosenberg shot him and he fell dead at his feet. The young officer at the door blanched with fear as another shot found its way into his chest.

Sarah screamed as the blood seeped onto the marble floor and spread like red arthritic fingers. "See what you made me do," he said with feigned sadness. "Had you not offered to ransom your family, and not given him this pretty bauble that he would have kept for himself, I would not have had to kill him."

Gretchen came running down the stairs, clutching small pieces of jewelry in her hands. With her eyes fixed on the dead officers, and a cold fear reaching up and strangling her heart, she handed what she held over to the man standing there with the gun. He looked at what she offered, and then back to her. "And this was all you could find?" he shouted.

"They must have taken the jewels when they left. I swear, I looked in all the places where their jewelry was kept. The safe was open and empty, and I didn't find any money, either."

"I trusted you Gretchen, I trusted you to learn all you could about where they kept their wealth. I singled you out for that purpose so I could single them out. And now you tell me that they took the gems and the money and fled?" Gretchen stepped back as if the small space between them could stay a bullet.

"But I did everything you asked me to do. I wrote down all the art they had and their furnishings. You can see how beautiful it is. This is what you told me to do."

"I'm very disappointed in you Gretchen, very, very disappointed." He was like a child whose sweet treat was taken away because he had misbehaved. "The Third Reich does not tolerate failure, and you have failed me by allowing the mother and children to get away."

"But I've been faithful...the sisters, speak to the sist..." and she turned to run. The bullet caught the fleeing girl in the base of the neck, and she fell to the floor.

Rosenberg turned to Sarah who was, to the Nazi's chagrin, loudly saying her final Shema, and sanctifying God's Name. "You've seen what I have done to three people who would betray me, and you know what I shall do to you if you don't tell me where they have gone. Wait, do you have sisters in Vienna? They went to your sisters?"

Sarah knew that her life was over, and her only thought was of her family and that she still might move this bloodhound onto a different path. She would lead him away from Vienna, away from the convent, and away from the train station. "Don't kill me," she begged, "promise not to kill me or my family."

"Tell me what you know, and if I like what I hear, I'll spare them. Where should they be, these sisters...where?"

"Yes, I have sisters living in Krems," she blurted.

"What are their names? Give me names?"

Sarah hesitated purposefully, hoping that the silence would be construed as reluctance. She was right. His fist smashed into her jaw, cracking a tooth. The pain radiated up the side of her face, and she felt herself tasting and swallowing blood.

"The name is... no, no I won't tell you." Now she felt the steel toe of a boot slam against her rib cage, she heard a crack, and a agonizing pain tore into her chest and side.

"Stop, stop," she pleaded, coughing up spurts of blood. "They live under the name Schimdt."

"There are a thousand Schimdts in Krems, you old hag. Where do they live?"

He was standing over her with his boot on her chest, pressing down. Her breath was shallow, and every gasp sent waves of agonizing pain thoughout her body. "Tell me, now, or I'll crush you with my foot."

Sarah did not want to die, and she knew that she was already entering the Valley of the Shadow. She tried to imagine her Reuben and her family waiting. She tried to imagine her children when they were young, playing happily in the field before the murderers came. As the pressure of the boot bore down, the images faded and she could feel everything in her chest collapsing. If she could hold on just a little longer so he would believe that she was willing to die to save them. Finally, when she was about to pass out, she motioned for him to bring his face closer. He knelt down with his ear next to her mouth. Rosenberg was almost gleeful. "They live in Sudtirolerplatz," and with her last strength, she spat a mouth full of blood into his face.

"Acch!" he yelled wiping the blood and sputum with his sleeve as he smashed at Sarah's head with his boot.

CHAPTER 28

August 18, 1939

My dearest brother,

First I must tell you that the reason this envelope and letterhead are on bank stationary is due to my firm belief that such official looking mail from reputable institutions are not opened or given too much scrutiny. Now, I must tell you that I am writing to you in Russian because if it is opened, no one will understand it. These are dangerous times, even in neutral Switzerland.

Ruth continues to recover. I have terrible news. A neighbor who escaped from Vienna, told us that Mama was murdered when the Nazis came to the house. We still have not told Ruth. Also, we still have not heard anything about Frederick or Heinrich. We are assuming the worst, and we continue to pray and make inquires. Ruth's comfort comes through Berta and Sigmund.

While we continue to be safe because we are citizens, so many others are in peril, especially Jewish children in Europe who have lost their parents. Jonathan knows people in Paris and Vienna who tell us of such things. It would seem that everyone knows what is going on, and no one cares. It shames me to say that this past year our government, the Swiss Bundesrat, asked Germany to put on each Jewish passport the letter "J" for Jude, which they happily did, and now it is easier for the border guards to identify and bar Jews from trying to enter Switzerland. We've heard that the Bundersrat forced at least 100,000 Jews back at the border, and this year all refugees without valid visas are to be evicted from Switzerland and forced back to France, Germany, or Austria, and to certain death.

On a more personal level, though we are both working and are able to support our family and Ruth's, the economy in Europe and here is growing dire. Jonathan is still head of security at the Schweizer Bankverein of Geneva, and I am still with the watch company, designing and making watches. What Ruth and her children brought with them will help us survive this war, and help others, but we could do more good if we had access to Frederick's bank accounts. We know what is there because when Ruth and her children first came to us, she had her bank statements and insurance policies that Frederick had taken out as a hedge against what he though might happen in Austria. Jonathan suggested that Ruth and I visit the bank where Frederick had made substantial deposits, and though Ruth produced proof of who she was, she was told that she could not access the accounts because the bankers insisted that only the owner of the account could withdraw the funds. They did say that if she could produce a death certificate for her dead relative, that would be a different case. Ruth collapsed in my arms at the thought that Frederick might be dead. The next time, Jonathan and I went to the Winterthur Insurance Company where Frederick had a large policy, to ask how his wife might receive the benefits. We were shocked to learn that the payment had already been made to the Third Reich because the Swiss insurance company, in collusion with Germany and Austria, declared that those Jews who owned policies were to be declared stateless and presumed dead. How they even discovered the policy is anyone's guess, and I'm wondering if men like Frederick, with substantial means, were targeted because someone working close to him had informed the Nazis when and where rich Jews had taken out policies. I suspect the

Nazis were given access to the files by Winterthur a long time ago, and as soon as Winterthur gave over the names, those men were targeted, murdered, and death certificates produced that the Nazis handed over to the insurance company for payment. I think they are funding their war with such treachery, and one day it will all come to light.

We have been meeting quietly with representatives of international Jewish organizations to alleviate Jewish suffering. Only Jewish refugees in Switzerland are excluded from state support regarding food, clothing, and shelter, and only Jewish refugees are required to reveal all their financial assets. Though we have raised 44 million Swiss francs to cover all refugee expenses, very little of that money has been used to alleviate their suffering. The government also put a head tax on wealthy Jews leveled at a little over one million Swiss franc. Also, tell your friends in America the following: Dr. Max Huber, the President of the International Red Cross, is sponsoring a program that allows foreign children to rest in Switzerland for as long as the war lasts, but Jewish children are excluded, so as far as I am concerned, the red color in the Red Cross symbol is made a deeper scarlet with the blood of the Jewish children they refuse to save. Sadly, it is only the International Red Cross that is still trusted to distribute money and food, and we have heard that people in America have raised money privately to save lives in Czechoslovakia and Poland. But word has come to us that someone in your State Department has tied up the application and no money has arrived. We have even heard that American officials argue that any money coming into Switzerland will help the enemy, because Switzerland extends credit to Germany. So again, Jews die. We are beginning to believe that this horror continues because no one out there really cares what happens to our people. We thought your government might be different, but it seems that even in America there are people who hate without cause, or are just shutting their eyes. Our involvement is very quiet because people who complain about the treatment of Jews here are sent to camps. Yes, even Swiss citizens are not safe.

Your loving sister,
Dora

CHAPTER 29

1939

Mrs. Schneeberger poured a cup of tea for Zeena. Somewhat bewildered as to why she had been invited to the offices of the World Jewish Congress, Zeena was especially confused when she was introduced to a rabbi named Stephen Wise who told her that he and his organization needed her help. Her curiosity was heightened even more when Armand entered the room and was warmly greeted by the others already assembled.

"It was I who suggested that you might be willing to help save Jewish lives in Europe" he said softly, after kissing her cheek. "We have word that something is being planned, something catastrophic."

Zeena looked into the face of her nephew, smiling at his resemblance to her brother, and wondered how he had become involved with this group. She would ask him at another time. "What can an actress hope to do for you?" she said smiling, doubting that she could possibly be of any assistance.

"Aunt Zeena," Armand responded, clearing his throat, "We've asked you here because we need your help and your talents. People here and in Europe acknowledge you as a great actress and an advocate for the arts. This, we believe, will allow you to enter certain circles we need to enter but cannot. I know you to be fluent in German, and I know that you have a photographic memory. All of us know of your courage and resolve to do what's right. The world may know you as Mademoiselle Marisett, but I know you as my dear aunt who helped free Alfred Dreyfus at great personal expense." He paused so she might digest what he had said.

"We are in receipt of reports from escaping Jews, informants still in Europe, the underground, and from the Soviets, that the atrocities committed against Jews are increasing, but we do not have any hard evidence that this is so. Too many in Washington are skeptical, especially in our own State Department."

"I assure you that what we have heard is not propaganda," interrupted Rabbi Wise. "We have it on the highest authority. Our representative in Switzerland, Gerhart Riegner, has been told by someone high in Nazi circles that the Germans plan to exterminate the Jews of Europe."

"But surely," Zeena replied, "the media can do a better job of ferreting out this truth than I can."

"The newspapers are just as skeptical, fearing the trap that such news may just be propaganda. World War I reporting taught them that lesson. Our own Jewish Hollywood moguls are so assimilated that they are more afraid of losing their overseas markets than they are afraid of losing Jews."

"And there are those Jews who think that it would be better to use movies and The Movietone News to unite the American people by emphasizing that the Nazis are the enemy of America," said Mrs. Shenberger. "While Movietone News pounds the drum against Germany, they are still not showing what is really going on, and the film industry is not portraying Jews in films or telling their stories. There are powerful Jews who have convinced studio owners that if they make this a Jewish problem, they would be hurting the war effort. America will not unite or go to war to save Jews, but they will go to war to bring down a Third Reich that threatens America."

"What can I possibly do?" Zeena asked. "I may fully support your efforts, and I will even appear on your behalf to raise awareness and money if that is what you want, but I can't see myself doing more. I am not quite as young as I was when I spoke out in Dreyfus's defense."

"No, we don't want you to raise any kind of awareness," said a young man with intelligent dark eyes and straight brown hair combed back. Josiah DuBois, an attorney and an Assistant General Counsel in the United States Treasury Department, had hitherto been silent. "We don't want you to be visible in any way or appear connected with us. In public, you must appear to act opposite to those feeling which you own. We ask you to do this because you are a great actress, and we need you to play a new role for us on a dangerous stage."

Zeena leaned forward, interested.

"Dear lady, in 1929, a Nazi named Alfred Rosenberg founded an organization called The Militant League for German Culture. He charged himself with the task of proving to the Germans that the Jews are in the forefront of creating degenerative tendencies in music, theater, in the visual arts, architecture and generally all areas of human endeavor. His purpose was to demonize the Jews as cultural aliens, claiming that Jews could only produce inauthentic imitations of their host cultures, and by acknowledging these Jewish efforts, Germany would become more susceptible to Jewish power. We have created an organization," DuBois continued, "that purports to be an American arm of Rosenberg's organization, and basically, we need you to travel to Germany as a representative of this organization and meet with Rosenberg to find out what his plans are. Rosenberg purports himself to be a lover of the arts. You are known as an advocate of the arts. We believe he will welcome your support. We believe that an eyewitness such as yourself has the gravitas to convince the people in our government that what we are hearing is absolutely true, and that the State Department must act to save whatever Jews can be saved." There was a long silence.

"Ah," said Zeena. "You are asking me to willingly enter the lion's den, perhaps to be discovered as a fraud, and made a prisoner or worse. But then again, you are asking me to possibly give the greatest performance of my life not having a script upon which I could rely. As you know, I am a secular person, but I am first a human being and willing to do what is right." There was another brief pause. "And here," she laughed, "I believed my career was coming to an end, yet today I am once again given the chance to perform on a dangerous stage. How can I refuse?"

The breath that was being held was collectively released, and smiles and nods were exchanged. "Naturally," Mrs. Shneeberger interjected, proffering the raised teapot to the others in the room, "you will incur no costs at all, and all arrangements will be made for you. In anticipation of your willingness to help us, we have created a well documented history of your involvement with the American German Bund and fake copies of your correspondence with Fritz Kuhn. These documents will also be on official Bund stationary. What we do need is a letter of introduction, signed by Kuhn, to be used as your introduction to Rosenberg. We have infiltrated Kuhn's office at the highest level so we can create a history for you. We have also contracted a young woman who will be your companion and a young man who will be your driver and protector. Both are German speaking Jews who left Germany as teenagers and are American patriots. They have both infiltrated the Bund on our behalf."

"The State Department is suspicious of our efforts and are not supportive," Armand continued, "so we have had to install our own people in certain places without the government being aware of it. Too many men in the government are pretending that the destruction of European Jewry isn't happening, and others know it is and stand by silently with a wink and a nod. They have made that abundantly clear to us through the barriers individuals have already set up for us in the Executive Office, in the Legislative Branch, and even in the Judiciary. But mostly, it's the institutional Jew-hatred of the State Department. We have few friends there, so we have to act on our own and in secret until our proof is so irrefutable that they cannot deny it and will be forced to act. We need you to get that proof for us."

"It will be necessary for you to meet with Mr. Kuhn," interjected Rabbi Wise "since he did visit the 1936 Olympics and did meet with Hitler and other high ranking Nazis. It would be important that you meet him, in the event that you are asked any questions related to his appearance."

Prior to her meeting with Kuhn, Zeena had studied the still photos and the moving pictures of the massive 1939 rally in Madison Square Garden so as to get a sense of this man and the charismatic hold that enabled him to gather almost twenty-thousand followers into one space. Office clerks, itinerant workers, mechanics, cooks, and waitresses rubbed elbows with a few professionals and technicians, but basically Zeena learned that Kuhn's followers, primarily disgruntled blue collar workers who, like their European counterparts, were looking for someone to blame for their desperate lives. Zeena had also made it a point to disguise herself as a house frau and convinced Chalfonte to also assume a character as they did back in Paris before Zeena became a star. Along with her bodyguard and new companion, the four of them attended a rally where Zeena was shocked to see large depictions of George Washington and the American Flag hanging amid black swastikas on blood red cloth. Men, wearing black pants and brown shirts separated by military Sam Browne belts and sporting garrison caps, stood on either side of the podium. These were the Ordungsdienst or OD for short, and Kuhn's attempt to ape Hitler's Schutzstaffel – the SS. Finally, there were the drummers, incessantly pounding out what became the unifying heartbeat of the hall, and Old Glory, companioned with the ubiquitous Nazi symbol, were both waved by the dozens of flag bearers. Finally, Kuhn, in an elaborate dress uniform, strutted up to the podium and thrust out his arm and palm in a salute familiar to his audience. But where Zeena expected the audience to scream "Heil Hitler," they screamed, "Free America, Free America." Free America from what? she wondered. From whom? Didn't they realize that as bad as things might be here, Americans were still better off than any other place in the world?

Fritz Kuhn, a rather pudgy man whose large stomach was further exaggerated by the same military belt the OD men wore, pushed his fleshy face into the microphone. His thick glasses precluded Zeena from seeing his eyes. Zeena paid little attention to the man's rant, having concluded quickly that his only message was to share his dream of an America that was Jew free and under Fascist rule. It did strike Zeena that the very Constitution he would so willingly destroy was the same document that allowed him to speak freely. There was something ironic in this she thought, and she wondered how many other times in the past or in the future, evil people would use the democratic freedoms granted them in America to overturn those very laws so they might establish dictatorships or theocracies.

"I had no idea that a person of your stature was interested in our cause," he said solicitously. "I am indeed honored that you would ask to see me." Kuhn, effusive and unctuous, brushed off the seat to which he had motioned Zeena. Her young companion, Helga Schwartzman, and bodyguard, Peter Lindzer, already known to Kuhn as loyal members of the Bund, quietly faded into the background. It was Peter who had informed Kuhn that a person of significance, a person who might be good for the cause and who also knew Helga, wanted to speak with him.

Zeena came right to the point and spoke in German. "I am part of a new organization we call The Kulturbund. It is our hope to break down the barriers between the German arts as they flourish here and as they flourish in the Fatherland. Ever since the Great War, there has been animosity between our two cultures, and my organization seeks to remedy that."

"I have never heard of this Kulturbund," he replied.

"That is because we are in our infancy. You might say we are extending the spirit of The Americans of Teutonic Heritage that attempted to combat the hatred towards us during and after World War I. They were once an infant organization, but I'm sure you've heard of them. I'm also sure you've heard of The Free Society of of Teutonia that became The Friends of New Germany which was also once in its infancy. Your own German-American Bund also had an infancy. But now look at it. It is my belief that I and my friends might become the cultural arm of the Bund and provide, shall we say, a more sophisticated face?"

The Bundestfuhrer leaned back in his chair, calculating how this renowned woman might well enhance his own efforts. He took off his glasses an squinted in her direction. His eyes were small and black. She knew that he was flattered, but sensed an ambivalence.

"I am an avid reader of Mr. Ford's, *Dearborn Observer,*" she added, "and I especially enjoy his essays called, *The International Jew*. I even wrote to dear Henry, suggesting that he publish them in book form." She lied, but knew that Kuhn had gotten his start working for the Ford Motor Company, and that Henry Ford was the one who introduced him to formalized Jew hatred. Suggesting that she also knew Ford might reinforce in his mind her devotion to the cause. "He said that he would consider it. I also understand that you met Herr Hitler himself at the Olympics. It is known among those who know your work, that the Fuhrer instructed you to go back to America and continue the fight. That is what I and my group also wish to do. I also know that you have designs on being on a stage much larger than the one in Madison Square Garden, and I can help with that."

She studied his face and saw that her hook had been swallowed and secured in his fat cheek. "Herr Kuhn, I can bring into your fold an entire new group of people, people with money and influence; people who can get things done and people who share your vision of freeing America from Jewish influence."

"And you will do this for me out of the goodness of your heart and for the sake of the German people in America?" he said with a slight smirk.

"Not entirely. I am wise enough to recognize a winner, and I am wise enough to bask in that glow. I am a winner. You are a winner. I know you. You are creating something that will be very powerful, and I know people who want to support you so they might benefit from what you will accomplish."

"And what do you want from me in exchange for your support?"

"A simple letter of introduction to Herr Rosenberg in Germany. I wish to go on, shall we say, a cultural mission and make the contacts I need to make so that my friends and I might better enjoy the success that will come to loyal Germans when there is a new order in America. As they say, 'a rising tide lifts all boats,' Herr Kuhn, and you are the tide that is rising."

Kuhn smiled. "Helga," he said, "will you prepare a letter of introduction for our friend."

CHAPTER 30

1939

Rabbi Stephen Wise did not know that Mademoiselle Marisette was the aunt of the ill-famed Abe Chernov, but the rabbi needed the right people for the right job, and with that in mind, he himself penned a note that was not on the stationary of the American Zionist Organization. In the note, he asked Abe if he might meet with him and another to quietly discuss a matter of grave importance. There was only that statement along with an address on the Upper East Side and apartment number. Abe wondered why such a revered man would want a meeting with him. His curiosity was such that he immediately responded that he would attend, and he would bring his younger brother.

The meeting was in the apartment of Judge Nathan Perlman, an important figure in the Republican Party of New York, and a former Congressman. Like Wise, he was a champion of Jewish causes.

After refreshments were served, Rabbi Wise came directly to the point. "I hope you can forgive our reticence to meet in a more public forum, Mr. Chernov, and I hope you can forgive our secrecy. Meeting with you and asking you what we must ask you, puts the judge and I at great risk to our personal and political lives. As the Talmud says, 'If I am not for myself, then who will be for me? And if I am only for myself, what am I?

And if not now, when?' The times are such when we must all be willing to go out of our comfort zones, and sacrifice for the greater good. Only in this way can we find out who we truly are."

"I appreciate your honesty, Rabbi. My father made me memorize that teaching a long time ago."

So what is the greater good that we are talking about here, Rabbi?"

"There are dangerous trends that we see today in America," he continued, "and these must be addressed in ways that may not be fully acceptable to the wider population." He cleared his throat. "What I'm talking about is the threat to the Jewish People and to the American way of life that a man named Fritz Kuhn and the German-American Bund pose."

"We are faced here with a difficult ethical problem," interjected Judge Perlman, "and we continue to wrestle with the ethics of it. We have agreed that the core of being an American is the duty that each of us has to everyone else, and the responsibility that everyone else has to each individual. The American Bund blatantly and shamelessly marches the swastika down streets of New York and Connecticut towns, spew their hateful filth, and train children to revere the most odious of values."

"We are crossing boundaries," interjected the Rabbi Wise, "into areas that we know are not ideal, but the situation calls for it. The Jews need to stand up for themselves and fight this plague. In short, Mr. Chernov, we want you and your associates to take action for us against these Nazis and those who sympathize with them. We have money and legal assistance ready if you will step forward as our militant arm."

Abe looked at Harry and smiled. "Remember when those Micks beat you and Sammy up and what we did to them so that they would never do it again? It seems like these gentlemen are asking us to do that again, only on a broader scale." Abe looked at the judge and the rabbi, both honorable men asking him and his brother to do something dishonorable, and totally against their moral code. Their inner turmoil was palpable. Deep in Abe's memory came another statement that he also heard from his father, insisting that "if a man come to slay you, slay him first." That seemed to resonate within him, because it said that each person had a right to protect himself, and that a murderer gave up his right to live just by his intent. At least, that's how Abe understood it. Abe knew enough about Nazis and certainly about Jew-hatred in the world and in America to know that the ultimate intention of such people was to murder.

"I am flattered that you invite us to do this, and I do understand why this must remain a secret. The good you do could easily be undone if you are associated with this. I thank you for your kind offer of money and support, but I think my brother and I would like to handle this ourselves. Let's just say you are giving us and our friends an opportunity to show those in the Jewish Community who do not like us, that they can still support us. After all, like us or not, we are all still Jews and at a certain level, we are all connected."

"I have one request of you," the judge said. "I do not want anyone killed in whatever you decide to do. You can beat them and break bones, but we must not be thought of as murderers."

"And I have one request of you," injected Harry. "Jewish mobsters attacking Jew-hating Nazis will make a great story, so we need you to do all you can to stifle criticism of us in the Jewish press." The judge agreed to do what he could. How ironic, he thought. To silence the free speech of one group, would lead him to try to dampen the free speech of another.

Joey, upon hearing about the meeting, wanted to bring in the Italians, but the Chernov brothers thanked him and insisted that this was something the Jews had to do for themselves. And do it they did, even allowing help from men, both young and old, who were certainly not part of the underworld. Training sessions in garages and in shul basements on busting Bundist heads were held, and nice Jewish men were taught how to use their fists, clubs, pipes, and feet. The warriors, in deep sleep within these observant and non observant men, awakened, grew restless, and took permission to rise up like the Maccabees of old.

As Abe had orchestrated the attack in the alley so many years ago, he also took a keen interest in the melees, wading into the fray along with his bat wielding companions. His silent partners had friends in both LaGuardia's City Hall, and in the police department, so when the Bundists were planning a march or a rally, Abe and Harry knew about them. Informed of the next big rally in Yorkville, they were also informed that a handfull of cops would be there as required by law. Lead pipes and bats had been concealed days before. At Abe's signal, stink bombs were simultaneously hurled through the windows, and the several hundred Bundist poured through the doors choking and holding their burning eyes. Benny Malin opened a bag of chicken blood and splatted his face with it, screaming to the cops for help. The confused cops at the door ran to him, and as they did, dozens of bat wielding Jews in the crowd, descended on the Bundists like the horsemen of the Apocalypse. Blood, teeth, and bodies lay everywhere, but no one was dead. Arms, noses, and backs were bruised and broken, but heads were never smashed. Abe was good to his word, and no one died. The first melee was a great success, and word came to Abe that his silent partners were well pleased.

Though Abe kept his bargain with Judge Perlman, the good judge did not hold up his end of the deal. The Jewish press saw each attack as newsworthy, and condemned this gang of unknown Jewish brutes for their uncivilized savagery. Abe's name had been leaked, and for the first time, he was linked in the papers to other well known Jewish gangsters like Buchalter, Reles, and Shapiro. When the American press picked up on the story, it became obvious to those who cared, that certain aspects of Gentile America were pleased to conclude that the wider

Jewish population were nothing but criminals. It was another rationalization for hating Jews.

Rabbi Wise recognized that the long term effects such news articles, and the mounting pressure put on him his peers, he was forced to declare publically that such behavior was immoral. Privately, he thanked Abe and Harry for what they had done, but nevertheless asked them to close down the operation. Of course, they did.

But the operation that Abe and Harry officially ended in New York filtered over into Newark, New Jersey where Longy Zwillman, a major Jewish bootlegger who had cops, judges, and elected officials on his payroll, would not tolerate the pro-Nazi factions and their regalia marching and rallying in his city and in nearby Irvington. So the Newark cops regularly informed Zwillman of a pro-Nazi gatherings, and Zwillman's Third Ward Gang, usually armed with stink bombs, bats and iron pipes, ravaged New Jersey bundists fleeing from the building. Zwillman had no restrictions on him as did Abe and Harry, so heads, legs, backs and arms got broken. And those who escaped the gauntlet, found their cars destroyed. And whenever any of the Third Ward Gang came before a judge, the judge gave the defendants no more than a slap on the wrist. The Newark judicial system supported the effort.

CHAPTER 31

January 18, 1940

My dearest brother,

Some of my news will fill you with pride and some will sadden you. To the eternal shame of the Swiss Government, our Budersrat voted unanimously to establish sixty-two labor camps into which Jews fleeing Nazi persecution are being placed. The chief architect of this disgrace is an official named Heinrich Rothmund, the same Nazi sympathizer who devised the idea of putting a "J" on all Jewish passports. I wrote of him in a previous letter. It seems this Rothmund made trips to German concentration camps and was so impressed, that he decided to establish them here. Of course they are called "voluntary," but anyone objecting is threatened with being sent back to Germany. So now Switzerland can proudly say that we also have slave labor working in our quarries, building our roads, and clearing our forests. And to further isolate herself from human compassion, the Swiss Government has abolished the six-year waiting period for residency requirement and raised it to a fifteen year waiting period. This will guarantee that no Jews coming into Switzerland will become citizens. We've been citizens for many years.

Now I must tell you about Sigmund and Berta. When they came to us, they were dressed as nuns, and that ruse saved their lives. They are both very brave to do what they have done. Sigmund's stature and soft features continue to allow him to pass himself off as a nun, and in this guise, he and Berta continue to assists children clandestinely over the border. Sometimes there are a dozen children in our house before we can quietly farm them out to others, be they Jewish or righteous gentiles who are willing to save a life. Word has come to us that Jewish children in Europe are disposable because they can't do the work. They are shipped to death camps in Germany and Poland to be murdered. Berta told me that before Mama died, she had given a mother superior in a convent in Vienna a nice sum of money and jewels so the convent might take children in and hide them. So Sigmund and Berta travel back and forth with a few children at a time with letters of transit so they might find rest in Herr Rothmund's convalescent camps. But they are spirited here. Rothmund knows nothing, so his staff does not anticipate arrivals from Vienna. I cannot tell you the danger they are in each time they get on a train. We are so very proud of them, and happily, Ruth is unaware of what they do. She thinks they are on business trips for their father.

When Berta is not moving children, she uses her disguise, and under the pretext of bring the word of God to the heathens in Swiss slave labor camps, she gathers information and reports what she is learning from the Jewish inmates to the Jewish organizations working in Switzerland and in America. She has already visited Gyrenbad and reported such primitive conditions that I cried. Here and in other camps, there aren't even beds. In one camp she found one hundred and thirty men sleeping on straw and wooden boards. One man told her that before the camp, he had spent months in a windowless cell in a local jail. The food is minimal, barely enough to survive, no medical attention, and not even changes of underwear. And wherever you look, armed guards. The money we have raised for the Jewish prisoners and given to the government, has not found its way to them to relieve their suffering. One man told her that he desperately tried to reach his wife who had appendicitis, and when he complained too loudly, he was put into solitary confinement and then sent to a mental asylum for two and one half months. On one visit to a camp, she actually met Herr Rothmund who said that if we make the Jews huddle on their straw as long as possible, they themselves will ask for permission to leave. He said he wants to teach them that Switzerland is no paradise, so that those who want to come in will be discouraged.

Thank you dear brother for the gift you enclosed in your last letter to me. It will go a long way to helping. I wish we could all be with you and your family in the safety of America, but we are safe as long as we are here. I wish I could say that for the children we rescue and the children who need rescuing. We are thankful that Zeena and David returned to you safely. Bless them for their efforts, but it is best that we now stay in Switzerland. We are citizens and protected, though no one knows that Ruth and her children live with us. Ruth doesn't leave the house, and when Berta and Sigmund leave, they leave through a garden gate and always in disguise so they are never questioned.

All our love,
Dora

CHAPTER 32

1940

Abe Chernov created Ginny's Place as a partial "thank you" to Virginia for agreeing to live the only life he chose to offer her, and for her willingness to abide by the conditions he had set out. Still, there was more. She was the mother of his only child, and what he felt for her was a mixture of appreciation and obligation. No doubt she was important to him, but appreciation and obligation are not love, and he knew he could not love her the way he imagined a woman needed to be loved; with total commitment, total trust, and a full heart. On more than one occasion he had invited her to leave him and find someone else, but she would not. So their relationship continued, and he came to respect her vocal talent, and appreciate her undivided attention to him when they were together. But he knew that something was missing. In his most private moments, he wondered if he ever could love anyone that way, and whether such love like that really existed.

Whenever Abe thought about love and relationships, he thought of his mother and father. His Mama was perhaps the only woman he had loved and trusted completely, and who had ever loved him unconditionally. And so he laughed when he learned that Leah did not include him on the census because in Leah's mind, if the government knew about your son, they would take him into the army for twenty-five years. As far as he was concerned, that was an act of love. But even remembering her, with her sad brown eyes always loving and calm, he could not forget the wistful pity there that seemed to silently whisper her disappointment for him not being able to become what she had hoped her eldest son would be. What he had become would not have pleased her as it did not please his father. He knew his Mama loved him, but her eyes sent that sorrowful message as if she had said out loud, "You are my greatest disappointment in life." As much as she loved him, that silent message was recorded on his soul. That important lady had expectations that he could not meet, and early on he concluded that if he could not please or fully trust this woman with his core, how could he please or trust any woman? He could not risk opening himself again. He would not risk it.

Abe had met and bedded dozens of women, and once or twice there were relationships that could have became serious. Still, he would never open himself fully to any woman because he basically did not trust. Never would he risk seeing that disappointment again in the eyes of a women he might have loved. Were his expectations of women unreasonable? Perhaps it were those old bitch teachers he had in school who reinforced in him the idea that women were judgmental, cruel, and could not be pleased or trusted; bitter old women who taught him subject matter and contempt.

It was no matter. His mother's disappointment was gone, those old bitter teachers were dead, and he was still alone. The fault was in him, not in Virginia or any of the others he had met. Causes could be found, and though not an easy thing to do, he came to believe that every human being secretly knew the root cause of his or her own problems, but just wouldn't face that truth let alone speak of it. Abe knew that he could not trust. Everyone was walking around in his or her own secret pain, reluctant to speak of the pain or to let comfort in. Comfort came with people, but if people could not be trusted, where was one to go with that conclusion?

Abe was a well respected man, well known, and quietly generous. There were small business owners he knew during the Depression who could not get loans from the bank, and on more that a few occasions, he put up the collateral for them without them ever knowing. His father was one of them, and in that transaction, Abe insisted that Jonah's bank never reveal to his father, where that money came from to save the school. He never spoke of his largesse, and people liked him just because he treated all people with fairness and respect. How much of this Abe Chernov was created to keep people from seeing the Abe Chernov that he believed himself to be, the inadequate child who could not read well, the man who would always see himself as someone not whole, set apart, even peripheral in his own family for how he made his living and what he had become. Had he not allowed himself love because of what loving and trusting someone might reveal?

So Abe compensated Virginia for not loving her as she wanted to be loved, needed to be loved, by showering her with the security of his wealth and the life that wealth could provide for her and their son.

Virginia, standing at the microphone, smiling at him from the small stage, finished "My Man," the song with which she ended each of her sets. She had first heard it when Fanny Brice sang it the Follies. Abe had taken her to the opening as a birthday gift, and he told her they were going backstage to meet an old friend. Fanny Brice was the old friend. Abe knew Fanny from the old neighborhood when she was Fania Borach, a skinny kid with spindly legs who shoplifted trifles with her younger brother, Louie, after school. They had stayed in touch over all these years. Fanny used to hang around because she had a crush on Maurice, but she never hustled one of the Chernov kids as she did others for change. Abe and she would sit and talk on the stoop and he'd listen to her dreams of being a star. He never judged her, and Fanny never forgot their friendship. Still, Virginia's singing "My Man" was an odd choice since the lyric was about a woman desperately clinging to a man who had other women he liked as much as he liked her. To Virginia, the song was a public statement of her love for Abe, her longing for him, and her resolve to be with him, no matter what. Initially, Abe felt the lyrics cut, but accepted them as a kind of punishment that he deserved, though he never said a word. Whenever she sang it, she rarely took her eyes off of him. Abe did not mind her gaze in which he read alternately both love and anger, and he relished the applause that washed over her as she came to his table after her set.

Ginny's Place was always awash in pink and peach lighting, that complemented her red hair. Small tables with peach underskirts to the floor were covered with white tablecloths. Each table held a small lamp with a red beaded shade that softly illuminated faces of laughing people, people in intimate conversations, and couples dancing. Patrons sat on gold painted spindleback chairs with burgundy cushions. It was all very refined.

In this place, Abe had deliberately stopped time, keeping the fantasy of an elegant speakeasy alive though prohibition was long over. The other speakeasies that contributed to his wealth and made him a celebrity in Manhattan and Brooklyn were closed long ago, but he had kept this one as a venue for Virginia. This cabaret was designed to be a throwback to the twenties, a frozen moment that gave him and his friends a weekly memory of being on top of the world, in control, and not under constant government surveillance. That wasn't to say that Abe and his friends were not still on top of the world and in control. They were, but times had changed, and they were closely watched by the Feds.

The Depression was winding down, and the government had become more watchful of less notorious gangsters because the lone wolf predators who had romanticized crime like Bonnie and Clyde or Baby Faced Nelson, were dead and gone. Big Al Capone was out of prison, dying in Florida from neurosyphilis, though his Chicago Outfit was still in business and going strong. Prohibition's drive-by shootings, targeted assassinations, massacres, and gang wars of the thirties in the big cities had put many in jail or in the ground. Prostitution, labor union racketeering, and gambling were still big and profitable, and that is where Abe, Harry, and Joey were now focused. J. Edger Hoover and the FBI were also refocused and had turned their attention to organized crime, just as violent, but whose leadership wore elegant suits and met in boardrooms; the Mafia, Murder Incorporated, and the people who straddled both. Abe, Harry, and Joey straddled both, and it was Harry, code named "The Bookkeeper," who was now insisting that they move their interests out of state to Las Vegas and also to Cuba where gambling was also permitted. Harry saw clearly what would be coming down on organized crime, and assured them that the FBI couldn't reach them in Cuba, and that Cuban banks were not open to the scrutiny of the U.S. Treasury Department. He pressed them time and time again that both Cuba and Las Vegas were open and eager to be developed, and both had government officials whose hands were both open and eager to be paid under the table for special treatment and for looking the other way.

Now, European nations were falling to the Nazi juggernaut, and war was imminent. England's Chamberlain had his admirers and supporters here at home, and the United States was hesitant of being drawn into another war on the Continent. With people fearful of facing new and harsher realities, the rosy aura that some placed upon the heads of gangsters gave way to a more sobering and less romantic view of law breakers. The Depression had left a deep scar on the American Mind, and though the New Deal was providing a dim light at the end of that long, dark decade, the people were becoming less tolerant of law breakers who were taking more than they were giving back.

So Ginny's Place, open only on weekends, was a place to go to remember the good old days when good whiskey and gin were smuggled in from Canada, where flappers with rouged knees danced the Charleston on tables, and where beaded dresses shimmered in the reflections of the mirrored ball that turned on the ceiling. The base, piano, drums, and horns wailed out jazz from the south or backed up Virginia as she breathlessly sang songs from Broadway.

Like the old days, the unmarked entrance was still hidden in an innocuous East Side alley, and the invitations had to be slid through a letter opening in the door where one of Abe's old bouncers gave the entry a dangerous authenticity. People loved it. For the women, flapper attire was required, and the men were required to wear tuxedos and black fedora hats. Like the old days, the booze was served in teacups and the cigarette girls sold their wares and themselves to the single men.

Each Saturday evening, Virginia, dressed in her speakeasy blue crystal beaded dress with a matching headband, stood greeting the guests next to a series of large glasses, one upon the other, that cascaded champagne. She smiled warmly, air kissed patrons, and alternately sipped the bubbly liquid, or took a puff from the long bejeweled cigarette holder she held.

Virginia had everything except Abe's name. She had everything a married woman could want out of life except the legitimacy of a wedding band on her finger. Though Leo bore Virginia's last name, Abe loved him unconditionally and created a substantial trust fund that would become available to him on his twenty-first birthday. In that way, Virginia who regularly doled out money to her predatory relatives, could not be prevailed upon to help them with any money that was held for Leo. Maurice was the executor of Leo's Trust. Abe neither liked nor trusted her Irish clan because he knew of their rapacious natures and Virginia's naivete to see her own for what they were. Abe provided everything a husband would provide for his wife, paid her bills himself, and gave her enough money to keep her and Leo living well, and out of the light that would have shone on them if they carried his name.

When Virginia left the Chernov house, she had gone back to her people, and Leo, for a time, became another kid running wild in the streets of Hell's Kitchen. As Leo got older, Abe saw that Leo was on a track that would lead him down the same dark road he himself had stepped onto long ago. So Abe imposed his will with threats of cutting them off if Virginia stood in his way of shipping their son off to a residential military academy in upstate New York. Virginia, whose survival depended on acquiescing to Abe's needs, and ever mindful of keeping the life style to which she had become accustomed, agreed and happily accepted a new rental apartment in Washington Heights so that Leo would not have to ever return to the West Side.

Under the watchful eye of the instructors, Leo learned to control himself and direct his energies into activities and studies. Leo excelled, moving from school rank to rank and grade to grade. The commander of the academy took notice of Leo's leadership skills, his spirit, and his intellect, and he prevailed upon Virginia to consider sending the boy to West Point. When she came to Abe with this proposal, the pride that Abe felt was like nothing else he had ever felt before. His son, in one generation, a full American, would be a West Point cadet with a career of proudly serving his country. He had been right not burdening Leo with his father's history or name, and perhaps Leo's accomplishments would bring him some redemption.

Now, at thirty-three, Leo had become a well respected officer in the Army and a source of great pride to his family. His star was on the ascendancy, but Abe feared for him because of the war that was coming.

Ginny's officially closed down at about one in the morning, and once the band had packed up, Ginny gone, the girls taking care of their business above the club, another clientele appeared at the alley door. Some of the men were known high rollers from the area, some were gamblers from out of town in for a short stay, some were rich marks, eager to rub shoulders with a seamier side of life that was dangerous and exciting, and some were old friends from the old neighborhood who had gone straight after Prohibition ended because they had married and settled down. All of them still liked a brief sip of something dangerous and illegal for old times sake.

Behind the little stage, a glass sculpted antelope looking intently at a glass moon hanging over a glass tree, was on a panel that swung open at the right touch to welcome the patrons to a gaming parlor with Tiffany shades hanging low above round poker tables and roulette wheels. Abe always sat with his back to the wall at one of the poker tables, a suggestion Joey had made to him when they were kids. Joey knew you always had to see what was coming at you, and a wall at your back was good insurance that no one was creeping up behind.

The cover charge was sufficient to cover the drinks and the late night noshes in case anyone got hungry. Cheese cake imported from Lindy's in mid-Manhattan was always on the dessert menu, and from Katz's Deli, imported from the Lower East Side, sandwiches of brisket, pastrami, and corned beef.

Everyone who was anyone knew of the back room at Ginny's, and from time to time, New York and New Jersey Congressmen rubbed elbows with judges, commissioners, police brass, members of the press, and stage and screen celebrities. Gamblers who had been told of Ginny's, always wanted to try their luck.

Abe sat stoically at his table, making mental notes of who came through the door, who they came in with, and where they sat. He smiled and nodded as he watched them place bets at the roulette table or toss the dice; they nodded back or waved. He was comfortable with those he knew, the regulars, but not quite as comfortable with the ones who appeared one weekend and never again. Most times, Abe viewed out-of-towners as hicks, even those from big cities, because he felt that anyone who was not born and bred in New York City just lacked real moxie, and therefore was to be viewed suspiciously. Still, each was greeted warmly at Ginny's. After all, their money was good and he liked separating them from it.

As he sat there waiting, one man came up to him wearing a cowboy hat and boots with spurs. He jingled. Abe assessed him and his wide toothy grin as more of a cartoon character who had gotten lost on the way to the rodeo. The man sat down and introduced himself as "Tex." Abe smiled to himself, sizing up "Tex" as a blowhard with a big wad of cash that he carelessly tossed on the table. A while later, another man came over, dressed in a tuxedo. He was very thin and seemed visibly nervous. He nodded at Abe, forcing a brief smile and sat down to wait. Abe vaguely recalled him sitting by himself, listening to Virginia sing. A man and a woman approached from different sides of the room. He, in a three piece, well tailored business suit, sporting a diamond pinky ring and wearing wire rimmed glasses. The woman had styled herself something like Joan Crawford, with padded shoulders, arched eyebrows, and scarlet red lips. On her upswept hair, sat a small black hat with a black egret feather and a veil that covered the top half of her face. Abe sensed an air of mystery about her, but he immediately concluded it was nothing but a sham when she introduced herself. Her accent revealed she was from somewhere in Brooklyn, or Jersey, or possibly West New York.

Nothing was wild in the games Abe played. Wild cards were for kids. Chips could be bought only in stacks of one thousand dollars, and that grand also bought you a seat at the table. A new deck was passed around for inspection and then opened. Each tossed in a one hundred dollar chip and Abe dealt two cards down. The four people tapped their response to be hit with another card. Abe thought that curious, and holding the deck, commented on what was on the table. The people again tapped their desire to be hit. Abe opened up a second card in front of each and commented again on the possibilities. He looked at his own hand, and checked. Again, there was the tapping of fingers and the pot grew. The final card was uncovered. Three of the players dropped out, leaving the Texan and Abe. Abe put in another hundred, and the Texan followed raising him two hundred. Abe looked at his cards and met the bet. Abe opened his hand, revealing two pairs, jacks high. The Texan had a full house. Abe smiled and shuffled the cards. Again, hundred dollar chips hit the green cloth and Abe dealt the second hand. Again, there was the tapping on the table for more cards, and Abe noticed that the tapping was somewhat different from the first hand. There were spaces between taps, long and short spaces. He found this curious, but continued. The cards were dealt, more taps of different combinations, and Abe lost again, this time to the woman. Abe summoned a waiter for another round of whiskey, and a new deck. He passed the cards to the man in the tuxedo. He wanted to focus not so much on the game, but on the tapping. Again, chips were tossed in, and the tapping began for cards. The dealer who had tapped once in the previous game, now called to be hit with two taps, a pause, and then a sudden third tap. The man in the business suit, after the first card was shown tapped three rapid times for another card. Abe was down five thousand dollars, and was suddenly aware that he was being cheated. Though these people came in separately, and appeared not to know one another, Abe was convinced that he was being conned by sophisticated card sharks who had devised some sort of tapping system where they knew when to stay in the game and when to fold. A fourth hand convinced him that they were passing one another signals. Again, he lost. He now owed six grand.

Slowly, Abe beckoned to one of the men at the door to come over, and motioning him closer, whispered something. In a few minutes, three other men appeared and each whispered to the three gamblers that if they did not get up at that moment quietly to be escorted out, they would be severely hurt. "You owe me money," the Texan growled, standing menacingly. The bouncer squeezed his upper flesh on his upper arm and he winced as he shook him away. At this, the woman calmly opened her purse, took out a gold compact, powered her nose nonchalantly, stood, and subtlety indicated with a smile how impressed she was with Abe's perception. She moved quickly toward the door. The man in the tuxedo put up his hands indicating that he did not want to be touched, and followed the lady to the open door that led to the alley on the other side of the building. The man in the business suit sneered at Abe, downed his drink, and threw his winning hand on the table. "You owe me for that!"

The Texan continued to eye Abe menacingly, and Abe motioned for the bouncers to take the cheat by his arms and unceremoniously throw him into the street. "Nothing to see," Abe said cheerfully to his gaping patrons. "Go on, enjoy yourselves."

In an hour or so, Abe said goodbye to the last of the convivial gamblers, waved off the bouncers, and sat in the dark, thinking about Leo, his father, his sisters so far away, and Harry's proposition to move the business out of New York. But New York City was where he breathed, and he didn't think he could breathe anywhere else and be happy. Perhaps it was time to retire. Already, he was on the north side of fifty. He certainly had enough money to retire and spend the rest of his life doing exactly as he liked. Harry could take over, and he would take a smaller cut. It was something he would think about.

He closed the door and it locked automatically behind him. Down the alley and across the street he could see his new Cadillac shining under a street lamp. He smiled faintly as he reached into his jacket for the keys, and then he heard a jingling sound. He stopped and listened, turning to inquire of the shadows. All was still. He took two more steps towards the car, and again the jingling. This time when he turned, the Texan emerged a few feet away.

"You owe us six large, mister, and you'd better pay us now!"

Abe looked at him directly. "I would have no problem paying you three times six grand if you won it honestly," he shot back. "Your little group is very clever and very impressive, but I don't pay off on fixed poker."

The Texan pulled a gun from his waste band and brandished it at Abe. "You will give me that cash now or you'll never see another poker hand."

Abe was suddenly a kid back in Brownsville confronted with Irish punks. He frantically searched for a rock or two by four, but there was nothing to be found. He was Abe Chernov. No one threatened Abe Chernov with a gun in an alley. This wasn't the way things were done any more. Didn't this sucker know who he was?

"You don't want to do this, mister," Abe said walking towards him with his hands up. "We can talk about this. Besides, I don't carry that kind of money on me, and if you kill me, you won't get any of it. Abe continued to slowly move towards him. "We can talk about this like gentlemen, can't we?"

The Texan stopped Abe with a bullet to his gut, a bullet that tore into Abe's coat, through his suit, and lodged somewhere near his liver and spleen. The Texan ran. A sharp, hot pain doubled Abe over and he clutched at at his midsection. He looked at the back of his killer with wide, disbelieving eyes, and then at the crimson stain that was dampening his coat. This wasn't the way things were done anymore, he thought. This wasn't the way he was supposed to die. Certainly he couldn't die here, not in an alley. No, he couldn't die. There was too much still to do. Too much to see. Too much to say. He staggered to the car, and he watched his bloody hand fumble for his keys. It seemed to him that somebody else's blood was on his hands and clothes, and it seemed that someone else's bloody hand shook the key into the ignition. He would not die now. And he repeated "I will not die now," over and over again. He pressed down on the clutch with a new agony coming from his stomach, and the hand moved the car into first and then into second. He pulled out. "I'll not die here," he repeated as if his resolve would make this his reality. The car moved into the street and he moved the stick into third gear. He wasn't far from his father's house. He would go there. Yes, he would go to his father's house.

CHAPTER 33

1940

Virginia's hands covered her mouth, but her scream was as silent as Abe's lifeless body, and before she could fully fill her lungs with air and wail her anguish, she collapsed into the arms of Armand and Maurice who carried her to a bedroom.

Jonah sat on the bed, rocking his son's body back and forth, desperately trying to will his own life force into Abe. In his desperation, he thought of Elisha who was able to bring the widow's child back to life. Why couldn't he? "Such a waste," he moaned. "Such a waste." A comforting hand touched his shoulder and he shook it off. The attempt to comfort seemed an intrusion. "I was there when he was born," he muttered softly to no one in particular. "I went for the doctor in three feet of snow." He started to tremble, and a wave of sickness gripped his gut and he doubled over Abe's body in anguish. Once again he was holding the lifeless bodies of his little twin boys who died so long ago, and once again he held the lifeless body of his beautiful little Jenny. The memory of those days, the mindless insanity of a child's death no matter what the age, just overwhelmed, and the hopelessness and injustice of the world coalesced deep within; his soul shuddered. "Lies. Now I know it is all a lie," he whispered to himself.

Somewhere behind him, his tortured brain thought he heard someone say, "He's in a better place."

"There is no better place," he cried out in anguish, and in that sudden release, Jonah Chernov affirmed the truth he had finally accepted. Everything he thought about life and death, good and evil, rewards and punishments were suddenly clearer to him than ever before. Everything was revealed as he held Abe in his arms. First, there was no reward in heaven because there was no heaven. Secondly, there was no justice from God because God was a human invention. And, if there is no such thing as God, than justice on earth was what those in power deem it to be. Millions were taken in the war, and millions more in the plague that followed. To what end? Was the world cleansed? Was there more food for the hungry because millions were dead? Were wars and plagues nature's way of providing? No! Evil still flourished, murderers still murdered and went free, and people still starved all over the world! He twisted his body to face those in the room. "What is the purpose of all this?" His family looked at him without understanding.

Now, he finally understood why people prayed to a God, and he understood the need for believing. He also understood the comfort one might have in believing that God had a plan for each human being, and each had a purpose. He had been brought up to believe such a thing, to believe in a God of goodness who watched over all, nourishing and protecting. For a time, when he was young, he held those beliefs despite the reality of what he saw daily around him. Then the darkness that covered Krivoser crept into his soul, and faith in this God wavered close to denial. Now, holding his dead son, his beloved son, Abe's pajamas wet with his father's tears, Jonah felt a physical and a spiritual revulsion at all the lies that were the foundations of all faiths, not only his.

All religions were no more than stories that were fantasy attempts to understand something that humanity sensed, yet that something remained totally beyond its comprehension. How naive to believe that some benevolent Being saw and constructed a future for each of us. It was becoming clear to Jonah that whatever significance to our pitiful lives there might be, we were the ones who designed for ourselves that significance and meaning. We live and we die. We make choices. That is all, and everything we are taught to believe is designed to give us false hope. At the end, we can expect nothing, and if we find meaning, it is meaning we have created for ourselves by seeing what needs to be done. Only we can give meaning to existence. But there was more. He knew there was more. There had to be more.

Armand and Maurice tried to take Abe from their father's arms, and Jonah swung his head around defensively. "Not yet, not yet," he cried.

"He's with Jenny, the boys, and with Momma," Fanny said.

He is nowhere, Jonah thought. And Leah was nowhere, and his twin babies were nowhere, and Jenny was nowhere, and his Zeydeh, and his Papa, and everyone else, were nowhere. They were dead, and death was the end. But though his brain and soul screamed this at Fanny and at the silent world, he said nothing because she believed, and he would not rob his daughter of whatever comfort their tradition offered in tragedy. But for him, the world was falling apart, and he did not know if he would ever be whole again. How do you continue when you see only emptiness? he thought. "I cannot live in a world where there is no meaning." he cried as his sons held him. They looked one another, again not understanding this cry of anguish and were greatly concerned.

The funeral procession turned left onto Madison Avenue and right again onto 59th Street towards the bridge to Queens. Jonah had a notion that he saw himself in a silent movie with somber faced black and white flickering people, silent tears, streaked cheeks, and mute sobs. Abe's was not the only funeral cortege on the bridge that day, and Jonah wondered who else was grieving a lost child or a parent. "Parents were not born to bury their children," he muttered to Marta, whose black laced hand gently caressed his own. Virginia sat opposite them, Leo at her side. Her face was covered in a black veil.

Harry made all the arrangements. He knew Abe would have wanted a traditional burial if only for his mother's sake. He, like his brother, had little interest in religion. Of course, his father would have insisted on a traditional burial if there were any questions on the matter, but Harry did not ask.

At the funeral home, Jonah noticed the throngs of men and women on the streets, waiting to pay their respects to his son. The few he focused on seemed dark and shadowy. Some of them he recognized from Brownsville, from newspaper pictures, hooligans; men whom other men spoke of in fearful, quiet tones. Their grim histories seemed etched in their lined and hardened faces. These were Brooklyn boys whose parents he knew had died, despairing at what their sons had become. Was Abe was such a man? Jonah was never quite sure. He knew the good Abe did, and he knew the bad. How does one love and rage at the same time? And the women there, too made up to be beautiful, and too well dressed for the times to be anything other than the women Abe knew from the gambling halls and from God knows where else. Were these the people who peopled his son's life? And why were there photographers flashing bulbs at him and disrupting the funeral? And why were people hiding their faces from the cameras? And who were the men on the periphery who were taking notes and watching the crowd? Were they the police, looking for Abe's murderer? Why were so many strangers pushing to get a look at Abie's casket as they left? Was there some fragment of his son's spirit they thought they might grab for themselves? And so many cars. Where did they all come from? What did they want?

Jonah had railed against Abe's life choice to become a gambler and cursed him for taking Harry into that life. Still, he had steadfastly refused to acknowledge or believe a decade's worth of allegations that accused Abe of racketeering, bootlegging, gambling, fixing sporting events, and even prostitution. No allegation had ever been proved against Abe in any courtroom because Armand quietly reminded Abe to plead the Fifth Amendment as a way of protecting him from self-incrimination. It worked as it had worked years ago when Armand first suggested it. Armand took it as a silent testament to his skills, that an idea of his had been upheld by the Supreme Court of the United States. Yes, his son was a gambler, but he also owned restaurants and hotel concessions that the IRS could not smear. Also, Abe and Harry were smart businessmen who made sound investments during the Depression when real estate was cheap, and Jonah knew that Abe had more money than he could ever spend and did good things with it.

The Texan who murdered his brother was hunted down by Harry and tearfully confessed what he had done before he was buried in a shallow grave in Carnarsie, but Jonah didn't know that. He did know that his son was murdered over not paying a gambling debt. So why didn't Abe pay that gambling debt? He could afford it. Was it a matter of honor? His murderer didn't care about honor; his murderer cared about money. What was honor worth when you were dead?

The entourage that followed the hearse down the great boulevard that roiled off the bridge like a smooth black river, made its way through the streets to the wrought iron gate of the Montifiore Cemetery on Springdale Boulevard in Queens. They waited their turn and finally were invited in to where the Krivoser Society had purchased land. Jonah, a founding member of this benevolent society, was there when the land was purchased. Few people had been buried until the flu and the war had caused markers to sprout up like unwanted weeds made of granite and slate.

Fanny had asked Rabbi Abraham Coleman from the shul on Sutter Avenue in the old neighborhood to officiate at her brother's funeral. His gentle dark eyes looked at her and the family sympathetically and led them saying, "Praised are You, O Lord our God, King of the universe, righteous judge." His withered hand held a shaking knife that made a cut in the garments they were wearing as an outward sign of their loss and grief. "We do not know why we are born," he began, "and we do not know when we shall die." He paused. "It is how we respond to death tells us a great deal about how we respond to life. As there is a way to respond to life Jewishly, there is a way of responding to death, Jewishly." Jonah silently rejected the rabbi's praise of God, but accepted the idea that there was a Jewish way of responding to life and to death. He still rejoiced in his traditions.

Rabbi Coleman intoned Psalm 23, "The Lord is my shepherd..." followed by Psalm 121, "I will lift up mine eyes unto the mountains..." Marta, stood next to her husband, her pale blue eyes focused on a distant place, another reality, and seemingly oblivious to the words over her stepson. Silent tears rolled down her cheeks, tears shed more for Jonah than for Abe, but she could not feel them. It was almost as if someone else was crying within her. Rachelann and Aaron moved closer to them, and stood quietly, each holding the hand of a parent. Elizabeth and Nathaniel stood near. Maurice, Sam, and Fanny, stood in a small cluster next to Rachelann while Harry stood a distance away, comforting Virginia and Leo.

As Jonah's estrangement with Abe grew, there were fewer and fewer opportunities for Virginia and Leo to meet with the family. Zeena and David were in Europe, trying to arrange the evacuation of Dora's family and Ruth's family from a Switzerland that was becoming less and less neutral and more and more under the influence of Nazi Germany. Armand stood farther away among family friends, his hat pulled down over his face. And though he ached to stand and comfort his parents and siblings, the politician in him knew that for the world to realize that the State Attorney General, Armand Duchamp and notorious underworld figure, Abe Chernov, were half brothers, his career and promise of a future in Congress would be in jeopardy. He knew he would have to leave the cemetery early, and enter his parent's home through the back garden. He knew that among the crowd were newspaper people and police in plain clothes.

"God, exalted and full of compassion, grant perfect peace in Your sheltering Presence, among the holy and pure, to the soul of Abraham Chernov, who has gone to his eternal home."

At the sound of Abe's name, Jonah felt a sudden weakness throughout his body and felt himself sinking. Maurice and Nathaniel rushed to help Aaron and Rachelann lift him up.

"May his soul be bound up in the bond of life," Rabbi Coleman intoned. "The Lord is his portion. May he rest in peace. Let us say: Amen."

The family murmured his last word softly, as the casket was lowered into the ground. Each one approached the mound of dirt and shoveled a clod of dirt onto the pine casket with the Star of David etched on the top. The first clod of dirt thumped loudly on the box and each following thump on the box seemed a ghostly echo. With each thump, Jonah winced as if being stabbed. He struggled to stop crying, and when the shovel was handed to him by Nathaniel, he pushed a large clump of dirt into the grave. This sound, this terrible thud and reverberation of dirt and stones hitting wood, shook Rachelann into the reality that she was actually putting her brother into the ground and would never see him again. With that truth, this respected woman who faced down brutal union busters and pushed back on police cordons, became a child again, and fell to her knees wailing for the brother whose handsome face and playful smile were gone. But there was a heaven, and she would see him there along with her mother and little sister and brothers. Jonah saw her anguish, and fearing she would faint, handed the shovel to Sam and moved to catch her. But Harry had emerged from the crowd and was already supporting her. Jonah looked at his son through tears, and gently patted his face. "We must bury our own. We must bury our own," he said to him softly.

The kaddish was intoned, and the good rabbi looked at the grieving family. "It is said that there is no comforting the bereaved when his dead is before him, and I have learned that when a when a child is lost, there is never any real comfort. It is an emptiness in space that is never filled. My friends, I can only tell you that we cannot understand why God gives and takes away. We can only look to Him for comfort and hope that the future will be better. To be sure, our faith teaches that we can strengthen one another in this time of loss. Rely on one another, have compassion for one another, and love one another." Then he looked beyond the immediate family to the crowd. "Do all you can do to console one another and the immediate family. We are taught that visiting the sick, dowering the bride, attending the dead to the grave, and comforting the bereaved, bring us rewards. What you are all doing here today is a great blessing to us all." He paused waiting for his words to take hold. He looked directly at Jonah. "There is one way to be consoled, that will go beyond yourselves and bring goodness in the memory of the dear son you lost, and that is to build something in Abraham's memory. Something that will light the world and reflect the goodness that you knew was in him. Something of meaning to you, for if you put your love for him and your feelings of loss into something good, you will be honoring his memory and at the same time you will be bringing light into a world that desperately needs light. Giving light where there is darkness, and bringing compassion to those who are lost and alone, will be a fitting memorial to the son and brother who was taken from you. We cannot wait for the Messiah to come, so doing something to make the world better in Abe's memory may hasten him. Such an investment of yourselves and the action that has at its core compassion for others, is what will help you through the emptiness you are feeling now. Build something, and be consoled by your efforts. Let us go from strength to strength, and strengthen one another."

There were soft sobs and the family turned and moved a short distance to Leah and Jenny's monuments to pay their respects and leave pebbles on their headstone. Harry was already there.

Rachelann had taken charge once the initial shock of Abraham's death passed. A week before, she and Fedya had returned to New York so that Fedya could see a heart specialist. He was in the hospital when Abe died, and he wasn't told because the doctor did not want him stressed. The trip form Jerusalem to New York was arduous and dangerous, and had to be attempted because without taking that risk, he would have no future.

So Rachelann moved between Mt. Sinai, and the Fifth Avenue house sometimes twice a day, but today, she stood with her family. It was Elizabeth and Rachelann who prepared the house for the shiva, and Elizabeth assured her that all would be ready when they arrived home. She would see to the preparations, and she brought with her members of her own staff bearing Kosher food for the family and friends who would return with the bereaved. Elizabeth had studied all the traditions, and all traditions were followed. There would be a laver and bowl at the door to wash away the impurity that death brings with it, and all the mirrors would be covered so the mourner's focus would not be shifted from grief to vanity.

The funeral cortege took another route back from the cemetery, holding to the tradition that the spirit of the deceased would only know the route that they took to the cemetery and not be able to follow them back home. Jonah thought this was nonsense, but agreed when Rachelann insisted on following the traditions her mother had taught her.

All who followed them back to the house, washed their hands and entered. Jonah, seeing the water at the door, the covered mirrors, and the dining room table laden with food, thanked Elizabeth and Nathaniel for their efforts, and kissed Rachelann's forehead. Marta busied herself with things in the kitchen, trying to focus on the needs of the guests and mourners. In reality, she wished everyone had gone to their own homes so she might comfort Jonah and hold him close. She knew that was what he needed. She also knew that this was his tradition, and she had always honored it. So when Jonah asked that he have a few moments for himself, she accompanied him to the library, and closed the door behind her, asking the family that he not be disturbed. She then, asked the family and friends go into the dining room, to have something to eat.

There was something he had to think about while the memories were still fresh. He needed to be alone and in silence. Rabbi Coleman, speaking about light and darkness, had given him a glimpse of clarity.

Jonah looked at the low wooden box he would have to sit on for seven days, and something in him said that the coming ordeal was part of an expiation of guilt for his treatment of Abe. The library had always been his refuge, but the peace that had usually enveloped him when he entered it, was not forthcoming. His anguish and guilt had become visceral and the pain would not be placated by books and old prints. He sat down on the hard box, leaning his elbows on his knees, covering his ears with his hands, thinking that by doing so, he could silence the voices, voices like mocking echos, that seemed to reverberate without end. "Why, Jonah?" they called. "Why another death?" they called. "What new truths are to be learned, Jonah?" they called. What truths are to be learned?"

"What truth?" he heard himself shout back. "What truths should be learned from children dying? You want to know my truth? I'll tell you my truth," he screamed silently. "Any God who could allow a man's children to die in agony before his eyes, is no God. Any God who is silent in the face of millions being murdered, is no God." A different voice screamed, a voice that was also his own. "Where are the promises of the psalms, Jonah? And what of the prayers of supplication sent out into the silent void? What of them? No one answers because there is nothing to hear them. Again, Jonah, what is to be learned? If anything is learned it is that any God worth being believed in would not allow such horror. And now, Abe's murder. Think, Jonah, think. What is to be learned? If there is nothing to be learned, than what is the purpose of living? Should I then learn that God had nothing to do with my children's deaths? Should I learn that God has nothing to do with deaths that wars, famine, disease, and disasters heap upon us? Have you been wrong all these years, Jonah? Has everybody been wrong? Does it all just happen for no good reason? Is it all just the way the world and humanity work? Can we just say 'it is what it is,' and let it go at that? That God has nothing to do with giving or taking life, or how life is lost? Is that the truth? Or is the truth in the light and darkness of which the rabbi spoke? If the wars, disease, and murder are the darkness, then what is the light? Beauty? Balance? Patterns? Order? Yes, that could be it; the light in us balances the darkness in us, and the universe impregnates both at birth. God has nothing to do with it. That's it. God has nothing to do with it. He lifted his head from between his knees and shook it, trying to shake off the questions and answers to the reality of the moment.

He thought of Abe's life as a life that moved dramatically between light and darkness. But it was the darkness that seemed to hold his son captive, even if his light broke through in his generosity. Abe was a confusion, a paradox of good and bad, of light and dark, and this realization about his son moved him to again struggle with the opposites that touched him this day; the opposites of life and death, good and evil, joy and sadness, alienation and involvement.

New images flooded Jonah's mind. When darkness comes, he thought, we incarnate as the light and the comforting hands that sooth. A person may find comfort in the belief that God might be with them because that is promised and that is what a believer believes, but Jonah now believed that true comfort came from the people who gathered around you. To be bringers of love and comfort that would help restore the balance between light and darkness, was the task of humanity.

That which people call God does not interdict the horror of the dark side that men bring into the world, but help comes only when good people, working from their own light, rescues and imposes order. Seeking that light within, and sending it out, was the true meaning of faith. There is something out there, something beyond the God his ancestors created so humanity could understand, and everything and everyone is part of whatever that is. Jonah did not yet grasp what this was, but he surmised it to be a presence that moved through all things, that animated all things, that elevated all things, that was infused in all things, and gave light to all things. This idea is what Jonah would carry with him, and it would sustain him. Other people might need a God they could imagine as a comforting father, one who promised to love and protect them, and that was fine for them. But for Jonah, that idea began to die in a burning Ukranian town when he was young, and it just kept eroding with each passing tragedy and disappointment. He had his traditions to keep the family together, and his traditions became his doorway to the transcendent. And now, he finally believed he was glimpsing what that transcendency might be; the reality beyond God. He had to tell Marta.

Jonah raised himself from the box, and walked over to the window and looked out. The trees were still, and a faint pale blue seemed to ease itself between the branches. Another season to visit him on the lovely street. Pattern emerging again at the bidding of the Presence, and his sad heart filled with a kind of gratitude and appreciation that he had never felt before. Suddenly, he seemed unfettered, like a pony breaking away from its mother and gamboling in some green field unencumbered and free. He no longer felt the anger or frustration that had haunted him in his struggle. He could bring his light to whatever effort he chose to undertake without the slightest need of future reward.

He walked back to the sliding oak door with beautiful inserts of spring and summer flowers executed so skillfully by Gilbert Lenett, and admired the excellence of the artist and of the light in Mr. Lenett that fostered such beauty, Jonah slid the doors open and smiled at the people who had brought their light, their compassion, and silent voices to comfort him and the people he loved.

CHAPTER 34

1941

Jonah fought the feeling of being overwhelmed and powerless to effect what was going on in Europe. He read and reread the letter from Dora about the abandoned children, wondering how he might make even a small difference. He blessed his nephew and niece in his heart for the work that they were doing in smuggling children and farming them out to righteous people in Switzerland who were willing to save innocent lives. The tragic truth Dora told, combined with the unbelievable story that Armand had revealed about the institutional anti-Semitism in his own State Department, convinced Jonah that he had to become involved. And as he sat in the comfort of his livingroom, he recalled what the rabbi said to him after Abe's funeral about moving on and building something worthy in Abe's memory. It was then that he decided that the money Abe had hidden could best be used to help orphans escape the hell in which they lived. He looked up with tears in his eyes.

"It is time we did something in Abe's memory," he said sadly. "The last letter we got from Dora has given me an idea, but I'm not sure where to begin."

"Tell me," Marta said, looking up from her crocheting.

"There are children in Europe who can still be saved, and I think I must do something about it. Marta, I want to organize something to save Jewish children."

Marta put down her work and smiled. Jonah was coming back into the light. "If it's going to be something about children, why not call it "Abe's Children?" That name would honor Abe and say something about the man few knew."

"I like that," he responded, becoming animated at the same time. He stood and walked to his desk and rummaged through a pile of letters that pled for funds. "Here it is," he said, crossing to her and sitting down. Wisps of silver hair fell onto his forehead and Marta's fingers put them back into place. "Here," he continued, "this is from the Joint Distribution Committee asking for funds. They were the ones who organized the St. Louis boat rescue, the one where the Jews were sent back to their deaths because no one would provide them sanctuary. This appeal says they are trying to rescue and support Jewish children in hiding, and are working to help thousands escape. They will be interested."

"And I think we must involve Armand because he knows the ins and outs of Washington and how to get things done," Marta added. "We need visas, and from what Armand has said, the State Department and that Brekenridge Long person who's in charge of them, is deliberately not issuing them, especially to Jews."

"I can tell you what that son-of-a bitch has done," Armand said, his face reddening. Congressman Emanuel Celler looked up from the papers Armand had put on his desk. The younger man was too upset to sit, so he started to pace and talk, initially pulling his first disconnected sentence from the air. "Did you know that the 1924 Immigration Act granted one hundred and fifty thousand immigrants a year to be legally admitted into this country?" His question was rhetorical, but the Congressman continued watching his agitated legal advisor with interest. Normally, Armand was the soul of composure.

"Just guess how many were admitted this past year?" he paused. "In the last year, only twenty-three thousand, seven hundred and twenty-five came as immigrants, and of these, only four thousand, seven hundred and five were Jews fleeing Nazi persecution. Do you believe that? And that bastard has the balls to say to me we that need to 'carefully screen' those coming in for the sake of wartime security! Are Jewish children a threat to our national security? Are all Jews potential German and Soviet spies? They are to Brekenridge Long! For ten years that despicable man and others like him in the Congress and in State have deliberately kept the numbers under quota. Those who might have done something are told lies, and the lies are believed without question because of who is telling them. And the lies go up to the White House and are still believed! We are to blame for not having shouted this from the rooftops when this first came to light, so we are also responsible for allowing America to turn its back on innocent people fleeing death. For what? To make sure we stay white and Protestant? The poem on the Statue of Liberty reads, 'Give me your tired and poor.' It doesn't say give me your white Protestants!"

Congressman Cellers stood, walked over to Armand with a glass of bourbon, and handed it to him. He could see the pulsating in Armand's jaw. "Sit down and calm down or you'll give yourself apoplexy. Brekenridge Long is a raging bigot. He certainly should not be Assistant Secretary of State, and certainly not the man to control quotas or visas." He paused in thought. "You are correct my young friend. If men of the temperament and philosophy of Long continue in control of the immigration administration, we may as well take down that plaque from the Statue of Liberty, blacken out the words you just quoted, and hang up another sign that reads, Golden Door Closed."

Armand sat, watching as his hand moved in a circular manner, causing the Scotch in the glass to become a whirlpool that reflected his thoughts. For a moment, he mused that the world was in this glass being swallowed by the vortex he had created.

"It would seem you have something to say to me, Armand. What is it?"

Armand emptied the glass of scotch with one gulp and told him of Jonah and Marta's plan. "I need visas," he said, "as many as you can get. I know there are people issued visas who never use them, so I know they are available." His voice became even softer and he leaned in. "Whatever can be done to get them, has to be done so quietly that Long and those who support him will not get suspicious."

"I'll talk to Eleanor and Sumner. I know that they will be supportive," Cellers said thoughtfully. "Wells already has a passionate dislike for Long, and Eleanor considers him an obstructionist of the worst order. In the meantime, as a Congressman, I can call for the lists of names of people who have been granted visas that have not been used. People die, people get arrested, and people go elsewhere. We can use these."

"I think Lyndon Johnson will also help." suggested Armand. "I know that from the minute he came into Congress, he has supported the naturalization of Jewish refugees. He was the one who saved Eric Leinsdorf' when our own State Department was ready to deport him back to Austria. Can you imagine? Very quietly, Johnson packed the conductor off to the Consulate in Cuba and got him a residency permit. Johnson's subterfuge saved his life. And a friend told me that in '38, Johnson provided a pile of signed immigration papers that got forty-two Jews out of Warsaw, while smuggling hundreds of other Jews into the Port of Galveston on boats and planes, hiding them, and finding enough money to buy false passports and fake visas in Cuba, Mexico, and Latin America. He must have saved four or five hundred Jews by himself, and he did it just because he could. I know we can count on him."

The house on Fifth Avenue again pulsed with life and expectations. Ladies, dressed in their Sabbath best, ladies who had originally moved from Krivozer to Brownsville and then to the Grand Concourse in the Bronx or to Eastern Parkway in Brooklyn, sat across from the fine Manhattan dowagers who had attended the Chernov Institute for Language and Travel. Jonah and Marta stood in front of the drawing room fireplace as their guests sipped tea and nibbled on dainty pastries.

"We have invited you here today because Marta and I have created an organization in our son's memory called Abe's Children, and we need your help. At this moment, I would like to read to you something from a memo written last year, the year my son died. The author is a man named Brekenridge Long who is the Assistant Secretary of State and controls the issuance of visas. This is what he wrote: 'We can delay and effectively stop for a temporary period of indefinite length the number of immigrants into the United States. We could do this by simply advising our consuls to put every obstacle in the way and to require additional evidence and to resort to various administrative devices which would postpone and postpone and postpone the granting of visas.' He was talking about keeping Jews out of America."

The looks on the faces of most of the women sitting before him was one of astonishment and concern. Some teacups rattled on their saucers and were set down. Some faces remained placid. "You see," Jonah continued, "because of Mr. Long's policies, I am assured that ninety percent of the quota places available to immigrants were never filled, which means that Mr. Long and those who followed his orders, have allowed hundreds of thousands of Jews to be slaughtered." He paused. "Many of these were children."

Marta stepped forward. "We have known each other for many years, and we are calling upon you today to assist us in our efforts to save the children who can still be saved. We have been able to acquire sixty visas to save sixty children, and if we are able to rescue them, we need signed affidavits that promise that there will be host families for these children. We're asking you to do nothing more than sign this statement, and as you do, we ask you to see each of your signatures as a lifeline to a Jewish child you would be saving." There was a murmuring among the guests. "If you cannot see your way clear to sign such an affidavit, perhaps you would be willing to help financially. Jonah and I are pledging whatever resources we have to this effort, but we really have no idea how much money we shall need. We anticipate that officials will have to be bribed at all levels, and we know that we will have to provide shelter, food, and comfort for those children who will be able to separate from their parents, probably forever. This is not going to be easy for us, for the parents, or for the children. Will you help us?" The room was silent, save for some muffled sobs, and the tinkling of stirring spoons. Then, a smattering of applause, and then the room echoed with support and appreciation.

Everyone from the Brooklyn and Bronx contingent signed an affidavit to welcome a child, and pledged financial support as soon as they could talk to their husbands. Most of the Manhattan ladies, not personally invested as were the others, did not sign affidavits, but did promise to send one of their servants with a check to support the effort. Some just smiled, finished their afternoon tea, and left.

Not long after that, Jonah and Marta set sail for Europe with cash, sixty American visas, and a man named Jim Novy. Jim Novy was a friend of Senator Johnson's, and the senator had suggested to Armand that Novy accompany his parents just in case there was trouble.

It was Eleanor Roosevelt and Sumner Wells who opened certain doors in the U. S. State Department that allowed Armand to discover that there were people issued visas who had died, had decided not to travel, had been arrested, or had gone elsewhere. He collected the names of these "missing" travelers and was moved along to like-minded government workers who willingly reissued these life saving documents that were all part of the legal quota.

It was to be a family affair. The money that Marta and Jonah had raised, the money Abe left, the money Harry and his friends contributed, ultimately amounted to tens of thousands of dollars. This amount was secreted out of the country to the one Jewish Swiss bank to which Jonathan had close ties. The money would be used to pay off the considerable number of people who needed to look the other way. And look away they did. Ruth's son and daughter continued to secret Jewish children out of Austria as Carmelite Nuns until they were stopped at the border, trying to enter Austria. It was a very close call, and the money they carried bribed the guard to allow them to go back to Geneva with the assurance that if he caught them again, they would be put in jail. When Dora and Jonathan approached them with their grandparent's plans, they themselves were figuring out a new plan and a new route of escape. Once they were told of their uncle and aunt's plan from America, they insisted on being part of it.

Berta and Sigmund, also part of an underground movement that did not despise Jews, knew the names of certain Vichy administrators who would be quietly willing to sell Jewish children scheduled to be sent to the camps in Poland, if enough money was being offered. Word was gotten to them that one key French Nazi agreed to smooth the way if the group agreed to take his own daughter with them. The child's mother was Jewish. They agreed.

The plan was fraught with danger. It would mean that someone would have to go into the heart of Nazi France, go to the concentration camp where the children were being held, decide on which children were well enough and still emotionally strong to withstand the trip, and decide from those interviewed, the fifty-nine who would be selected. The thought of a triage for Jewish Children was repulsive, but Berta and Sigmund had been forced to do just that when selecting the few children who would cross with them into Switzerland each time they made the trip back into Vienna. The job of getting the visas finalized would be left to Jonah and Marta. Then they would take them to Vichy to meet with Phillip Petain, the newly appointed Nazi sympathizer who was charged with controlling the southern part of France which was not occupied by the German military. That would be equally dangerous, though they both spoke French fluently from their years living in Paris, and could easily pass as ex-French patriots from America, wanting to save French orphans from the horrors of war.

When Petain took over, his first order was to fully control the economy and the workers, and immediately recognized that he would need a flow of capital to win the favor of the French he was now subjugating. Even though the media he controlled was rabidly Jew-hating, he did see the reasonableness of getting rid of Jews and being paid by Jews for the privilege of doing so. This was business, and what Berlin didn't know about, or what the Germans who ran the rest of the country from Paris didn't know about, would not hurt them or him for that matter. The sale of fifty-nine Jewish children could earn him thousands and buy him admiration.

Marshal Philippe Pétain transformed older military camps in Southern France and used them to intern Jewish people, Gypsies, and various political prisoners. In fact, the opening of camps became part of his economic plan since it provided ongoing jobs to the French who were more than willing to supervise the dispatching of Jews to Auschwitz and Treblinka. Camp de Rivesaltes in the Pyrénées-Orientales held children to be rescued, and was identified as the best place because of its proximity to the Spanish border and less of a distance to travel than to Switzerland. Since the guards and other workers in the camp were Catholic, Berta and Sigmund insisted that they were the ones with the skills to carry off the deception. If the camp administrators believed that little Jews were being transferred to a convent so they might be converted to the true faith, two nuns appearing to accompanying them would give a veneer of truth to the lie. They and the children would be packed into the same boxcar, but that car at a certain point would be separated from those who were heading to their deaths, and put on a track heading south to the Spanish border where they would meet up with Jonah and Marta who held the approved visas that would allow them to leave the country.

There wasn't much of an underground resistence force in France, and those who did claim to hate the Vichy Government, hated Jews as much, so the underground could not be trusted to speed their journey in safety. But there were Jews and righteous Christians who had something of their own underground, and they had been contacted a month before by Brith Shalom, a national Jewish service organization who had heard of Jonah and Marta's efforts to raise money for this project. Brith Shalom became the funnel for the transfer of funds to these righteous partisans, and these people were provided guns and provisions to help guide the children across northern Spain and ultimately to the Portuguese boarder where other righteous partisans would lead them to Lisbon. From there, they would embark on a boat for Liverpool and then on a boat for New York City. That was the plan, and it was a good, well coordinated plan had treachery not reared its head.

Berta, Sigmund, and the children disembarked from the train at a small train station high in the Pyrenees where they were met by a group of men and women who had been paid to escort them over the border. Jonah, who had been ailing, decided that the trip across the rugged mountain range would be too much for him and for Marta, and he gave the visas to Sigmund and Berta after having painstakingly written the name of each child onto each visa. They then chartered a plane in Vichy and flew to Lisbon to wait the children's arrival.

Trouble was waiting for the children and their protectors at the French border. One of the French guards, an ideological Nazi, declared that despite the visas, the children could not pass over because they were Jews and had to be returned. The partisans, dressed as peasants, crowded close to the guard rails that separated France from Spain, pretending to be upset by the hold up. The Vichy guard raised his gun menacingly, sensing danger, and other guards came running to his aid. From the rear of the crowd, a shot rang out and the French Nazi fell dead. The children began screaming, and more gun shots surprised those who had come running. The small contingent fell. Berta grabbed the hands of two of the children and Sigmund yelled for the others to follow him around the barrier arm that remained closed. Several of the partisans, seeing the children running towards the Spanish side and not knowing how this hoard of ragamuffins would be perceived by those who had pledged their allegiance to Franco, raised their guns at the Spanish guards in the event that the Spanish guards would fire at them. Suddenly, one by one, the Franco loyalists were felled by shots coming from behind them, and when that contingent had fallen, other partisans emerged from the trees on the Spanish side and welcomed the terrified children. A group of men on each side of the border, dragged the bodies of the guards into the woods and tossed them down ravines where their corpses could not be seen by anyone passing by. It would appear that they abandoned their posts for one reason or another, and officials from both countries would curse them.

 The French partisans returned to France and dissolved into the dense forest, while those on the Spanish side led Berta, Sigmund, and the children to a bus where they were provided with uniforms from a Catholic school. The children were instructed to speak to no one, and they understood the need for secrecy and obedience.

 The bus carried the faux nuns, the faux Catholic children on holiday, and the faux Spanish parents accompanying them through the rugged terrains of Huesca and Navarra where sunburned towns clustered around Medieval churches and monasteries with orange tiled roofs and thick walls. They refueled in Pomplona near the great Gothic Cathedral, and then rode southwest towards Segovia. The children marveled at the Roman aqueduct and asked if they might get off the bus, but the adults smiled and said that it was not possible. Further to the southwest they went through the Avila and Caceres regions, and finally to the Portuguese boarder, where another bus and a change of clothing also waited for them. From there to Lisbon and freedom.

CHAPTER 35

1941 - Berlin

"Yes," Zeena said looking into the young faces that had been focused on her for the better part of the two hour workshop that she had been invited to give. "And never forget that it is and will always be, a very insecure profession."

There was a smattering of laughter and murmurs which she had expected, and she waited for a moment until the class settled. "Now," she continued, "our time together is coming to an end, and I want to share with you what I have learned over the years." Again, all eyes were riveted on the elderly lady seated before them. As she looked at them, she wondered how many of their Jewish classmates had disappeared without a word. She wondered how many had been dismissed from the school by daring to inquire about their whereabouts. They were like young people all over the world, caught in the throes of a whirlwind that was not of their making or of their choice.

"The world," she began, "The world you wish to create on any stage through your craft, must first and foremost be a true world and thoroughly human if your audience is to discover something new, something significant, and something extraordinary through your effort." She paused, allowing the message of honesty to take hold. "This world you create must be unique and unlike any other world your audience will ever experience, and if you are good at your craft, and if you are in a good play, you will unify these strangers before you in a way they have never been unified before."

Zeena leaned forward as if to share a secret with them, and they unconsciously responded to her subtle and deliberate movement by meeting her with their own.

"You all aspire to be actors," she said almost in a whisper. "But I tell you now that everyone connected with the theater aspires to be an actor. Know that only you few have the right look, the presence, the drive, and the talent to achieve that." A muffled, embarrassed laughter followed, and she smiled at the expectant faces. "Also, you must never be ordinary," she continued. "You must always keep your distance and create that mystery around you that can only be defined as glamour. What is glamour?" she asked rhetorically. "You will know it the moment you step out of an elegant car and see the people behind ropes clamoring for a whiff of the air you breathe." Again, there were the embarrassed smiles on the faces of those who surmised she could read their thoughts and dreams.

"I warn you that there are difficult moments ahead. Many of you may be wonderful actors and actresses, but you will be turned down because you are unknown. Fate is a hard mistress who smiles on one and frowns on another. Much of life in the theater has to do with chance, so I tell you now that if and when you are selected for a role, you must enter that role fully and honestly by constantly testing your soul and your inner strength. You must constantly evaluate yourself in light of the person you are creating, and if necessary, dismiss what you thought you were. Take nothing for granted. To be great, you must face yourself, accept what you are, and grow in your craft by changing who you are to fit the life you are newly creating."

She took a breath and scanned the group for a light in their eyes that would tell her that they knew what she was saying to them. Some had that light, and some did not.

"Every new play," she continued, "will demand this very personal sacrifice of you because you are creating truth and giving the audience a totally new view of life and of themselves. The author has created a character, but you will be creating a new life, a new human, never before known and never to be known again. You are not giving the audience you, but a new being. You become instant parents, and all your experiences, and memories, coalesce into a child only your uniqueness can create."

She looked at them softly, as if these strangers had been her own children, thinking of the years in which she had learned a craft that she was now sharing. She hoped they took her words to a deeper meaning. They were destined to create new worlds on the stage, but they were also being called upon to create the world outside the walls, to evaluate themselves constantly and to create something of value and of beauty. Outside the walls they must look for the truth, and reveal it for what it. By seeing the truth and acting, perhaps they could be saved.

She finished talking, and the young people before her sprang to their feet applauding, and Zeena stood, and laughing, took an elaborate bow. They rushed to her talking at once, but were cut short by a commanding voice from the rear of the room. They froze, stood at what almost seemed like attention. As the heavy footsteps grew louder, the students fell away from Zeena as petals fall away from the center of a flower. They did not look at the man who approached, but they quickly made a path for the person walking towards them. Suddenly, fear replaced levity and enthusiasm, and they lowered their eyes to become invisible.

"Herr Rosenberg," said Zeena, extending her gloved hand. "How kind of you to come for me personally."

"And Fraulein Marisette," he responded. "For an American, your German is impeccable."

The last strains of Wagner's overture to *The Flying Dutchman* receded in the background as Alfred Rosenberg ushered Zeena into a large drawingroom that was old world and elegant. "You might not know this," he began, "but you're listening to Herbert von Karajan, who's conducting the Berlin Philharmonic. He is our Fuhrer's favorite kapeppmeister, and conducts Wagner only as a true Aryan can. Few people outside of Germany know that he's been with the Nazi party since 1933, and is one of our strongest supporters."

Zeena's smile hid her disgust for this racial ideologue and propagandist who sat himself in a large leather chair once owned by a Jewish merchant in whose home he lived. The roaring fire in the hearth turned the purloined brandy in his glass a deep gold, and she imagined him choking on it. He looked at Zeena over his round metal rimmed eye glasses that were strangely small and seemed purposefully to accentuate the intense focus of the two tiny, dark dots that were his eyes.

"Let me first respond to your question about the art you see by saying that the Furer trusted me to create the *Einsatzstab Rosenberg* so there would be an organized effort devoted to gathering great art to a central location in Germany for the pleasure of those who could really appreciate it. You see, my dear, I am in charge of the territories where inferior races tried and failed to create high culture. Since inferior people cannot appreciate even what they see that may be of value, it is my task to bring it to those who will appreciate it. Of course you understand that by inferior races, I mean primarily Jews."

Zeena felt as if she were playing a game of chess, and her next gambit was to make him reinforce his own feeling that he was the only important and interesting person in the world. "I do believe that you are called 'the arch-priest of Nazi culture.' Are you not?" she replied. "You are even known in America as the author who espoused the superiority of Aryan culture over the Jewish race." His smile revealed his smug satisfaction.

"They know me in America?" he asked, obviously pleased that his reputation had traveled so far.

"But there are still those who still think of Herr Goebbels as the great art connoisseur." Zeena sipped her wine and over the rim of the glass watched his mood darken.

"Goebbels knows nothing of art," he sneered, and Zeena knew she had touched a nerve that she could exploit. It was obvious that Rosenberg did not wish to expand on his distaste for Goebbels, possibly out of his own fear of this man. He changed the subject quickly.

"To answer the question you asked me in the car as to why we think we have a Jewish problem," he began, "I must first tell you a secret." He waited as she leaned forward and placed her own glass on the table. "You see Fraulein Marrisette, at our core, true Nazis are pagans who wish to return to that blissful state where humanity was not fettered with the condemning God the Jews foisted on our beautiful world, and their damn morality that Christianity foolishly accepted as its own." He paused and leaned in. "And on top of these, the Jews birthed this damned Jesus Christ that we were taught to worship. Woden and Thor are much more to our liking and our Nordic temperament."

"But I see no evidence that you are trying to resurrect the old religion," Zeena interrupted with a hint of a smile. "Your support in Europe comes from Christians. Do you think they would support you if they knew you wished to resurrect Woden and Thor?"

"It is true that they might not support us if they thought we wanted to return to paganism, but as for supporting us concerning the Jews, they are already running to do that. Jew hatred was ingrained in their faith from their beginnings, and not by pagans. Did you ever read the Gospels themselves?" He lit a cigarette, proffering one to her which she declined. "My Christian brothers and sisters were taught to hate Judaism more than they were taught to hate paganism. Beyond that, they were taught to hate Jews more than they were taught to apply the loving words of their Messiah to all people. Besides, paganism is so far removed from their lives that they give it no thought, but the Jews are a constant presence that has continued to plague them for centuries. We are merely giving our fellow Christians permission to do what they have always wanted to do, but were checked by foolish rights granted the Jews by governments, and a ludicrous morality from their Bible. Besides, didn't our beloved Fuhrer say something like 'we are only continuing to do what the church began to do centuries ago?'"

"I still do not see," she responded, feigning ignorance, and hoping he would reveal more of the Nazi intent. "Are they not an insignificant minority?"

"Yes, they are a minority wherever they are, but never insignificant. You will agree they have infested the earth. Yet despite the handicaps place upon them, they have occasionally achieved some note wherever they were tolerated and allowed to put down their roots. This separate nation within nations, having its own laws, its own God, its own visions of itself as a distinct and chosen people became, and continue to be, a perpetual reminder that they rejected Jesus, rejected what the Catholic Church taught about their new God, and by doing so, refused to validate Christianity. Certainly, you can understand the animosity that that generated throughout time. People just don't like being told that they are wrong, especially the people who have the power of life and death over you as we now have over them."

He turned his head upward, exhaled a long stream of smoke into the air and admired the painting of Muses surrounding Wisdom painted on the ceiling. Zeena followed his eyes upward and immediately recognized the irony. Here sat a man filled with hate and destruction who wished to be known as a great lover of the arts, speaking about the rationalization of murdering an entire people, admiring Wisdom painted on a ceiling.

"Jew hatred has been there since the beginnings," he continued after another sip of the brandy, "and when you combine the old Catholic hatred that the Church Fathers created with the newer Protestant hatred that Martin Luther created, you have the very force we needed to execute our plan.

That's the religious piece of it, but equally important is how we were able to bring the non-religious Europeans to our cause."

"I should like nothing better than to learn that also," Zeena replied, remembering her own experiences with the Dreyfus Affair in Paris so long ago, and the secular men and women who railed against the Dreyfusards and cursed Dreyfus solely because he was a Jew from Alsace and really not a true Frenchman.

"We can start with your great Voltaire who described the Jews as 'the most abominable people in the world.' He even claimed that Jewish priests sacrificed human victims! If the father of the French Enlightenment can tell us that the Jews possess a vile nature, and ascribes their hatred of other people to their religion and its laws, who are we to argue?"

"Are you suggesting that Voltaire was something of a link between the old Christian animosities and the secular world by ruling the Jew to be outside of enlightened society?"

"Exactly," he said, somewhat excitedly that she was seeing what he saw. "It was our very own Neitche, the father of our true German Enlightenment, who brought all the pieces together by teaching us of the Aryan master race and declaring that God was dead. He finally gave Germany its voice. Once you believe that God is dead, and therefore no judgment and no authority behind a Biblical moral law that has suppressed our natural instincts for millennia, we now had the permission we needed to declare what is right and what is wrong. We replaced the God of the Jews as the arbiter of good and evil. And if we declare it good to murder Jews, then it is good."

Zeena felt her stomach involuntarily turn as her eyes murdered the man who now sat smugly before her. She knew she would be taking a gamble with what she would say next, but it was unavoidable. "I can now see how the currents of religion, history, and culture can culminate in the present situation. I have heard it said, unofficially of course, that the time is ripe for what is being called, 'The Final Solution' to what we all know as 'The Jewish Question.'"

Rosenberg nodded, closed his eyes and smiled. "Ah, yes, the Jewish Question," he said. "I'm not really supposed to talk about that, but I will only say that Germany will regard the problem we have with the Jews as solved when the last Jew has left greater Germany."

"But there are those in the West who believe that Germany means to make all of Europe greater Germany." Zeena said. "Where will you put them all?" Her nervous laugh was by design.

"One day, there will be no more Jews where Germans breathe because there will be no Jews left in Europe with breath. I cannot say much more than this, but there is talk." He thought for a moment, and not being able to stop himself from bragging. "To that end, I have been put in charge of gathering their archives, their art collections, and their ritual items for the purpose of scientific and cultural research. With each country that we envision occupying in the future, we will dispose of the Jews and keep the best of what they own. I already know my targets."

"But are there enough German soldiers to dispose of so many people and confiscate their belongings?" Zeena countered. "I would imagine you would need thousands upon thousand of loyal Germans in each country."

"We have thousands upon thousands of loyal people, but they call themselves Austrians, Hungarians, Czechs, Frenchmen, Poles, Belgians, Dutch, Greeks, and on and on. We don't need only Germans to carry out our plans when we have those in Europe who share with us a common hatred. It is hate that binds us together so it will take almost no convincing. They will round up the Jews for us, or murder the Jews themselves, or stand quietly by while we murder them. They will happily give up their Jews if we give them what their Jews have after we take what we want."

"Surely you can't believe that the man in the street holds..." Rosenberg interrupted her.

"The people in the street, the good Christians, the good secularists, and even the good Nazis, have not the slightest clue regarding history, religion, and culture. Theirs is not an intellectual hate with a philosophy behind it. These people hate because they were raised to hate; their parents hated, their priests and ministers hated, and their teachers hated. Their reasons are most superficial, but it serves our purpose. We are going to exploit this natural inbred hatred that comes to them as naturally as breathing. The Nationalist Socialist Party is merely giving them the voice and the arms and legs for them to do what they've always wanted to do. Now they will be able to do it just because we will tell them that they can. Ask the man or woman on the street, and they will blame the Jews for the economic depression, or the corruption in government, or the dissipation of our society, or that old canard that they killed Christ. These people have no need for philosophy because they already have their truth. But what they do desperately need is some group upon whom they could blame their failures, their inadequacies, and their despair. We are giving them permission to act on those fears and hatred with impunity. What will be amusing is that even after the Jews are gone, there will still be economic depression, hunger, and injustice. They may think that by getting rid of the Jews their lives will be better, but they'll still feel the same despair, even if there isn't anyone to blame it on. Even that will not stop the hate, and they will never realize or allow themselves to see that they were wrong. Remember, God is dead. No one judges. In the Jews, we have a ready made enemy that has been with us for centuries."

Zeena sat back in her chair smiling because she sensed that he was about to reveal something that had not been revealed before, and she was preparing an empty tablet in her head where each word would be recorded.

"You see," he said, "we have formulated a theory that is unlike any theory in the world. We have picked up on an old idea that the Jews are a race, but unlike other races who are known by their skin color, or eye shape, or hair texture, the key racial identifiers of the Jew are the ideas and the values that the Jew holds. To us, the Fuhrer and the Third Reich are the arbiters of what is good and what is not. That's the core of Fascism. To the Jew, the arbiter of what is good and what is not, will always be their God. They hold their God above society, and they believe that their God continues to judge men, and governments, and whole societies. Surely, you can see the conflict. This is an idea we cannot tolerate, and the only way to eliminate such an idea is to eliminate the people who hold such an idea." He paused so there would be a silence in the air that would prepare her for the ultimate truth of what he would say next. "You see, my dear, we must destroy the Jews if we are to destroy this idea of a judgmental God. The Jew is the constant reminder that God is not dead, that our Neitche was wrong, and that we are not the moral authority for what will be the new world that we envision."

Zeena felt her eyes widen with this new revelation. What insanity, she thought. "But certainly all Christians do not believe that God is dead or believe that if you kill people you will kill an idea?"

"Of course they don't," he quickly said, "but understand that those believing Christians are too busy worrying about their after-life with Jesus to notice that they have completely missed the point of what Jesus taught. Some will care about what we are doing in Germany and what we will be doing in the rest of Europe, but most will not. Some will speak up, but most will not. Some will even risk their lives trying to hide Jews, but most will not. Besides, remember that the underlying hatred for the vast majority is always there, and that is what we are counting on. Good Christians as well as bad Christians will smile and be our best supporters because we will be getting rid of the Jews for them, and we are giving them the privilege of helping us. In their hearts, the great majority believe that is a good thing to do. I assure you of that. And we do believe that there are a great many good Christians in America who feel the same way, and we keep in close touch with them." He paused for a moment fully confident and fully assured that he had made the case for her to bring back to Nazi sympathizers in the United States.

Zeena looked directly at him. "Herr Rosenberg, I am confused about something. For centuries, Christianity demanded that if the Jews give up their law and their idea of God and converted, they would not be harassed. In the Nineteenth Century they were asked by the secularists to give up their concept of being a distinct people if they wanted to enter society. Many converted and many became secular. You do not allow them these opportunities, and I don't fully understand why."

"Again, I am amazed at your perceptions," he said as he placed his hands on his knees and pushed himself up. He was now standing in front of her. Zeena moved slightly back in her seat. "Few have asked because few care to know." He cleared his throat like a professor beginning a lecture and smiled at the thought of what he was about to reveal. "We believe that once you are a Jew, you cannot not be a Jew, for the things the Jew hold as his or her truth is indivisible like red is to blood. Who they are is embedded in their blood and in their brains. They cannot separate their blood or their brains from their beliefs no matter how often they kiss a cross or denounce their way of life. I would go so far as to say these things, these beliefs, these attitudes, these thoughts, are in their very cells and are passed along through conception. A Jew is a Jew is a Jew and cannot be anything else. When you combine these ideas with the character traits demanded by their sacred texts, and the horrendous belief that there is a God above who judges everything, the only way to stop them is to kill them. Our scientist tell us that even having one Jewish grandparent or even great grandparent does not cleanse you of the infection. We are in the business of murdering an idea."

The insanity and lies that this odious man was spouting as if they were truth, caused Zeena's breath to come more rapidly and heat flush her face. It was her nature, in such situations, to confront and attack, but she knew she could do neither if she were to gather the information she was asked to gather. She had had enough of this man for one evening and for a life time. She was confident that she could report back the full intentions of the Third Reich regarding the Jewish People, her people. Now, for the first time in many years, Zeena saw that these people were also her people.

"I do want to tell you how much we appreciate your willingness to come to Berlin and perform for us and teach a master class," he said, tiring of the topic and changing it to one he preferred. "I know this was an arduous task for a woman of your years, but you are still considered one of the greatest living actresses today. By accepting our invitation for this cultural exchange with our American friends, and by gracing the stage here in Berlin, you let the world know the German culture continues to revere the arts, even as it finds the need to eliminate those within our society who make art degenerate."

"You are too kind in your flattery of an old woman," Zeena responded, her rage barely contained. "When I speak with our friends in the Bund and with Mr. Kuhn, I assure you that I shall share my memories of you and of Germany and her culture exactly as I have witnessed it." Zeena was calling upon all her resources to control her revulsion. The last time she had felt this was at her final meeting with Ezra at his trial. But even Ezra with all his evil did not come close to the insidious horror and depravity of this man and those who were part of his circle. A beast wrapping himself in the trappings of culture and of art. Such men, she thought, continue to prove that there is no relationship between loving the arts and decency.

"But let's not talk about me, my dear Alfred," she said, forcing a change of subject. She stood and he offered her his arm. "You did ask me to accompany you here because you wanted me to see something that you said you obtained in Paris from Le Jeu de Paume." She steadied herself on her cane and smiled assuring him that she did not need his support. The thought of touching him was obscene.

"As you well know, I am something of an art connoisseur fraulein, and while I would have no difficulty dealing with deviant Jews the likes of Chagall, Soutine, and Grosz if I could get my hands on them, there are some of their work I do find quite exceptional even if they do not glorify the values of the Third Reich as our Arno Breker does. Of course, degenerate art can still garner a nice price for the German treasury if it is sold, shall we say, privately? We have set up a wonderful system for dealing with art which has been liberated from the homes of rich Jews and European museums. It is all first sent to Paris to be recorded, sorted, and temporarily housed at that lovely little museum in the Tulleries Gardens in Paris under the watchful eye of my friend, Bruno Lohse. The Fuhrer is also planning to build The Fuhrer museum where the greatest treasures of Western Civilization will be ultimately housed. The pieces there will be so well known that we cannot touch them. A few of us take lesser known works, first for our own collections, and then Lohse auctions off the rest to other officers of the Third Reich, wealthy friends, and some covetous art dealers for the foreign market. I myself have employed art dealers such as Gurlitt, Buchholtz, Moeller and Boehner whom I have authorized to appropriate and auction off other lesser works that were confiscated to benefit the German treasury. Of course, Herr Gurlitt will occasionally secret away for me something special for my own personal delight though I'm sure he is secreting away some paintings for his own secret collection. But tonight, I want to show you my prize. As he spoke, he beckoned Zeena over to a wall between two windows upon which hung a painting she recognized as a Pissarro. "Yes, I know he was a Jew," Rosenberg said, "but considering that he was the father of the Impressionist Movement, I believe that for history's sake, there must be samples of his efforts. The one under it is by another Jew Impressionist named Pascin and it is also a good representation of the period. Yes, yes, I know that they should have been burned, but I just couldn't bring myself to do it. Of course, in the future, no one will know the artist's religious origins, but only the place the paintings hold in art history. You know," he continued parenthetically, "that the Fuhrer wishes to establish a museum in Prague dedicated to a defunct people and an art museum in Paris to show the decadent art that once flourished and rotted the souls of good Europeans. That's why, wherever we go, we take the finest Jewish ritual objects and ship them to Prague, and their best art to Paris. Both cities are becoming store houses, and there are caves and mines holding other great treasures. You would not believe how much we have already gathered. What is good is stored for the future, and what is not, is melted down or burned." He winked at her and playfully put his fingers to his lips, reminding her not to reveal his little secret. As he spoke, he looked hungrily around the room at what he or Gurlitt had stolen. "The Paris museum will not only display the art of Jewish degenerates like Chagall, Epstein, Lipchitz, Modigliani, and Gottlieb, but degenerative art by painters like Picasso, Braque, Matisse, Ernst, and Gris. I guess you don't have to be Jewish to be a degenerate artist." He laughed.

Zeena noticed that as he spoke of the art and the artists, he seemed to breathe faster, like a man, who having undressed a woman, sits back to contemplate her and satiate himself. This strange man possessed these paintings as if they were indeed each a woman to be caressed and finally seduced.

When she looked at them, she saw only the devastation and death of innocent people whose lives were ripped apart.

"But my prize painting in my entire collection is by an Austrian artist named Gustav Klimpt who thankfully was not a Jew. This particular painting will not be in the Fuhrer's museum, but hangs here in my own home. Thankfully, Klimpt took commissions from wealthy Jews, for if he did not, this masterpiece would not exist, and I would not own it." He moved is arm to the far side of the room." This portrait I personally took out of the home of a wealthy Viennese merchant whose name I think was Kreiten. I believe it is of his young wife. Would it please you to look at her?"

Zeena followed the flowing gown of gold, russet, yellow, and orange boxes and circles from the base of the canvas up to the serene face of a red haired woman who leaned her head casually against her hand while looking out with eyes that embraced the viewer with acceptance and compassion. Zeena saw the cane in her hand begin to shake, and she felt her knees buckling. It was the painting that hung in her sister's salon. It was the painting of Ruth that her husband had commissioned for their fifth anniversary after the birth of their first son.

"What is wrong Fraulein ?" Rosenberg said with false solicitude. "You are suddenly pale."

"It must have been the wine," she said as she took a seat in front of the full length portrait. "I can understand why you love this painting," she said, accepting a glass of water. "Her eyes are so compassionate." She paused. "Do you know who she was and what became of her and her family?" she said, desperate to know more than she already knew.

"If I recall correctly, her name was Ruth Kreiten. The story that came along with the portrait was that the SS, after some convincing, plied from a nun in a convent near their home that she and her two children escaped into Switzerland disguised as nuns. She may still be alive because she left Austria before Switzerland closed her borders to Jews. While officially neutral, the Swiss are not really neutral when it comes to saving Jews. They're profitting too much from Jewish money in their banks that will never be reclaimed. We did pick up the husband who I was told was a friend of that lunatic Freud, and the older son who was one of those piano prodigies you hear about. The old man was sent off to one of the camps in Poland, though I forget which one. I do recall that the son was sent to Theresienstadt where we sent whatever Jews we could find who had exceptional talent. For a while, we used that place as a model community so the gullible people who came there like the Red Cross would believe that nothing bad was happening to the Jews elsewhere in Europe. I met with a group once, and believe me, they didn't want to see anything other than what we wanted them to see.

They asked few questions and smiled a lot. We knew they would give a good report. Secretly, I think they were with us."

Herr Alfred Rosenberg seemed to reflect for a moment on his several visits to the camp and continued with a satisfaction that hinted of nostalgia. "I myself was in the audience when the inmates performed Verdi's *Requiem Mass*, which I thought was a rather brave thing to do. I imagine they believed that such a performance would remind us of God and take pity on them, but actually we found it quite amusing because right up until the performances, we deliberately began killing off their singers and musicians. Yet they continued, and they did perform which I myself must admit showed their tenacity. Little good it did them. It always struck me strange, that none of them seemed to know why they were really there." He stopped for a moment, and almost as an afterthought he said, "And if I am not mistaken, I once may have heard this Kreiten woman's son playing Chopin. He was really quite brilliant; such a feather like touch on the keys. I think they cut off his hands and hanged him. Don't you think it a terrible waste that such a talented young man was born a Jew?" He chuckled.

Zeena moved to the closest chair for fear that she would collapse. There was a knock at the door. A note was handed to Rosenberg. The soldier saluted, clicked his heels, and turned.

"I'm afraid I must leave on some urgent business," he said. "My car will take you back to your hotel." He also clicked his heels, turned, and left.

Zeena had no time to be outraged or to cry for her nephew or her sister's husband. She had to find some tangible proof that she could convey to Riegner at the World Jewish Congress before a soldier came into the room. She stood, shaking, and opening the leather binder on the desk, rummaged through the papers. Lists of murdered Jews and the art they owned were meticulously listed. Then, in the center draw, she found exactly what she wanted. There were copies of two memos, the first a directive to Reinhard Heydrich dated July 31, 1941 from Goring and it read, "I herewith commission you to carry out all preparations with regard to...a total solution of the Jewish question in those territories of Europe which are under German influence...I furthermore charge you to submit to me as soon as possible, a draft showing the...measures already taken for the execution of the intended final solution of the Jewish question." The second document described a meeting of Hitler's henchmen at the Berlin villa of Wannsee in which was devised "the Final Solution" to the "Jewish Problem."

When Zeena reached London, she dictated the message to Samuel Silverman who sent it on to Rabbi Stephen Wise at the World Jewish Congress.

> "DICTATED TO SAMUEL SILVERMAN AUGUST 29, 1942 TO STEPHEN WISE (% MRS SCHNEEBERGER 250 WEST 94TH ST.)(WORLD JEWISH CONGRESS 330 WEST 42ND STREET. HAVE RECEIVED THROUGH FOREIGN OFFICE FOLLOWING MESSAGE FROM RIEGNER GENEVA STOP. RECEIVED ALARMING REPORT THAT IN FUHRER'S HEADQUARTERS PLAN DISCUSSED AND UNDER CONSIDERATION ALL JEWS IN COUNTRIES OCCUPIED OR CONTROLLED GERMANY NUMBER 3-1/2 TO 4 MILLION SHOULD AFTER DEPORTATION AND CONCENTRATION IN EAST AT ONE BLOW EXTERMINATED TO RESOLVE ONCE FOR ALL JEWISH QUESTION IN EUROPE. STOP. ACTION REPORTED PLANNED FOR AUTUMN METHODS UNDER DISCUSSION INCLUDING PRUSSIC ACID. STOP WE TRANSMIT INFORMATION WITH ALL NECESSARY RESERVATION AS EXACTITUDE CANNOT BE CONFIRMED STOP INFORMANT STATED TO HAVE CLOSE CONNECTIONS WITH HIGHEST GERMAN AUTHORITIES AND HIS REPORTS GENERALLY RELIABLE STOP INFORM AND CONSULT NEW YORK STOP FOREIGN OFFICE HAS NO INFORMATION BEARING ON OR CONFIRMING STORY."

"Paul, I come to you with this information because my own organization is too cowardly to do anything about it, but for the sake of my preservation, my name must be kept out of it. Can I rely on you to do that?" Carl Burckhardt, vice president of the Red Cross, nervously lit a cigarette. His voice shook. "Hitler has issued a written order to make Germany 'Juden-frei,' and I was told this by two very well informed Germans in the ministries of war and foreign affairs. I am telling you, Paul, that the word "'extermination'" or something very close to it was used. They made their intent quite clear to me, and I am in a position to confirm this but only in private as I am doing now, and certainly not for publication. They told me that since Jews have no place to go, and since there is no place for Jews to go because no country wants them, extermination is the only recourse."

Paul Squire, the American consul in Geneva, ran his hand through his hair, and leaned back in his chair, studying the bespeckled and neatly appointed man before him. Consul Squire, on other occasions, had passed on information from this man to his embassy regarding Swiss responses to the refugees, but was told through official channels to remain "neutral." To the outside world, he appeared to be as neutral as Switzerland itself, but there were back channels and underground networks with which he was aligned, and it was through him that hundreds of Jewish children were saved. So the word "extermination" struck something deep within, and he knew that this information was not something that could be ignored by anyone who believed in God or who had a conscience. "What do you mean that your organization is too cowardly to do anything about it?" he said, looking with intense interest at Burckhardt, and feeling his jaw beginning to twitch with rage.

"Before coming here," Burckhardt said, "I met with the ICRC and appealed to them to save German Jews and to speak out against this slaughter, but I was rebuffed. I couldn't believe what I was hearing. I was told that intervening would serve no purpose, rendering the situation even more difficult, and it would jeopardize all the work undertaken for the prisoners of war and civil internees, the real task of the Red Cross."

"Carl," Squire began, "I will leave your name out of this as my source, but this information must be sent to my Ambassador in Bern." Squire took a sheet of paper from the desk. "Leland Harrison will know that the term Juden-frei is the Nazi's way of cloaking their intentions of genocide, and he will pass this on to our Department of State for instructions on how we are to respond."

CHAPTER 36

1941

Dearest Jonah,

Bless you and Marta for the work the two of you have done in saving the children, but I fear that it is becoming much too dangerous for your work to continue. Word is coming to us that the Nazis have put into place something they call "The Final Solution," which we are told will eradicate all the Jews of Europe. You must not return, but work from America to save our people, and please get word to us that Zeena has returned safely.

I must confess to you that while it saddens me that America was attacked by the Japanese, I must also confess that I'm glad they have been pushed into this war because without America, we are all lost. Now we have some hope that perhaps some of us will survive. If America doesn't come to our aid, and the Nazis win, Switzerland will give up her Jewish citizens as quickly as the French and Poles did the moment the Germans asked. Of that I have no doubts.

Jonathan was invited to handle the security of a special international banking conclave here at the Schweizer Bankverein this past week, and was questioned by an American banker named Carlos Neiderman about bank security. This Neiderman person is the branch chief of Chase Manhattan Bank in Paris, and in conversation with other managers that Jonathan was part of, bragged that top German officials hold his bank in high esteem, and as a result, the Nazis have made large deposits of gold with them. Neiderman then said to the Barclay representative that his Paris branch had already seized and handed over to the Nazis about 100 accounts held by Jews thus far. He also said that they are collaborating with the German authorities in freezing Jewish assets. Barclay's manager responded that they were doing the same in France, and at the same time also revealed that J.P. Morgan, Guaranty Trust Company of New York, Bank of the City of New York, and American Express are taking similar actions in order to garner favor with the Third Reich. I wonder if the American and British Governments know of their traitorous actions or this banking conspiracy?

Jonathan also told me that he was asked to supervise and make secure what amounted to 280 truckloads of looted Nazi gold that they had stolen from the banks of the countries they occupied and looted from the bodies of victims. The gold was being transported to Spain and Portugal as payments for imports to feed their war machine. He saw papers that clearly stated that top Nazi officials, including Goering and Goebbels, are using Swiss Diplomatic pouches to spirit out their stolen, blood-soaked assets to Argentina via the Dresdener Bank of Berlin and the Schweizer Bankverein of Geneva.

I must end here. Give my love to your beloved Marta, my sister, and the rest of the family. I pray each day that the decent people of the world will one day rise up and stop this evil. I've loved this country and the people in it for many years, but the past few years have opened my eyes to this government and a hatred that seems to have become institutionalized. If we do live through this horror, we will come to America. A government which would collaborate with those who would murder innocent men, women, and children because they are Jews, is no government to which I can be faithful. If you know of anyone who can help us with the paper work here, please let us know so we may begin the process.

Your loving sister,
Dora

CHAPTER 37

1942

St. Peter, the head waiter Sherman Billingsley hired as his Cerberus to guard the gates of the Cub Room, the sanctum sanctorum of the Stork Club, made a deferential bow of his head and lifted the golden rope when he saw Harry approaching. Here, at 3 East 53rd Street just east of Fifth Avenue, Café Society gathered and ogled one another and relished being ogled in return. Billingsley, a corn fed looking former bootlegger from Oklahoma with a high forehead and perfect teeth, moved around the big dining room, obsequious to some, condescending to others, but always pampering the old rich and the newly rich. Based on the clientele he allowed in, one could easily see that he was a bigot, and those few black or brown faces that did get in were ushered upstairs and out of sight. That was clear to all, and those who knew Billingsly really well also knew that he was a closeted anti-Semite. But Billingsly knew that he and his supper club would not have become the focus of New York's society elite were it not for Jews like Abe and Harry. The Chernov brothers had supplied him with liquor, protection during Prohibition, and a wealthy clientele. Still, it was Walter Winchell, the most famous gossip columnist in the country and a Jew, who really put the Stork Club on the map and made it an American destination, as much as the Empire State Building was, by broadcasting his show from Table 50. So when the likes of Winchell, and other Jews such as Leonard Lyons, Al Jolson, Bert Lahr, and Ethel Merman, who brought other Broadway stars with them to the golden cord, Jews or not, they were afforded the same respect as were the more desired WASPS, declining Euro-trash royalty from Europe, and the captains of industry who all wanted to be seen and talked about.

The Cub Room was away from the prying eyes of the public, and that was where Winchell wrote the copy for his column and broadcasted his radio show. As Harry approached the table, the writer looked up from his notes, smiled, and motioned for Harry to sit while he finished his phone call. Winchell was the first to laud Abe and Harry's involvement in his column even after the *Forward* and other Jewish newspapers had declared that they would not support Jewish violence, even against the Bund. But Winchell was unabashedly supportive, and as a result, he and Harry became friends. This friendship worked well, for the newspaper columnist was given access to Harry's world, a world in which Winchell delighted, and Winchell gave Harry access to a world of celebrities and politicians. Both benefitted from their association.

Harry had always felt comfortable in this windowless supper club, decorated with elegant wood paneled walls and hung with portraits of beautiful woman. Billingsly spared no expense on flowers or food to delight the senses of the elegant patrons, and Harry was as delighted as the next one to be part of the scene. Billingsly owed Harry big time for being instrumental in freeing him when he was abducted by mobsters, and Harry used that as a chip whenever he needed something Billingsly could offer. Harry didn't like bigots of any kind, and knew Sherman for what he was.

Everyone Harry watched from Table 50 seemed to be furtively looking around and speaking softly, probably about other guests, happy to recognize a starlet, or politician, or famous entertainer from Broadway, or a film star from Hollywood, happy to think they were being recognized themselves. But since he was the one sitting at Winchell's table, he knew it was he they were wondering about. Something in Harry was pleased about that.

Harry's revery was shaken when a beautiful young girl with long legs and red hair approached the table. "Cigars, cigarettes, cigars, cigarettes? Oh, how nice to see you again, Mr. Chernov," she said, with a genuine smile on her face, her eyes softening affectionately.

"It's nice to see you, too, Ginger," Harry responded. "How is your mother doing these days?"

"I think she's really going to get well this time, Mr. Chernov, thanks to you. That doctor you called took mama the next day, and he said not to worry about payment." Tears of gratitude were welling up in her eyes.

"You cry and you'll spoil your make up," Harry cautioned. "I'll take a pack of Lucky' Strikes." Harry tossed a fifty dollar bill on her tray. "Keep the change, and buy your mother some flowers from me."

Winchell put down the phone and leaned in. Harry opened the pack, thumped one out, lit it, offering one to his companion. "So how's 'the mouth that roared' tonight?" Harry said smiling. "I hear that's the latest thing they're calling you."

Winchell laughed and took the cigarette. "That's one of the nicer things they call me," he laughed.

"First off Walter," Harry began, "I want to thank you for the kind words you wrote after Abe passed. I should have thanked you a while back," Harry said, releasing two streams of smoke through his nostrils.

"Look, Harry, everybody knew Abe as a racketeer, but people should know that he was also patriot. Had it not been for him and you for that matter, the Bund would still be marching down Broadway. People should know what he did for the March of Dimes that FDR and Cantor put together. Abe was a complex guy."

"Me and my father were most appreciative."

Winchell smiled and continued. "Your brother had real style, and did more to class up Broadway and New York than most people. I was happy to have known him." Harry smiled briefly. "Now while I love looking at your ugly kisser, Walt, what did you drag me down here for? I got other things on my plate, and you'll be the first to know if it's news worthy."

"Are you a patriot, Harry, like Abe?"

Harry was taken up short by the sudden question seeming to come out of nowhere.

"You bet your ass I'm a patriot," Harry said indignantly. "You know I tried to enlist, but they said I was too old and too short." Winchell smiled and continued.

"So you know that the government thinks it was sabotage that burned the Normandy."

Winchell's question seemed out of left field, and Harry was caught up short.

"Where is this coming from Walter? You can still smell the stink from the soot and the ash on my piers. I'll tell you and anybody else that it was Nazi sabotage. What's your point?"

"Okay, okay," he responded. "While I cannot say who approached me," Winchell continued leaning in, "I will say that the Office of Naval Intelligence's, acting on the highest authority, is interested in talking to you about helping to watch out for and stop German infiltrators masquerading as dock workers. They think these krauts infiltrate on submarines, and that's how Washington thinks they got to the Normandy."

"Are you saying that the United States Government is coming to me for help?" Harry laughed in delight.

"They know what you and Abe did in getting rid of the Bund, and they think you can help them in some counter espionage efforts."

Harry sat back and laughed again, but this time at the irony. Here was a government, bent on putting him and his organization away for life, coming to him because he had an organization that they needed. Of course he would do it, he thought. He would do it for America because he was an

American. Patriotism was what it was all about. There would be a couple of conditions.

He leaned into Winchell, took another drag on the cigarette, and cleared his throat. "You tell your Navy high command, and you tell whoever asked you to contact me, that I would be honored to serve my country. But you also tell them that I have a couple of conditions." Harry paused, searching Winchell's eyes for an invitation to continue. "They're not impossible conditions, but conditions." Harry felt he had good cards in his hand. "The first is that Joey DiAngelo is moved to a minimum security prison and then, early release. You tell your Navy friends that if they get that done, I will assure you that Joey will also show his appreciation to America in the same ways I can. The second thing has to do with a letter I got from my sister in Palestine. The Jews need guns and people, but those British bastards have set up navy blockades and quotas for Jews coming into the country. I plan on sending stuff, and I want assurances that any containers off my dock to Palestine and to a particular import/export dealer, go through customs here without incident or inspection. If the Navy makes good on both of these conditions, Di Angelo and me will assure you that there will never be another Nazi sabotage or infiltration on any dock where water touches American soil."

Winchell reported back to his contact in Washington, and Harry contented himself with thinking that it was FDR himself. In a few days, Harry got a phone call from Joey's wife that Joey had been transferred to a minimum security prison, and the following week, when certain dock workers were found acting suspiciously while loading a certain boat, they were apprehended and convinced that assisting the enemy was the wrong thing to do. These men never returned to the docks. They couldn't. What the stevedores also discovered was a shipment of arms to an Arab Palestinian merchant, and this startling event gave Harry another idea to address his sister's ongoing request to help his people.

The hidden armaments were unloaded, secretly transferred onto another boat that was also heading to Palestine, but to a very different organization. A telegram was immediately dispatched to the offices of the Joint Distribution Committee in Jerusalem with the name of the Arab receiver and the address to where the shipment was to be sent. Hidden within the telegram was Fedya's code name, so the person receiving it at the JDC knew to whom it had to be sent. Harry knew that when Fedya got the information he would turn it over to the Freedom Fighters for Israel, a break away group from the Irgun that were known as the most unrelenting fighters against the occupying British and the hostile Arabs. This particular group were viewed as terrorists by both adversaries, and by some Jews as well. Harry gave orders that the original containers be filled with stored, broken weapons scheduled to be melted down, and these he shipped to the Arabs. His message to Fedya was that the FFI should watch the address. When the shipment arrived, the suggested they could take out the Arab terrorists as well as those receiving the shipment. No one would be the wiser. From that moment on, all crates destined for Palestine were carefully inspected by Harry's men. Since all shipments to both Arab and Jewish ports in Palestine passed though the docks, Harry made sure that they bypassed customs agents. Having mentioned this to Armand one evening at their father's home, Armand related that his friend in Washington, Lyndon Johnson from Texas, also secretly raised thousands of dollars for Israel, and shipped heavy crates of guns marked "Texas Grapefruits" to the Jewish underground.

As long as the war raged, Harry saw to it that there was a steady flow of ordinance, weaponry, and occasionally a vehicle that found its way through the British blockade of Jewish ports. The ships were always off loaded in the dark onto innocuous fishing boats and hidden under stinking fish before the ships landed and were searched. This was the same procedure he had used in getting liquor into the country from Canada. Everyone involved knew that the biased British, who turned up their noses to Jews and Arabs alike, would not wade through stinking fish.

While Harry's focus was on smuggling and making Nazi supporters disappear, Joey, his sentence commuted to time served, continued to keep the docks free from saboteurs, relying on his contacts around the country.

Though Harry and Joey knew they would never receive any official recognition for their efforts because the government would never admit that it was in cahoots with the Italian and Jewish underworld, both knew what they had accomplished for America. By helping to destroy the American German Bund and keeping the docks free of saboteurs, Harry felt as American as an elected official. Joey's contacts in Sicily provided him with the movements of Nazi shipping and Axis troop movements, and these he handed off to a grateful government, and again, no recognition was given. Still, the friends knew that they had contributed to the safety and success of America's fight against the Nazis, and in their minds, they were American patriots in the truest sense of the word.

CHAPTER 38

1943

Eight or so years had passed, enough time for tempers to cool, for people to move on, for people to forget, and for wrongs to be righted. Sam painted as he wished, when he wished, and what he wished, continuing to dismiss Surrealism, Dadaism, Abstract Expressionism, and a variety of other isms that he felt did not move the viewer to a deeper understanding of the human condition. There was still not much of a market for social realism, even though canvases did sell. He pieced together a living accepting mural commissions, and by teaching a class or two at Pratt. But Sam found his true satisfaction, as he did when he was little, in the cool and cavernous basement of the Met where he also worked part time assisting the curator of the European Collection. Mostly, his task was to piece together and identify works of art from private and public European collections in the hope that whatever had fallen to the Nazis could one day be restored to their rightful owners.

His reputation as a painter, a fine arts historian coupled with his work ethic, brought him to the attention of Francis Henry Taylor, the Met's Director, as his reputation had brought his name to the head of the WPA years ago. When Sam learned that their mission was to save as much of European culture as they could while the war was still being fought, he decided that this is what he wanted to do. Like his brothers, he had also tried to enlist in his country's service, but was told that he was too old. But the Monuments Group had no age restriction on the members of its teams, and doing something that hinted of heroism and adventure was something that resonated with him. He also saw it as a way of being part of history, of being part of something that was truly important. Tomorrow he would be leaving his family to fly to London, meet with other representatives from allied countries, and begin the massive documentation, location, and rescue of what was stolen during the Nazi occupation.

If ever a truth was spoken, it was the one that proclaimed that there is virtually no relationship between love of the arts and decency. Sam knew this from his long years of working with desperate artists during his time with the WPA, but he came to fully understand that idea as he toyed with the possibility of joining the armed forces despite his age.

As an artist and something of a curator, he had become painfully aware of Germany's ravishing of European art for the glory of the Fuhrer. In fact, it was Hitler's love of art and his never ending anger at the Academy of Fine Arts of Vienna for rejecting his application for admittance to that august institution which he firmly believed was run by Jews, that made Sam first take notice of what was going on. Hitler loved art, and yet that did not stop him from being the most despicable and evil man on earth. The idea that the arts made people decent was a fallacy. The man loved art and set out to eradicate entire populations that he considered inferior. Art taught him nothing. It was known in art circles that the Fuhrer's vision was to recreate Rome in Berlin, with himself as the emperor-artist. It was this vision that prompted the rape of museums and private collections. As part of his vision, Linz, his adopted Austrian town, would become the art center of his empire, with the Fuhrermuseum; the grandest and most comprehensive art museum in the world as its epicenter. Here would be displayed the greatest works of art pilfered from museums and from ownerless Jewish property. It would house his own private art collection, and he urged the Nazi high command to begin collecting on their own. Years before, he had sent German art scholars to secretly create inventories that recorded the art, its location, who owned it, and its value long before his advance to conquer Europe began. In this way, as soon as a country was overrun, his agents knew exactly where to go. As countries were absorbed, so were the art works, and these were gathered up and secreted back to Germany and hidden until that moment in time when they could come out and be hung in the Fuhrermuseum. This artistic rape of European art was not lost on those who headed the museums of America.

"Sam," said Director Taylor, "the board and I have agreed to close the museum at dusk. We fear theft or injury in the event that there is a blackout. The Frick has blackened all their skylights and windows already, and MoMA's paintings are in a single space and surrounded by sandbags."

"What can I do?" said Sam, waiting to be invited to be seated in the dark oak paneled Edwardian room of the director's office.

Taylor motioned for Sam to sit. "Sam," he began, "as head of The Association of Art Museum Directors, I've invited my fellow administrators to a meeting. Paul Sachs, the grandson of Marcus Goldman, the banker who is one of our greatest benefactors, will also be there. I believe you met him when you studied with George Stout, his conservator at the Fogg Museum at Harvard."

"Yes, I did," Sam replied. "Museum Work and Museum Problems given by Stout at Harvard was Sachs's design. He's very knowledgeable."

"Yes, and because of what you learned with them, the Met has benefitted. Paul knows you as a student, and I want you there. I will need your opinion and help." He paused, gathering his thoughts. "The directors from the most prestigious museums in the country" he continued, "are coming to a presentation showing what is going on in Europe and what is happening to the great collections. As they watch it, I need you to be my eyes and ears. I need you to judge the acceptance or rejection of what is said by watching and listening to their responses and conversations. I need you to formulate what you, as 'the man in the street,' might feel about what is going on."

On the day of the symposium, Sam did as he was asked, and watched the faces who watched with horror the slides of Rembrandt's *The Night Watch* being rolled up like a carpet and put in a narrow box, and Michaelangelo's *David* being encased in brick. He saw on their faces the dismay when they saw the shattered glass covering the floors of The Tate Gallery, and the vast salons of the Louvre containing only empty frames.

When all except Taylor, Stout, and Sachs had gone for the day, Paul Sachs approached Sam. "What do you think?" he asked. Sam smiled at the diminutive five foot two man before him who had so influenced the museum world of America, that pictures were hung on American gallery walls much lower than they were hung in Europe in deference to his height, and as a gesture of appreciation.

"I think," Sam began, "that if your intention was to galvanize the energy here, you did that. I think they agree with you that museums are a bastion of our history, our freedom of expression, and our values, and must remain open. But if you want me to speak as an administrator might, I would tell you that I would keep the museums open, and I would make preparations for war by boxing up and secreting away the best of the best and shipping these out of town." He paused. "And again speaking as just a man in the street, I'd like our museums to be open in the event that I needed strong walls to shelter me from a bomb blast."

"We hope it won't come to that," said Taylor who had walked over. "I agree with what you are saying, Sam, and I think it would be in the best interests of the museum and the people if we followed your suggestions."

George Stout, impeccably dressed in a double breasted black pinstriped suite joined the conversation. His chiseled features and pencil thin moustache gave him the air of a dandy, but he was in fact a man who had no difficulty in getting his hands dirty. "We are involved in the most dangerous upheaval in the history of Western art," he repeated from the speech he had delivered earlier, "and we need to put the art world right again. To safeguard these great treasures, we will be showing respect for the beliefs and customs of all men and will bear witness that these things belong not only to a particular people, but also to the heritage of mankind." These were the words that had resonated with Sam, and encapsulated the objectives of the meeting.

"Gentlemen, I want you to know that I have begun gathering together the next generation of art conservators and restorers because I fully believe that the solution, or at least part of it, rests in the immediate training of a large new class of conservators which I call my special workmen. I did this because I saw what the fascists did in Spain with their tanks and airplanes. I saw what they did to Guernica. It should be clear to us that the continent's great art and architecture are susceptible to being destroyed if no one stands up to speak for them and make some attempt to rescue them."

Lieutenant James Rorimer, a powerfully built, barrel chested man, waited for Sam Chernov and George Stout on the beautifully symmetrical black and white tile of the foyer of The Algonquin Hotel on West 44th Street. James Rorimer, whose family name was changed from the Jewish sounding Rorheimer so he might get into Harvard, was a young dynamo in the art world. With ambition more than most, he had risen to the position of curator of medieval art at the Met in only seven years, and was the lynch pin in developing the Cloisters in upper Manhattan. He was now about to leave for the European Theater, one of the select few to carry Stout's vision of saving as much of European culture that they could save while the war was still raging. If the vision could come to fruition, Stout believed that men like Rorimer, a man with pitbull intensity and devotion, could bring it about.

Sam had not seem James since James had joined the Army. Now, on leave before shipping out, Rorimer was Stout's ideal for the Monuments, Fine Arts, and Archives section; an arts warrior who seemed to thrive in the military. The three waited patiently for a table. This famous sanctuary, still viewed by New Yorkers as holy to the literary giants of the 20's and 30's, was still a favorite place for drinks and lunch. Today it was crowded with many men and women in uniform being treated by their parents or friends to something special while on leave. The three were ushered to a table in front of an artfully crafted half wall into whose four oak panels were imbedded ebony stylized lotus flowers encased in ebony rectangles. On either side stood four large mahogany columns rising to heavy mahogany beams.

"James, Sam," Stout began, smiling, "we three are art world grunts, so let us raise our glasses to the grunts of the world who get the job done." The three martini glasses clicked in the air. "To the grunts," they said simultaneously. "We," Stout continued, "like to get our hands dirty, and we come out of a blue collar world which is the very opposite of the world from which come the directors we serve. Did I say that correctly? Anyway," he continued, "we are not the people who enjoy the endless committee meetings, or the endless cocktail parties where we cultivate donors." He motioned for another round. "I have something important to tell you." He took another sip, and dabbed his moustache with his napkin. "I have to tell you that I have run up against walls and down blind alleys to get this project off the ground, and I've come to the conclusion that only by working through the armed forces will we be able to accomplish anything of lasting value. There are forces out there that prefer working with high commissions composed of elite directors who will bend to please whoever holds the purse strings." His voice cracked slightly, and the corners of his eyes teared up. "But the truth is that I'm making no headway, and even Kenneth Clark, of the National Gallery in London, said my idea of a conservation corp was ridiculous." He took a deep breath as if to re-inflate himself. "I still believe that there is much that can be done, and I will not give up on the idea that if we can get artists or architects to accompany our invading forces, they could tell the military to try to avoid destroying some important monument, and we will have done a great service. I've trained plenty of people for the job, but my efforts continue to fall on deaf ears. I am frustrated beyond belief. A man has to do something, and therefore I have applied for active duty in the navy." He raised his glass again, laughing. "And so my dear friends, let us lift a cup to me and to all those brave fellows who are willing to do something significant."

Sam, without reservations, respected these men, not only for their exceptional talents, but for their foresight and patriotism. He could do no less. Sadie was gone, and the girls were living well and happily with Jonah and Marta. George Stout had taken the step, and so would he. He would enlist and do his part, hoping that if the monuments effort would ever get off the ground, he would be invited by Stout to be part of it.

CHAPTER 39

1944

Sam barely made the cut off date for enlistment, and even if the Monuments Group never got off the ground, he would at least have served his country. Happily for Sam, the Monuments Men as they were called, did get off the ground, and placed no restrictions on the ages of those who were promised a place on the team. As a soldier, he would be automatically elevated to officer status, and he was elated when his commander called him into the office and handed him his papers to fly to England. Tomorrow he would be leaving his family, flying to London, and meeting with other representatives from allied countries, so the massive documentation, location, and rescue of what was stolen during the ongoing Nazi rampage could begin.

Harry's phone call to Sam asking him to come up to the New York Apartment for a farewell drink, came as a surprise since the family had gathered only a few days ago at his parent's home. Harry lived with his wife and sons in Scarsdale since the Depression in a 1920 Tudor mansion. He was able to buy it after the crash at a good price from the widow of a man who had hurled himself off the roof of his office building two days after the stock market fell. Molly, his wife, was a full time homemaker. Two of their three sons, Ralph, and Milton were serving their country in the Navy and the Army, split between the Pacific and Europe. Paul, their eldest, had two children of his own and was exempt from service. Molly did not have a good night's sleep since her two sons went off to war.

After Prohibition ended, and before Abe's death, Abe and Harry's business ventures diversified, and they used this apartment as an office, a place for meetings, and a place to sleep when their varied enterprises kept them from getting home. They put it in the name of Sally Flowers, the young waitress Abe had met so many years ago, the woman who had been running the concession business for them for decades. Sally also kept the set of books that were not in Harry's head, the books on the legitimate businesses the brothers owned that laundered the money generated by the not so legitimate businesses. Harry came and went with none the wiser, and everyone in the building believed that the nice, older woman who gave nice tips at Christmas, lived there alone, and occasionally had a gentleman visitor. On those weekday evenings when Harry couldn't make it back to Scarsdale, he would stay over, but weekends when his sons were young, he would always make it his business to be home with Molly and the boys and working in his garden. Now, two of his sons were working for Uncle Sam, Paul was married and into his own life, and Molly was busy with her temple's sisterhood, her Hadassah work, her book clubs, the war effort, and a host of other things that kept her busy and out of the house. In truth, Harry was too involved in his new enterprises to care much, and over the years they had grown apart.

Sally opened the door when Sam knocked, exchanged pleasantries, ushered him into the livingroom, and disappeared. Sam found himself in an artfully decorated room, but one where there were absolutely no hints of anything personal like a photograph or a memento from a trip that would give a visitor any sense of the people who lived there. Sam had seen such rooms in the furniture departments of department stores. It certainly had style, and Sam sensed that these Art Deco pieces were selected by Fanny who loved that sleek period. He used paint to create on a canvas, and Fanny used furniture to create on square feet. There were two club chairs, one in green and one in gold horsehair, and a red couch in the same material. These focused in on a pale yellow faux fireplace that he knew hid a radio in it behind a sliding panel. Beneath it were faux logs hiding orange and red bulbs that flickered as an electric wheel turned. On either side of the iron and brass andirons were two oriental vases, and on the fireplace mantel were two stylized women, one holding a lyre, and one a violin. Above the mantel, in a polished black metal frame was the very painting he had done of the city that Sadie said no one would buy. But it seemed that Harry did, or at least Fanny did, though she told him that the buyer wished to remain anonymous.

Sam sat down in one of the club chairs, and while admiring the painting, experienced a flood of memories of the tempestuous years with Sadie when it was painted. He searched for happier moments, but they all took him into their bedroom, and Sam just didn't want to go there even in memory. The banker she thought would marry her did not, and Sam let her know that he was not about to come to her rescue. Though she tried to revive their relationship, Sam was having none of it. He did see her on rare occasions, like his daughters' bat mitzvahs, and each time he felt a mixture of pity, repulsion, and strangely, guilt. Few of the images of those years were good, and he tried to change his focus.

He could hear voices coming from another room, but could not make out what was being said. So he turned his attention to the three books on the end table next to him, and he wondered why Harry would have bought the tragedies and comedies of Shakespeare and the short stories of Guy de Maupasant. Harry would never have read these, so he thought it may have been Fanny's attempt at humor to have placed them there. They sat between two book ends that Sam found as curious as the books. Each had a man, standing on a pile of books, against a tall bookcase. Each had a skull like head made of ivory, and Sam found himself twisting one of them off and twisting it back on to pass the time. Then he heard the apartment door close, and silence. Soon Harry entered the room carrying an army issued backpack. He was wearing a three piece black pinstriped suit with a grey tie that had at its center a tie tack composed of a small ruby surrounded by a circle of diamonds. Harry walked to the window, pulled back the gold fringed, dark green curtains, and watched a figure walk out of the building and hail a cab. He turned and lit a cigar.

"You going some place?" Sam said hesitantly, looking at the backpack. There had always been a vague discomfort when he was alone with his older brother because of what Harry did and who he was. Since Abe's murder, Sam had noticed a subtle darkness bear down on Harry that seemed to rob him of his humor and make him slightly sinister.

"No, the backpack isn't for me, Sammy, it's for you."

"I've already got one, and it's packed to go," he responded, his discomfort increasing.

"It's a very simple thing I'm going to ask you to do," Harry said, glancing at his watch and walking back to the window nervously. "You're traveling to England, right? Your plane lands at Heathrow, right? You take a train that takes you to track eight in St. Pancras Station, right?"

"How do you know this, Harry?" Sam said in a voice that did not hide his suspicion or his anger. For security reasons he had been asked not to share the details of his trip, the mission, or the work he was to do.

"Never mind how I know," Harry said through a veil of cigar smoke. "A man named Reuven Dafne will meet you when you get off the train in London. He will identify himself, and you don't even have to speak to him. That's all there is to it. You carry the backpack onto the plane at Idlewild. No one will check a soldier's backpack. You don't let it out of your sight, and you give it only to Dafne. Duplicates of everything you need in the backpack that you have at home will be waiting for you in your hotel room."

Harry placed the backpack on the coffee table in front of Sam and opened it. Sam's eyes widened and he looked at his brother with astonishment. "This is just too much, Hesh," he said looking at what had to be thousands of dollars in five, tens, and twenty dollar bills. Did his own brother want him to risk everything that was important to him just to deliver his dirty money to some other criminal over in London? "I've too many important things to do, and too much to lose to become involved with your underworld friends. I won't do this for you, Heshy, I just won't."

"You'll do it when I tell you what the money is for," he said quickly and with authority. "This is not what you think it is. This is all legit. Well, its not really legit if you're those bloody bastards in the British Home Office who don't want this money going where it's going; to the Jewish resistance." He waited till the information sank in, and then he continued. "What I'm asking you to do has nothing to do with my business. It has to do with saving Jewish lives."

Harry waited for this last piece of information to be absorbed. Sam's eyes narrowed with all the possibilities of something going very wrong. "Like Papa and Marta," Harry continued, "I have been quietly involved in rescuing Jews and fighting Nazis in my own way. Abe did also. And I've been quietly helping Rachelann and Fedya create a homeland where our people can be finally safe. Millions of our people have already been murdered. What you see in front of you is fifty thousand dollars that has been quietly collected, and it needs to reach the Jewish Underground." Again, he paused, studying Sammy's eyes for some connection to what he had just said; to the reality of what was going on in the real world outside the world of Sammy's narrow world of art. "Brother, the Arabs are waging a relentless war to obliterate the Jews in Palestine and do in the Middle East what the Nazis are doing in Europe. We have to stop them. Me, you, Papa, Maurice, and everybody else, we have to stop them. Reuven Defne is an officer in the Jewish underground, and this money will go a long way to buy supplies and weapons to stave off the ongoing attacks from all sides. Sammy, you may not like the world I live in or my life style, but how I make my money has nothing to do with the good that my money can do. I've been involved in smuggling arms and people to Israel for years, and no one questions how it's paid for as long as it's paid for. Now I'm asking you to take advantage of your position with this group of yours and do something that will save lives. Think of it as saving Rachelann and her family. I'm asking you not to wait to become a hero later by saving paintings. I'm asking you to be a hero now and save Jewish lives." Harry walked over to the desk in the corner and took out several pages. "Papa got this from Rachelann last week, and I want you to read it. Then you decide."

Sam reached out for the letter, and sank further into the chair. It was dated months ago.

September 11, 1944

Dearest Papa and Marta,

Again, as always, my heart is so filled with love and appreciation for all you and the family are doing for us here in our homeland. Fedya is feeling much better since the procedure he underwent during our last visit, but we know we shall have to come back in the future for yet another procedure. Fedya, I, and our children are hanging on and we are all learning how to defend ourselves. How sad it is that my sons have to be soldiers when they have the souls of farmers.

There are things happening that I'm sure are not being written about in America. The White Paper that the British issued further restricting the limited quota of Jews they will allow into Palestine of which I wrote to you long ago, has truly consigned European Jews to the slaughterhouse and the ovens. While few come legally, we've had to smuggle in many more thousands, but five of those rescue ships were deliberately sunk by the guns of the British blockade, murdering 3,000 of our people who only wanted to survive. It breaks my heart that the same government that issued the Balfour Declaration, has blockaded the Palestinian coast and have interned thousands of Jews into detention camps on Cyprus. But at least they're alive if not free. What great compensation could the Arab nations be offering the British Government that the British would willfully collude to seal the fate of European Jewry?

Our sons are part of the underground movement, risking their lives every day, fighting the occupying forces, and the Arabs. While the movement has been successful in smuggling Jews past the blockades, much more needs to be done.

Fedya and I are now members of the New Zionist Organization, and our friend, Zev Jabotinsky remains our devoted leader. There is such conflict among our own people, and we broke off from another group to form this one when they refused to define the aim of Zionism as the establishment of a Jewish State in all of Palestine on both sides of the Jordan River. We do not want Palestine partitioned.

Our brave men and women have been fighting on two fronts; the British and the Arabs. The Palestinian Arabs look to an Egyptian named Hassan al-Banna, who years ago created something they call the Muslim Brotherhood. He maintains that it is the nature of Islam to dominate and to impose its laws on all nations. The Jews of Palestine stand in his way since he believes that every piece of land that was once ruled by Muslims, must be ruled by Muslims again. He wants to reestablish the Caliphate which ended when Turkey fell. As I said, the Jews stand in his way. We know there are already thirty-eight branches of his group here now, and they are secretly training fighters, smuggling weapons, and training assassination squads and suicide bombers. And now, word has come to us that this al-Banna has entered into a political and military relationship with Hitler. We have learned that their intelligence service collects information on the Egyptian Government and the movements of the British army and offers these to the Germans for the powerful connections and advantages Germany can offer. So the British are now fighting them and us.

The British, out of hatred for us, appointed a rabid Jew hater named al-Husseini to be the Mufti of Jerusalem, and in one of his broadcasts, after praising the Nazis because they "know how to get rid of Jews," he said, "Arabs! Rise as one and fight for your sacred rights. Kill the Jews wherever you find them. Kill them with your teeth if need be. This pleases Allah, history, and religion. This saves your honor." We have even discovered that he has plans for a death camp, modeled on Auschwitz, to be built near Nablus. What more can I say? We are surrounded by hate, and it is only those people in America who give us hope. Give my love to all.

Your devoted daughter,
Rachelann

Harry watched tears run down Sam's cheeks as he put the letter down. He wondered why his father and brothers had not involved him before, and he suddenly felt peripheral in his own family. Harry poured him a glass of scotch and one for himself, handed it over, and made an air toast to his brother.

"Can we drink to the success of another mission, Sammy, or are we drinking just a goodbye toast?"

"Let's drink to the success of the mission," he said. "What else do I have to know?"

CHAPTER 40

1944

Not long after George Stout had enlisted and was assigned to developing paints for camouflage, he received a letter from a friend that let him know that Colonel James Shoemaker, head of the United States Military Government Division, had heard about Stout's idea for Monument Men, was interested, and had requested all information available about the concepts of monuments and conservation. Not much longer after that, Paul Sachs wrote excitedly to him that President Roosevelt had appointed a commission to protect and salvage artistic and historic monuments in Europe, and that he had been asked to be a member of that Commission. He implied that this "Roberts Commission" would impress the military high command and garner their support. "My dear George," he wrote, "your baby is about to be born. You should be very proud."

He looked up into the clear cloudless sky over Shrivenham, England, and laughed to himself, still not believing that his government and England's too, would now agree to put together a unit of artists, technicians, and architects who would be commissioned as officers, and attached to army units who could actually influence what might be saved. Now Sam and James would be appointed officers and billeted to Shrivenham, along with Marvin Ross, Walker Hancock, and Robert Posey, the other Americans. The Brits, Lord Metheun, Squadron Leader Dixon-Spain, and Ronald Balfour were already there and all would be under the command of Geoffrey Webb, a professor from Cambridge, acknowledged as one of the great scholars of his country.

No one expected Lieutenant Samuel Chernov to be on Dover Beach in England waiting to be taken to Utah Beach in Normandy the second day of the invasion, so when Sam arrived at the port with his orders, there was no one there to verify that he was expected to join a particular unit or point him in a particular way. His mission to join the Monuments Men was unique, and no one knew anything about it. In truth, no unit had been assigned to them. Sam and the others involved had fallen through the cracks. He stood there turning this way and that with his papers in his hand, and as far as he could see, a sea of khaki and camouflage frantically swirled haphazardly around him. Someone in the Quarter Masters Corp saw his confusion and thrust an ammunition box under his arm and pushed him into a line of soldiers boarding one of the thousands of crafts bobbing up and down in the surf. This was one of the landing ships, that carried the tanks. The great mouth of the vessel closed slowly after a tank juggernauted its way onto the boat, sending soldiers scurrying like ants to the rails for safety. Sam made his way to a low bench that was quickly filling up, un-shouldered his rifle, and placed it and the ammunition's box in front of him. Like swarms of angry wasps, wave after wave of RAF planes, along with the 101st and 82nd Airborne divisions, droned overhead, carrying the thousands of men who would be parachuting behind the enemy lines that very day. Sam, who did not hold much with prayer, silently wished them well, knowing that some would never see their families again. He might never see his family again for that matter.

"Can I sit here?" cracked a voice, shaking Sam out of his sudden awareness that he might never make it back.

"Sure, kid, sit down," he said, glad to be interrupted and glad to have someone to talk to for the trip across the Channel.

The motor, which had caused everything to vibrate, grunted and they felt themselves moving through the churning surf and turning east towards France. The young man shivered.

"You want a smoke, kid?" Sam said, offering the kid a Lucky Strike. Clearly, Sam out ranked this buck private, but Sam didn't care for formalities. Besides, this kid knew where he was going and what he was going to do. Sam didn't even know that much.

"I don't smoke, thank you."

Sam read the name on the young soldier's jacket. "Rappaport," Sam said, "I grew up with a Rappaport family who lived a block away."

"Where was that?" the boy responded.

"In Brooklyn, the Brownsville Section."

"That's where I live. My parents still live there."

"Did you ever shop in the candy store on the corner of Stone and Pitkin? I was born in the back apartment, and when I was a kid, before I moved away, I played with a kid named Irving Rappaport."

Arthur Rappaport looked at the name on Sam's jacket. "That's my uncle, Irv. Ain't it a small world, Lieutenant Chernov." The young man started to stand and salute, but Sam motioned to him to sit down. "But the people who ran it when I was growing up weren't named Chernov. When I was really little my Momma took me there, but then she stopped. The place closed down sometime in the 30's. I think it was a front for something, but my parents would never tell me."

Sam smiled to himself at the memory of the candy store, the friends, the street games, and the smile faded when he thought of it as the White Mountain Dairy and Abe and Harry's business venture. He was glad his family name was no longer associated with what went on in the basement, or behind the secret wall, and the upstairs brothel.

The young man took off his helmet and ran his fingers through his sandy blond hair. "I was really afraid when I got on this boat," he said, tears at the corner of his hazel eyes. "It suddenly all became very real and I felt sick. Before I left, the doctor had to give my Momma medicine to calm her down, and Papa couldn't make her stop crying. Either could I. I think I know now what she must have been feeling. My older brother is somewhere in the Pacific, and every time we got a letter from him, she would read it over and over and then she'd go to bed and cry. Papa told her that she should be happy that they hear from Leon, but I know she'll never be happy again until we are all at home at the Shabbos table. We're her whole life."

Sam looked at the young man, suddenly realizing the horror that every man in a flack jacket and every family who sent him off, faced. He looked around the boat. He was the oldest man there. Most were eighteen or nineteen, their entire lives ahead of them, and many of them would die without ever having lived, tasted the sweet lips of a true love, the tender touch of a wife, the scent of a newborn baby, the satisfaction of a job well done, a home. War murders dreams, he thought. War kills entire worlds.

The beach was littered with the carcasses of bombed out vehicles, and the sands were still red from the blood of fallen warriors who had come across in the first wave. There was a heavy, unmistakable stench of burned human flesh mixing with the acrid smoke from charred and broken fortifications. Overhead, the constant drone of aircraft, wave after wave, darkening the sky as they flew towards the front lines; flying towards glory or death. The giant moving machines and cranes, now off loaded, were lifting and carrying twisted debris to dumps and out of the way to make the landing easier for the next wave of men. He could hear the distant whizz of bombs dropping from the skies, the rush of explosions, and he could see the mine sweepers further up the beach in either direction and hear the boom they made when they exploded. In training, he had been told that mines could be found in places as innocent as in a church pew, or as deceptive as under a dead body.

The buildings of the town on the top of the ridge were charred hulks, except for a small stone church in the distance that seem to have escaped. He made a mental note to visit it to see if anything could be salvaged. Sam found a munitions depot being built at the foot of the rise, close enough to it to be well out of the range of German artillery. There he placed the cartridge box, but not before relieving it of a string of bullets. He swung his pack off his back and rested his rifle against the rocks and breathing heavily, collapsed onto the sand. He had no idea where he was to go, and since no one seemed to be expecting him, he would not be missed. He sat down to catch his breath, but the scene before him did not let him breathe easily. It seemed to him like one of those surreal paintings he loathed. Thousands of silver balloons, an overhead ceiling obscuring the beach from the enemy, floated and danced in the wind like metallic clouds against an innocent clear blue sky. These watched over a horrific scene of organized confusion; men wading off the boats desperately trying to keep up with their units, the still smoldering craters scaring the sand and choking the air with soot. Then there were the tractors, tanks, and heavy guns being off loaded, the medics carrying the injured off to makeshift hospitals, and priests bending over soldiers giving them the last rites. The absurdity before him sent his mind spinning, and the vision reinforced his belief there was true evil in this world, a thing that men created for their own gain, and such men and such evil had to be confronted and stopped. War was the last option. Again, the cacophony brought to him by the relentless din of aircraft overhead, the exploding bombs in the distance, the exploding mines, were all a reminder that all of this had to happen for evil not to triumph.

Even though he had no specific assignment, Sam knew that he would have a zone of responsibility to cover, and since he had no specific army unit, he attached himself to the first convoy moving out in the direction of a town called Carenten, a village in his assigned zone. He had been assured that he would be behind the front lines, but the front lines kept changing, and the rapid advances that the army thought it would make did not come to pass. On too many occasions, sniper bullets whizzed over his head, and on more than one occasion, he found himself cowering at the base of the hedgerows that crisscrossed the countryside like overlapping spider webs. His ultimate goal was Deauville where the rendevous was set, and after inquiry after inquiry, he discovered that the 87th Division, 34th Regiment, Company K Weapons Platoon would be moving in the direction of Deauville before moving into Germany, east of Metz. All the men around him were green, frightened kids, like Arthur Rappaport who Sam knew was assigned to the 87th but not in his platoon. And then it began to rain, and he found himself slogging through mud that was soon ankle deep. If any of the boys around him had any fantasy of adventure and glory, it soon was washed away, leaving a kind of numbness and fear of what lay ahead. They passed soldiers of what was left of the 26th Division. Half their men had fallen in the brief time that they were there. These young men had seen death, and they silently nodded as they passed, seeming to say to them that "very shortly you, too, will know what we know, and you'll never be the same."

Sam and Company K marched for hours, rested, and marched again. The night, which should have provided some respite, seemed endless with the vague din of explosions in the distance, and the acute sharpness of the German bullets that swished above their heads in the trees hoping to find some mark.

By daybreak, the rain had stopped but the morning was grey. Sam knew that even if the sun were out, it would not take away the dampness that he felt to the bone. They moved into an open field, a field littered with the rotting carcasses of cows and horses blown up from bombs dropped over the course of the last few days. The platoon was ordered to advance, take the next hill and dig in in preparation for a counter attack. Bullets continued to whiz over his head, and he found himself moving past fallen men, some silent, some screaming for a medic. His soul wanted him to stop and comfort each one, but there was an inner voice insisting that he had to survive, and this thing in him insisted that his only salvation lay in getting to the next ridge for protection and digging in. Mortar shells fell like meteor showers, and Sam fell to his face as he heard one zoom past his helmet and explode several yards away. Thick, brown mud, flung up from the explosion, fell on his back and legs, and when he finally opened his eyes and blessed whatever was to be blessed because he knew he was still alive, he saw a severed arm only two feet away from his face. His stomach lurched into a gag, and he vomited where he lay. Sam seemed outside of himself, and in that state, he noticed an intermittent lull in the bombardment. He picked himself up, and zigzagged to the next rise. There, he fell to his knees, and saw his hands grasping his shovel and frantically spitting dirt into the air like some crazed dynamo. It was as if this out of body someone were digging this foxhole. His throat burned from the acid that he had brought up, but his canteen was empty. He remembered crossing a small brook on his way up the rise, and he waited again for a lull in the fighting before he thought it safe enough to retrace his movements. This time he would move on his belly back to the stream. Then word came to the men around him that there would be no counter attack, and for a time, the fighting was over. Slowly, the men in the company stood, like the vision of the valley of the dry bones, and looked around, dazed. Whatever cows that were alive when they entered the pasture, now lay still, and soon, some soldiers were butchering them for their meat. Others had the same idea as Sam and headed for the stream with their canteens. Dazed and shaken, few of them spoke to one another. Around him lay young men crying in pain and screaming for anyone to help them. And then, there were the dead, the boys who would never cry out in pain or in joy. Already, those who were assigned to those details were in the field carrying the moaning and the silent away on stretchers with only the bloodied mud to attest to their sacrifice. First, Sam knelt down on his hands and knees and drank his fill. Then he put his canteen into the water and watched as the water displaced the air in the form of bubbles. He thought it strange to notice such a simple thing like bubbles at such a moment, and yet this simple awareness made him feel connected to his old self. He stood, and saw two older men lifting the body of a young man whose skull was partially blown off, onto a stretcher. Arthur Rappaport had been sent out as a scout and became one of the first in his platoon to fall. Sam lurched forward, sloshing through the water to the other side, barely able to control himself. He had made a connection with this kid in the time he sat with him on the boat, and he knew the people he came out of, his heritage, his family's hopes for him, and the devastation for that family that would accompany his death. One of the stretcher bearers was fiddling with Arthur Rappaport's dog tags. "He a Jew," the soldier smirked as Sam approached. "We can start a Jew stack if we can find another," responded the other soldier. "Thought Jews bought their way out of service."

"You insensitive fuck," Sam screamed at the startled soldier. "He's a kid who just died for you, and for me, and for our country. Your blood any redder or more American than his? Look at him, damn you," and Sam grabbed the soldier's neck and pushed his face down to Arthur's pale cheek where the boy's seeping blood was mixing with mud and caking. "Your blood any redder, you bigot, you fucking bigot?" He continued screaming as other soldiers started to gather. "Who the fuck taught you to hate like that? Your parents? Or did you learn to hate in Sunday School? Is your so called Christian compassion reserved only for other Christians? This kid died protecting you, to keep you and your fucking family safe, and all you can see is that he was a Jew? Do you even know any Jews, or do you just hate because that's just who the fuck you are?"

Sam felt a restraining arm on his. "Lieutenant, we don't have time for this, now." Sam looked up at the stripes on the officers jacket, released the soldier, stood, and quietly walked back to his foxhole. He was weeping softly, thinking about the world that would never be descended from Arthur Rappaport.

CHAPTER 41

1944

"Armand, I feel as if I'm in trench warfare with my own countrymen," Josiah DuBois stood up, and forcefully thrust into Armand's hands a copy of a report proving the U.S. State Department's deliberate obstruction in the effort of saving European Jews. DuBois, the Assistant General Counsel in the U.S. Treasury Department, working in the Foreign Fund Control, began to pace, periodically stopping and pointing out to his friend and colleague special blurts of newly revealed truths. "Look at that memo about the $600,000 offer from the World Jewish Congress to ransom Romanian Jews. Those son-of -a- bitch Jew hating bureaucrats deliberately sabotaged that offer by not conveying that message to the Romanians, and now those people are probably dead." He walked to the window and looked out on a day that seemed as bleak as the words he had shared with Armand. "Our Department of State, as well as the Red Cross knew of the genocide back in 1942 when the WJC made it public," he continued. "The State Department knew about the Final Solution discussed and finalized in Wannsee, and still refused to speak out against it while millions were being slaughtered. Look where it says, '... what is unquestioned is that the Red Cross and the U.S. Government were aware of Hitler's genocidal intent.' Paul Squire in Geneva sent a memo about a meeting he had with the Red Cross' vice president, Carl Burckhardt, where Squire was told that in 1941 Hitler called for Germany to be Juden-frei by the end of 1942. Burckhardt assured Squire that this information had come from two very well placed officials in the Nazi hierarchy, and when Burckhardt brought this information along with a request to help Jews thoughout the world to a full meeting of the International Red Cross Committee, his request was rejected for the ludicrous reason that it would 'make the situation more difficult,' and that 'it would jeopardize all the work undertaken for the prisoners of war and civil internees – the real task of the Red Cross.' Can you believe that? How much more difficult could it get? Those sanctimonious Swiss hypocrites were using rationalizations to cover an institutional Jew-hatred that is comparable to that of our own Department of State's."

Throughout Josiah's diatribe against the mindless bigotry he encountered daily in his relationship with the State Department, Armand felt his face flush as he perused the papers before him. How different things might have been had our country done something meaningful after it learned of and confirmed the Nazi genocide. And how different things might have been had the Allies issued their joint declaration condemning "Germany's bestial policy of cold-blooded extermination of the Jewish People in Europe." And how different it might have been if Pope Pius had spoken out against the slaughter and threatened those Catholics who supported the Nazis with excommunication. Now it was too late, and he knew that if rescuing Jews had been given to the Treasury and not State, perhaps another million lives could have been saved. How strange, he thought. Between the Department of State's deliberate efforts to stall any effort to mobilize assistance, and Congress' refusal to suspend immigration quotas even to save children, so many lives could have been saved.

"Not only that. That closed door bullshit twelve day Bermuda Conference our State Department and Britain cooked up to appear that they were concerned about the genocide, was just a sham because I was told that our state delegates were directed by our State Department to accomplish nothing! That's why they rejected any Jewish representation. It was set up to fail from the beginning, and the specific proposals from the Jewish community given to the representatives were used to wipe their collective asses."

"What can I do?" Armand said quietly.

Du Bois smiled. "I need your help to build a case against the State Department for willful treachery. I'm passing this information to Morganthau. He has Roosevelt's ear, and I know that once the president knows what his own State Department officials have done, he'll be supportive of making the needed changes to do what can still be done. Those bastards will appear in front of a congressional committee to answer for their own crimes against humanity."

CHAPTER 42

1944 - The Oval Office

"Franklin, I'm the closest friend you have in this government, and at the risk of upsetting you, I'm going to upset you." Henry Morgenthau, Roosevelt's Treasury Secretary, stood in front of the man who inhaled through his iconic cigarette holder. "I would not be your friend and concerned about your legacy if I did not."

"Henry, don't you worry about my legacy," he said, bending down to scratch Fallah's ears before lifting the dog onto his lap. "Social Security, the WPA, the public jobs promised and delivered by the New Deal, are what will be recalled once this damn war is over."

"That's not the only legacy you'll be leaving, and now I'm speaking to you as your confident, and as a Jew." Roosevelt lifted his head.

"What are you saying, Henry?"

"I'm saying that you've been deliberately lied to by the State Department, and in the minds of many of my people, the statement that '20,000 charming Jewish children would all too soon grow into 20,000 ugly adults', uttered by your cousin, Laura Delano, is viewed as a reflection of your own thinking."

"That's nonsense," the president said, angrily stamping out the cigarette in an ashtray. "My cousin was foolish to say that, and what she thinks and what I think are two different things. Besides, you know as well as I that we're doing all that we can do considering the circumstances and our limitations."

"I would have agreed with you last week about doing all we could to save the Jews of Europe, until I was handed the papers I have in this case by one of my own. And after reading them, I can truthfully tell you that we have done very little. Franklin, I'm telling you as your confidant and friend that history will forget the names of the people in the War Department who advised you not to bomb the Auschwitz gas chambers because it was 'too far away,' and would 'divert man-power.' But you and I now know that 500 pound bombs carpeted factories not five miles east of that death camp. Eventually, the world will come to know that, too. The fact that key railroad stations that could have been bombed to stop the deportations of Hungarian Jews to Auschwitz were not, will also be laid at your feet with the allegation that you let Jews die because you didn't want anything detracting from the greater war effort. You listened to the wrong people, Franklin, and while they will be forgotten by history, your name will be associated with the State Department's institutional anti-Semitism that has fueled their anti-immigration policies and their inaction for all these years."

Franklin Delano Roosevelt pushed back on his wheelchair and moved around the desk and onto the carpet. His brow was furrowed at the accusation Morganthau was making at his efforts and those of the Department of State. "What proof do you have?"

"Proof? I'll give you plenty of proof," Morganthau asserted, opening up his briefcase. "Here is the dossier with the names of the two Slovakian Jews who not only escaped from Auschwitz, but gave us its secret location. They also warned us that the Nazis planned to exterminate the entire Jewish population of Hungry. He put the papers onto the president's lap. "And here are the letters from Jewish groups begging the War Department to bomb the gas chambers and the railroad lines that were being used to bring Jews to Poland. Yet McCloy, your esteemed

Assistant Secretary of War, discounted any intelligence regarding Jews. He was the one who claimed that we could not divert our bombers from the war effort, and that Auschwitz was out of range. You accepted his word, though it was a bold face lie. Here's the proof, the reports proving that on August 20th, 127 Flying Fortresses dropped 500 pound bombs on the factories near Auschwitz and then made another run three weeks later. You were lied to deliberately, Franklin. How many Jews do you think the Nazis murdered in those three weeks when we could have bombed that death camp?" Henry Morganthau suddenly stopped. "And now for the part I cannot understand, Franklin, and perhaps you can explain it." He swallowed. "Now I also happen to know that you met with McCloy, and he raised this very issue about bombing Auschwitz with you, and that you rejected the proposal, insisting that all efforts had to be channeled into winning the war and that the Germans would only order the Poles to build another one. Was he carrying out your orders, or were you acting on his suggestions?"

The President Roosevelt's jaw tightened. "That information was highly classified, damn it," he said indignantly deflecting the question. "Who told you that?"

"I'm a cabinet member, Franklin. I'm the Secretary of the Treasury. I have the highest clearance one can have in this government, and no one stands in the way of my investigations. For years you and Churchill have been receiving secret evidence that Hitler is rounding up Jews and murdering them. I know this because Churchill told Anthony Eden that Hitler was waging a war against the Jews, and that the magnitude of this slaughter should be viewed as the greatest crime ever committed in history. I also know that when Churchill said that death camps could be eliminated by our bombers if you approved, you did not give that approval. How could you not have done that? But don't think that England is clean in this. That fiasco last year called the Bermuda Conference on the refugee problem was deliberately held out of the public eye. Without Jewish organizations present, America and England could then rationalize why they were not willing to buy Jewish refugees being offered for sale, as well as quietly resolving that there would be no changes made to absorb Jewish immigrants or increase immigration to Palestine."

Roosevelt's hands tightened on the wheels of his chair, and his normally placid face was red. His eyes seemed off in a distance, seeing the moments Morganthau was forcing him to recall. "Henry, I could bring you up on treason for revealing to me things that I considered top secret and not to be known."

"Franklin, you have nothing to worry about from me. The New Deal legacy for the American People will not be tarnished by what has transpired between us, and our history books will never reveal what went on between you, Churchill, and McCloy. But there is a truth that must be told now, something that I will not leave to be discovered long after we are all gone. I have here the summary of an indictment proving how our own State Department deliberately sabotaged any and all efforts to save whatever Jews could be saved from the gas chambers and the machine guns. This indictment is free from any mention of you, but it does name names, and the major name is that of Brekenridge Long and his minions whose policies of deception, overt lies, and inaction, have led to the direct murders of thousands of people who could have been saved. There will be a public hearing that will expose the actions of these insidious men, and when that is done and they are out of power, they will be blamed and you and your legacy will be safe. When this is all revealed, and credit given to your administration for revealing and prosecuting their treachery, we will create something that will be called, The War Refugee Board." He pulled another document out of his case and handed it to the president. The document said that this board's objective will be to "rescue, transport maintain, and relieve, the victims of enemy oppression and establish havens of temporary refuge for such victims.'"

"You seem very sure of yourself, Henry, and just a little bit presumptuous."

"Mr. President, if I were aware of what the State Department was doing for these past years, I would have been presumptuous years ago. Pillorying Long is just, and you have to be seen by America as being a righteous man. Someone must take the blame for this, and it cannot be you."

"And if I do not choose to create this so called War Refugee Board, or choose to hang Long out to dry, or choose not to bring shame upon my Department of State or on my Presidency, what will you do then?"

"What will I do, Franklin? I will release Long's dossier to the press, and then they will be in control of the narrative and not us." He paused for a moment. "You are not the only one to be concerned about the legacy you leave. You will be remembered for bringing our nation out of the Depression and giving us Social Security. I want to be remembered as one of the men who did not stand by and do nothing as innocent men, women, and children were being slaughtered." He paused and looked at the tight jawed man stroking his dog's back. "You know what is ironic, Franklin?" A small, smile played at the corners of his mouth. "Right now, and for years to come, most American Jews will proudly call themselves Roosevelt Democrats because of Social Security and other New Deal programs. Still, I wonder if you would be so revered if they actually knew that you could have saved their relatives in Europe and chose not to do so."

CHAPTER 43

December 1944: Senate Committee on Foreign Affairs.

"Don't you dare judge me, Bonnington," Breckingridge Long blurted out suddenly. "I am a man under siege by liberals like you, and under constant attacks from left wing radicals and the Jewish press for doing what I think is best for my country."

"Mr. Long, let us not forget why we are here," the senator retorted in a voice that trembled on the edge of exasperation. "You have heard Elan Steinberg, the executive director of the World Jewish Congress, state before this committee that the U.S. Government was fully aware of Hitler's genocidal intent, and that we learned of it from their operative in Switzerland in August of 1942. Furthermore, you know as well as I and as well as all the members of this committee that our government's objective was to work out programs to save those Jews of Europe who could be saved. Yet you mouthed this policy, and at the same time, deliberately put up barriers to implementing this policy. And now, because you actually went so far as to prevent our government from rescuing Jews from Nazi occupied Europe, our own government will have to share, for all time, responsibility for this extermination. That is one of the reasons why you sit before this committee today. And now, let me finish reading from the charges: '... guilty not only of gross procrastination and willful failure to act, but even of willful attempts to prevent action from being taken to rescue Jews from Hitler."

Long's eyes bulged at the formal allegation and he stood pointing his finger at the committee. "This doesn't lay at my feet alone, senator," he shouted. "If this government knew what was going on, why didn't the Congress act to change the immigration regulations that would have opened the gates to these people you now claim to support?" There was a muffled commotion and flash bulbs exploded at the senators who sat stone faced before the defendant's table.

"As I said before, Mr. Long, the U.S. Congress will have to deal with this eternal shame at a later date, but right now we are looking at what could have been done for these people that you and the U.S. State Department would not permit to be done. You have not only deliberately prevented the public from learning about German initiated atrocities, you and those who support you at State have deliberately undermined the government and private rescue efforts." He paused and took a breath. "Mr. Long, I have before me a memoranda that you had the gall to send to your cohorts. Will you read it or shall I?"

Breckinridge Long's face showed no regret. The state of his tie and suit showed no crumpled response to the hours of listening to himself and his colleagues being vilified for their brutal indifference to the lives of innocent people. He sat there with a look of contempt for his accusers and a smug indignation that he was being reprimanded for doing exactly what any good or true American in his position would have done. America was for Americans, and he, through his actions, was keeping America safe.

"Then let me," Bonnington continued. "We can only delay and effectively stop for a temporary period of indefinite length the number of immigrants into the United States. We could do this by simply advising our consuls to put every obstacle in the way and to require additional evidence and to resort to various administrative devices which would postpone and postpone and postpone the granting of the visas.' Did you write that Mr. Long?"

Long leaned over to his council and exchanged whispers. "Now, all America knows," continued the senator, "that ninety percent of the quota places available to immigrants from countries under German and Italian control were never filled. If they had been, an additional 190,000 people could have escaped the atrocities being committed by the Nazis."

Senator Bonnington studied the face of the white haired and bespeckle man sitting several feet away from the raised dais upon which he and the others sat. Here was a man who fancied himself as an entitled aristocrat, a man who saw himself as a true American; a white man, a Protestant man, a man of property, a rich man who forgot that his own ancestors had fled persecution for the same safety he had single handedly denied others. "History has a way of forgetting people like you and me, Mr. Long," he said in closing the day's proceedings. "Most people become memories or nameless faces in family picture albums, spoken of for a brief time, and then lost to memory. But while you and I, and what we are about here today, may never make it into the high school history books, I can guarantee that we shall become footnotes that some future scholars will seek out when the full story of this war is written. Our descendants will no doubt read of us and what we have done. We will be judged by them, Mr. Long, as we will be judged by history. Those who ultimately do find out about you, will catagorize you among the worst of our generation. You personally led an underground movement of vicious, mean spirited men who not only revealed themselves to be accomplices of Hitler, but are war criminals in every sense of the word! You and people like you have made America complicit in genocide."

Brekenridge Long sat near a roaring fireplace in the comfort of The Laurel Park Race Course Club, and this cloistered oasis of elite civility held at bay the pounding questions and hostility of those on the Committee on Foreign Affairs. Here, in this bastion of homogeneous Anglo Saxon society, in the presence of superior people like himself who disdained people outside their circles, people of quality and breeding, educated people from the best schools who could trace their lineages to the beginnings of the nation, he felt safe. The festive Christmas decor, the fine cognac reflecting the dancing flames, the soft instrumental music, all shut out the ugliness of human variety that he had tried to keep from encroaching into his America.

His demeanor changed when he picked up the Washington Post on the table and read the headline: "State Department Officials Willfully Fail To Act," and under the headline, in smaller type, the line, "Brekenridge Long obstructed rescue attempts, drastically restricted immigration, and falsified figures of refugees admitted." He exhaled a deflating breath, sipped again from his glass, and looked around to see if he was being watched.

"Hello old boy, and a Happy Christmas to you," said Chandler Washburn, forcing a smile at his long time golf companion. Long looked up to see three of his country club golfing and riding friends standing above him with martini glasses and smiles that hinted at what could only be described as freudenshas. Long's eyes swept over the three comprehensively, and immediately thought of Job's friends who had come to blame him for his troubles. Winnie Cranchester and Augustus Williams sat down on the club chairs opposite him and Chandler Washburn sat next to Long in a leather wing chair.

"Seen the paper today, old boy?" said Chandler, pressing out a cigarette in the ashtray.

"I was just about to read it when I was interrupted by the three horsemen of the Apocalypse, old boy," Long responded in a low, gruff voice. "Are you here to support your friend, or are you here to get an inside account that will become locker room gossip?"

"You cut us to the quick, Brecky. Why would you think that of us?"

"Because I know who you are, and because if any of you were in my position, I would be gloating as well. That's just who we are among ourselves."

The other three men looked at one another and laughed. "So what went on behind closed doors?" asked Winnie. "Did they really accuse you of gross procrastination to save Jews from Hitler, and a wilful attempt to obstruct any attempt to do so? Not that I'm judging you. We don't judge our own. But I must say..."

"What must you say, you damn hypocrite? Last week you insisted that we support you in blackballing that new CEO of Reinbeck Coorporation because you found out that his wife was a Jewess, and as I recall your exact words, 'We don't need little Jew brats dunking themselves in our pool.' Of course, that's not what you said at the board meeting, but everyone knew what you meant."

"Water under the bridge, Brecky. This little oasis we have here takes us away from having to brush up against Jews, Catholics, Negroes, Irish, Italians, and the like so we can retain our sense of balance and so our children can meet their own kind of people. But keeping someone out of your club is a little different from getting them murdered. Don't you think?"

"I was keeping them out of America," he said sharply. "Soon America will be filling up with people not like us, and you mark my words that if we don't stop this influx of riffraff, we'll be in the minority in a few years, and they, not us, will be running America. If you were in my shoes, you'd have done the same."

"But we've opened our doors to Jews like Kurt Weill, Einstein, and Otto Klempere."

"Yes. People like them are people who have something to offer. In my mind, they are not Jews at all. They have risen above their race, and aren't like the rabble who sell rags on New York City streets. The rag pickers are the ones I am keeping out. I'm keeping America for people who can become real Americans."

"Have you forgotten who is fighting right now to keep America for Americans?" Cranchester interrupted. "American men and women over there are fighting for you and me, and not one of them is fighting based on their religion or ethnicity. They're fighting because they want to keep America from people like Hitler, Tojo, Mussolini, and Franco; not from tailors and peddlers. But you seem to be waging your own little war against Jews under the guise of keeping Americans for Americans. What do you think gives you the right?"

"You all disgust me," Long countered. "I'll admit that I'm a bigot, and I'll admit that my parents taught me who real Americans were by the time I was five years old. At least I know who I am. But you smug fakes pretend you have no feelings of repulsion or any vague concern for your position on the top of the food chain every time you encounter anyone who isn't an Episcopalian. And that makes each of you a bigot and a hypocrite."

"Now wait a minute, wait a minute," interjected Williams. "Some of my best friends are Jews. I roomed with a Jew in college, and my dentist is Jewish, so don't lump me in with bigots like yourself."

"Just by saying, 'some of my best friends are Jews' tells me you are. So why have I never seen you golfing with your dentist here, or entertaining him and his wife for dinner at the club? Would he be uncomfortable, or would you be uncomfortable?"

"Okay, okay, Brek," Chandler said, and his eyes moved around the circle as he briefly assessed his companions. "Let's all admit that we all voted to keep that Jewish guy out and support this being a restricted club. Let's all admit that on one level or another, we are all bigoted against people who are different from us. And let's all admit that each of us harbors anti-Semitic feelings. But our prejudices are not quite as lethal as yours are Brek because our actions may keep a Jew out of our club, but yours kept Jews out of the country and got them murdered. I think there is a cognitive disconnect in you, Brekenridge that you either don't accept or just don't see. Blackballing Jews from joining the club because you don't want them swimming in the pool or their sons dancing with your daughter, is different from deliberately signing their death warrants by sending them back to Europe or not granting them visas so they can come in."

"Brek," Cranchester interrupted. "Did you really order the American mission in Switzerland to stop sending any reports about the Nazis' extermination of the Jews so you could plausibly deny the atrocities, and tell anyone who inquired that there was no foundation to the allegations that hundreds of thousands were being murdered and starved, or was that one of your colleagues?"

Long stood abruptly, his jaw tight and his eyes like ice blue rocks. "I see what's going on here," Long said defensively. "If I let in thousands of Jews, it would be as if I were extending an invitation to Germany and the Soviets to inject spies among them."

"But why blackball the children? Did you think the children were German or Soviet spies? No Brek," Washburn continued, "You're a special kind of anti-Semite. You, Henry Ford, Father Coughlin, the Grand Wizard, you go beyond anything we closet bigots would ever do. We'll smile at them and then make jokes about them behind their backs, and we'll have a friendly drink or lunch with them and still blackball them. But what you did was in a whole different class. I think it was Shakespeare who said of one character that he 'Out Heroded, Herod.' You've joined that company."

Washburn was also on his feet uncharacteristically pointing a finger at Long's chest. "I remember that in Dante's lowest ring of Hell was a three faced Satan, and out of each mouth protruded a man who had betrayed his friend. If memory serves, one was Judas, Jesus' betrayer, and the other two, Brutus and Cassias who betrayed Caesar. If there is a Hell, Brecky, I do believe that you will also be in that lowest ring for your betrayal of humanity, and you and Hitler will be protruding out of Satan's anus."

CHAPTER 44

October 18, 1946

My dearest Papa and Marta,

First off, thank you for the money you send us monthly. Without your support, we could not easily survive. I wish I could say that things were going well. Of course, I and the boys are well and doing what we must to keep the animals at bey, but Fedya is not doing well again, and the doctors say that if he is to live, he must return to America because he needs care that they cannot provide. It is not only the anxiety and stress that he is constantly under working for our survival, but the doctor thinks he might have picked up something while he was in prison that has further weakened his body. The British do not treat Jewish prisoners well, and there is not always access to decent food or medical attention. I'm positive there is something wrong with his lungs, but the doctors here cannot find the cause for his cough. Though we are needed, there are others who can pick up our work, and I have decided to take Feyda back to New York to see a specialist in the city. Our American passports, will make things easier for us. If he needs to be hospitalized, Mt. Sinai Hospital is not far from you, and I'm hoping you will make room for us for the time we need for him to get better. Perhaps you might contact someone who will be willing to look at him. We would very much appreciate that.

We are so very much looking forward to seeing the family again, and catching up. Since the end of the war, we have been able to get letters to Aunt Dora and Aunt Ruth. Ruth's son, Sigmund, came in as a tourist on the Austrian papers that they had taken with them from Vienna, but Berta, remained behind to take care of their mother. Ruth, she wrote, is physically in good health, but she still has not been able to deal with the deaths of Frederick and Henrik, and does not like to be left alone. Two of Dora and Jonathan's sons, Saul and Max, also came in on their Swiss papers, masquerading as Red Cross workers, but they could not say that they were Jews or the British would have immediately suspected them. They stayed with us for a week, and then joined the resistance. I'm not sure where they are. I pray for all the boys each night. Jonathan has advanced in his position at the bank only because Swiss Jews have major shares in it, and Dora's skills as a watchmaker and designer still earn her high praise and a very good salary. Grandpa Reuben would have been so proud of her. My lovely Liora is engaged to be married to a fine man named Menachem Mendel who was smuggled in from Poland. He is a scholar and lucky to be alive. When her first husband, of blessed memory, was murdered by Arabs, I wondered if she would ever recover. She is only twenty-six with two little children, and knows that she must get on and make a life for herself and for them. This man lost his own wife and children in Poland, and is happy to fill the emptiness in his heart with another man's children who need to be loved. Of course, they plan to start a family together. My two middle children, Asher and Benjamin are with the Haganah somewhere in the Galilee fighting to free Safed, but our twins, Joshua and Caleb, are still too young to go off to war, so they will be coming with us to visit. I will need them to help with their father and the luggage. They are excited to make such a trip, but also reluctant to leave. So "Mr. and Mrs. Edward Davidson" of New York City" will be coming back for a visit shortly. I'll write again when there is more to tell.

Things seem to be in a spiral here, ever moving forward, but returning on itself sometimes with a vengeance, so I do not know how things will turn out for us here or for our brethren in Europe. We must keep moving forward because we must become a place of refuge. To that end, there are some countries and individuals within those countries who are willing to help us, and some are not. Over the years we have had it reinforced time and time again that the current British Government officials are not our friends. On a more positive note, refugees secreted into the country have told us that the Czech Foreign Minister Jan Masaryk is providing trains to the Haganah to transfer Jews from Poland to the U.S. zone in Germany because there are still anti-Jewish riots in Poland, and some who have returned to take back their homes and possessions have been murdered. It may not be news in America, but we have also heard that there was a pogrom at Kielce where the Poles murdered Jews who had come out of hiding because there was a rumor that the Jews were murdering Christian children and using their blood for their rituals. Can you believe such ignorance still exists and is still used against us? Even the most ignorant Jew alive knows that any blood is forbidden to us, so I lay those murders at the feet of the Catholic Church and their Popes who never denied such allegations even though they know that the prohibition of drinking blood of any kind is one of God's commandments. It seems that the deaths of millions are still not enough.

Even now, to calm Arab fears, the British continue to intercept survivors in order to return them to the charnel house we call Europe. And to justify this horrendous behavior, the British Foreign Secretary Bevin is now claiming that Brittan never promised to create a Jewish state, and has actually said that Jews trying to leave Europe should not push their way to the front of the line. One newspaper here in Jerusalem reported that Bevin charged the United States with agitating for Jewish settlement in Palestine because, and I quote, 'they do not want too many of them in New York.' And this is how I think the spiral works. Following Bevin's remarks, the Haganah blew up the guard station on the coast that was part of the lookout for refugee ships. I don't know if that was cause and effect or not, but it seems that when the British act despicably out of their own self interest and without compassion for what we have been through, our Palmah troops and the Irgun troops harass them even more. England sides with the Arabs against us, and they must be forced out.

So the next turn of the spiral came with the blowing up of the radar station on Mt.Carmel, and the Irgun raided and destroyed twenty-two aircraft of the Royal Air Force. It is all spiraling out of control and too many are dying. You know, Papa, that I have always aligned myself against those who oppress others for their own gain. I can understand why the Arabs hate us. They are insular and still tribal. But why the British? What are they getting out of it? They may have fought gallantly against Hitler, but I assure you they did not do that for us, and by this denial of our rights to a homeland, and their open hostility to us, they continue to carry out Hitler's design. They are confining our people to camps here, and are building them on Cyprus. Though they are not gassing our people, I'm sure there are those among who would and not look back. We are still not free to become what we must become. We are not free to become what God wants us to become.

Through his work, Feyda has been in contact with the Anglo-American Committee of Inquiry whose task was to examine the situation of the remaining Jews in Europe and the Palestinian question. They recommended that 100,000 displaced persons and refugees be admitted to Palestine, and that the ban against Jews buying land be lifted. President Truman approved, but Attlee of Brittan will not act on the recommendation, again fearing Arab anger and reprisals. Perhaps it was in response to that, the Haganah blew up ten of the eleven bridges that connected Palestine with its Arab neighbors. And the spiral moves forward.

I'm sure the news has come to you about the recent tragedy regarding the King David Hotel. I must tell you that Fedya and I are not in favor of such deliberate carnage. I do not know if the Irgun's actions at the hotel were the direct effect of the British beginning a two week search for our military leaders and for arms, but over 2,500 of our people, including Fedya, were arrested. Fedya insists, and I believe him, that the Irgun gave plenty of warning that the hotel, which acted as British military headquarters, was to be attacked, but the British deny it. I really think they were just too over confident to think the Jews would dare attack them in their own headquarters because their disdain for anyone not British is matched only by their arrogance and condescension. Now, Tel Aviv is under curfew as thousands of British troops, now forbidden to have any social or business relations with us, are searching for the Irgun.

In closing, my dearest father, we send our blessings to President Truman for endorsing our right to a homeland being established here on this sacred land, and to your governor, Mr. Dewey, for bravely insisting that hundreds of thousands be allowed to come to us. A very happy 5746 to you, Marta, and the family.

Your loving daughter,
Rachelann

CHAPTER 45

1947

The door slammed. The startled family looked up from their dinner as Maurice careened into the dining room. His face was dark, and he appeared unsteady on his feet. "Do you know what those inconsiderate evil sons of bitches did?" He gave no one a chance to guess who the sons of bitches were or what they did. "They awarded thirty-four million dollars to Austria. Can you believe it! Austria, a country who welcomed the Anschluss with open arms and fought with the Nazis, is being compensated by the Tripartite Gold Commission because they claimed the Nazis looted their treasury. Austria gave them their treasury! I warned them against including them, but those idiots didn't listen and let them have access to the reparations agency. And now that nation of Quislings are going to get restitution! The nerve! The chutzpah! We excluded the Eastern Bloc, and I begged them not to reward Austria, but they didn't listen. On top of this, mind you, no individuals will be compensated either, no people like Ruth or her children will get anything back, but those Nazi loving bastards in Vienna will be getting millions." He walked over to the sideboard and not caring what he was pouring, downed whatever was in the glass in one gulp. Then he poured another.

"Come sit down, Maurice and have something to eat," his wife said, getting up from the table. "Your face is almost purple and your pressure is probably sky high. You'll get a stroke if you keep ranting like this."

"And Italy is getting six million. Italy, one of the Axis Powers who helped create the horror, is getting six million dollars, but not one cent going to any Italian Jewish families who survived the war."

"Sit," Shirley commanded, taking his coat and hat and hanging them up.

Maurice, crestfallen, tossed back a second shot which he now knew was brandy. Shirley, the woman he married after his beloved Rose was taken from him in the great flu epidemic, took an empty soup bowl and ladled into it the hot borsht with flanken and potatoes that was one of his favorite meals. Maruice sat, knowing his wife was correct in her warnings and request, and took several deep breaths. The somewhat sweet and somewhat sour red liquid played on his tongue, and he closed his eyes and he was back as if in his mother's kitchen. He took another calming breath and another spoonfull.

"The other representatives of our government had nothing to say about that?" said Jonah, who was motioning with a frail hand for another ladle of soup.

"They were all for the distributions because they got their cut. America's coffers as well as those of England and France can all use an injection of gold, and these millions are a windfall. I've seen U. S. State Department documents showing that two tons, about twenty-eight million of Tripartite Gold will be going to the U.S. Federal Bank Reserve Bank in New York, and the Bank of England will be getting twice that amount. The greed at that table tonight was palpable, and believe me, none of them are friends to the Jews. Yes, Europe's displaced person's camps will be getting twenty-five million to support the immediate survival for both Jews and non-Jews, but not a red cent will be going directly to the survivors of the death camps or the survivors who came out of hiding to help them rebuild their lives. Everything's been taken from these people, and greed is keeping them from getting what is rightfully theirs."

CHAPTER 46

1948

The Chernov family continued the tradition of gathering in the parlor around the RCA radio on Sunday as it did on most Sunday afternoons during the war years. Earlier in the day, after lunch, the women and children had worked in the kitchen, opening up bags of Bohack coffee, and stuffing packs of cigarettes and dollar bills in them for those few family members they could locate who had escaped the Holocaust and were still in displaced person camps. The children thought it was fun, having no idea of the reality that existed for these distant relatives. And why should they? Should they have been allowed to hear the stories of the mindless brutality and hatred told by those who were lucky enough to make it to America? Should they know about an infant cousin being tossed into the air and caught on a German bayonet? Should they know of another being hacked in half in front of her parents? Should they know what it was like to breathe out of a reed under brackish water so the dogs wouldn't be able to sniff them out and tear them to pieces? These were not stories that children should know.

Walter Winchel, Gabriel Heater, and Edward R. Murrow continued to be the trusted source of news in the extended family as they were to most Americans, and the conversations following their broadcasts heard raised voices with challenges of pin pointed logic from the older generation to their younger adult children. Jonah, the proud patriarch, sat on his chair smiling at the points made and the counter points made, remembering when such dinner table conversations were the norm. Now, another generation of men and woman sat his table, thinking and arguing, and making themselves interesting; interesting people and interested in the world. As he sat there, his great granddaughters passed a comb through his silver white hair, and twisted strands of it into curls around their little fingers.

"Stop bothering my husband," Marta said, smiling as she passed, carrying a tray of freshly baked ruggelach, tantalizing them by extending the platter and moving it away, but only the boys left off annoying their great grandfather and followed her in the hope that she would reward them with the sweet nut and chocolate delicacy.

Jonah waved her off, loving the attention, and allowed the three little girls to treat him as though he were a living doll. This is what he had lived for, though he was saddened that he had never seen all of his grandchildren or great grandchildren in the same place at the same time, and never would. He relished the memories of the Passover Seders, when his American children and grandchildren made their way to his table. At least now Rachelann, Fedya and two of their sons were here though the other three children were away defending Israel. Now Dora and Jonathan were here with David and his family, but their other sons were also in Israel. He looked at Ruth, his beautiful sister Ruth, sitting next to her daughter, her eyes dreaming of a time long passed, smiling faintly at this happy group of people, yet not fully knowing who they were. Her Sigmund and Berta were somewhere in Europe, devoting their lives to settling refugees and aiding survivors. Sam and his girls were sitting on the floor near the radio, playing with Armand's youngest. Of course, Abe was gone, and Leo was still in the Western Sector of Berlin, overseeing something he could not write or talk about. And Harry's life had him moving between Cuba and Las Vegas, still doing God knows what. Happily, Harry's children found the time to visit.

"I think it's coming on now," Maurice said. "Sam, turn up the volume."

There was a bit of excitement as the children were ordered to sit and listen to a moment in history, though they had no comprehension of what that moment meant. The rest of the family squeezed onto the couches or seated themselves on the floor with their little ones on their laps. There was a pause, and then a voice announced, "We now take you to the Municipal Museum of Tel Aviv in Israel where David Ben Gurion is reading Israel's Declaration of Independence." A moment of silence and then a rasping static followed by: "We, the members of the National Council, representing the Jewish People in Palestine and the Zionist Movement of the world, met together in solemn assembly today, the day of termination of the British mandate for Palestine, by virtue of the natural and historic right of the Jewish People and the Resolution of the General Assembly of the United Nations, hereby proclaim the establishment of the Jewish State in Palestine, to be called Israel."

"I think I remember him from when I was a young man," Jonah said to the children on his knee. "When I was young, I knew them all."

"I never knew that," said Aaron, lifting his daughter from her grandfather's lap and sitting down on the armrest of the old man's chair.

"It is from another life," Jonah said, somewhat wistfully, looking back into dusty memory at things that never happened but might have happened had other choices been made. "You know, Aaron, that I've always supported the Zionist movement, and when I was young, I met with many of the early founders." A faint smile crept across his lips. "In fact," he hastened to add, "Theodor Herzl himself asked me to work with him to interest people into going to Israel. That was many years ago."

"Then that could have been you on the radio, Zeydeh?" interjected one of the older children. Jonah smiled at the thought of what might have been.

"So, Papa," Aaron continued. "Why didn't you go and work with him?"

Jonah thought back to an ancient compartment in his brain that held a diatribe from Leah where she threated to leave him and take the children to America if he decided to follow Herzl. That decision to go to America took him away from his dream of becoming a name, but it was also the one that took him down a path that led to being surrounded by great grandchildren, grandchildren, and children in a comfortable room on a spring afternoon in May. Yes, he could have insisted, gone off with Herzl to be counted with the likes of Ben Gurion and Jabotinsky, and Ussishkin. Certainly, he had the knowledge, the skills, and the heart to become something more than a teacher of languages to wealthy women. But looking back and seeing what had happened in Europe to his people, he knew Leah was right to insist that he find another path, one that would not imperil his wife and children. She saw what he did not, and he knew she was right. Her path was better for all of them.

"Sometimes, dreams are a luxury you just can't afford, Aaron, and you have to make due with what comes your way. The path I was on brought me to America and here I found your mother, and you were born. How can I regret anything when I look at her and at you?"

Aaron Chernov was what Jonah laughingly called "the child of his old age," though only a handful of years separated his youngest son from Sam, the last of his children with Leah. He became a different father with Aaron, a better father, because once the burden of living hand to mouth was lifted, there was time for the attentiveness and affection he could not shower on Rachelann, Abe, Maurice, Fanny, Harry and Sam when they all lived behind the store and he worked fourteen hours a day. Maurice, Fanny, and Sam, the children who lived with him after he married Marta, welcomed it, and Jonah could be to them the way Reuben was to him. Armand was already grown when they met.

Armand and Aaron, brothers separated by two decades, never knew the whip of depravation, so both entered their lives with the confidence that the world was theirs. Both were remarkable men; both lawyers. Armand, who worked with the Department of Justice, had access to the movers and shakers of the world and had their respect. Aaron, tall and handsome, with his mother's light complexion and high cheek bones, his father's bright blue eyes and sandy colored hair now showing strands of grey, had excelled at whatever sports he played, and had a wall covered with testaments to his academic acuity. His ability to see abstractions, coupled with his logical mind and sonorous voice, first catapulted him to the position as captain of his college debating team. In law school, these same qualities brought him to the notice of his professors, who made it a point to attend when Aaron stood for mock trials. Upon graduation, he was immediately hired by a very prestigious Jewish law firm with a promise of rising quickly. More established law firms had offered him positions, but he did not want to be the token Jew they would point to with pride, and he knew he would never be allowed to rise higher than associate.

"Aaron," Jonah said, returning to his question. "You know I don't believe that we are fated to do or be anything in particular. We are born into certain circumstances and to certain people who are burdened with their own circumstances, and out of this morass, we are supposed to find ourselves and our own way. If we are lucky, we meet people along the way who help, or sadly, hinder us. In theory, we have the power to change our circumstances, and we always have the power to dream. But as I just said, there are obstacles placed in our way in the guise of people or circumstances, and we sometimes encounter moments in life when one must look at the world and say to ourselves, 'We are what we are, it is what it is, and we must move on.' This I have learned in my eighty four years of being on this earth. So why didn't I go to work for Herzl and become what I dreamed

I might have been? Because it would have been a selfish thing to do to my wife and children; draging them all over Europe, keeping them uprooted, and not in a place where they could go to sleep at night and not be afraid. A man must recognize his responsibilities to others and act. That's what makes a man a man; being responsible even at the expense of his dreams. I did not have the right to do that to them, but look around, Aaron. It was the right choice, and for someone who started out as a poor tailor in the Ukraine, I didn't end up too badly. For that, I am grateful to my first wife, and eternally grateful to your mother for loving me and helping me not to be afraid."

"I understand, Papa," Aaron said. "It's like what happened to Cousin Nathaniel after the Seligmans drowned on the Titanic. He wanted to be a concert pianist, but he had to give up that dream because he had to run the family business."

"Yes," Jonah smiled. "You understand. But look what happened. Then, a hundred or so people depended on that store for a living, and now, thousands of people work for him because he was the one who dreamed that there could be a Seligman's Department store in every major city in America. Because you may not fulfil one dream, it doesn't mean you can't have others, and new dreams can come true."

"So the effect of Nathaniel's dream not coming true resulted in a thousand people being able to fulfill their own dreams because he provided them with good jobs."

Jonah's shaking hand reached out to pat his son's cheek. How proud he was of this man, and how much he loved him.

Loud static from the radio focused their attention to the corner of the room, and someone was saying "Breaking news."

"Ladies and gentlemen. In Washington, President Truman speaking for the United States Government, followed through on his promise to Chaim Weizmann, the newly elected President of Israel by declaring de facto recognition of the State of Israel, because the United Nations defeated the American proposal to establish a trusteeship type regime for Jerusalem. Truman warned he would do this in April, and he has done it to the chagrin and wonder of the world. News has come that the British Government would withhold recognition for the time being, and Andrei Gromiyko of Russia said it recognizes the existence of the new state, but is not ready to announce formal diplomatic recognition. And this just in — In other news, Prime Minister Nokrashy Pasha speaking from Cairo, said that the Egyptian armed forces had been ordered to enter Palestine to 'restore security and order.' The Arab armies of Transjordan, Syria, Lebanon, Saudi Arabia and Iraq have begun their invasion. Jerusalem is under siege. Additional news will follow."

"You know," said Maurice, "that England has been winking at the armaments that are flowing to their Arab friends secretly for years, while they've done their best to relieve the Jews of theirs. Did you know that our own government has an embargo on sending armaments to Jews, and has refused to lift it?"

"You're getting yourself into a state, Murray," Shirley reminded him as she passed with a tray of teacups and saucers. "Your face is getting red, and the vein in your temple is starting to pulse."

Maurice paid no attention to his wife's comments. "I would not be surprised if there are people in our own Department of State who are in collusion with people in the U.N. who share the goal that the Arab armies will do for the world what Hitler started but could not finish."

"You are misinformed, my dear brother," Fanny said.

Maurice stopped mid-thought looked incredulously at his sister. "What are the chances that I'm misinformed, Fanny?" Maurice rejoined with a slight shaking of his head. "Do you know that while we have an evenhanded embargo on armaments to the Jews and Arabs in Palestine, $37 million of arms sales from us have already gone to the Arab League. Do you see the evenhanded logic of our State Department? It won't sell to Jews or Arabs in Palestine, but surely you see the problem with this evenhandedness and how it works against Israel. Had you been French, Fanny, you would probably have thought that the edict issued that forbade both rich and poor to sleep under the Paris bridges at night was even handed. Are you oblivious to irony?"

"I wasn't talking about bridges in Paris, Murray," Fanny said. "Did I say anything about bridges?"

"Look, Fanny, the point I'm trying to make is that evenhandedness can really screw one of the parties; mostly the weaker one. The Arab League is composed of all of those nations ready to go to war against Israel. The weapons we sold the League and those the British willingly winked at that flowed into Arab hands, are now turned towards our people. Do you doubt that is not by design? That someone in our State Department and in the British War Office were not in collusion? God bless Harry and his friends for doing what those bigoted bureaucrats didn't have the guts to do. I wish he was here so I could thank him myself."

"I never thought you would subscribe to conspiracy theories Maurice, and I certainly..."

Marta came into the room and interrupted Fanny in midsentence. "Coffee, tea, and desserts are served. Sam, Aaron, will you help your father out of his chair?"

Later that evening, after Armand and Aaron had helped Jonah up the stairs to his bedroom, and after Marta made sure he took his heart medication, she climbed onto the old oak bed next to him. Jonah had flatly refused to get rid of their original bedroom set when the styles changed. While the fashionable people were buying the sleek Art Deco bedroom sets of the 20's or the inlaid veneered French styled bedroom sets of the '30's, the tall, solid golden oak head and footboard of the double bed he and Marta shared were elegant enough for him. Aaron was born on that bed, and on it, he and Marta had nursed each other back to health. The entire room itself, the warm tones of gold and beige with hints of claret in the curtains and the bed cover, comforted him whenever he entered it. Here hung the European etchings they had collected, also in warm tones and gold frames that reminded him of the lovely canals of Bruge along which he and Marta strolled years ago. Here also hung the two sketches of them by Van Gogh and Degas that had been done a lifetime ago in Paris. Around these were family pictures facing the bed. The room had a timelessness to it, or at least a moment that captured time, and whenever he entered it, he felt at ease. Jonah had told Marta that when the time came for him to die, he wanted to die here, and something of him would always be in this place if she wanted to talk to him. She said he was a foolish old man to talk of such things.

The electrified hurricane lamp on the night table cast a soft glow on the elderly couple, as Marta pulled the covers up to Jonah's chest.

"You want to fool around?" Jonah said softly.

"You remember how to fool around, you silly old man?" Marta said, laughing as she adjusted his pillow and then hers.

"I don't think I remember, so you'll have to show me." He started to laugh.

"You want to die tonight? The doctor said you were not to get excited."

"I promise you I won't get excited. I haven't been excited in years, but I think to be excited just one more time would be worth the risk."

"At our age it's a risk for both of us, and from what I remember, it's not worth dying for."

Jonah laughed. "Such a thing you say to a dying man?" and as he said this, she took his hand and placed it on her breast. She smiled at his familiar touch, and moved closer to him.

"Dying now would be a terrible inconvenience," she whispered, re-straightening her own pillow as she turned off the light. "And you're not dying. You just say that to get attention. I know you, Jonah Chernov. Besides, I haven't a thing in the house for anyone to eat. That's if anybody came to the shiva. And without food to serve, I'd be terribly embarrassed. Certainly, you would not want me to be embarrassed, would you? Give me a few days to shop, and then you can die." As she leaned over to kiss him goodnight, his hand moved and lingered on her face, and he held it there so his fingers and lips might again memorize her the softness of her cheek. The bed creaked as she moved, and her head rested on his chest so she might listen to his heartbeat. "Please stay beating," she whispered to the air. "You can't die. You can't leave me."

"I was thinking today, that we have never seen all our children, with our grandchildren and the great grandchildren in the same room at the same time." He said after a silence. "You know what I'd really like, Marta? I'd like that to happen even though I know some won't be there. But maybe most will."

"That's a nice idea," she responded. "But you have to promise me that you'll live."

A pale winter light from the moon, stealthily, like a white cat, eased its silent way over the blind slats and into the room, vaguely illuminating the sepia tinged photographs on the wall opposite the bed. Old photos of Chernovs in Europe brought over, newer ones from Austria and Switzerland, photos of the family sent from Israel, and photos of Chernovs taken in America. How many were there in the family now? Eight children, eighteen grandchildren, and five great grandchildren? So far, thirty one, though there were others who were lost. And how many more if the twins and Jenny had lived? Had Henrik lived?

Marta also studied the pictures through the haze, and remembered again just how grateful she was for having met this decent and loving man on a train so many years ago; how, over the years, his children had come to accept her. How in her heart they became hers as much as if she had carried them under it. The little ones called her Bubbie.

"Shall I write to Harry?" she said, as her eyes moved to the ceiling. "You haven't seen or spoken to him since their divorce. I'm not sure Molly or the boys would want to be here if he is. She was so hurt, and the boys are still so angry with him. You don't think he'd bring that Las Vegas showgirl with him, do you? I don't know what he was thinking."

"Well, you know he wasn't thinking with his brain," Jonah said knowing she would get his allusion. "But I'll tell you Marta, I miss my son, and I miss him every day as I miss Abe every day." Again he paused. "But what they did, and what Harry still does, gives the lie to everything I hold dear. I try to think about the good things they did; the things that makes a father proud of his sons, but the other things, the people they hurt, the people they used... I can't even talk about it."

"Then you don't want me to write to Harry?"

"No, I didn't say that," he hastened to add. "Let me think about it."

"It was nice seeing Zeena tonight," she said, changing the subject. "For a woman in her eighties, she looks like she's in her sixties. I think it's the way she puts on her makeup, and I think she pulls back her face and neck with tape. Do you think I should try that?"

"I like your face just the way it is," he said softly. "It has character." He paused. "Do you know that the last time Zeena introduced me to someone, she said I was her older brother. Can you believe that? We're twins. How can I be older?"

"I love you, Jonah. Now go to sleep."

CHAPTER 47

1948

As Jonah Chernov lay there, sinking into a quiet death by degrees, the vague shapes of people in the room around his bed began to merge with shadows of memories he thought were long forgotten. He could hear the sounds of quiet sobbing, and the soft intonation of someone chanting a canticle that pleaded for his soul's rest. Beyond the footboard of the big oak bed stood ill defined outlines of ghostly faces and shapes; faces and shapes seemingly summoned by some unseen conjurer not of this world, and mouthing words he could not discern. Were they loved ones come to say goodbye, or were they the ghost of his past, newly summoned by that sorcerer so they might pounce on him all at once; pointing out all his flaws, all the pain and shame he caused, all the errors he had made, and all the secret inconsistencies that filled his life? But why conjure these, he thought, when there were other faces and images that were so good? Why should a man focus on the bad at the end, on his regrets? Might such memories also be a reminder that is also a step to whatever redemption there was to be? What nonsense. Even now, such nonsense.

In the distance, beyond the open door, he heard the sound of a solo violin. He smiled. Marta had remembered and the Victrola in the parlor was brought upstairs and placed outside the bedroom so he could hear the plaintive notes of one of his favorite pieces of music, Massenet's *Meditation* from *Thais*. Jonah believed that there should be music to accompany the great rites of passages for one's life; something grand, something by Verdi to accompany one's entrance into the world, and something plaintive like the *Meditation*, for one's exit so the person dying could at least enjoy his passing.

Through the dim light, he saw the outlines of the pictures that he knew to be his life. He had memorized them, and as he recollected each one in turn, they seemed to magically animate, as if they had become a silent movie. In his mind, each picture became a door to a room, a door through which he might go. First he saw the picture his mother insisted be taken of the family when an itinerant photographer came to Krivoser. That door opened into a room before he was married to Leah, before the world exploded and he was forced to flee into whatever life held for him. And that picture morphed into a small farmhouse with familiar mixing bowls, the candlesticks, the samovar, his loft, and his sisters chasing him, laughing. The room was filled with the presence of his mother, like a giant roosting bird, and his Papa, quietly reading a book. Next to that, he saw the picture of his first family with little Sam on his lap and him sitting upright wearing a high starched collar with Leah's hand on his shoulder as the other children clustered around them. That picture was also the door that closed on their Paris apartment and opened into the candy store and their early life in Brownsville; a life of deprivation, agonizing guilt, a life of loss. And then the picture of Marta, Armand, and little Aaron that they sat for when Aaron was three. A door opening into another room in Paris, and then a life that brought him support, affection, security, and purpose; a life that gave his children with Leah opportunities they would never have had before. And the wedding photographs: Elizabeth and Nathaniel's, Rachelann and Fedya's taken in Israel, Fanny and her Freddy, Maurice and Shirley, Sam and Sadie, Harry and Molly, Armand and Beatrice, and Aaron and Mamie. Family pictures had been sent from Geneva, and from Vienna, too. There was a portrait of Leo, his eldest grandson standing next to Abe. Abie, his son Abie. His beloved son.

Jonah had fantasized that with his death, the demons of regret and the distant voices of condemnation that continued to cling to his life like parasitic vines, would vanish. Were they there in the shadows, waiting in some extended purgatory? He wanted death to be silent; soft, like Marta's caress, like the *Meditation*, a death of velvet blackness, of eternal nothingness where history and memory dissolved. Indeed, his early life and the memories of it were a road that was pitted and littered. It was a road with sharp rocks sticking out of the earth, and shards of glass ready to cut. And how he had been cut. Still, he had maneuvered this path, but only he knew how deeply scarred he really was from the trek. And the secret of his survival was to keep the scars hidden deep where they would not be exposed by any antiseptic and revealing light. He had won. His secrets remained his own. He had played by his own rules well enough so that his past with its lies, his inadequacies, and the deaths he had caused so long ago would die with him. The pain and the deceptions that haunted him would be over, and these would not follow him into the darkness. This was his hope. Death would end it all. And yet, the child in him did want there to be something more so he and Marta could continue in some way. If there was something else, he could be with Abe again and with Papa and Zeydeh. What if the afterlife you created for yourself would be the one to which you would go? With an afterlife of his own creation, he would eliminate the inadequacy, the guilt, and shame of his early years. In such an afterlife, there would be no eternal accuser. There would be no Leah or Sarah. There would be no burning peasants. There would be no Ezra. Again, such foolishness. Even at the end he was still a foolish child filled with fantasies.

He turned his head to the right and slowly made out the faces of Zeena and Elizabeth with Marta in between them, their arms around each other for support. Armand and Aaron stood behind them. Armand, the surprise of his life, and Aaron, the unexpected miracle and joy he and Marta shared later in life, were standing close to one another with their heads lowered. To the left he could make out the faces of his children; Rachelann, Maurice, Fanny, and Sammy, each so different, each such a source of pleasure and pain. He tried to imagine his little Jenny standing with them, but he had lost her so long ago, he could not even imagine what she might look like middle-aged. And his twin sons, never even reaching their first birthdays. He lingered on each face as he did when they were children reciting their lessons to him. How old they looked; hair streaked with gray, faces lined. Wasn't he too young to have children so old? The thought amused him. And wasn't he too young to be a great grandfather? How many? Four? Five? Six? He didn't remember, but he did remember how it felt to have them sit on his lap.

He had lived to see all of them prosper in just one generation of being Americans, some from being recognized and rewarded for knowledge and skills in their fields, and two prospering though infamous choices that he decried. Still, he could honestly say that he loved them all even if he was not proud of them all. "Where's Abe and Harry?" he said to the air. "I don't see Abraham and Harry. Marta, didn't you invite Abe and Harry?"

Marta moved over to him. "Of course I invited them," she reassured him, turning towards the children with a look of profound sadness.

"I'm here, Papa," said Harry, making his way through the daughters and sons-in-laws standing behind their spouses. "I'm here, Papa."

"I'm so sorry, Harry, so sorry," Jonah said, trying to rise but only able to clasp Harry's hand. "I was angry, and my anger pushed you and Abe away and broke the family. I'm so sorry."

Harry knew how his father felt about the path he had chosen, and the estrangement became palpable. But for Jonah, how far was a man to go in forgiving his children when his children willfully brought dishonor on their family? Now he regretted the harshness of his words and actions. "Family is family no matter what," he said. "I pushed you and Abe away. I didn't see how fast the time goes. I broke the family." Tears ran down Jonah's cheek. "Where is Abe. I have to tell Abe I'm sorry."

Harry looked across the bed at Marta. She nodded, and silently gave her permission. "Abe's on his way, Papa, but he told me that it is good between the two of you. He knows you love him. He'll be here soon." Harry normally did not cry, but he did at that moment.

Soft lips descended on Jonah's forehead, gentle hands patted his own, and soft words of love cracked through tearful voices. I am not really ready to die, he mused. Another emotional contradiction. Was anyone ever really ready to die? He wanted the soft blackness, yet to have it, he would have to leave his Marta and his family. Marta leaned over and kissed the tears on his cheek. This was a different kind of pain, a loving pain. This was the pain of loss and of losing.

One by one, sons, daughters, sons and daughters-in-laws, grandchildren, and great grandchildren moved forward to the bed he had shared with Marta for the past forty-four years, sat briefly on it, smiled at the creaking, made their final farewells, and retreated back into the shadows with the ghosts.

A blast of late December wind shook the window frame and the heavy damask curtains warred against the cold intrusion.

"Marta," he said weakly. "Marta, come sit and hold my hand."

The slender woman, her light blue eyes glistening with tears, came to his side and sat down. The bed creaked again and they laughed.

"I'll fix that tomorrow," he said, a smile playing around his dry lips.

"Do you promise? You've been saying that for forty-four years." He laughed and his laugh turned into cough. She moved closer and raised his head.

"Here, Jonah, take some water."

He sipped from the glass and motioned with pursed lips that he didn't want any more.

"Do you remember the joke about the old man on his dying bed who asked his wife for a piece of ruggelach she was baking because he wanted to die with the taste of her ruggelach on his lips, and she said he couldn't have any because she was saving it for the shiva? I want a piece of ruggelach."

"The doctor said it wasn't good for you."

"I'm dying, Marta. Do you think a piece of ruggelach will make a difference?"

Marta laughed at her foolishness, her reddened eyes suddenly light again with humor. "Fanny, please bring up some ruggelach for your father." Then she turned back to her husband. "Yes, I remember that joke," she said, her heart breaking at the thought of what it would be like not feeling his touch, not hearing his voice ever again, and not laughing at his fanciful imaginings. "You are not taking this very seriously," she replied, knowing full well that he would discount her admonition with more humor.

"And why is this moment different from any other moment," he paraphrased. "Aren't we dying every day we live? He could sense his lips moving as he murmured faint responses to the soft kisses and the gentle touch on his hand. "Did I make you happy, Marta?" he heard himself say to her, or did he only think he said it? "I could never make my mother happy, and it seemed that I could never make Leah happy. So, did I make you happy?" How odd, he thought, to be dying after living a lifetime, and the only question on his mind was whether he made another person happy? Was that what life all came down to? Making another person happy? "Did I make you happy, Marta?" he repeated.

"Yes, my beloved. You made me very happy. Now go to sleep."

"Will you miss me, Marta?"

She felt as if her heart would rupture.

"Why are you taking such a long time to answer?" he quipped. "How much time to think do you need?"

"Not very much," she laughed, brushing the tears out of her eyes. "From time to time I may miss your humor, and your little blurts of unexpected philosophizing, and your gentle touch. Yes, my dearest husband. I shall miss you with all my heart." She gently put her head on his fragile chest, oblivious to the dozen or more people who watched their parting moments.

"Then it's been a good life with me, hasn't it, Marta?" he said, again asking for some reassurance, for some indication that some of the choices he had made had been the right choices and that his life had meaning. "We made a good life together and we made two beautiful sons, didn't we?"

"Yes, my Jonah. Yes, we made a good life together."

"Put down your hair, Marta. I want to see you as I saw you the first time I came to visit you. Do you remember that day?"

Smiling at the memory, she reached up to the pins that held her abundant silver and white tresses and allowed them to fall onto her shoulders. Jonah weakly reached out for a lock of it, moved it between his fingers, and drew it to his face to smell it and kiss it.

"Thank you for the world you gave me," he said. "I am very tired now and I want to sleep. "Armand," he said, his hand gesturing weakly, "you watch over mother and Aaron and you keep the family together. When everything falls apart, it's family that remains and keeps you strong. Abie isn't coming?" he said suddenly to Rachelann who had moved closer. "Abraham must be here. I never meant for him to leave. It was so long ago. I forget. I must tell him... I must tell him..." and his voice trailed off. He started to pull himself up, his frail limbs struggling against the sheet.

"Sha, Papa," Rachelann said softly, gently pushing against his frame. "Abie will be here," she said, looking over at Marta and Harry, her eyes pleading.

"It's not good to lie to a dying man," Jonah rejoined.

"You're not dying," she continued, unable to bring the reality to her lips. "Just as Marta says, you just like attention."

"Rachelann," he whispered. "Listen to me. If Abe doesn't get here in time, I need you to tell him that I need him back here and that I want him to forgive me. You are the eldest, so you know that family is all there really is. We came through half of this terrible century because we are a family of strong people, but we'll be strong only if we stay together as a family. When I am gone, you must tell them what I said. You must tell them that bad things happen to people who leave their family. I see that now so clearly. I made mistakes, but you and Armand can make it better."

Jonah's voice trailed off and his last words were barely audible. His breathing was shallow and that part of his spirit that wanted to live, fought against the blackness that was closing in on him. All stood motionless around the bed and muffled their sobs.

"Look, Abie is here," he said, motioning with his finger towards the footboard. And then there was silence.

EPILOGUE

"Jonah," a voice called.

"Here I am," he heard his mind respond as if he were a Patriarch hearing a call. His eyes remained closed, yet he clearly saw a tall figure standing in an unnatural light with a naked sword in his right hand.

"You're not God, are you?" he imagined himself saying, his voice more curious than trembling.

"No," the figure answered as he revealed a pair of large white wings. "But Ayn Sof, the Eternal, the Endless One, moves me to talk to you. I am the Angel of Death."

Jonah's mind raced to a midrash about a Rabbi Ben Levi, and suddenly, he heard his voice strong and young again saying, "You swore that no man would ever look upon you." It was almost a challenge.

"Ah, yes. That wonderful old legend. Actually, I prefer what Longfellow did with it," the angel replied. "Let me think. 'The angel took the sword and swore, And walks the earth unseen for evermore.' Of course, the poet took some liberties, but they wouldn't be poets if they did not. Besides, you are very close to not being a living soul, so I can take some liberties, too. It's a good poem, but for glimpsing the really important truths about 'life, the universe, and everything,' I think it was Wordsworth who really came closest to it. Ever read *Tintern Abbey*?"

Jonah smiled at the thought of imagining not only a conversation with the Angel of Death, but at having imagined an Angel of Death who liked poetry.

"Am I dead?" Jonah asked.

"Yes and no. It's hard to explain," the angel replied. "Most things in my business are hard to explain."

"Then why are you here if I'm not dead?"

"Because death is a process, and before I take you, I am bidden to hear your story so Ayn Sof might know you."

Jonah thought for a moment. "What do you mean 'So Ayn Sof might know me?' What's this Ayn Sof? Are we talking about God?"

"We are talking about that which you call God," the angel replied, "but your word God, is so limiting and so filled with anthropomorphic images, that it loses the essence of what Ayn Sof really is."

Jonah had never heard of this Ayn Sof, but nevertheless was delighted that the Angel of Death knew the word anthropomorphic.

"Well if this Ayn Sof is the same as God, isn't He supposed to 'know me' from birth, and when do I get to meet Him?" Jonah was strangely excited. Was there really a celestial being talking to him, or had he conjured this image because he was truly afraid of a final nothingness and the dialogue was a way of postponing the end?

"Meet Him?" the angel said. "Know all about you personally?" The angel's voice was laden with incredulity. "Do you know how big the universe is? Do you actually think this little blue dot is the only experiment in existence? Let me put it in words you can grasp, Jonah. I just record the stories, take the story tellers, and pass them and their stories on. To know where the story of your life goes, or where your soul goes for that matter, and what happens to them after I leave you, is above what you would call my pay grade."

It occurred to Jonah that he was not going to get the answers he wanted.

"Now I need you to start with after Leah took you out of the hospital in Paris. Everything before that was recorded and passed on when you didn't die. Why you didn't die then is a long and complicated story, so let's not talk about it because it was rather embarrassing episode for me personally."

The angel hastily changed the subject. "But I'll tell you what I found interesting from that incident. After recording your history till that point, and your anger with what you call God, I also recorded that you never really did lose your faith. People do not rail and curse something in which they do not believe. Oh, believe me, Jonah, you're not alone in the paradox. Lots of people have that kind of relationship with The Endless One. Only true atheists ignore Him, and that is what a true atheist should do, but doubters do not ignore, and I do believe they find some solace in hurling their rage up to heaven. The interesting thing about you and so many others like you, is that despite your so called loss of faith and rage, you continued to live a moral life. You continued to accept the Torah's moral laws, knowing that there was a need for there to be an Authority behind those moral laws, and yet, at the same time, you rejected that Authority as your personal God. The idea that people can still be good without professing belief in a God who demands goodness is a human paradox, and something I've been told that is unique in the universe."

"Wait a minute," interrupted Jonah, "I still don't understand this Ayn Sof who we call God. Isn't He suppose know all the details of my life already? I was taught there was a plan, and that I was set on a particular path for a particular reason to achieve a particular end. Are you telling me that Ayn Sof doesn't have a plan and doesn't know me? Isn't He supposed to know everything? Isn't it ..." Questions poured from his mind like a sudden cloud burst.

The angel would have sighed if angels could sigh. "It's hard to explain," the angel interrupted, so let me try again. "The Being you refer to as God, angelic beings call Ayn Sof. Abraham sensed His presence, and because of human limitations, gave

Ayn Sof a human voice, human actions, human expectations, and entered into a dialogue with Him. The confusion came with the idea that this dialogue is with something out there when it is really a dialogue with the aspect of Ayn Sof that is within each of us. All things in creation are composed of, and moved, by Ayn Sof. The dialogue, be it formal prayer as you call it or just talk, is an inner conversation with the Him. You call the Ayn Sof within, your soul. Ayn Sof is outside of you, inside of you, and surrounds you. This is what makes everything, one. The universe is a unity. I'm using the word 'Him' because humans understand gender, but Ayn Sof has no gender. I can't explain it any better than that, so don't ask. Angelic beings are not clear on how the process works, but we do know that the idea you call 'God' is a human construct of what cannot be grasped by humans or by angels. You talk about a plan. I know there is a plan, but it is a plan for the workings of the universe. Ayn Sof is the universe. His creations, you and I, are the sentient aspects of His existence. As I said, it's very complex, and knowing about how things actually work is still beyond my understanding. Besides," the angel replied, "you concluded a long time ago, and quite correctly, that The Eternal doesn't know what will happen, so why should He intimately know you or what your life was going to be? I surmise such blurts of human awareness regarding His nature are what makes people like you and other thinking humans interesting and probably why He puts up with all your nonsense. But that's just conjecture. Again, I really don't know. But I do believe that your continued existence rests on the fact that you are a perpetual source of astonishment and wonder, and if I might go out on a limb, amusement. It's all about free will and the choices you make with that terrible gift. Personally, I think that giving free will to primates was a big mistake. Primates are too unpredictable. Fish would have been a better choice. Fish are nice and they don't cause trouble."

Jonah felt his lips smile at the thought that God didn't know the future. Jonah was right to have concluded that years ago.

"Yes, yes, you were right in surmising that," the angel said, reading his thoughts. "You were correct in concluding that what humanity continues to call God actually doesn't know what humans will do next or why they do what they do. The whole Eden story with the snake is a metaphor for that. Same thing with Cain and his brother's whereabouts. Do I make my point? He doesn't know what human beings will do until they do it. It is only then that the Ayn Sof within becomes aware of their freewill choice. I wish everyone understood this so they would stop blaming Him and start taking responsibility for their own actions. Jonah, it boils down to this question, and this question will give you a hint of your value and what the angelic hosts surmise is His interest in humanity: Is it illogical that with what human beings do to one another, and a realization that prayers are not answered, people still continue to pray and continue to keep moral laws though their God remains silent? Why do you continue to believe there is something out there in the face of His silence? You must admit it does seem a little illogical, does it not? Remember that defining moment back in that burning field when you raged at Ayn Sof for the first time and came to know that He was silent in the face of human tragedy? That's when you first started understanding. It wasn't fated that Krivoser would be attacked, and it wasn't fated that the flaming stick you hurled into heaven would fall into the field and burn those peasants to death. It was then that you started to recognize that people made their own destinies. It was at that moment you became a deeply religious man even though your heart walked away from prayer, and that a concept of a God who decreed what a person's life was to be at birth. No reasonable person would continue such a dialogue or relationship unless he or she saw the reality beyond the reality; the Ayn Sof idea beyond the God idea. You kept your people's ritual observances because you recognized them as a doorway to the transcendent that was beyond the God of the Torah. You instinctively knew the value of keeping these traditions in your life. I personally find your inconsistency fascinating, and something to ponder. You are more interesting than most, Jonah Chernov."

The angel moved closer to the bed and sat down, leaning the sword against the night table. Jonah took notice that the bed did not creak. His family, unaware that their patriarch had already stepped into the valley of the shadow, continued their silent vigil until Marta began to usher them out, telling them that they had to have something to eat. Only Marta and the man intoning psalms remained.

"Jonah, let me explain what's going to happen. You know how people who have a near death experience say their life flashes before them?" the angel asked reflectively. "Well, that is really one of my kind recording the story of their lives so it can later be absorbed by Ayn Sof. That's what happened to you in Paris. Think of your life being recorded on one of those records you're so fond of. I and my kind are charged with making the recording so Ayn Sof can play it and absorb it when He has time."

"You mean the Ayn Sof is like a big record cabinet of people's lives?" Jonah said cautiously. Again, the synapses in his brain began making unlikely connections. "You mean He'll put the record of my life on some Victrola, listen to it like it's a popular song, and memorize it?"

"That's an over simplification," the angel replied, "but comes close to a piece of the totality." The Angel of Death smiled. "I'll confess to you again that I don't even know how the system works. No one does, and there is no one to ask. We just know what we have to do and we do it. Now, see your life flash before you from Paris onward, and then we can be off. Now it's time to finish up."

"Isn't she beautiful?" Jonah said, imagining Marta, and trying to prolong his time with her on earth. "I shall miss her and our life together."

"Then why did you wish for oblivion? What if I told you that you were correct to imagine that the afterlife you envision is the one you will get? What if I told you that I am also here to move you to one who will help you create that afterlife? Just imagine that Marta is with you, and when her time comes, she will be there next to you for eternity if that is your desire."

Jonah was comforted. "You know, this is good," he said, never taking his eyes off Marta's image while addressing the angel. "You see that if you exist, then it is real proof that this Ayn Sof exists, that something exists, and that I wasn't insane to argue and rail against that something whose existence I doubted."

"No one ever said you were insane," the angel countered. "No one is insane who talks to The Eternal. That's called prayer, and prayer is directed either within or without. Reviling is also a form prayer. Reviling The Eternal says you care about His world. Still, you could be considered insane, and you would be, if you actually thought that The Eternal talked back to you."

The angel sensed a vibration and knew he was spending too much time with this soul. He had to move on. "Humanity will eventually discover that all human beings are hard wired to the universe with an inborn inclination to believe in something beyond themselves. You and I and everyone for that matter are the Ayn Sof's sentiency. His sentiency was built into our original design, yet some humans fight that truth because some humans cannot deal with the intangible. The inclination to doubt was also built into your design to make things more interesting."

"But what if I were only hedging my bets?" Jonah said, fully believing that his deception to refocus the angel from his task was working. "That's what Pascal told humanity to do? What if you are only a figment of my imagination, 'a piece of undigested beef' like Scrooge said to Marly's ghost?"

"Jonah," the angel said, "Now you're just stalling, and we really must get on with it."

"So you're telling me that because I raged and argued, I must never have truly doubted The Eternal's existence? As a Jew, as a human being, it was my right to be angry with what I believed was doled to me. I was especially angry for being taught to believe that God was in fact in control and would keep those promises of protecting me, and those I love. I truly believed that 'God never slumbers or sleeps." I believed the promise that God would destroy our enemies. Those promises were not kept. I had a right to be angry. We all have a right to be angry."

"Jonah, no one is saying you didn't have a right to be angry considering what you were taught and what you came to see as reality. What's interesting is that your disappointment from promises not delivered resulted in an anger that became the chain that tethered you to Ayn Sof. At the same time that you were attached by anger, you still ascribed the beauty of life and family, and the wonders of nature to Him, so you were also attached by gratitude. It's complex, but it's all one, and now that it has all come together, you can be at peace."

Jonah's breath became labored with the memories of his early life in Krivozer, in Paris, and in Brooklyn. "Things happened to me and to the people I loved that shouldn't have happened to people who truly believed. We truly believed and we were abandoned. I truly believed and I was abandoned. God had to answer for that."

"Now you're getting upset and losing your philosophy," the angel replied, "and you might as well finally accept the idea that Ayn Sof doesn't take responsibility because humanity creates its own problems, not Ayn Sof. Ayn Sof is neither just nor unjust. Ayn Sof just is. Ayn Sof is existence; pure and simple so there is no point in demanding answers. You read the *Book of Job* and the answer that was given to that ancient man is still the same. Who are you to demand answers? Nothing has changed. You will not learn why you were born, you will not learn why you were here, you will not learn why the things that happened to you happened to you, and you will not learn why you had to die. I don't know the answers either. No one does, but seeking some kind of understanding and answers to those questions while you live, is what makes life meaningful. Jonah, by that criteria, you had a meaningful life. The best answer I can give you is an understanding that you took the cards the world dealt you and with them chose to make a decent life for yourself, despite what those cards said. That counts and that's what I need to hear about. That's what will tell Ayn Sof who you truly were. Our time together is running out." There was a second vibration, and the angel picked up his sword. "You don't want to exasperate me, Jonah, because if I get exasperated and take you before the entire story is told, Ayn Sof will not be increased by your life, and what you lived through will not have any meaning in the great scheme of things."

Jonah did not understand. Was the angel saying that we increase or decrease Ayn Sof by our lives? Did Ayn Sof need human experiences to grow or expand in some way? Were we mere physical extensions so that Ayn Sof might feel and be more than just spirit? Again, Jonah's mind began to race, and more questions spewed out in rapid succession from his silent lips.

"Look, Jonah," the angel said, moving closer. "All that the angels can surmise is that Ayn Sof is the process that allows for existence. That's it. Humans exist, and by virtue of your existence, you are part of Ayn Sof. Then you make decisions as to what shape that existence will take. Conditions outside of your control sometimes force you to make decisions. You can act on your decisions and even change your mind. We, on the other hand, are compelled to perform the function for which we were created. We have only glimpsed why we are compelled to do what we do, and we have no idea as to what the end of this is all for. That's why we admire humanity and resent you at the same time. You can decide to act; we are compelled to act. Ayn Sof is a mystery, even to us." He paused. "Jonah, I would give up this sword if I could be human and make my own decisions and then die. None of you realize what a gift that life, choice, and death are, and so many of you squander the opportunities that angels never have. Listen to me. All your questions have no meaning any more. Questioning is what the living must do. The dead don't need the answers; you had them while you lived. Existence holds the answers to everything, but most are afraid to see the answers in front of them. Now tell me what I need to know, and begin where I told you to begin."

"If I give it all up to you, the entire truth of my life, will I, while I'm still alive, be free of the memories for just a moment?" Jonah countered. "I am more afraid of the pain of eternal memory than I am afraid of eternal death."

"You will be free," the angel said in a low voice that hinted of sympathy. "That's death's reward for living. All pain and painful memories cease to be." The angel took his sword and touched Jonah on the forehead.

"Why is Marta weeping on my chest?"

"You have passed away," Death said.

"But I can still see her and my family in the other rooms. Why can I still see them?"

"Because you and I are not finished."

"What will happen to my Marta and my children when I am not here?"

"No one knows, not even the Eternal. That is something that people on this side still do not understand."

"But that means," Jonah blurted, "that Ayn Sof..." and Death cut him off.

"That means that they will make their choices, and those choices will move their lives in a particular direction. Ayn Sof will know what those choice are only after they are made, and only after I, or one like me, takes their stories when it is their time. What you must understand is that if what you said and did while in this world was seen by your family as being good and of value, they will act that way to honor you. What they will carry on into their own lives that they learned from you, is a key piece of your legacy and your immortality. It will guide them. Eventually, you will be forgotten, but how you acted in this world will be your legacy if the behaviors are replicated from generation to generation. I wish people knew this at the beginning."

"But..."

"Jonah, it is time for you to enter eternity. Let me take your memories and pain. There are others I must free."

Edwards Brothers Malloy
Thorofare, NJ USA
February 11, 2016